PRAISE FOR THE NOVELS
OF THALASSA

A Beggar at the

"Beautifully written, this novel transports ... ...the 19th century, British imperialism and the pull of two cultures in an ever-changing world."—*Lancashire Evening Post* (UK)

"Set to a backdrop of the Raj in the immediate run-up to the 1838 Afghan War, *A Beggar at the Gate* details in depth and with intelligent sensitivity the increasing desperation felt by an Englishwoman torn between two cultures. It is a story of love and understanding, of duty and honor, of spirituality and redemption, painted beautifully and vividly with deft soul strokes. The prose is as eloquent as the rounded characterizations, and when a novel can find contemporary relevance despite its historical content, it's marked as a work of some power."
—*Big Issue* (UK), (4 stars)

"Thalassa Ali is uniquely positioned to take us through an honest account of life during the British Raj. From the spectacular Charak Puja to the sati rites at a maharajah's funeral pyre to the descriptions of living quarters and the fashions of the times, Ali creates a believable world with sights and sounds buried in the annals of time."
—*Libas* (Pakistan)

"Ali tantalizes her readers from the first page. . . . The poisonous political atmosphere of the Punjab after the death of Maharaja Ranjit Singh is captured vividly in this book and Thalassa Ali's eye for fine detail and archaeological insight is unparalleled."—*Dawn* (Pakistan)

"Ali's portrayal of Islamic society is nuanced and sensitive."
—*India Currents*

"Ali centers her story on Mariana, whose love for Saboor and Hassan tears her apart just as India is torn asunder by the British, Hindu and Muslim factions. The quick pace and rich detail, along with her insightful characters, will have readers eager for more. SWEET."
—*Romantic Times Bookclub* (4 stars)

"*A Begg...* ...rites with more confiden... ...at portrays the positive ... ...l tolerance that are its tru... ...Islam that has emerged...

"*A Beggar at the Gate* is a terrific insightful historical tale with a touch of romanticism that brings to life mid-eighteenth-century India. The story line moves rather quickly yet not only has full-blooded key characters, but also provides a deep window into two peoples at a point of major strife seemingly ready to turn deadly.... Readers will beg for more sequels, especially what happens to the fascinating Saboor as an adult."—*Midwest Book Review*

"The journey that Mariana embarks upon here is magical, mystical and almost sensual."—*Pakistan Link*

"This whole allegory is beautifully done, and one gets the feeling that Ali has hit her stride here. Her prose is simple and elegant...a pleasing offering."—Bina Shah, *Hindustan Times*

"Thalassa has done well to capture the spirit of the land, its customs, smells and sounds and the enchanting spiritual and mystic culture."
—*Nation*

"A load of historical detail that lifts the story."
—*Sunday Express, Indian Express*

"*A Beggar at the Gate* is such a blockbuster, literarily speaking.... An epic with a splash of East-meets-West romance—albeit more historically accurate and sans heaving bosoms... Ali's propensity for historical detail is a pleasure."—*Herald* (Pakistan)

"An extra pleasure to read because much of the landscape still exists today...an enjoyable read."—*Books, Etc.*

"Expertly weaving historical fact with a rich, exotic setting, Thalassa Ali holds her readers captive in this intriguing novel."
—*Paperback Shelf, Mid County Post*

"Full of beautiful historical and visual detail."
—*Historical Novels Review*

A Singular Hostage

"Lyrical and zippy . . . this richly populated novel is notable for . . . compelling mysticism . . . convincing historicity."—*Publishers Weekly*

"Colorful."—*Kirkus Reviews*

"Enlivened by captivating descriptions, Ali's seductive tale is a wonderful blend of adventure, court intrigue, historical fact, and Sufi mysticism, and it will appeal to fans of M. M. Kaye's *The Far Pavilions*."
—*Booklist*

"Eminently readable."—M. M. Kaye, author of *The Far Pavilions*

"A sweeping pageant of life in the British Raj, and one woman's attempt to realize her destiny. Mystical and romantic in a way that recalls *The Far Pavilions*."—Stephanie Barron

"An excellent book, beautifully researched and charmingly written, which does justice to both English and Indian cultures. I was particularly impressed by the matter-of-fact mysticism and spirituality. Lovely."—Barbara Hambly

"A rare book indeed. It combines extraordinary characters, a riveting plot, a rich historical backdrop, Sufi mysticism, and the allure of an exotic oriental court, and is eminently readable. . . . The reader will be tempted to devour it in one reading. . . . Outstanding . . . Thalassa Ali has truly mastered the storyteller's art. . . . We breathlessly await the sequel."—*She* magazine

"[A] distinctive setting . . . [and an] intriguing first novel."
—*Washington Post*

"This mesmerizing tale helps readers better understand a vitally important area of the world."—*School Library Journal*

ALSO BY THALASSA ALI

A Singular Hostage

A Beggar at the Gate

Companions

of Paradise

Thalassa Ali

BANTAM BOOKS

COMPANIONS OF PARADISE
A Bantam Book / April 2007

Published by Bantam Dell
A Division of Random House, Inc.
New York, New York

Excerpt on page 3, from *An English Interpretation of The Holy Qur'an with Full Arabic Text* by Abdullah Yusuf Ali, Sh. Muhammad Ashraf publishers and booksellers, Lahore, Pakistan, 1975

Excerpt on page 28, fragment of Sa'adi, translated by Samuel Robinson of Wilmslow, 1883

Excerpt on page 43, from *An English Interpretation of The Holy Qur'an with Full Arabic Text* by Abdullah Yusuf Ali, Sh. Muhammad Ashraf publishers and booksellers, Lahore, Pakistan, 1975

Excerpt on page 74, fragment of Jalaluddin Rumi, translator unknown

Excerpt on page 78, from *The Mystic Persians—Rumi* by F. Hadland Davis,
Ashraf Publications, Lahore, Pakistan, 1967

Excerpt on page 86, from *An English Interpretation of The Holy Qur'an with Full Arabic Text* by Abdullah Yusuf Ali, Sh. Muhammad Ashraf publishers and booksellers, Lahore, Pakistan, 1975

Durood on page 96, translation by Syed Akhlaque Husain Tauhidi

Excerpt on page 100, from a pamphlet by the Afghan Antiquities and Museums Service and Instituto Italiano per il Media ed Estremo Oriente, 1966

Excerpt on page 212, fragment of Jalaluddin Rumi, translator unknown

Excerpt on page 238, fragment of "Hohenlinden" by Robert Campbell

Excerpt on page 245, from *An English Interpretation of The Holy Qur'an with Full Arabic Text* by Abdullah Yusuf Ali, Sh. Muhammad Ashraf publishers and booksellers, Lahore, Pakistan, 1975

First excerpt on page 283, fragment of Jalaluddin Rumi, translator unknown

Second excerpt on page 283, fragment of Sa'adi, translated by Samuel Robinson of Wilmslow, 1883

Excerpt on page 307, from *An English Interpretation of The Holy Qur'an with Full Arabic Text* by Abdullah Yusuf Ali, Sh. Muhammad Ashraf publishers and booksellers, Lahore, Pakistan, 1975

Excerpt on page 316, from *An English Interpretation of the Holy Qur'an with Full Arabic Text* by Abdullah Yusuf Ali, Sh. Muhammad Ashraf publishers and booksellers, Lahore, Pakistan, 1975

LIBRARY OF CONGRESS CATALOGING-IN-PUBLICATION DATA
Ali, Thalassa.
Companions of paradise / Thalassa Ali.
p.   cm.
ISBN: 978-0-553-38178-8
1. British—India—Fiction.   2. Afghanistan—Fiction.
3. Punjab (India)—Fiction.   I. Title.

PS3601.L39C66 2007
813'.6—dc22   2006048502

Printed in the United States of America
Published simultaneously in Canada

www.bantamdell.com

BVG   10 9 8 7 6 5 4 3 2 1

*To all those who have been brave enough to speak the truth
in the face of opposition*

ACKNOWLEDGMENTS

First, I want to thank my fabulous editor, Kate Miciak, who bought The Paradise Trilogy from a rookie writer, and never looked back. Kate, if it weren't for you, *A Singular Hostage, A Beggar at the Gate,* and now *Companions of Paradise* would never have seen the light of day. Thanks also to my energetic agent, Jill Kneerim of Kneerim and Williams, who took me on, and had the very good sense to show my first manuscript to Kate.

I owe much to my friend and consultant on all matters Afghan: the excellent historian and editor Kamar Habibi, and to my writing teacher, the late, incomparable Arthur Edelstein.

Thanks to my writing group, who stood by me as I struggled and complained my way through all three books, including *Companions of Paradise:* Lakshmi Bloom, Elatia Harris, Cathie Keenan, Kathleen Patton, Pam Raskin, and Jane Strekalovsky. Each of you has made a valuable contribution to this trilogy. Thank you all from the bottom of my heart.

There are many others who have helped me in varous ways:

My dear, patient friend Zeba Mirza, who was left out of the acknowledgments for *A Beggar at the Gate.* Shelâlé Abbasi, Gillo and Ali Afridi, Dure Afzal, Shehryar Ahmad, Faqir Syed Aijazuddin, Bunny Amin, Kathleen Baldonado, Bill Bell, Brian Bergeron, Upty Clouse. Lenny Golay, Tariq Jafar, Farida and Asad Ali Khan, Judy and Bazl Khan, Tahireh and Zafar Khan, Jessica Lipnack and Jeff Stamps, Janet Lowenthal, Erika McCarthy, Cornelia McPeak, Rashid and Bano Makhdoom, Azim Mian, Kyra and Coco Montagu, Fauzia Najm, the Pakistan Mission to the UN, Ann and Frank Porter, Sharon Propson, Samina Quraeshi, Meheriene Qureshi, my sister Ala Reid, Sam and Juliet Reid, Sally Redmond, Shakil and Rehana Saigol, Mansoor Suhail, Javed and Farida Talat, Audrey Walker, Serita Winthrop, and Joyce Zinno.

And of course my greatest allies, my children Sophie and Toby Ali. Thank you, thank you, thank you all.

HISTORICAL NOTE

For all its remoteness and high, inaccessible mountains, Afghanistan played an important role in the Great Game—the epic, nineteenth-century struggle between Britain and Russia for control of Central Asia.

Afghanistan's value lay in its trade routes, for it stood at the heart of a network of ancient caravan tracks known collectively as the Silk Route. Those narrow, treacherous roads connecting Russia and China with India and Rome had been used for thousands of years to transport rock salt, lapis lazuli, tea, and silk, but they had also served as invasion routes for the armies of Alexander the Great, Genghis Khan, and other conquerors.

By the late 1830s, the British had established colonies in much of southern and central India and had begun to look north, toward the rich kingdom of the Punjab on the Afghan border. But even as they approached Afghanistan from the southeast, their rivals, the Russians, were moving down from the northwest, and had begun to threaten Persia.

It was not difficult for the British to convince themselves that the Russians would soon take over Afghanistan, invade India, and snatch away Britain's possessions there. Their solution was to preempt this threat by deposing the Afghan king, Amir Dost Mohammad, and replacing him with Shah Shuja, his British-leaning rival.

In 1839, the British implemented their plan. Having driven out Amir Dost Mohammad and declared Shah Shuja king, they settled their army and ten thousand camp followers into a cantonment, or fort, north of Kabul, and sent for their wives and children.

Two years later, they paid dearly for their folly.

Of the characters in *Companions of Paradise*, Akbar Khan, Abdullah Khan, Aminullah Khan, Shah Shuja-ul-Mulk, Sir Alexander Burnes, Sir William Macnaghten, Lady Macnaghten, General Sir William Elphinstone, General Sale, his wife Lady Florentia Sale, his son-in-law Captain Sturt, Brigadier Shelton, and Major Wade are all historical figures.

Mariana Givens, her uncle Adrian Lamb, and her aunt Claire Lamb are fictional characters, as are Harry Fitzgerald, Charles Mott, Hassan Ali Khan, his son Saboor, his father Shaikh Waliullah Karakoyia, and his aunt Safiya Sultana, Munshi Sahib, Haji Khan, Nur Rahman, and all the servants.

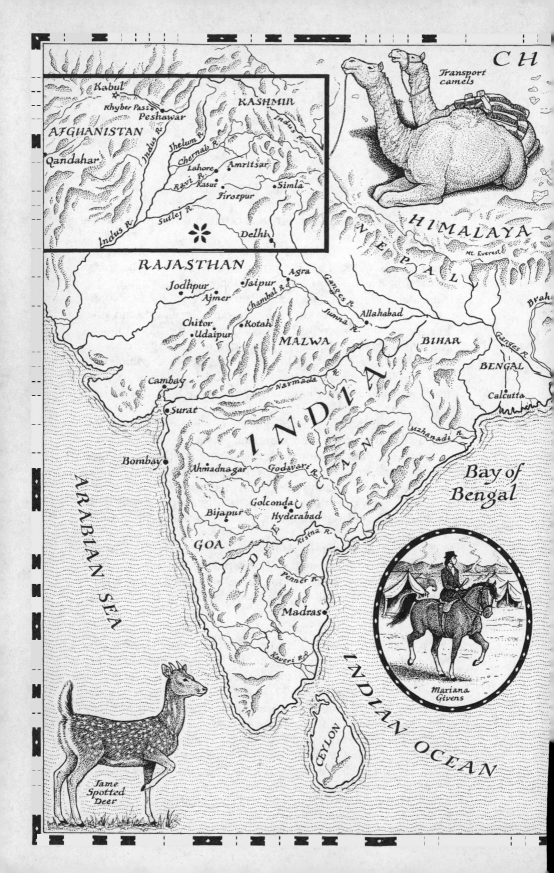

Transport camels

CH

KASHMIR

AFGHANISTAN

Kabul

Khyber Pass
Peshawar

Qandahar

Indus R.

Jhelum R.

Chenal R.

Lahore   Amritsar

Ravi R. Kasur

Firozpur   Simla

Sutlej R.

Indus R.

Delhi

HIMALAYA

Mt. Everest

N
E
P
A
L

Brah

RAJASTHAN

Jodhpur   Jaipur   Agra

Ajmer

Chambal R.

Ganges R.

Allahabad

Chitor   Kotah

Udaipur

MALWA

Jumna R.

BIHAR

BENGAL

Calcutta

Cambay

Surat

Narmada

I
N
D
I
A

Ganges R.

Bombay

Ahmadnagar   Godavari R.

Mahanadi R.

Bay of
Bengal

Golconda

Bijapur   Hyderabad

GOA

Ristna R.

D

Pennet R.

Madras

Kaveri R.

ARABIAN SEA

Mariana
Givens

CEYLON

INDIAN OCEAN

Tame
Spotted
Deer

Lanchow
Kabul
Khyber Pass
Peshawar
KASHMIR
AFGHANISTAN
Indus R.
Jhelum R.
Chenab R.
Qandahar
Amritsar
Lahore
Ravi R.
Kasur
Simla
Firozpur
Sutlej R.
Indus R.
Delhi
BURMA
Mandalay
Hanoi
Andaman Islands
N
Scale of Miles
0
50
100
200
300
INDONESIA
Illustrated by Laura Hartman Maestro 2002

Companions of Paradise

Prologue

Mariana Givens sat at a small camp table inside her tent doorway and looked uneasily at the stony landscape in front of her.

She could see nothing unusual about the caravan halting station of Butkhak. Its scrubby, sloping hills seemed to fold into each other in the same way as those she had seen at every stopping place between India and Afghanistan. The walled town itself looked unremarkable. Even the ragged nomads with their black tents, their camels, and their herds of jostling sheep were identical to the ones she and her English traveling companions had encountered for the past six weeks.

She shivered, and adjusted her shawls. Why, then, did this place, only a day's march from Kabul, tug insistently at her imagination? Perhaps it had been responsible for the strange, upsetting vision that had come to her a few nights earlier, as she lay waiting for sleep.

Mariana was no stranger to prescient dreams, for they had come to her before, but no previous vision of hers had been as troubling as the great funeral procession that had appeared without warning and passed before her—a silent horde of English people, its leaders on horseback, the rest of the mourners in carriages or on foot, all wearing solemn black, down to the tiniest bonneted girl.

To what melancholy destination had they been going as they filed down a rock-strewn slope, and out of sight? And why had her queasy dread at the sight of them been accompanied by a quickening in her heart, as if something quite different and very important was about to happen to her?

A folded paper lay in front of her on the table. Covered with elegant right-to-left script, it was her Persian poetry lesson for the day. As she glanced at it without interest, a discreet shuffling came from outside.

A moment later, an elderly man appeared, shoeless, in her doorway. He wore the characteristic long shirt and baggy trousers of northern India and Afghanistan. A shawl lay draped across his shoulders.

"*As-salaam-o-alaikum, Bibi,*" he offered mildly, and he stepped inside.

Mariana leapt to her feet, her skirts swaying, the fingers of her right hand pressed to her forehead in greeting. "And peace be upon you, Munshi Sahib," she replied, glad that her aunt Claire had not witnessed such respectful treatment of an Indian native.

Her munshi was exactly the person she wanted to see.

At first glance, Mariana's language teacher seemed no more than a wispy old man with a three-day growth of beard and a *qaraquli* hat set squarely on his narrow head, but Munshi Sahib was far more than that. He was a Follower of the Path, and a custodian of secrets that Mariana longed to learn.

He did not sit down, although she had invited him to do so many times. Instead, he came and stood as usual beside her chair, rocking a little on his stocking feet, his hands clasped behind his back.

"Have you finished your translation, Bibi?" he asked, inclining his head toward the paper on the table.

"I have, Munshi Sahib," she replied, frowning up at him, "but today is not a day for mystic poetry. There is something else I need to know."

Her dread returned as she told him of her dream. While she spoke, he shifted his gaze to the doorway and looked outside, as if he were imagining the same column of black-clad mourners marching noiselessly past her tent.

"Can you tell me what it means?" she asked, when she had finished.

He looked into her questioning face, his expression unreadable. "I can, Bibi," he replied gently, "but not today."

"Please, Munshi Sahib," she begged.

"I will say this much," he said gravely. "Whatever may happen in the future, you must not fear for yourself. You must allow yourself to be drawn toward your destiny."

He straightened his shoulders. "I will recite a verse," he announced. "It does not explain your dream, but it offers knowledge that may prove useful to you when the time comes."

With that, he began to declaim in a language Mariana did not understand, his eyes half closed, his voice a minor singsong. He drew out some sounds and hurried past others, producing the same throaty vowels and half-stops that had beckoned to her ever since she had first heard them.

He was speaking neither Urdu nor Persian, for she had studied both languages.

"I have recited a small portion of the Holy Qur'an in Arabic," he said when he had finished, confirming her guess.

"Like all Qur'anic verses, this one has multiple meanings," he added. "I will give you the most straightforward of them. You must keep it in your heart."

She nodded, wondering why he looked at her with such intensity.

"*I call to witness,*" he intoned, bringing his hands in front of him, moving them in arcs as he drew out his words, "*the ruddy glow of sunset;*

"The Night and its Homing, and
The Moon in her Fullness;
Thou shalt surely travel
From stage to stage."

She nodded, then unable to help herself, she blurted out her other question, the one she had wanted to ask ever since they left India, three weeks earlier.

"Please tell me, Munshi Sahib," she pleaded, certain he could tell her, but equally convinced he would not, "will I return to Lahore? Will I ever see Saboor or his father again?"

Her teacher smiled. "That, Bibi," he said gently, "is for you to discover yourself."

Why had he chosen that particular verse? she wondered, as he vanished around a corner of her tent after bidding her a polite good-bye.

Did it explain her dream? Did it reveal her future?

❦

THAT SAME afternoon in a bright courtyard in the walled city of
Lahore, a merchant raised his voice.

"Speak to us of Paradise," he said.

He wore gold rings and an intricately embroidered shawl, but for
all his obvious prosperity, the merchant lowered his eyes before the
man in a tall, starched headdress who sat before him on a padded
platform, the sun warming his back.

Shaikh Waliullah, leader of the Karakoyia Brotherhood of Sufis,
nodded gravely.

As he surveyed his seated followers, several of them exchanged
meaningful glances. "Have you noticed?" they murmured. "Have
you seen?"

The object of their gossip was the Shaikh's powerful gaze. At once
intimidating and healing, it had been feared and venerated throughout the walled city for thirty years.

In the past few weeks it had softened.

Some said this change was due to the sweet presence of the
Shaikh's successor, his four-year-old grandson who now sat beside
him, listening, round-eyed, to each afternoon's conversation, a small
hand resting on his grandfather's knee.

Others believed it was due to worry, for the Shaikh's son lay in an
upstairs room, recovering from grievous wounds. Still others blamed
it on grief, for the old man's foreign daughter-in-law, the woman
who had once rescued Saboor from certain death, had abandoned
the family, and run away to Kabul with her own people.

The Shaikh cleared his throat.

"Paradise," he began in his deceptively light voice, "is the Garden
of the Beloved. Its very air is filled with Divine Love.

"Nowhere on earth," he added, as his audience sighed in unison,
"will you find its equal—not even among the fertile valleys of Kashmir. Our finest fruits—our mangoes and grapes, our melons and
blood oranges—are but a weak imitation of the glorious fruits of
Paradise.

"In the Garden, the fortunate will find loving companions. They
will drink from the fountain of Salsabil. And those who have striven
hardest will have the greatest reward of all, for they will come face to
face with the Beloved."

The child Saboor shifted at his grandfather's side, and looked up
into his face.

"What is it, my darling?" inquired the Shaikh looking down at this small interruption. "What do you wish to know?"

"Is An-nah coming home soon?" the child whispered.

"He wants his foreign stepmother," murmured the followers. "He wants her to return."

The Shaikh frowned. "You have not been listening, Saboor."

The little boy hunched his body. "I am afraid," he said in a small voice. "I am afraid for An-nah."

"Ah," the followers whispered uneasily, "the child knows something. He has seen into the future."

Chapter 1

March 22, 1841

Mariana Givens rode into the capital of Afghanistan on the morning after the Afghan New Year. Riding sidesaddle next to her aunt's palanquin with its twelve trotting bearers, and followed on foot by a tall groom and a tough, albino mail courier, she played only a modest role in the dignified procession of English people that paraded past the great, frowning citadel, then turned toward the British cantonment.

Sir William Macnaghten, the Political Envoy, and his beaming, newly arrived wife, led the march on an elephant, preceded by a cavalry escort. Mariana's uncle rode behind them on horseback with his foppish assistant, Lady Macnaghten's Charles Mott, who was also nephew. Mariana and her aunt came next, followed by more cavalry and a long line of trudging servants and coolies and scores of pack animals carrying the camp tents, Lady Macnaghten's silver, bone china, and Bohemian glass; the household goods of Mariana's family; and enough champagne and brandy to last the Residence for a year.

Aunt Claire held the curtain of her palanquin aside, and put her head out. "Sir William seemed very pleased to see his wife again after all these months," she observed in the sonorous tone she reserved for the discussion of senior officials and their families. "And Lady

Macnaghten appeared especially happy this morning as we were leaving Bootik, or wherever that was. She looked positively girlish!"

Mariana did not respond. Instead, she glanced behind her, over the heads of Yar Mohammad and Ghulam Ali, past the cavalry and the baggage train, toward the forbidding Hindu Kush Range that divided India from Central Asia. Those mountains, whose stony valleys and dangerous passes they had crossed so laboriously, seemed no farther behind them than they had been when the travelers had set out from camp four hours earlier.

She blinked, hoping it was only the bright, deceiving air that made them seem to follow her, then drew her shawls closer about her, longing for the warm plains of India, where she had left her heart.

Dust storms would rise soon from the flat plain of the Punjab, turning the sun to a red disk and filling the air with fine grit that irritated people's eyes and crunched between their teeth. The hot weather would bring the dreaded *lu*, the hot, arid wind that killed children and old people, and dropped farmers dead of heatstroke in their fields. But for all the discomfort of India, if Mariana's circumstances had allowed it, she would gladly have abandoned her aunt and uncle and the rest of Lady Macnaghten's traveling party and turned back to Shaikh Waliullah's house in the walled city of Lahore. There, while the dust blew in through the *haveli*'s shuttered windows, she would have sung nonsense rhymes to little Saboor, and laid cool compresses on Hassan Ali Khan's forehead—that is, if he had wished her to do so.

Surely she would find a way to return there, and atone for her mistakes....

Ringed by snow-topped mountain ranges and watered by a winding river that bore its name, the city of Kabul stood six thousand feet above sea level. Bounded on the northwest by the Kabul River, on the south by the Sher Darwaza heights, and on the southeast by the Bala Hisar, its great fortress of kings, the city occupied a roughly triangular area on the western edge of its high, fertile plateau.

When Lady Macnaghten's traveling party emerged from the mountains and onto the Kabul plain, its members had found themselves in a demi-paradise. The sky above the tree-lined road was a sharp blue, quite different from the bleached sky of India. Bright light fell upon vast mulberry and apricot orchards, still veiled in the wispy red that precedes the green of spring. The skirts of the surrounding hills, some still boasting ancient fortified walls, were beginning to turn green, while here and there tulips and hyacinths pushed their way up through the soil. The air was so clear that Mariana easily made out the facial expressions of three men standing on a distant road.

Traveling west from Butkhak, they had crossed the Logar River at Begrami, then paraded past the frowning Bala Hisar before turning northwest toward the Kohistan Road and the newly built cantonment, symbol of the recent political triumph of the British, and their powerful military presence in Afghanistan.

Men passed on the road, their loose garments flowing about them, carrying loads on their heads or leading strings of camels. Mariana studied them, amazed by how different they were from the Indians she was accustomed to.

Bristling with weapons, their backs upright, these men moved swiftly, with fluid, ground-covering strides, their eyes fixed on the distance, unlike the Indians, who moved about unarmed, their shoulders hunched thoughtfully.

A stocky fellow stepped toward Mariana. Greasy hair hung below his loosely tied turban. The handle of a knife protruded from an opening in the man's coarse, woolen coat. His face was narrow and harsh. Mariana saw that his eyes were circled with black kohl. He was followed by a youth with a large bundle on his back.

"*As salaam-o-alaikum,* may peace be upon you," she offered politely.

He strode past without acknowledging her, but the youth behind him paused. He stared into her face with startlingly beautiful eyes, his heart-shaped face intent. Before she had time to nod, the older man looked over his shoulder. His mouth twisting, he reached for his knife. The boy dropped his gaze and hurried after the man.

There had been something odd about the boy.

"What are you doing, child?" Aunt Claire inquired, putting her head out for a second time between her palanquin curtains. "Surely you were not speaking to the *natives*!"

The British cantonment and its neighboring residence compound for government staff stood on the Kohistan Road, a mile north of the Bala Hisar, where the new British-approved puppet king had been installed. A walled parallelogram built to accommodate the British army and its twelve thousand camp followers, the cantonment was surrounded prettily by irrigated orchards and overlooked by the nearby Bibi Mahro and Sia Sang hills.

Mariana's old interest in military matters quickened as the cantonment's long ramparts became visible through the trees. She studied its fortifications, remembering the books she and her father had read together, imagining the questions he would ask in his next letter.

A large bazaar had been built outside one of the fort's heavy corner towers. Through several openings in its mud brick outer wall, Mariana glimpsed narrow, busy streets filled with small shops displaying colorful wares. Peopled by the artisans and shopkeepers who had accompanied the British army, the bazaar looked like any Indian town; indeed, it was larger than many towns, for it housed several thousand souls. As the procession passed by it, the air that had been perfumed with the scent of poplar balsam took on the added tang of wood smoke, sewage, and spices.

After the procession had halted, and the Macnaghtens and Charles Mott had been ushered ceremoniously away to their grand house in the Residence compound, Mariana frowned.

"I had thought the walls would be higher, Uncle Adrian," she said thoughtfully. "After all, we are invaders here. And I wonder why the surrounding ditch is so narrow. It seems to me—"

"You and the Would-Be-General must wait for that information," her uncle replied. "Once we are settled, you will have plenty of time to pepper everyone with your military questions. As for me, I shall barely have the time to fulfill my own duties. I understand that only a few of our people here are able to speak Farsi, and hardly anyone knows a word of Pushto."

"Poor Uncle Adrian." Mariana dropped her voice. "I don't suppose Charles Mott is any use, either."

Her uncle spread his hands. "Charles Mott holds Lady Macnaghten's elbow, that is all."

The polyglot population of Afghanistan had two principal languages. Of these, Farsi, or Persian, would always do as a court language, but Pushto was spoken by all the tribesmen who lived near the border with India—the same area the British army had passed through on its triumphant march to Kabul.

"How will you be able to communicate with people and gather information?" she asked.

Her uncle shrugged. "We can use Farsi," he replied, as they followed a young officer to their assigned bungalow in the Residence compound. "But if we cannot understand the subtleties of a man's own language, we will never know what he is thinking."

❧

"I UNDERSTAND," Mariana's aunt Claire declared two mornings later, as she, her husband, and Mariana sat on mismatched chairs in their dining room, "that Kabul is becoming quite a gay station. It is no wonder that our officers are now sending for their wives and children. They are playing cricket and putting on theatricals. They are even arranging picnics to lovely places within reach of the city."

She sighed happily as an elderly manservant poured her a cup of coffee. "I shall be delighted to stretch my legs, now that we are away from that stifling Indian heat."

"There is to be a race meeting tomorrow," Uncle Adrian put in. "I understand that Afghan horsemen will participate."

"A race meeting?" Aunt Claire sniffed. "I have no intention of attending a third-class horse race with a lot of Afghans. Besides," she waved toward a heap of bundles on the drawing room floor, "we haven't even had the carpets unrolled, and that hunched-over servant of Mariana's pretends not to understand a word I say. How will I have the pictures hung if you're gone all afternoon?"

Uncle Adrian signaled for more toast. "Shah Shuja, our new Amir," he said, "is expected to be present with his court. All our senior officers will be in attendance on the king, but there will be a separate tent for the other officers and all the ladies. Both Lady Sale and Lady Macnaghten are expected."

His wife sat straight in her chair. "Why did you not say so?" she cried. "Of course I shall be delighted to—"

"Now, Mariana," he went on, "you must be *very* careful at the race meeting. Do not speak to the Afghans, or meet their eyes. In Central Asia it is considered extremely bad manners for a woman to look openly at a strange man."

"Adrian, I am shocked!" The edging on Aunt Claire's lace cap quivered with indignation. "Surely an innocent Englishwoman may look at whomever she pleases!"

"Furthermore," he persisted, "the good opinion of our own officers is vital to your future, Mariana. You must do your utmost to behave correctly. Your reputation has suffered considerably in the past two years. And you must *on no account* reveal that you are technically married to an Indian native."

Mariana laid down her fork. "Uncle Adrian, there is no need to remind me—"

"You are the only eligible Englishwoman in Afghanistan, and since young Lieutenant Fitzgerald may be coming tomorrow—"

"*Fitzgerald?*" Aunt Claire's pudgy face turned radiant. "If there is the slightest chance Lieutenant Fitzgerald will be at the horse race tomorrow," she announced, "then I would not miss it for *all the world.*"

"I AM looking forward to my first public appearance," Lady Macnaghten confided as she and Mariana perched together on a sofa in the Residence's sitting room. "I shall wear my blue watered-silk, and a few feathers. As my husband is to be seated in the royal enclosure with the Shah," she added with a little sigh, "I shall have to manage without him."

Mariana smiled politely. What time was it? How long would she have to listen to Lady Macnaghten talk about herself?

As if she had heard Mariana's thoughts, Lady Macnaghten leaned toward her, close enough to reveal a few faint lines around her eyes. "Lieutenant Fitzgerald has returned from Kandahar," she whispered meaningfully. "I have told him that he must on no account miss the race meeting. You must therefore look your *very* best. I am sending Vijaya to you this afternoon."

Fitzgerald. The person Mariana most dreaded seeing. If the lieutenant came tomorrow, her appearance would be the very least of her worries. "That is very kind of you, Lady Macnaghten," she demurred. "But I am sure I shall manage perfectly well."

"Perfectly well will *not* be good enough." Lady Macnaghten waved a manicured hand. "Your hair and skin are dry. You have let yourself go entirely since we left India. When Vijaya is done," she added confidently, "you will look as pretty as you did then. And after tomorrow, it will be only a matter of time before Fitzgerald proposes.

"And of course," she added, ignoring Mariana's stricken face, "I shall not mention this to a soul."

Mariana got hastily to her feet. "Thank you so much, Lady Macnaghten," she said firmly, "but I must leave. I fear my aunt is waiting for me."

Proposes. If Lady Macnaghten, or the British community, learned the truth about her marriage to Hassan, they would stop forcing her on Harry Fitzgerald.

If they knew, they would never speak to her again.

Two hours later, she sat at a makeshift dressing table in her bed-room, a towel about her shoulders while Lady Macnaghten's silent, sari-clad maid combed henna paste through her hair.

Only Lady Macnaghten, who herself made good use of Indian beauty tricks, had noticed Mariana's transformation after her visit to Lahore, from clumsy English girl to elegantly cared-for native wife. She alone had seen that transformation fade, then disappear, on the journey from Lahore.

Mariana did not need to look in her hand glass to know how much she had changed since her arrival in India three years earlier.

On that first day, twenty years old, pink-cheeked and clumsy, she had flung herself into Aunt Claire's arms, certain she would be mar-ried to a handsome English officer before a year had passed. Young, and optimistic, she had believed she had nothing to lose.

But she had lost, then lost again, and with each failure she had given up a little more of her innocence about herself.

Her face had thinned a little in that time, and her rosy cheeks had turned to ivory, but her skin already felt smooth from Vijaya's efforts, and after a tortuous session with a cat's-cradle of twisted string, her brows now formed graceful arches over her eyes. The henna would tame her curls, and make them shine.

By the time Vijaya left, Mariana would, ironically, look once again like Hassan's wife.

Of course, myopic Aunt Claire would be unlikely to notice any of these changes. Only yesterday, as she poked fretfully through her jewelry, she had listed the same tired complaints she always made concerning her niece's looks and deportment.

"I hope you will listen to me this time," she had warned. "As you are about to make an entirely undeserved new start in British society in Kabul, you must rein in your outspoken manner. Cultivate de-mureness. And for goodness sake do something about that huge, un-fashionable smile of yours."

Mariana had sighed as her aunt swept from the room. The new start that Aunt Claire referred to was more than undeserved. It was a sham.

Three weeks after she had taken painful leave of the unconscious Hassan, his luminous little son and his fascinating family and joined Lady Macnaghten's traveling party, Mariana had gathered her courage and swept into her uncle's tent. Expecting no sympathy from her cholera-ridden uncle or his exhausted wife, she had gone straight to the point.

"I must tell you," she had blurted out, without any softening preamble, "that I did not divorce Shaikh Waliullah's son while I was in Lahore. He may have divorced *me* since then, but I do not believe he has."

As she spoke, she had reached up and touched the bodice of her gown. Under the fabric, her searching fingers found the gold medallion the wounded Hassan had sent after her, carried by the courier Ghulam Ali.

A wavering note had accompanied his gift. *For my wife,* it had read.

Giddy with happiness, she had sent Hassan a passionate, gushing letter of thanks. In the five weeks since then, he had not replied.

"He might also," she had added, her voice dropping, "have died."

Uncle Adrian's face had changed color. "You *never* divorced that man, after all the trouble we went to?" he had croaked from his pillows.

"I tried, Uncle Adrian, I really did. There was fighting in the city and my husband was constantly—"

"Never mind 'fighting in the city,'" Aunt Claire cut in from her folding chair. "For the past weeks you have led us to believe that all was accomplished, that you were free to marry an Englishman once we reached Afghanistan. *You have lied to us,* Mariana."

"I merely avoided the truth. Uncle Adrian has been so ill. I did not wish to burden you with more than—"

"I should have insisted." Aunt Claire's chins wobbled with outrage. "I should have questioned you as soon as you returned from the city." Her eyes narrowed. "Mariana, I demand to know the truth. Did you ruin yourself while you were there? *Did you allow your native husband to take liberties with you at his father's house?*"

"Please, Claire. Adil is here." Uncle Adrian signaled to the elderly manservant who hovered, fascinated, near the doorway of the tent.

"I allowed nothing," Mariana snapped, as soon as the servant had gone. "With Lahore under attack, there simply was no time for a divorce. Besides, my husband was wounded during the battle at the Citadel."

"But we told you a thousand times that your *one* chance at happiness depended upon the dissolution of that hateful native alliance of yours. Even with your uncle half-dead with cholera I should never have trusted you. My mother-in-law," Aunt Claire said cruelly, "told me *never* to trust a woman with green eyes. Everyone thinks you are free now," she added mournfully. "Lady Macnaghten has told me herself that Lieutenant Fitzgerald is waiting anxiously for you in Kabul."

She found her handkerchief and dabbed her eyes. "*Why* do you do these things? *What* will your mother say? I promised her I would look after you—"

"Why should we tell anyone?" Uncle Adrian interrupted. "People will not talk about something they do not know."

"Oh, but they will, Adrian, they *will*! But wait—" Aunt Claire's tired face had brightened. "Perhaps you are right."

"Aunt Claire. I—"

"No, Mariana. You must listen to us. That native wedding of yours was a fraud from the beginning—nothing but mumbo jumbo recited outside a tent by a native in a headdress. Since you were never really married, there is no need for a divorce. We shall go on exactly as we had planned," she concluded firmly, holding up a silencing hand when Mariana tried to speak. "*No one* is to learn what you have told us. They must continue to believe your marriage has been dissolved. As far as we are concerned *you are free to wed an Englishman.*"

After leaving them, Mariana had stopped outside, straining to hear what her aunt would say next, then jumped back, stung by what she heard, and furious with herself for listening.

"Nothing would make me happier," her aunt had declared, "than to learn that the man is dead."

Three weeks later the camp had folded its many tents and set off for the Khyber Pass and the journey into Afghanistan.

Chapter 2

By the end of March, Kabul's bazaars and caravanserais echoed with the shouts of merchants from India and Arabia selling chintzes, indigo, drugs, and sugar, or perfumes and spices. To the north, the caravans from Russia and China, from Orenburg, Bokhara, and Samarkand, had already begun to thread their way down through the high, icy passes of the Hindu Kush mountains, bringing Chinese crockery, tea, bales of silk, and fine Turkmen horses.

Even without the northern traders, the city bustled with more excitement than usual, for the royal race meeting was expected to attract horses, riders, and serious gamblers from far outside the capital.

From every direction, heavily armed men and boys streamed toward the city.

The races were to be held on a flat plain in the shadow of the brown Bibi Mahro hills that rose from the flat plain north of the city. There, the old racecourse ran in a straight line from west to east, ending almost at the brick ramparts of the British cantonment. Two miles long, it offered plenty of room for horse and camel races, wrestling, and *naiza bazi,* the graceful game of tent-pegging.

On the morning of the meeting, Mariana crept about the house hoping to avoid her aunt, but to no avail. "Come and join us in the verandah," Aunt Claire hallooed after breakfast. "It is so lovely here in Kabul," she murmured, adjusting her shawl as Mariana sat down in a basket chair. "With such delightful weather and clear air, I have quite forgotten the discomforts of India."

Mariana nodded warily. *Please do not mention Fitzgerald,* she pleaded silently.

"And now, my dear," her aunt continued, in a voice that must have carried all the way to the road outside, "we have just learned that *he* will be present tomorrow. This is very good news, all we could wish for. You and Lieutenant Fitzgerald are to meet again at last!

"Of course the meeting will not be quite as I had imagined," she added severely, "but the important point is that you will meet. You must heed our advice. Do *not* mention your current situation. No one must know of it, *no one.* And do not be too free with the lieutenant on your first meeting."

Mariana stiffened.

"Now, Mariana," her uncle begged, "we encourage you to be careful only because we know how much this meeting means to you. After all, whether we like it or not, you are well-known for your indiscretion.

"And now," he added, rising from his seat, "I must be off."

"I shall be *more* than discreet with Lieutenant Fitzgerald," Mariana retorted. "I shall barely speak to him."

"What nonsense." Aunt Claire peered into Mariana's face. "What have you done to your eyebrows?"

Mariana jumped to her feet. "I must change," she said hastily.

"Whatever you do," her aunt called after her, "remember to behave normally."

Normally. Mariana closed her door firmly behind her. What was normal behavior in a person who might still be married to a native man, but was not allowed to say so? She jerked open her latticework window shutters and leaned outside, her face to the sun.

Her aunt was correct about one thing. Whether she wished to or not, she would have to face Harry Fitzgerald.

He had been handsome, with his straight blond hair and fine Roman profile. He had been good-humored and unconcerned by her less than perfect appearance when she lost her hairpins or buttoned her gown wrong. Like her, he was fascinated by military history. His high-collared blue jacket, the uniform of the Bengal Horse Artillery, smelled deliciously musty. Harry Fitzgerald had been the perfect husband for her, or so she had thought.

Then a piece of false gossip about him had surfaced that had ruined their prospects. Forced to give him up, she had thought she would die from the pain.

She sighed and turned from the window. Now, too late, he had been redeemed, and everyone from Aunt Claire to Lady Macnaghten was anxious to see them engaged.

Had she married Fitzgerald, she would have been a military wife for the past year—stitching embroidery all day, and paying calls on the wives of senior officers, none of whom knew, or cared, about India. She would already have endured months of loneliness, while he campaigned in Afghanistan.

Perhaps she would not have minded.

But she had not married him. Instead, she had gone from adventure to adventure, and become a different person in the process. She had also done more than fail to divorce Hassan Ali Khan.

I allowed nothing, she had lied when Aunt Claire had demanded the truth. But the fact was that three days after she returned little Saboor safely to his family in Lahore, Hassan had slipped into her bedroom, and she had given herself to him without a murmur.

As sweet as musk, she is, he had whispered that night.

She reached absently into a tin trunk, pulled out a silk afternoon gown, and shook it out. Of course her life in Lahore would have been largely confined to the Shaikh's upstairs family quarters, and she would have spent much of her time waiting for Hassan to return from his work or his travels, but she did not care. Any amount of confinement would have been worth it, if she were Hassan's wife.

Besides, there was so much to learn in the Waliullah house. Among the Shaikh's family women, she would have found a whole world of knowledge to absorb—poetry, philosophy, and the mysterious science of healing. At night, Hassan, long-limbed and compelling, would have bent over her as he had once before, his bearded face intent, his warm, inviting perfume barely covering the scorched scent of his skin.

That night, he had called her *Mariam.*

She had foolishly lost him the very next day, but perhaps not forever. Perhaps he would change his mind, and come to find her. . . .

She looked without interest at the striped, silver-gray gown in her hands. Lady Macnaghten had already complained that its color was too dull, but Mariana did not care. She buttoned herself into it, twisted her curls up and pinned them to the top of her head, found her fine straw bonnet and left the room.

If only people would stop interfering in her private life....

She sighed as she approached the drawing room where Aunt Claire sat with her sewing. She should tell Fitzgerald the truth. Before he showed interest in her, she should tell him that her marriage to Shaikh Waliullah's son had not been the repugnant mistake everyone thought it was, but an accident of fate that she hoped had set her on the threshold of a new life. She should apologize for any past misunderstanding, and state firmly that although her marital state was unknown, her sole ambition was to return to a comfortable old haveli in the walled city of Lahore.

But the cost of such honesty would surely be too high. Tainted by her association with natives, called a liar by people who thought she had divorced Hassan, she would be ostracized—flung to the bottom of an invisible social ladder, to be trampled by everyone but the natives themselves.

And by association, her aunt and uncle would suffer, ignored, insulted, and barred from the company of "decent" people.

To them, her marriage to Fitzgerald was a social necessity. To Lady Macnaghten, arranging the marriage of a social inferior was a pleasant way to pass the time.

Mariana sighed again as she opened the drawing room door. If Hassan did not take her back, her feelings would cease to matter, for Harry Fitzgerald would represent her last chance to marry and have children of her own.

BY THE time Mariana and her aunt arrived at the race meeting, the morning's events had already taken place.

As her trotting bearers huffed their way toward the spectators' tents, Mariana opened the side of her palanquin, and peered disobediently out.

Tea sellers with tall, brass samovars and hawkers of trinkets and tobacco were everywhere. Men in loose gray or white clothes and embroidered waistcoats squatted beside pits of hot coals, threading bits of mutton and goat's meat onto long, wicked-looking skewers.

Others sold dried apricots, raisins, and roasted pine nuts from the backs of donkeys. On a low rise near the tents, a group of white-bearded men sat beneath a spreading plane tree, sharing a water pipe, their eyes on the pairs of boys who wrestled below, in the time-honored way, each one gripping his opponent's arms, trying to throw him off balance.

The crowd thickened. Mariana's palanquin slowed. As her bearers shouted for room, someone bent to look inside.

"*Mairmuna,*" he cried, blocking her view. "*Mairmuna!*"

It was the slim boy with the heart-shaped face whom she had encountered three days before. As her palanquin began to move again, he kept pace with it, talking rapidly and unintelligibly, his urgent face a foot from hers, his clothes smelling unpleasantly of unwashed human skin.

"I have no idea what you are saying," she told him in Farsi, waving him away.

For all his fuzzy-chinned youth, the boy gave off an odd depravity. He looked at her exactly as he had on the road, his arms loose at his sides, his whole being focused upon her.

Unnerved, she banged on the roof above her head, signaling her bearers to hurry.

"*Khanum,* lady!" he cried after her, as the palanquin surged through an opening in the crowd, using, too late, a word she understood.

The spectator tents stood twenty feet apart on sloping ground above the racecourse. Between them, British civil and military officers clustered, laughing loudly, the sound of their voices drawing stares from the Afghans.

The Shah's splendid enclosure of densely embroidered woolen hangings put the British family tent, a mess tent commandeered for the occasion, to shame. As she passed it, Mariana glanced guiltily inside. The pudgy, nervous-looking Afghan who sat on a dais covered in gold satin must be Shah Shuja. The king's turban was pushed well back above a sour face, revealing a bulging forehead and a shaven hairline. Other Afghans sat around him on the carpeted ground, while folding chairs held rows of British officers in morning coats and top hats or dress uniforms.

The Amir's chiefs were quite unlike the officials of an Indian maharajah's court. Accustomed to the style of the Punjab, Mariana would have been unimpressed by males covered in jewels and silks, but here was something very different. These men were not showily attired, although their long, fur-trimmed coats looked soft and expensive, and their turbans were all of striped silk. Most were handsome, with strong features and full beards—even the evil-looking old man with missing ears, who bent, whispering, over his king—but more than their appearance, it was the Afghans' watchful tension that caught Mariana's eye, so different from the relaxed, almost languid poses of some of the British officers.

The bespectacled, top-hatted Sir William Macnaghten sat on one side of the king, accompanied by a rotund younger gentleman who lounged, smiling, in his chair, one foot extended in front of him. He must be, Mariana concluded, Alexander Burnes, the British Resident, and Macnaghten's second-in-command.

At the Shah's other side, resplendent in gold epaulettes and many medals, three senior army officers looked stiffly out at the crowd. Mariana identified the first easily. An elderly, wizened general, he was surely the old Commander in Chief, who might soon be leaving for India. An officer, also a general, with a long nose and a scarred face, might be Sir Robert Sale.... Mariana stared at him, fascinated. Now known as the Hero of Ghazni, General Sale had personally led the charge that had captured the great fortress by the same name, as he traveled north to Kabul with the invading British army.

A real, fighting general—she must find a way to converse with him. Her father would be so pleased.

The last of the three—a sour-looking one-armed brigadier—turned to speak to someone behind him.

Mariana ducked hastily into the shadows of her palanquin. That someone was her uncle.

Inside the second, plainer tent, a double row of chairs faced out at the racecourse, where quicklime had been used to mark off lanes and starting lines. There a few ladies and uniformed officers stood uncertainly, as if waiting for someone important to arrive.

Lady Macnaghten swept inside on her nephew's arm a few moments later, feathers bobbing in her hair, her blue watered-silk rustling. Before lowering herself into an armchair in the front row, she offered Mariana and her aunt a discreet nod of greeting.

Charles Mott offered Mariana a longing glance.

Aunt Claire beamed with pleasure at such public recognition, then bent toward Mariana as a tall, plain-looking woman strode in, escorted by an army major and followed by a young, sour-faced version of herself.

"That is Lady Sale and her daughter, Mrs. Sturt," Aunt Claire murmured, as the two women were handed to front-row seats.

Mariana studied the new arrival's angular profile. No one could have been less like the manicured Lady Macnaghten than the wife of the Hero of Ghazni, with her thin-lipped face and unbecoming gown. As Mariana watched, Lady Sale nodded abruptly to Lady Macnaghten, then, without another word, raised a pair of opera glasses and surveyed the racecourse.

"I find her quite difficult," Lady Macnaghten had confided to Mariana. "She says whatever she chooses, whether it is rude or not, and she discusses military matters as if she were an officer herself. And if you can imagine it, she had her portrait done while wearing a man's striped turban!"

A moment later, wedged into a folding chair between her aunt and a pregnant woman with gray hair, Mariana craned her neck toward the track, looking for a sign of horsemen.

Lady Sale beckoned to the stiff-backed major. "What is the purpose of those?" she inquired, pointing toward four small tents that had been set up opposite them, along the margin of the course.

"I have no idea, Lady Sale," the major replied, standing at attention. "They were not here yesterday."

Martial music sounded in the distance. The crowd fell silent. Nearly hidden by a cloud of dust, a mounted procession had begun its approach from the far end of the racecourse.

A group of smartly uniformed British officers came first, riding glossy horses and carrying the regimental flag of the 5th Light Cavalry. They were followed by bearded Afghans, whose handsome, brightly dressed mounts were easily as good as those of the British. Each group had its own colorful triangular standard, and each of its four riders carried a nine-foot lance with three prongs at its end. A second lot of British officers came next, then a few more Afghans, followed by members of the Irregular Horse, and finally, a large, disorderly group of tribesmen on showily caparisoned horses, carrying the same unusual-looking lances.

Mariana looked carefully at the Afghans as they rode past, each one radiating a careless self-possession. Hassan had been wounded in the Hazuri Bagh; the Afghans who had saved him had looked like these men.

She thought of them now, carrying him through the dark, violent city, risking their lives for a man they hardly knew. . . .

As the second group of British officers passed by, Lady Macnaghten drew herself straight, her feathers quivering. "Why," she trilled pointedly, "I believe that is the Bengal Horse Artillery!"

"Where?" Aunt Claire's fingers closed on Mariana's knee.

Mariana started. Lieutenant Harry Fitzgerald was passing not a hundred feet away, on a gray gelding Mariana recognized from two years earlier. How could she have missed that distinctive uniform with its black, shiny helmet and long, scarlet horsehair plume? How could she have missed Fitzgerald's handsome Roman profile or his strong, stocky body, so different from Hassan's long slim form in its flowing Eastern clothes?

Panic overtook her. She looked away, unable to speak.

Aunt Claire pinched her leg. "Is *he* among them?"

"Do they not look handsome in their dress uniforms?" fluted Lady Macnaghten.

Lady Sale sniffed audibly.

All the participants had ranged themselves along the sidelines, to wait for their events. Fitzgerald now stood near the finish line, among a group of British officers.

To her relief, he did not turn or look upward toward the tents.

He was not in the first event, a display of charging drills by the 5th Light Cavalry. Nor was he in the second. Keeping her eyes from him, Mariana tried to summon her usual curiosity as preparations were made for the third event.

Men had been hammering tent pegs into the ground fifty yards down the course, each peg marked with a colorful flag. Twenty yards beyond the pegs, two more flags marked a finish line. More men appeared beside the track, with drums of varying sizes suspended from their necks. As they beat a steady, hypnotic rhythm, four tribesmen rode toward the starting line, each man carrying a lance.

"They call this naiza bazi," Lady Sale's officer said helpfully. "Each horseman must ride down the course, spear one of the pegs at full gallop, then carry it over the finish line without dropping it."

"There is no need to tell me," snapped Lady Sale. "*I* know tent-pegging when I see it."

Lances upright, the riders turned their backs to the course and waited for the signal, their horses dancing, shoulder to shoulder.

"But those horses are all entire," Lady Sale cried over the din of the drums. "Stallions, all of them. How extraordinary!"

At a squealing trumpet blast from the Amir's enclosure, the four animals spun about and charged in perfect unison down the course, their riders bent low over their necks, lances lowered and ready.

The drumming rose to a crescendo. As it did, all four horses launched themselves into the air as if they were clearing an invisible jump. An instant later, they landed and galloped on as all four lances swept upright, a tent peg impaled on each one.

"Ah," cried Lady Sale, "what horsemanship!"

"How romantic," sighed Lady Macnaghten.

After three more rounds of tent-pegging, it was Fitzgerald's turn at last: a four-mile race. Mariana watched reluctantly as he rode to the starting line with several other officers: two from the 5th, and two others whose uniforms Mariana did not recognize. Other horsemen joined them, a pair of wild-looking mustachioed men from the Irregular Horse, and a handsome Afghan boy on a tall black mount.

"Another stallion," observed Lady Sale.

"They are to ride to the end of the course, circle a plane tree at the end, and then return," said the officer.

Another trumpet blast and the horses were off in a thundering line. The young Afghan was in the lane nearest the tents. Mariana saw his whip arm rise and fall.

Fitzgerald must have known she would be among the spectators, but he had not looked up to find her. Mariana searched the galloping crowd, a hand to her eyes, but could see only dusty confusion as the field pulled away.

A cloud of fine grit rose over the spectators and filled the tent. Lady Macnaghten and Aunt Claire held lace handkerchiefs to their faces. The pregnant woman coughed noisily.

Lady Sale took no notice of the dust.

Thousands of Afghans stood on the slope below the tents and all along the edge of the course, watching as the horses returned, strung out in a line by now, a cavalry officer out in front on a tiring bay. Mariana looked for Fitzgerald's gray gelding, but could see only the big black stallion closing in on the lead, his young rider standing in the stirrups, his clothes billowing as he drove his horse to the finish, a thin arm lifting and falling in time with his horse's stride.

A moment later it was over. With a burst of speed, the black stallion overtook the bay. As it charged across the line, the boy rider threw his head back and spread his arms in victory.

"I should like to see," Lady Sale said tartly, "how that native child would have fared if *he* had been wearing a tight uniform and a dragoon helmet."

Fitzgerald was eighth.

After a few shorter races, all won by British officers, the meet was finished. The winners pushed their way up the crowded slope to receive their prizes from the Amir.

Lady Macnaghten yawned delicately behind her fan. "I suppose—" she began.

Whatever she supposed was interrupted by a fresh wave of sound from the plain below. The drummers were at work again, in greater numbers than before.

Pounding their double-ended drums, dancing to their own rhythms, they were certainly celebrating something, but what was it?

The crowd below was craning toward the far end of the course.

"What is this?" shouted an officer, as a line of horsemen appeared in the dusty distance. "The races are over. No one else is supposed to—"

Long lances at the ready, twelve horsemen galloped in single file toward the four small tents that had appeared so mysteriously, their guylines pegged out in a vulnerable line along the margin of the track.

One by one, the horses jumped. One by one, their pegs removed, the little tents trembled, then collapsed.

The riders pulled up dramatically, their horses rearing, in front of the royal enclosure. As the drums continued their din, their leader, a burly man with a thick black beard, wrenched the peg from his lance, hurled it toward the fallen tents, then galloped away, his henchmen behind him.

"Those tribesmen did *not* seem friendly to our cause," observed Lady Sale, when the drumming had ceased. "If I were Envoy," she glanced pointedly at Lady Macnaghten, "I would make sure they were brought round, whoever they are."

"Who were those horsemen?" Mariana murmured to her uncle's assistant, as they waited for the palanquins to arrive. "Did you and Uncle Adrian know of them?"

"No, Miss Givens." He flicked dust from his sleeve with nervous fingers. "No one has said a word. Miss Givens," he added, "would it be—"

"Charles! Charles Mott," Lady Macnaghten called out petulantly. "Stop talking to Miss Givens, and help me into my palanquin."

Mariana watched with relief as he rushed away. During the long journey from Calcutta, she had seen enough of her uncle's damp-faced assistant to last a lifetime.

A knot of officers had been standing a short distance away. One of them detached himself from the group and approached her, a black dragoon helmet beneath his arm.

It was Fitzgerald.

Mariana stiffened.

He bowed smartly. "Miss Givens," he said, "how delightful to see you here in Kabul."

He looked heavier than Mariana remembered. His straight, fair hair gleamed in the sun. He offered her a careful smile.

Mariana touched her aunt's arm. "Aunt Claire, may I present Lieutenant Fitzgerald?" she said, equally carefully.

"Oh," exclaimed her aunt. "Oh!"

"He is so much handsomer when seen face-to-face!" Aunt Claire burbled ten minutes later, as they got out of their palanquins. "Did you see his smile, so gentlemanly, so restrained? I cannot wait for him to call on us!"

Mariana did not reply. As she had stepped into her palanquin, Fitzgerald had offered her a second, different smile, a crooked, knowing one that she had nearly forgotten.

He was a living, breathing person. Until this moment, she had not even considered that fact.

Chapter 3

The following morning, the sound of someone scuffing off his shoes outside her door announced the arrival of Mariana's man-servant with her coffee.

Dittoo was a champion talker, whose many opinions were best heard when one was properly awake. As usual, as he pushed his way inside, the tray rattling in his hands, Mariana closed her eyes and feigned deep sleep.

He dropped the tray noisily onto her bedside table. "This house," he announced, ignoring her subterfuge, "is not good enough for you and your family, Bibi. The dining room is too small. Only five servants can fit inside while you are eating. Ghulam Ali says that open verandah will fill up with snow in the winter, and there are only these two bedrooms.

"As to the servants' quarters," he went on. "They have given only six rooms for forty servants, including the sweepers! I do not know where Ghulam Ali and Yar Mohammad will sleep, since they are Muslims, and—"

"Enough, Dittoo," she snapped. "We will build more quarters. Now go," she added firmly.

He leaned closer. "This is a dangerous place, Bibi," he whispered hoarsely.

She opened her eyes.

Her servant's ill-shaven face was bunched with anxiety. His shoulders drooped beneath his shabby uniform. He glanced over his shoulder. "Everyone is talking," he went on, "about the Afghan chief who came to the races yesterday, and swore his revenge against the British and their new king. These Afghans do terrible, cruel things. Your British people should never have come here, and thrown out their real ruler."

She sat up, the quilts to her chin, and swept the hair from her eyes. "That chief did not swear to anything," she declared. "And even if he had, we have an enormous fort, and a great army. With such protection, why should we fear one Afghan, even if he is a chief?"

She frowned as he hunched his way out of her room without replying.

"I thought they *wanted* us to come here, Uncle Adrian," she said later that morning. "I thought the Afghans had invited Shah Shuja to be king."

"Some of them had." Her uncle shrugged. "But some had not. In any case, we only invaded Afghanistan to prevent the Russians from taking the country over for themselves. No one wanted them threatening our possessions in India."

"And were the Russians really coming to India?"

He ran a hand through his fringe of hair. "It was never certain that they would. I understand," he added, "that yesterday's tribesmen were Achakzais from the Pishin valley, and their leader is the chief there, but he is not Shah Shuja's only enemy. Aminullah Khan from the Logar valley is another. Aminullah was one of Shuja's greatest allies at first, but he now has left in a huff, and we fear he has changed sides. People say he is old, palsied, and very deaf, but they also say he has ten thousand fighting men at his command, and is well-known for his cruelty."

Remembering Dittoo's fears, Mariana glanced toward the window. Outside, newly sown grass had begun to sprout in front of the verandah. Past the nearby houses, the high walls of the Residence rose protectively around Sir William Macnaghten's vast garden. It all seemed so peaceful.

"Macnaghten and Burnes do not seem to understand the locals," her uncle continued, "not even the previous royal family. I discovered only yesterday that Dost Mohammad's eldest son has not gone into exile in India with his father, but has vanished instead into the mountains north of here. No one seems to know, or care, where he is. If he is like other Afghans, he will not forget the injury we have done his father. I fear," he added thoughtfully, "we may have failed to understand the depth of these people's pride."

Pride. Mariana's munshi had told her that pride meant everything to an Afghan. Any one of them, especially a Pashtun tribesman, would willingly throw away his life to prove a point or defend a principle. He would never forget a service, would defend a guest to the death, and would offer asylum to anyone who asked properly, even someone who had murdered a member of his own family.

"If an Afghan's honor requires revenge," her old teacher had told her, "he will exact it, whatever the price. We have a saying in India: *May God save me from the fangs of the snake, the claws of the tiger, and the vengeance of the Afghan.*"

If all this were true, she thought, Afghanistan would be no easy country to control.

FOR SIXTEEN hundred years, through the coming and going of kings great and small, through endless destruction and rebuilding, the Bala Hisar had stood upon a high spur of the Sher Darwaza heights, overlooking the Kabul plain.

Its mud brick walls and heavy corner bastions had suffered considerable neglect in Dost Mohammad's time, but even in its dilapidated condition, the old citadel still cast a formidable shadow over the city at its feet.

Inside its walls, the Bala Hisar was crowded with buildings. Palaces, barracks, courtyards, stables, gardens, and municipal buildings crammed its lower reaches, while above them, the fort, with its armory and its fearful dungeon, looked out upon its long, crumbling, fortified walls that even now climbed up and down the distant hills, protecting the Kabul plain from the ghosts of long-forgotten marauders.

On the morning after the horse races, Shah Shuja-ul-Mulk, King of the Afghans, sat on a raised platform in the frescoed audience hall of his largest palace, his ministers ranged behind him. Sunlight entered the breezy clerestory windows above the king's head, glanced off his great striped turban, fell onto the shoulders of his embroidered coat and the silk bolster he leaned against, and bathed the rug where he sat, turning its tribal dyes to the color of precious stones.

Two black-coated Englishmen sat on chairs before the king's platform, their own retinue of officers behind them.

Shah Shuja regarded his guests with unhappy eyes. "Victory," he announced in high-pitched Persian, "has become dust in my mouth."

The British Resident and the British Envoy glanced at each other. "Dust, Sire?" the Envoy repeated.

"The chiefs," the Shah responded impatiently, "show me no respect. You saw what Abdullah Khan did yesterday. Why should he, or anyone else, honor me when my enemies are still alive and unblinded?"

The king's ministers nodded, their eyes on Macnaghten and Burnes.

"We do not," replied the bespectacled Sir William Macnaghten, "believe it necessary to kill chiefs simply because they do not like us. Besides, Highness, they are paying their taxes. They would not be doing so, or offering you respect, if they were dead."

"Or if their eyes had been put out," added the round-faced Sir Alexander Burnes.

"Taxes, taxes." The king raised beringed hands. "The Pashtun chiefs should not pay taxes."

"But," argued Burnes, "the chiefs *must* pay you. You are their sovereign."

Shah Shuja's hands dropped into his lap. "I am elder among elders, chief among chiefs. I am no despot, to be wringing money from tribes who share amongst each other. Wherever I look, I have new enemies. If you would let me charge the customary duties on your trade caravans, I would not need these taxes."

"Sire," said Macnaghten in his smoothest tone, "we cannot allow you to tax *our kafilas*."

"If I may not charge your kafilas, then you should give me the money I need. India is a rich country. Ahmad Shah Durrani supported this kingdom for years by plundering India. Now your people are enjoying its wealth, but you are not sharing it with me."

The king gestured about him. "Look at this household," he said, his voice rising. "I have three hundred retainers to maintain, not to mention the royal guard or the women. What of my ministers and their families? Surely, with all the millions of rupees that pour into your Indian treasury, you have enough to spare for these."

"As I have said, Sire," Macnaghten insisted, "the chiefs are paying their taxes."

"Then," Shah Shuja said wearily, "we are doomed."

"But why?" his visitors chorused, disbelief on their faces.

"The Eastern Ghilzai chiefs must be given gold to keep the passes open between here and India, while others must have their gold taken from them. Why should we take gold from one man, and hand that same gold to his enemy? Mark my words, the chiefs will not endure this inequity for long."

"We have heard your complaints, Sire," Macnaghten said a trifle sharply, "and now we must confer with our generals. If you will give us your kind permission, we shall return to the cantonment."

After the British delegation had been seen out past the intricately carved doorway of the audience chamber, the Shah turned to his elderly, earless vizier.

"Humza Khan," he sighed, "these *feranghi*s will be our undoing. Only their useless elephants will remain here in the Bala Hisar, devouring camel-loads of fodder each day, a testament to British folly and arrogance."

"Ah, Sire," replied the old vizier, "who can tell the future?"

ALTHOUGH THEY had been assured that none of the Shah's court understood English, Macnaghten did not speak until they had trotted their horses through the Bala Hisar's high main gate.

"First Shah Shuja wishes to kill the chiefs," Macnaghten said at last, "then he objects to taxing them. The man makes no common sense."

"And the money he spends!" Burnes shook his head. "His ministers were all wearing imported silks again. What have you heard from Calcutta?"

"I had another letter this morning, demanding we reduce our expenses." Macnaghten sighed. "If he had any political imagination, Lord Auckland would send *more* troops and *more* money. If we captured Herat and Peshawar, we would control this whole part of the world."

"Quite true, but impossible, given the visionless government we have," agreed Burnes as he steered his horse past an obstacle course of rocks.

Macnaghten shook his head. "I have no idea what to do now," he said heavily. "I suppose we could always turn our backs on Shuja, and return to India."

"And if we did," Burnes reminded him, "he would lose his head, and we would lose Afghanistan. Worse, we would no longer have the fruits and pleasures of Kabul to enjoy."

He smiled broadly as they and their escort clattered under the Lahori Gate and into the walled city. "Ah, Macnaghten," he cried, "how I love this country!"

Chapter 4

That night, at the sound of a string bed creaking in the darkness of her bedchamber, Shaikh Waliullah's twin sister opened her eyes.

Hassan was awake. He sat hunched over on the edge of his bed, his hair tangled, his bearded face scarcely visible in the starlight from the window, his heavily bandaged leg at an awkward angle from his body.

Dawn was far off, Safiya Sultana guessed, for she felt no instinctive urge to rise and wash for the pre-sunrise prayer. Instead, she raised herself on an ample elbow and studied the nephew she had nursed for the past nine weeks. "What is it, my dear?" she inquired. "Are your wounds troubling you?"

"No, Bhaji," Hassan Ali Khan replied softly. "I am thinking of Yusuf."

Safiya nodded. "May Allah Most Gracious bless and keep your dear friend."

"It was my fault," he said abruptly. "It was I who killed him."

Fully dressed, as always, in a comfortable *shalwar kameez*, Safiya sat up and cuffed her bolster into a more comfortable shape. "Nonsense," she declared. Her voice, as deep as a man's, echoed in the small chamber. "You and Yusuf were both shot in the Hazuri Bagh. You lived and Yusuf died. That is all there is to it."

He dropped his head. "They shot him because of me."

So that explained why Hassan's wounds were taking so long to close. Remorse was certainly no aid to healing. Needing time to think, Safiya offered her nephew a noncommittal grunt.

Memories of the recent civil strife that had led to Hassan's wounds and Yusuf's death were still raw in the walled city of Lahore, indeed in the whole kingdom of the Punjab.

It had taken Maharajah Sher Singh, the present king, three savage January days to wrest the throne of the Punjab from his hated rival, Rani Chand Kaur. While Sher Singh's gunners shot down into the Lahore Citadel from the high minarets of the old Badshahi Mosque and his artillery sent cannonballs through its smashed-in Alamgiri Gate, damaging the royal palace and military buildings and slaughtering courtiers, soldiers, and servants, thousands of his own hungry, unpaid soldiers found their way into the old city that shared the Citadel's ancient, fortified wall. There they had rampaged, uncontrolled, through the city's bazaars, invading its houses and murdering its citizens.

The wounds remained.

It was only through Allah's Grace that the Waliullah family's old haveli had been spared.

Hassan's odd English wife had proved useful more than once during that time. For all her odd behavior, the girl had her good points.

During the battle for the throne, an ambitious Englishman had tried to murder Maharajah Sher Singh. Learning of the plot, Hassan Ali had braved the fighting in the Hazuri Bagh with his friend Yusuf and two Afghans. Together, they had managed to thwart the assassination, but at the cost of Yusuf's life.

The Afghans had since disappeared, leaving the wounded Hassan the only witness to what had happened that day.

Afterward, wracked by fevers, Hassan had left that story to the imaginations of others. Too ill to care, he had ignored the speculation about his complicity in the assassination attempt, and the gossip that his English wife had sided with the British plotters and persuaded him to kill the Maharajah himself. Later, after Sher Singh had learned the truth, and the city had covered him with glory, he had still remained silent.

He had borne without complaint the surgeries that had rescued his left hand and cleaned out the wide, putrefying flesh wound on his leg. He had cried out, of course, as the surgeon plied his knives and his cauterizing tools, but to Safiya's ears, Hassan's groans had sounded like those of a man who knew he deserved punishment.

"I should never have gone to the Hazuri Bagh that day," Hassan said harshly. "I should have let Yusuf, Zulmai, and Habibullah do the work of stopping the assassination. Unlike me, they were well versed in the art of killing."

"It is true that you are no soldier," Safiya agreed, "and that the battlefield is no place for the Assistant Foreign Minister. And it is also true that Yusuf was a fighter, but what of your Afghans? I thought they were mere traders, men who come to Lahore every year, bringing saffron, rubies, and horses."

"Zulmai and Habibullah are merchants, but they are hard men, and expert shots." Hassan shook his head in the dimness. "If I had stayed in this house and not insisted on joining them, Yusuf would still be alive."

"Then why *did* you insist?"

He made a tired gesture. "I do not know, Bhaji. I thought they needed me—"

Whatever Hassan's secrets might be, they were doing him no good. "Speak of that day, my boy," Safiya Sultana ordered. "Tell me your story."

He sighed raggedly. "The Hazuri Bagh, where the battle took place," he began, describing from habit a place that Safiya, a lady in *purdah,* had never seen, "is the rectangular walled garden lying between the entrance to the Badshahi Mosque and the main, Alamgiri Gate to the Citadel. It is a small garden, only about a hundred paces broad and fifty paces deep, filled with old trees and ruins, with a pavilion at its center. With its high, surrounding walls, it is a dangerous place for a battle.

"We knew the four assassins would arrive early, and hide in the garden, and so we went there the night before Sher Singh began his attack on the Citadel. At first light, as the fighting began, we paired off and began to search for them. Within an hour, three of the four were dead, killed by Zulmai, Habibullah, and Yusuf.

"I saw the battle with my own eyes," he added. "Sher Singh's cannon fired first, splintering the huge wooden doors of the Alamgiri Gate. Then his best Nihang soldiers tried to storm through, but the

Rani's guns had been set up just inside the gate. When they fired, hundreds of Sher Singh's soldiers were killed instantly." He shuddered. "There were great billows of smoke. The timbers of the gate caught fire. Severed limbs and heads flew into the air and fell to the ground. It was deafening and horrible.

"Sher Singh fought on that morning, but he had lost control of his assault. When the defenders began to fire down into the garden from the surrounding wall, Sher's troops realized they were trapped. They panicked and ran, climbing over each other to get out through the side gate of the Bagh."

He fell silent.

Only two things disturbed Safiya Sultana's customary stout calm: lack of food and lack of sleep. Although she would never admit it, the difficult work of nursing Hassan had nearly exhausted her strength.

"Go on," she urged, "tell the rest of it."

"We were now desperate to find the fourth sniper. Sher Singh had kept out of sight until then, but we knew he would want to see the disaster at first hand. At the exact moment that he appeared under the arches of the garden's pavilion, Yusuf and I found the last assassin. He was crouched behind a tree, a child too young to wear a turban, his musket pointed straight at Sher Singh."

He shifted uncomfortably on the edge of his bed. "We both raised our weapons, but Yusuf, may Allah bless him, must have wanted me to have the glory of saving Sher Singh's life. He held his fire and told me to shoot."

"And then?"

"I could not do it, Bhaji. The child was dressed in rotting rags. He was shivering with cold. I wondered what he had been offered to do this terrible thing. He was in my sights, an easy shot, but I was powerless to pull the trigger. I could not breathe. Yusuf repeated his order to shoot, but I could not move even one of my fingers.

"In the end, Yusuf killed the boy, but not before he got off a wild shot that wounded someone near Sher Singh. When the guards looked to see where the ball had come from, they must have seen us, not the dead child. Yusuf shouted, but it was too late. They all fired at once. I was knocked to the ground. From where I lay, I could see only Yusuf's foot, but even then I knew he was dead. Zulmai and Habibullah came running, and pulled me to safety. If they had not done so, a second volley from the guards would have killed me." He raked his fingers through his hair. "If I had been less of a coward, Yusuf would still be alive."

Safiya held out a hand. "There is no point in—"

"I am not a hero," he interrupted, "whatever they say in the bazaar. Of the four of us, I alone did nothing to stop the assassination. My only contribution was to get poor Yusuf killed."

"I did not know you could shoot," Safiya remarked, to divert him. "I thought you were all brocades and diplomacy."

"*He* taught me." Hassan's voice broke. "We were fourteen."

"And what happened after that?"

"I do not remember," he said curtly.

Safiya did not reply. Both of them knew well that Hassan's story had not ended when his Afghan friends dragged him, shocked and bleeding, from the Hazuri Bagh. Both knew that, guessing where he lay wounded, his wife had rushed out into the dangerous city streets that night, and found him in a house by the Delhi Gate.

Without her, he would have died of infection as Sher Singh's soldiers rampaged through the streets outside.

For all his misplaced guilt and the loss of his burly, good-natured friend, Hassan had been a fortunate man.

" *Al-Hamdulillah*, Allah be praised," Safiya murmured.

"I see no cowardice in your story," she went on in a normal tone. "You, a courtier with no history of soldiering, risked entering a battle to stop an assassination. When the moment came, you felt your opponent's humanity, and could not bear to take his life. Do not forget, Hassan," she added, her deep voice echoing in the small bedchamber, "that you have served the Punjab and this city for seven years. I remember the day you went to join the great Faqeer Azizuddin at court.

"How many Punjabi Muslims have worked as you have, side by side with the Sikh and Hindu nobles of the court, to bring peace and well-being to this kingdom? How many have negotiated with the Pashtuns in the north, the British in the south? How many have spent night after sleepless night struggling against the ill luck that has brought one wrong person after another to the throne since Maharajah Ranjit Singh's death?"

Hassan made a small, disbelieving sound.

"You should have told me this story weeks ago. And now," she added, yawning, "I need my sleep. Your explanation of why you went to the Hazuri Bagh in the first place must wait until tomorrow."

Hassan drew in his breath. "Bhaji, I—"

"Not another word." So saying, Safiya Sultana stretched out on the groaning bed and closed her eyes.

A moment later she began to snore.

"WHAT GIBBERISH are you talking, child?" Safiya demanded the following afternoon of the four-year-old in rumpled muslin clothes, who bounced beside her on the sheet-covered floor, babbling aloud in a foreign tongue. Around them in the upstairs ladies' sitting room, women fanned themselves and talked in low tones as they waited for the afternoon meal.

"An-nah taught it to me," Saboor said gravely. "It's called 'Hey, Diddle Diddle.' It is about a cat who plays a *sarod* and a cow that jumps so-o-o high!" He flung his arms over his head. "And a small dog who—"

"Enough, child!" Safiya rumbled. "I am too tired to listen to such nonsense. Ah," she glanced through the curtained doorway, "your father has come. See how well he is walking now."

Watching her nephew approach, Safiya rejoiced in Hassan's improvement since the previous night. He had bathed. Someone had washed his hair and combed it back, so that it curled behind his ears. His beard was neatly trimmed. Dark circles still lay beneath his eyes, and his broad, fair-skinned face had thinned, making his broken nose more prominent than before, but in his fine, embroidered muslins, he looked almost like himself.

Allah be praised, his wounded thigh was no longer hugely swollen and inflamed, with pustules breaking out all over it. For the past week, he had been able to sleep on his back, not stretched out on his stomach. All that was needed now was for the open wound to finish closing safely. He had also begun to use his injured left hand.

It had taken all Safiya's healing arts to keep him alive after he had been brought into the haveli, sixteen hours after his battle. It had taken all the family's prayers to drive away the illnesses that had later threatened his life.

As Hassan stepped out of a pair of embroidered slippers with up-turned toes, Saboor ran to him. "Abba!" he cried, flinging his arms around his father's waist. "You are all dressed! You are wearing your nice shoes!"

"Yes, I am, my darling." Hassan stroked his child's curls with a hand that would have been beautiful, had it not lost its middle finger.

Safiya's heart went out, as it always did, to the man she had adored from the moment he was born. Her twin brother's only child, Hassan had been the one she turned to after cholera had killed her two little daughters and left her starving for a child to love. Only six years old then, and with a mother of his own, Hassan had understood her need. For hours at a time during the first terrible days, he had sat beside her, one small hand resting on her knee.

Saboor, two years younger than his father had been then, already promised to be as loving as Hassan.

She caught the scent of musk. Hassan was wearing perfume. That, too, was a good sign. Of course if he were in the Maharajah's presence, he would also be wearing jewels: his heavy, waist-long pearl necklaces, *kundan* earrings set with rubies and emeralds, enameled bracelets, gold rings...

Jewels gave elegance and power to a man who knew how to wear them.

"You need feeding," she said gruffly, enjoying the perfume's forceful, heady sweetness. "You are a skeleton under those fancy clothes."

"Yes." Safiya's gap-toothed sister-in-law nodded vehemently. "He must have plenty of *yakhni* and meat dishes to strengthen him."

"You are going to Peshawar when you are well again, are you not, Bhai Jan?" asked one of the children.

"I do not know, Mueen, I may go there, or to Multan, or somewhere else." Hassan grimaced as he settled himself on the floor, his little son at his side. "But I will not go anywhere until I can ride again."

Saboor sat up. "When my Abba goes, I will share his saddle," he announced, his eyes bright. "We will ride and ride on his beautiful gray horse, and then we will send for An-nah, and she will live with us!"

Safiya saw Hassan's fingers stiffen on the child's shoulder.

"Will you take me with you, Bhai Jan?" asked Mueen.

"I do not know, my dear." Hassan smiled carefully. "I am not sure you should come with me. I will be traveling much of the time while I am there."

"But I can help you," the boy insisted. "I can carry your things."

"I'll carry Abba's things, too!" Saboor looked eagerly from face to face.

Hassan did not reply.

Safiya, too, kept her silence. Keeping the peace in the restive Punjab was an unsafe and thankless enterprise, especially now, with so much turmoil at the Citadel. Wherever he went, Hassan would have to deal with never-ending complaints about taxes and the unpaid soldiery. Dealing with angry landowners and villagers would mean taking an armed guard when he left Lahore, not a pair of children.

Saboor peered eagerly at his father. "When will we see An-nah? Will we go to Kabul to bring her home? Will it be soon, Abba?"

Hassan smiled vaguely. "I do not know yet, my darling."

"But I want to see An-nah *now*. I want to tell her—"

Unable to bear the pain on Hassan's face, Safiya made a kissing sound. "Do not worry, my darling," she said in the singsong tone she reserved for pacifying children. "*Inshallah,* you will see your An-nah soon. Go to my room." She pointed to the verandah beyond the curtained doorway. "You will find a paper on my bed, with my newest poem written on it. Take it downstairs and show it to your grandfather."

Saboor's face had begun to crumple. "But, Bhaji, I—"

"Take him with you, Mueen," she said firmly.

As the child shuffled away, bent-shouldered, his cousin holding his hand, two or three of the ladies looked up from their conversations. Safiya's sister-in-law leaned forward eagerly, sucking on her teeth. "What did the child say?" she demanded. "Is Hassan *not* going to bring his wife back from Kabul?"

Ignoring the questions, Safiya raised a hand. "Hassan and I," she announced pointedly, "have an important matter to discuss."

As soon as the ladies had removed themselves disappointedly from earshot, Safiya turned to Hassan. "And now," she said, tugging a bolster toward her, "you and I will finish our conversation of last night. Your ill-considered presence at the Hazuri Bagh had something to do with your wife Mariam, did it not?"

He looked at her hollowly. "It did, but, Bhaji, this is a very painful—"

"Out with it," she ordered. "For nine weeks you have had poison in your mind. You must tell me what it is."

He sighed. "Very well, then. I was not in my right mind when I insisted on joining Yusuf and the others. I was very angry with Mariam. Earlier that day, she had overheard me speaking to Yusuf about the assassination attempt. Without waiting to discover the truth, she had made up her mind that *I* was—"

"Plotting to kill her uncle and aunt and her other English traveling companions at their camp in the Shalimar Garden." Safiya nodded. "Yes, I know all that. She told us herself. She has admitted her evil suspicions and recanted her accusations. I myself was horrified to learn how stupidly and badly she had treated you, but she was so remorseful that I forgave her.

"Of course," she added meaningfully, "it was not my forgiveness, or your father's, that she wanted most."

"She demanded to know whether I planned to kill *her*, as well." Hassan's eyes blazed. "How could Mariam have believed that of me, of us? How could she have uttered those ugly, hysterical words on the morning after—"

He dropped his gaze.

Safiya did not need to ask what he was referring to. The entire Waliullah household knew what had occurred between Hassan and his beautiful, difficult wife on the night before her mad outburst. What a fool she had been to throw away her success. . . .

"She accused me of only pretending to like her, of luring her into this house with lies." He opened his hands. "In my rage, I consented to the divorce she had asked for, and then I insisted on going with Yusuf to the Hazuri Bagh."

"And so Mariam is to blame for Yusuf's death?"

"No, Bhaji." He sighed again, heavily. "My anger is to blame, for I allowed it to impair my judgment."

Safiya nodded. "And what do you propose to do about her now? Do you still wish to divorce her?"

"I propose nothing." He reached with his good hand into a pocket in his clothes. Safiya heard the faint crackling of paper between his fingers.

She frowned. Perhaps Mariam's behavior had driven him past some invisible point. She had seen this happen with others in the past, over lesser matters. Once Hassan turned his back on a person, that person was finished for him. . . .

He took his hand from his pocket. "Mariam and her family will, *Inshallah,* return from Kabul within a few months. The British will use their army to keep Shah Shuja on the throne there, but they will not need her uncle, who is a civil officer. When she returns, the future will be decided."

"And what of poor little Saboor, who waits for her?"

"Bhaji, I do not know. It pains me to see him longing for her so, when I—" His voice trailed away.

"You should act," Safiya decreed. "There is no sense in making the child wait. Whatever your decision, you might as well take it now.

"But before we speak any more of your marriage," she decided, "we must dispose of your remorse over Yusuf's loss. Whatever you may believe at this moment, neither you nor Mariam is to blame for what happened to him. It is time for you to hear the story of my mother's death. It has meaning in your case."

"As you well know," she began, "your father and I are twins. At the time of our birth, Wali came out at once, but I, who was second, hesitated. As the attending women tried to drag me out, one of them made an error that caused our mother to bleed severely. The most experienced women were called, but she died within hours.

"Your father and I were turned over to the family ladies. As you are aware, our older cousin, who later married your grandfather, treated us as her own children. But when we were a little more than three years old, I stopped eating. Our cousin used to follow me from room to room, trying to tempt me with milk and sweets, but I would not touch food. Wali was fat and healthy, but I became so weak that the ladies feared I would die."

"You were weak, Bhaji?" Hassan stared. *"Thin?"*

"I was," Safiya intoned, "for I believed I had killed my mother. Because of that belief, I suffered from a stomach pain that stopped me from eating."

He drew in his breath.

"The story of our birth and her death had been told and retold in my hearing. Over and over again, people pointed to me. *It was she,* they said, *who caused her mother's death.* People can be cruel to children. I was not deaf; nor was I stupid. By the time I was three, I could no longer live with my agony.

"In despair," she continued, "our cousin sent me to your great-grandfather, Sheikh Abd Dhul-Jalali Wal-Ikram. He, of course, used to sit, as your father does now, on a *takht* in the courtyard, surrounded by his followers. I vividly remember burying my face in my elder brother's shoulder as he carried me out into the courtyard, for I could not bear to see my grandfather's hatred."

She sighed at the memory. "His beard was pure white, and his mouth drooped on one side. I was too frightened to speak when I was handed to him, but he needed no words from me. He took me onto his lap and smiled with such luminous kindness that the pain in my stomach began to melt away. In that moment I understood that there was no blame on me for my mother's death.

"He recited something, then he blew into a tumbler of water and gave it to me to drink. I was told later that he had prayed all the previous night for me. That I cannot confirm, but to this day I remember the relief I felt the moment I was brought into his presence."

"And was that when you decided to become a Follower of the Path?"

Safiya nodded. "It was. But I have more to say. You, Hassan, are suffering as I did then, from a grain of truth. In my case, while it was true that my stubborn refusal to be born had brought the careless midwife whose action killed my mother, it was she, not I, who made the fatal mistake. In your case, your anger drove you to the garden, and then your inability to shoot a child assassin began a chain of events that led to Yusuf's death. But it was the guards, not you, who killed him.

"We must not allow ourselves to be led into despair by a grain of truth, for a grain can become a boulder that crushes the soul. Perhaps you were foolish to go to the Hazuri Bagh, my dear," she added, "but the truth is that the bigger fool was Yusuf, may he rest in peace, for he allowed you to come with him and then, at the critical moment, asked you to do the impossible. After all, he had known you since childhood.

"As to your wife," she said after a moment's pause, "for all her outrageous behavior and her mistrust of you, she has saved both Saboor's life and your own. That is no small thing. Perhaps in the end you will reach some accommodation.

"It is clear that she does not fit into our household, but it also seems that she fits in no better with her own people. A person with no real home always thirsts to belong somewhere. I believe that with encouragement and training, she may learn to belong here."

He had watched her steadily throughout her story. Now he dropped his eyes. She watched his chest rising and falling beneath his long, embroidered shirt.

Irritated by his silence, Safiya pointed an upturned hand at his chest. "If you do not like your wife," she said crossly, "then why did you send her your gold medallion with the verses from Sura Nur carved into it? Why send her such a powerful token of your regard? And why have you never taken off the silver *taweez* she took from her own neck and gave you when you lay wounded?"

"I do not know, Bhaji." He reached up and touched the small silver box on its black cord, then stared out through the curtained doorway, his gaze far away.

A moment later, his hand returned to his pocket where the hidden paper crinkled again.

It would be a pity if he did not forgive the girl. Saboor would certainly suffer without her, but so would Hassan, wifeless for the second time in less than three years.

Mariam was certainly in desperate need of training, but she had courage and a good heart. And although Safiya herself gave little importance to outward appearances, it was clear that with her creamy skin, soft brown curls, and broad, transforming smile, the foreign girl was as beautiful as any young woman in Lahore, or would be if she paid more attention to herself.

Safiya sighed. There was no more to be said. She craned her neck, searching for a helpful child among the whispering groups in the sitting room. "Mehereen," she called, "go and tell them to bring the food."

An olive, she said to herself, remembering the verse inscribed on Hassan's gold medallion, *neither of the East, nor of the West . . .*

Chapter 5

April 15, 1841

As a horse and rider approached, Nur Rahman Khan sprang up from his vantage point beside the Residence's guarded entrance gate, and narrowed his eyes. To his relief, it was the foreign lady, returning at last from her outing. Sitting sideways in her saddle, dressed in heavy black with a veiled riding hat, she walked her fine mare unhurriedly toward him, ignoring the misty rain that had turned the Kohistan Road to mud. Behind her strode the same pair of Indian servants who had accompanied her when she left: one man tall and long-legged, the other burly and pale-skinned beneath his turban, with a beard the color of corn silk.

Nur Rahman stepped into the horse's path on his quick, dancer's feet, his slender body taut with tension. He must time his move exactly. If he approached the lady too early, while she was too far from the gate, he would risk being set upon by the servants before he could get inside. If he waited too long, she might ride through the entrance without him, leaving him outside to be manhandled by the pair of aggressive-looking sentries who stood by the gate, smart in their red woolen coats and white cross belts.

Later, friendless and without shelter or safety, he would be hunted down. . . .

From the day of her arrival in Kabul, Nur Rahman had included the lady in his plan. The polite greeting she had offered to Painda Gul on that first morning had caught the young dancer's attention, for only an extremely courteous person would have addressed such a man at all. Later, Nur Rahman had learned in the bazaar that the woman and her uncle were two of only a handful of English people in Kabul who spoke any local language.

One of the foreign women, they had said, *speaks both Farsi and Pushto.*

What a pity, they had added, *that of the few foreigners who can speak to us, one should be a woman!*

Her uncle, the gossip ran, was an intelligence agent. Nur Rahman knew this to be the truth, for on his very first day in Kabul, the old man had gone straight to the bazaar, where he had questioned several shopkeepers in rusty, accented Farsi.

Wherever he went, he had inquired about Wazir Akbar Khan.

Only this newly arrived Englishman, people said over their glasses of tea in the *chaikhanas* of the city, *asks about the son of our true Amir, who even now waits to wrest his father's throne from the hands of the unbelievers. Only this man knows what is in our hearts.*

Only he, agreed others, *understands the danger to his people.*

In the crowd at the horse races, Nur Rahman had seen the English lady getting into her palanquin. Calling out to her in the Pushto of his people, he had rushed to her side. She had not dismissed him then, although she had not understood him. He had realized too late that the bazaar gossip had been wrong, that she understood only Farsi. Her bearers had carried her away by that time, but he had known then what he must do.

It was she, he realized, and no other person in all of Kabul, who might, in the proper circumstances, save his life.

It was a gamble, of course, but he was Afghan, and used to gambling, and the odds were not entirely against him. Perhaps, if she were as kind as she appeared, and if Allah Most Gracious willed, she would accept his request for *panah,* the hospitable asylum that must be given to those who ask properly, even those who have committed unspeakable offenses.

She, of course, was not Pashtun. She might fail to understand this ancient duty, but he had no better hope at this terrible moment than a young, black-clad Englishwoman and her newly built, well-guarded fort.

As her horse approached the gate, Nur Rahman kept his distance from the guards. He knew what they thought of him. Somehow, what he had become was written plainly on his face. But it was not his fault. He no longer remembered clearly how Painda Gul had enticed him away from the safety of his family when he was very young. Perhaps the older man had offered him sweets, perhaps a new kite. It no longer mattered. What had mattered was the desperate grief he had suffered, torn from the love of his mother and small sisters and the protection of his father and brothers. Now, even if he knew the way back to his ancestral village, he could never return there. How would his family, even his mother, receive him after the terrible shame Painda Gul had forced upon him night after night, until he no longer recognized himself?

He was a dancing boy now. Trained with beatings and curses, he whirled and stamped, dressed as a woman, at weddings and the births of other men's sons. He himself would never have a son, although his beard was starting to grow. Who would give his daughter to a grown-up child-slave of Painda Gul?

At last, after all his years of rage and waiting, Nur Rahman was armed and free. His patron's cruel knife with its ten-inch blade lay hidden in his clothes, still streaked with the blood of its former owner. With that same knife, Nur Rahman would defend himself from further harm, perhaps even from the insults he endured wherever he went. He might be a dancing boy, but he had his pride.

But now he needed help, for at this moment Painda Gul lay, eyes staring, his throat slit, in the same city hovel where he had first brought Nur Rahman as a child of six. When his body was discovered, no one in Kabul would doubt the boy's guilt. After all, who had not known the story of the wolf-faced Painda Gul and his *bacha*?

"*Ya Hafiz. Ya Hafiz,*" the boy whispered. "O Protector, come to my aid."

The lady had nearly reached the entrance. Her servants trailed behind her, relaxing their vigilance as she approached the sentries.

"Khanum, oh, Khanum!" Forcing himself to breathe, Nur Rahman flitted to her side.

She started in her saddle, her eyes wide behind the veil that hung from her stiff black headdress.

He reached out and gripped her stirrup. "*Panah,*" he murmured.

Her eyes widening, she kicked out at him. "Let me go!" she cried.

Ignoring her dismay, he took the hem of her heavy skirt in his other hand and raised beseeching eyes to her face. "*Panah,*" he begged again, tightening his grip as the mare jerked sideways. She *must* know what the word meant.

Her servants were already sprinting toward him, shouting unintelligibly, their heavy sandals slapping the wet mud. The sentries stared from the gate.

"Only three days." He held on, gasping with pain as she brought her riding crop down upon his wrist. "Three days, Khanum, I swear it."

The pale-bearded servant arrived first at Nur Rahman's side. Seizing the boy's fingers, he began to pry them from the leather strap. When their hands touched the lady's boot, she cried out again, her voice filled with outrage.

The tall servant arrived. "*Rokho,* Ghulam Ali," he said. When the first man moved aside, he stepped behind Nur Rahman and seized him in a long-armed grip, dragging him away from the woman and her mare, forcing him to loosen his hold on the stirrup.

"Wait," Nur Rahman gasped, "I mean no harm, Khanum-Jan! I ask only for protection from my enemies!"

Fearing he had lost his chance, he reached out to her, tears welling in his eyes.

She frowned behind her veil. "If you wanted protection, why did you not say so?"

"But I did," he protested. "I—"

Silencing him with a wave of her riding crop, she spoke sharply to her two servants. The tall one released Nur Rahman. The pale one set off toward the gate, signaling outrage with every movement of his stocky body.

"You are fortunate," she added, returning to Farsi and glaring at Nur Rahman, "that we did not turn you over to the guards."

Hope flickered in the boy's heart. For all her obvious annoyance, the lady's face was full of curiosity.

But her expression held something else as well. She wrinkled her nose. "Do not touch me again," she ordered, turning her mare aside.

"We will remain here," she added, her eyes averted, "until someone comes who can tell me what all this is about."

Nur Rahman stood motionless, his eyes lowered, afraid to breathe. Surely if the lady had intended to send him away, she would have done so at once. But who were they all waiting for, the lady sideways on the mare in her strange-looking saddle, the tall groom watchful beneath his untidy turban, the red-coated sentries glowering from beneath the brims of their tall, black uniform hats?

After a long interval, during which Nur Rahman glanced fearfully several times up and down the road, the lady's servant reappeared, followed by an elderly Indian gentleman in a golden qaraquli hat and a pair of woolen shawls.

As he stepped unhurriedly through the gateway, the old man brought with him a wave of peace so powerful that it seemed to perfume the air around him. Nur Rahman filled his lungs with it. "May peace be upon thee, Father," he offered giddily, a hand over his heart.

"And upon thee," the old man replied kindly. "What is your name, child?"

"Nur Rahman," the boy breathed.

The lady bent over her mare's neck. "I am sorry to disturb you, Munshi Sahib," she said in Farsi, her voice soft with respect. "This boy has been clutching at me, begging, I think, for asylum. I need your advice."

"Ah." The old gentleman turned to Nur Rahman. As he did so, the dancing boy's heart came near to breaking, for there was no disgust in that gentle gaze, no turning away. If Nur Rahman had had the courage, he would have thrown himself right then at the old man's feet.

"And is it panah that you want?" the old man inquired.

"Yes, dear Father, for I have killed a man." Nur Rahman swallowed. "I slit his throat this morning. But Father," he added desperately, putting his stained hands out of sight behind his back, "by my head and eyes, it was necessary. He was evil. He had, he had—"

Nur Rahman turned away, his throat closing. It was no good. For all that he seemed to know the meaning of panah, it was clear that the old gentleman was no Pashtun. Why, then, should he honor the code, especially for a murder whose cause was too shameful to relate?

Without the truth, Nur Rahman could expect no asylum, no mercy, but how could he reveal his agony in front of this female foreigner? How could he describe the events of the past month, when the hair had lengthened on his face, and the city barbers had called out to him that it was time for the dancing boy to shave his beard? His patron had become more brutal than ever during that month, swearing he would throw Nur Rahman out, threatening him with that terrible knife, telling him he had grown too old, too old. . . .

Sweat trickled down the dancing boy's spine.

He had made up his mind only two days before, in Istalif, where he and Painda Gul had gone to entertain at a wedding. As Nur Rahman danced for the men in his shiny woman's clothes, his arms moving sinuously over his head, he had seen his patron talking to a little boy, a lovely child of five or six years, who gazed, wide-eyed, into Painda Gul's grinning face. Turning from the child, Painda Gul had glanced at Nur Rahman.

At that instant, the dancing boy had understood. That sweet little boy was to be his replacement. Soon, perhaps tomorrow, Painda Gul would return, stealthily, to Istalif. Soon, abducted from his confused and grieving family, the child would lose his innocence in Painda Gul's bed. Like Nur Rahman, he would spend his childhood weeping for his lost family.

And what of Nur Rahman, who had been Painda Gul's boy for the past eleven years? How would he survive, thrown out of Painda Gul's hovel, alone on the cold streets of the city?

After his dance, Nur Rahman had slipped outside and vomited.

They had returned from Istalif the following night. After the older man fell asleep, Nur Rahman had crept through the darkness to the hook where Painda Gul's long-bladed Khyber knife hung in its scabbard. He had never killed before, but his Pashtun blood had told him what to do. Grasping a handful of greased hair in one hand, Nur Rahman had jerked Painda Gul's head back, then drawn the fierce Khyber blade across his knobby throat, slicing through the great blood vessels connecting head and body. Painda Gul had opened his eyes too late.

Now, Nur Rahman shuffled his feet. "I cannot say more," he murmured.

"There is nothing more to say," the old gentleman replied.

"What is he talking about, Munshi Sahib?" inquired the lady from her saddle. "What does he want?"

"This boy," the old gentleman replied, glancing at Nur Rahman to make sure he understood, "is a Pashtun. Pashtuns live by a code of honor. A provision of their code is that protective asylum must be offered for three days to someone who asks for it, even if that person has committed a crime, provided that the person tells the truth about his circumstances. The boy has told us enough."

Enough. Relief flooded over Nur Rahman.

"Now he wants us to keep him safe from his pursuers for three days."

Three days. What a princely time that would be....

When he had arrived at the gate, Nur Rahman's sole concern had been the saving of his skin. But now that his dancing boy's heart had gone out to this peaceful old stranger, a new need thrust itself upon him, blocking out even his desire to survive.

Oh, Allah, he prayed, *do not take this old man from me!*

"And what," the lady replied, also in Farsi, "do you recommend that we do?"

The old gentleman joined his hands behind his back and rocked on his heels. "I leave the decision to you, Bibi," he said gently. "My only duty is to explain what he wants."

The lady's mare pawed impatiently at the dust. The tall groom spoke quietly to her. A cold breeze blew through Nur Rahman's thin clothes. He waited, holding his breath, refusing to shiver.

"He may come inside, but only for three days."

The lady addressed herself not to Nur Rahman but to the old man, but the dancing boy did not mind. He lowered his head to conceal his joy, imagining himself sitting at the feet of the old man, serving him....

"He may stay for three days," she repeated, "and not a moment longer. He will sleep in the storeroom at the end of the servants' quarters, but he is *not* to mix with the servants. He should understand that if my aunt discovers he is here, he will have to leave immediately."

The old gentleman turned to Nur Rahman. "You have understood the lady's instructions?"

Unsure of his voice, Nur Rahman cleared his throat. "I have, dear Father," he croaked, before following them inside.

Chapter 6

As she rode into the cantonment, Mariana glanced behind her in time to see her odd new guest hurrying to join her munshi. They made a curious pair, walking through the rain together, her irreproachable elderly teacher and this young Afghan with his fluent Farsi, whose dissolute face she could scarcely bear to look upon.

The boy must have been beautiful once, with those great, soulful eyes and that perfectly carved mouth. What could have happened to him, she wondered. What poison had he absorbed to make him so curiously repellent?

And what would happen, now that he had been granted his three-day asylum? Would he make impossible demands of her, or somehow contaminate the other inhabitants of the servants' quarters?

Both her servants had stiffened visibly when she agreed to let the boy inside. As he walked behind her mare, Yar Mohammad kept his eyes averted from the boy, and Ghulam Ali scowled with disapproval.

Only Munshi Sahib had seemed unperturbed by his presence. Indeed, something about the old man's manner had encouraged her decision. Even now her teacher seemed to have no difficulty allowing the boy to take his arm and help him past a muddy hole in the road.

Since that was the case, she would leave the boy and his troubles, whatever they were, to Munshi Sahib.

A moment later, she passed through an opening in the thick rampart wall that divided the cantonment from the walled Residence compound.

As her mare splashed along a broad path leading past Sir William Macnaghten's walled garden, Mariana wondered for the hundredth time why the British civil officers had been housed outside the sheltering fortifications of the military area. In contrast to the cantonment, whose ramparts were surmounted by a stone parapet, the Residence compound was furnished with no more than a plain six-foot wall on its three exposed sides.

There must have been a good reason for such an optimistic plan, although Mariana could not fathom what it was.

A broad avenue ran parallel to the rampart wall, dividing the Residence compound into two parts. Sir William's grand house and spacious gardens with their concealing compound wall took up the area next to the cantonment, while the seventeen hastily built offices and houses of the civil staff, including Mariana's uncle, took up the other. Farthest away, against the useless outer wall, a series of shambling buildings housed the many hundreds of servants who staffed the Residence compound.

But it was not the geography of the compound that occupied her thoughts as she rode, followed by her two servants, past the offices and houses of various secretaries and doctors. Since their brief encounter at the race meeting, she had received no word from Harry Fitzgerald.

According to Aunt Claire, who had managed to keep track of his movements, he had left the next day with his horse artillery, to put down some fighting in the north.

He could have written from there, but he had clearly chosen not to. So much, therefore, for Aunt Claire's dream that he had been waiting, lovelorn, for the past two years.

But Fitzgerald had good reason to dislike Mariana.

Soon after gossip about him had forced their separation, she had snatched little Saboor to safety from Maharajah Ranjit Singh's neglectful grip, then become entangled with his mystical family. Later, believing she was aiding the British invasion of Afghanistan, she had announced in front of a large crowd, including Fitzgerald, that she was engaged to Saboor's father. That sensational disclosure had made Fitzgerald's humiliation even worse. Unsurprisingly, he had soon afterward sent her a bitter, reproachful letter.

In spite of Fitzgerald's anger then, and his failure to write to her now, he had seemed genuinely pleased to see her at the race meeting.

Unlike Lady Macnaghten's nephew, the groping, pallid Charles Mott, whose aunt would have fainted dead away at the thought of his marrying Mariana, Fitzgerald had been both attractive and intelligent. He had laughed with her, and told her of his dreams. Before their hopes of marriage were dashed, they had spent hours together, arguing happily over the great battles of history—Marathon, Tours, the defeat of the Athenians at Syracuse—as she and her father had done in his vicarage study from the time she was twelve. Those conversations, and Fitzgerald's hot, hasty kisses, had provided her with some of her best moments in India.

Harry Fitzgerald could explain the British defenses to her. He could give her vivid battle descriptions to send to her father.

She lifted the rain-dampened riding veil from her face, and turned her mare into the lane where her uncle's small bungalow stood in its garden.

If Hassan still loved her, nothing else would matter. If he had divorced her, she must find a way to love Fitzgerald again, and to make him love her.

If only Hassan would write...

The rain had stopped. An Indian *dhobi* saluted as he passed Mariana in the lane, bent over beneath a great bundle of washing, his bare feet covered to the ankles in mud. Someone coughed hollowly behind a mud wall.

Uncle Adrian sat on a chair in the sun, deep in conversation with two ragged Afghans who stood in front of him. A pair of carved *jezails* had been propped against a verandah pillar. All three men glanced up as she approached. The Afghans turned their heads away immediately.

As she handed her reins to Yar Mohammad, the drawing room shutters banged apart, and Aunt Claire appeared, red-faced, in the open window.

"*He* was here!" she exclaimed, a plump hand fluttering at her breast, ignoring her husband's furious glare. "Lieutenant Fitzgerald came to call not half an hour ago. I tried to make him wait for you, but he said he was expected elsewhere. He is to leave again tomorrow." She turned from the window as Mariana entered the house. "Where *were* you? *Why* did you take so long?"

A few hours later, she knocked at Mariana's bedroom door. "You must hurry, my dear," she called. "We are to be at the Residence at six o'clock sharp."

"M-m-m!" replied Mariana through a mouthful of pins as she hastened to fix her curls to the top of her head.

A liveried servant had come at the very last moment, bearing the heavy, cream-colored invitation on a tray. Uncle Adrian was not a senior officer, so it had been clear that it was his family, more than himself, that was wanted at Sir William's table. This was no surprise, since Uncle Adrian's household boasted two of the eleven English-women residents in Kabul.

Fitzgerald was to be there. This Mariana had learned when another of Lady Macnaghten's servants had arrived on the heels of the liveried man, a private note in his hand.

Look your prettiest, the note had instructed. *Lieutenant Fitzgerald has accepted our invitation.*

"It doesn't matter if there are creases at the back," Aunt Claire snapped, just before six o'clock, as Mariana turned obediently in front of her. "They'll think you have been sitting down in it. Oh, I wonder what *he* will say, when he sees you are there!

"Ah," she added rapturously, "how thrilling to dine at the Envoy's table!"

In her palanquin, Mariana breathed in slowly to quell the tightening in her stomach. She was a fool to bank on a future with Hassan. Silence was all she had received from him since he sent her the delicately carved gold medallion that even now lay hidden next to her skin, suspended from its simple gold chain.

How silly she had been to send such a gushing response to his gift! How foolish to copy that old Persian poem into her letter, so full of references to the pain of separation and the soul's longing for union! How idiotic she had been to dream of him on the stony road to Kabul, waiting fruitlessly for a sign of the love she had once seen on his face. . . .

Had he already divorced her as he had said he would, on the day she had run away from his house? And if he had, why had no one told her? Had his family somehow failed to inform her, or had their messenger died or been killed on the dangerous roads between the Punjab and Kabul?

If she were already divorced, she had only herself to blame. Again and again, she had catalogued the blunders she had made in Lahore, beginning with the ill-fated announcement of her coming marriage.

That revelation had done more than hurt Harry Fitzgerald—it had humiliated Hassan as well. She clearly remembered the rustle of silks, as Maharajah Ranjit Singh's bejeweled courtiers had turned in the crowd to stare at one of their own.

And what of her own attempt to divorce him without cause? What of the furious accusations she had made after leaping to the conclusion that he planned to kill her family? What of her needless escape from his walled city house, when there had been nothing to fear?

And finally, what of the clumsy, unseemly part she had played in his rescue on the night after he was wounded in the Hazuri Bagh? Looking back on that event, she saw clearly that she should have told someone in the Waliullah household that she knew where Hassan lay wounded, instead of rushing out into the dangerous streets of Lahore on that bloody night, and fainting dead away in front of two dozen heavily armed Afghans.

If she had curbed her impulses, if she had thought before she acted, everything would have turned out differently. Now, no amount of painful longing or regret could alter the sad truth that Hassan had no reason to take her back.

What would become of her then? A woman alone with no money, she must depend upon her uncle and her father until they died. After that, without a protecting husband, she would disappear into isolation and poverty.

She stared into her looking glass, at her uselessly dewy skin and glossy curls. She knew what her family would say: that she would not be young for long, that she should think of her future.

Life with Fitzgerald, however dull, would be far better than traveling from house to house among her relatives, getting older and older, a pathetic spinster aunt who earned her keep by caring for the aged and the sick.

If she had fair-haired babies, perhaps they would be enough to make her forget her darling, round-eyed Saboor, who must miss her even now.

How she longed to wrap her arms about his energetic little body....

Her huffing bearers stopped. She sighed, pinched her cheeks until they were rosy, gathered her yards of striped taffeta skirts, and stepped out of her palanquin in front of Sir William Macnaghten's handsome portico.

"I believe our new Commander in Chief will be present," Aunt Claire said in a stage whisper.

"If General Elphinstone is dining with us," Uncle Adrian replied, "then the only other senior officer at dinner will be General Sale."

The Commander in Chief *and* the Hero of Ghazni! Mariana brightened.

"That is," her uncle added, "because Elphinstone's second-in-command, Brigadier Shelton, despises him for a fool."

Mariana frowned. "Brigadier Shelton *despises* General Elphinstone? But why?"

"They loathe each other. In fact, they—"

"Be quiet, you two!" whispered Aunt Claire, as the Residence door swung open, and turbaned servants stood aside to let them in.

Chapter 1

All the senior-most English people in Kabul were here, in one
room! Mariana looked eagerly about her, taking them in—Sir
William Macnaghten, smiling at his guests from beneath beetle brows;
Lady Macnaghten, radiantly pretty in rose satin and pearls, fluttering a peacock feather fan; General Sale, the scar-faced Hero of Ghazni
and his formidable wife; and General Elphinstone, the frail new
Commander in Chief with his pained expression and heavy limp.

The presence of these luminaries would have been exciting
enough, but across the drawing room, deep in conversation with her
uncle and Charles Mott, stood the only Englishman in Kabul who
had lived in Afghanistan before, and who spoke both Farsi and
Pushto—the rotund, voluble British Resident, Alexander Burnes.

Others were there, as well. Mrs. Sturt, the Sales' sour-faced daughter, and her husband, Captain Sturt, stood in a corner, talking to
Alexander Burnes's lanky friend, Captain Johnson, who lived near
Burnes in the walled city, and managed the funds for Shah Shuja's
court and army.

And then there was Harry Fitzgerald.

Mariana sensed Fitzgerald's presence before she saw him. He
waited behind the others, then stepped forward and bowed, unsmiling, in her direction.

"And you, Lieutenant," Lady Macnaghten trilled, fluttering her fan for emphasis, "are to take Miss Givens in to dinner."

"I should never have allowed you to do your own hair," she added fiercely, into Mariana's ear. "It's all lopsided. Let us hope he does not notice. Other than that, you look lovely. I'm sure he is as good as won!"

The business of lining up for dinner seemed to take forever. As Lady Macnaghten fussed over the pairing of her remaining guests, Mariana stood self-consciously at the back of the group, a wary hand on Fitzgerald's blue-clad arm. She risked a sideways glance, and saw that his Roman profile was as perfect as before, but his body had thickened in the past two years. No longer an eager young officer, he now gave off a heavy, male assuredness.

In the dining room, a lovely pair of Bohemian candelabra dominated the damask-covered table. Around and between them, a flock of silver birds gleamed in the candlelight. Crystal and bone china glowed at each place. At a signal, a dozen Indian servants stepped forward and pulled back the dining chairs.

Mariana arranged her skirts, patted her hair experimentally, and turned her attention to the conversation around her.

"You must have no fear, General Elphinstone," Sir William Macnaghten announced from the head of the table as he unfolded his napkin. "We all understand your hesitation in taking up this post after so long an absence from combat, but you have nothing to fear here in Afghanistan."

Absence from combat? How long had it been since General Elphinstone had fought a battle? Remembering their shared fascination with military history, Mariana caught Fitzgerald's eye.

After a tiny hesitation, he bent his head toward her. "The Envoy means to say," he murmured, "that General Elphinstone has not seen active service since Waterloo."

"*Waterloo?*" she whispered. "But that was twenty-six years ago!"

She would have said more, but the Hero of Ghazni cleared his throat beside her. "And why," he asked gruffly, "is there nothing to fear?"

"All is at peace in Afghanistan." Sir William perched his spectacles upon his nose and surveyed his guests. "Seeing the vast superiority of our force, Amir Dost Mohammad has surrendered his throne and departed Afghanistan for India with most of his family. We have persuaded Shah Shuja *not* to secure his sovereignty by killing or blinding his enemies. He has shown magnanimity toward all. As a consequence, the whole country is as quiet as one of our Indian possessions—and more so."

"That is not quite the case," Fitzgerald murmured. "On his first day in Kabul, Shah Shuja had fifty Ghazis hacked to death behind his tent, young men and old. I saw it happen."

Mariana caught her uncle and Charles Mott exchanging glances across the table.

Sir William smiled expansively. "Our work in Afghanistan," he said, "is nothing more than a grand military promenade. Just imagine—we have lost only thirty-four of our officers to date, and only five of them in battle!"

"Exactly. Yes, indeed." Alexander Burnes nodded vigorously over the rim of his wineglass, his round face already flushing. "The Afghans, with a very few spoilsport exceptions, have fully recognized the advantages of having Shah Shuja for their Amir, and us for their allies."

Mariana opened her mouth to ask precisely what advantages he meant, but the elderly Commander in Chief spoke first.

"That may be, and I certainly hope it is," General Elphinstone observed in a kindly tone, "but nevertheless, it seems to me that there are too many small Afghan forts near our cantonment. I suggest we arrange to buy them all, and raze them to the ground. We would also be wise to throw a bridge over the wide irrigation canal that runs close to our eastern boundary."

"Yes, a bridge would be useful," returned Sir William, "but I am unsure, General, what the government in Calcutta will say about the little forts." He signaled to a servant to refill Alexander Burnes's wineglass. "Surely there is nothing to be feared from a few small buildings, even if they are occupied by Afghans."

Mariana frowned. He and Burnes were certainly sanguine over the arrangements for the cantonment. She glanced across the table at General Sale's son-in-law, in time to see a fleeting bitterness darken his face.

Captain Sturt, she remembered, had been the engineer in charge of building. From his expression, the cantonment's plan had not been his. Who, then, had been responsible? Was it the recently retired General Sir Willoughby Cotton, now replaced by General Elphinstone? And who had put poor old Elphinstone in charge of the British force, with his gout and his shaking hands?

"There is nothing to fear!" Alexander Burnes declared. "To date, our enterprise has been so successful that we have nothing to do but enjoy ourselves. *I* spend most of my time planning dinner parties at my house in the city. You have no idea how many Afghans are in attendance. I would say they compete for my invitations!"

"I quite agree," put in his friend Captain Johnson. "It is quite wonderful how *interesting* Kabul can be."

Lady Macnaghten gave a little tinkling laugh. "But you must be joking, Captain. From what I hear, Kabul is as filthy as any Oriental town." Peacock-feather eyes rolled as she waved her fan.

"I understand," Uncle Adrian offered quietly, "that one of the more difficult chiefs has been seen several times north of here, in Kohdaman."

Sir William smiled expansively. "Do you mean the insolent braggart who gave that unexpected tent-pegging exhibition at the horse races a month ago?"

Uncle Adrian nodded.

"Believe me, Lamb, that fellow is no threat to us at all. He does nothing but ride about the countryside with a handful of men. If it came to a real fight, he would run like a rabbit. Besides, he returned last week to the Pishin valley, where he belongs."

"It is a wonder," Burnes put in lazily, changing the subject, "how easily one can obtain brandy and cigars from India these days."

On Mariana's right, the Hero of Ghazni shifted heavily in his seat. Needing distraction, she turned to him. Here was someone worth speaking to: General Sir Robert Sale, who had been made a Knight Commander of the Bath two years earlier, after his successful siege of the mighty fortress of Ghazni ninety-three miles south of Kabul. It must have been a great sight—the invading British Army of the Indus moving north toward Kabul on its way to oust Dost Mohammad from his throne, taking every fortress in its path....

"I am delighted to meet you, Sir Robert," she began eagerly, imagining the letter she would write to her father in the morning, describing their conversation. "I understand that the fortress of Ghazni had never been taken until your successful action two years ago. Your victory certainly parallels that of—"

"My dear young lady," he interrupted, loudly enough for everyone to hear, "I never discuss military matters with females. Let us speak instead," he added, gesturing carelessly, "of something nearer to your heart—bonnets, perhaps, or the best view for an afternoon outing."

She stiffened. "Sir Robert, I—"

"My wife," he went on, glancing down the table, "is the only woman who knows a jot about war." He smiled, one of his eyes closing due to the long scar down one side of his face. "Now *there* is a woman who understands a good fight."

Stung, Mariana raised her chin. "In that case, General," she replied, "I shall save for Lady Sale my comparison of the storming of Ghazni to the Siege of Constantinople in 1453."

Hero of Ghazni, indeed.

"What?" He cleared his throat. "The Siege of Constantinople, you say?"

"Yes, indeed." She leaned forward. "Here, the naval element was missing, but the fortifications at Constantinople can scarcely have been stronger than the ones at Ghazni. In your case, of course, there was a weakness in the Kabul Gate, while in their case it was the Kerkoporta that had been—"

"Yes, yes," he barked. "And now, may I ask why you are so interested in military history, when you should be finding yourself a husband? My daughter here," he flapped a hand toward the plain young woman seated opposite, "was married when she was seventeen. You look much older than that. How old *are* you?"

Perhaps Sale was a good general. Perhaps he looked after the men under his command, but Mariana no longer cared. Her face heating, she turned smartly away from him.

On her other side, Fitzgerald was busy with the doddering old General Elphinstone. Until that conversation ended, she and General Sale seemed doomed to sit side by side, trapped in uncomfortable silence.

They were not. "And now, Lady Macnaghten," he trumpeted, turning casually away from Mariana, "how did you enjoy Peshawar when you were there? I found the Sikh governor most hospitable when I was there."

As Mariana toyed angrily with a plate of river fish, Fitzgerald turned toward her.

"I wonder, Miss Givens," he murmured, "if you would like, some afternoon, to hear *my* account of the storming of Ghazni."

"He knows nothing about Mehmet the Second's Siege of

Constantinople," she whispered furiously. "He does not even know that it marked the end of—"

"—the Middle Ages," they said in unison, then smiled together for the first time in over two years.

He smiled crookedly. "General Sale does not need to know anything. He's a fighting general, not a thinking one. He makes certain he is wounded in every battle. His men will do anything for him." He dropped his voice. "No one will tell you this, but he nearly lost the battle at Ghazni. Fortunately everything turned out all right in the end."

Mariana stared. "He nearly *lost*?"

"He ordered his men to retreat when they should have advanced, but changed his mind at the last instant. It was lucky for him."

As if by magic, Lady Macnaghten's voice rose above the hum of conversation. "Now, General Sale," she fluted, "*do* tell us all of your exploits at Ghazni. We understand you were *exceedingly* brave, as always."

"Ah." General Sale smiled again, his face bunching around his scar. "They were nothing. I was wounded in the foot, at first, but that was nothing. My one moment of danger came after I was felled by a blow to the face." He gestured carelessly. "Major Havelock should be credited with saving my life. He turned up, usefully, as my assailant and I were grappling upon the ground. I ordered him to run his sword through the body of the infidel. He did so, and I escaped."

"Hah!" crowed Burnes. " 'The body of the infidel'!"

Infidel? Without faith?

"Then they were pagans?" Mariana heard herself ask. "But I had thought they were all—"

"Mohammedans, of course," Sale interrupted heartily. "Wretched, godless Asiatics, every one of them." He gave a satisfied grunt. "There was great carnage. They all fought like mad dogs. Some of the wounded tried to escape by the blown-in Kabul Gate, and fell onto the burning timbers, where they were roasted in their sheepskin coats. It was most satisfying."

"Hear, hear." Lady Sale raised her wineglass.

"Hear, hear," repeated the others, all except for Mariana, who dropped her fish knife noisily and deliberately onto her plate.

The table grew silent. Sir William Macnaghten peered in her direction, his glass still raised. At the table's far end, Lady Macnaghten frowned, her fan motionless in her fingers. Across the table from Mariana, Aunt Claire made little flapping gestures, begging her not to speak. Beside her, Fitzgerald cleared his throat warningly.

But what if she did speak? What if she told these self-satisfied, overstuffed people that the Afghan "mad dogs" they referred to had only been defending their own fortress, that Muslims were very far from godless, that it was *not* satisfying for human beings to be roasted to death?

What if she told them of the horrors she had seen in Lahore?

She imagined the terrible scene that would follow her outburst— the accusations of brash ignorance, of disloyalty to the Queen, of siding with the enemy. Who would speak first, General Sale, his features swollen with martial fury, Sir William Macnaghten, his thick brows knitted in disbelief, or Lady Sale, whose attack would be the deadliest of all?

What right, they would say, had she, an unmarried woman, to voice an unfavorable opinion about a British army action? Who was she, a person of no great fortune or family, whose reputation had already been blackened once by scandal, to criticize her elders and betters?

All this would mean the ruin of Lady Macnaghten's carefully arranged party. Lady Macnaghten, who was generously trying to help her, would never speak to her again.

But General Sale, it seemed, was too intent on his remembered triumph to take her breach of manners into account. "The horses were a different matter," he boomed, shaking his head. "Dozens of them had been wounded in the assault. When we entered the fort, we found them galloping about, hysterical and dangerous. In spite of all our efforts to spare them, quite a number had to be shot."

"A pity," agreed Burnes.

Macnaghten nodded sorrowfully.

Mariana gazed from face to face, searching for someone who shared her feelings.

"I shall be leaving for Kandahar in the morning." Fitzgerald leaned toward her, interrupting her troubled thoughts. "I do not know when I shall return. May I write to you while I am gone?"

"Yes, of course." She nodded absently. She had studied military strategy since she was twelve. All that time she had likened war to a game of chess. . . .

General Sale turned to her. "And now, young lady," he trumpeted, "may I ask if you have seen our cantonment?"

"No, Sir Robert, I have not," she replied flatly.

"Since you have such a keen interest in military matters, if you will present yourself at the gate at three o'clock sharp tomorrow afternoon, one of my subalterns will bring you inside and show you about. And bring your uncle. I like him."

"Thank you," was all she could manage.

Chapter 8

Now, Mariana," her uncle told her as they rode under the archway of the cantonment's main gate, "as we shall not be invited again to see the workings of the cantonment, I encourage you to examine it thoroughly. It *is* rather impressive, is it not?" He flushed happily beneath his top hat as he surveyed the huge, enclosed military compound.

Mariana smiled carefully, not wishing to disturb his expansive mood. Several times recently, she had caught her uncle staring into space, his face creased with worry. He never told her what information he had gained from his informants about the true state of Afghanistan, or whether Sir William Macnaghten had paid attention to his warnings. But whatever her uncle's concerns were on that score, she could see that he had every confidence in the safety of the cantonment.

This was no time to tell him how puzzling and unwise she found the location of the cantonment and Residence compounds, both overlooked by nearby hills and surrounded on every side by occupied forts.

Why on earth had Sir William Macnaghten so airily dismissed General Elphinstone's plan to buy and destroy those buildings?

Furthermore, the ground on which the cantonment and Residence

stood seemed to have been chosen for its beauty rather than its util-
ity, for it was wet orchard land, full of trees and covered like a
checkerboard with deep irrigation ditches.

How did they expect to move heavy guns about on this sort of terrain?

She would also not mention that the very length of the cantonment's outer walls, enclosing an area nearly a thousand by six hundred
yards, would make it extremely difficult to defend in the event of
trouble.

She looked about her. To her left, past a small artillery park with
thirteen guns of various sizes, an orchard had inexplicably been left
standing, rendering the high rampart between the northern end
of the cantonment and the Residence compound nearly invisible
through the trees. To her right, neat rows of mud brick barracks and
officers' quarters occupied a large area. Behind them she glimpsed
the walled compounds of the generals. Straight ahead of her on a
large parade ground, groups of red-coated infantrymen wheeled to
shouted orders. In the shade of the barracks, other soldiers sat in
groups, cleaning weapons and polishing brass.

Pack mules filed past, their harnesses jingling, led by grooms
in loose, native clothes. A troop of mustachioed cavalrymen trotted
toward the parade ground on tall, handsome chargers. Camels
strode through a side gate, carrying heavy sacks of foodstuffs.

"I shall ask our guide," her uncle continued, in a businesslike
tone, "to show you the full view from each corner bastion, and to
give the measurements of the surrounding rampart wall and its para-
pets. You have already passed the commissariat fort between here
and the city many times, of course, and you know that the fresh water supply comes from the irrigation canal outside our eastern wall."

He looked about him. "I am certain we shall be allowed to watch
the infantry drilling while we are here, but I doubt we shall see an artillery practice today, since no one seems to be anywhere near the
guns. Even so," he added happily, "that should be enough to satisfy
you and the Would-Be-General."

Lost in thought, Mariana nodded again.

She did not have to climb the cantonment's corner bastions to
know the location of the several small forts that Macnaghten had
taken so lightly at dinner. All were within a few hundred yards of the
outer walls, one of them almost between the cantonment itself and
the commissariat fort where all the food supplies had been stored.

"Here comes our guide." Her uncle gestured toward the curly-haired youth who hurried toward them. "It is a pity Fitzgerald has left us for Kandahar. A horse gunner would do a better job of explaining our artillery than this poor little infantryman."

Mariana sniffed to herself. Thirteen guns scarcely qualified as "our artillery."

She returned the young officer's bow. She must stop worrying and pay attention. After all, Papa would like nothing better than a detailed account of the cantonment.

But as the young man began to speak, she did not hear what he was saying, for the vision she had seen all those weeks before at Butkhak returned without warning. It filled her mind's eye with mourning figures, and her heart with dread. She blinked, begging it to leave her, but it remained—the same black-clad funeral procession her munshi had refused to explain, marching somberly past her and across the empty parade ground, to the beat of invisible drums.

Her uncle silenced their guide with an upraised hand. "Is something wrong, my dear?" he asked her.

"Nothing, Uncle Adrian." She pressed a damp hand to her forehead. "Nothing at all."

He nudged his horse closer, his face full of concern, then signaled to their guide.

"Forgive us, Lieutenant Mathieson," he said. "Miss Givens is not at all well. We must return to the Residence compound at once."

"No, Uncle Adrian," she objected. "I—"

"Nonsense," he interrupted firmly. "You have gone quite white."

As he led her slowly home, Mariana noticed her munshi walking in the lane, on the arm of their strange young visitor.

What did Munshi Sahib know? she wondered. And why had he given her that hollow look, his hand tightening on the Afghan boy's shoulder?

"I DO not like the boy," Dittoo said firmly, as the English lady and her uncle rode toward the bungalow.

He spoke with the conviction of a man experienced with foreigners. "Bibi," he declared, "knows nothing of these people. Without knowing it, she has let a thieving little dancing boy into this house. And I can tell you something else. Now that he is here, he will be difficult to get rid of."

Having said his piece, he hawked and spat into the dust beneath the tree where he squatted with his two companions. Birds chattered above his head. A goat bleated in a neighbor's garden.

Ghulam Ali grimaced. "I would have told her not to take him in," he pointed out, "but she sent me inside to fetch Munshi Sahib."

"You should have said something, Yar Mohammad," Dittoo added accusingly. "You had the opportunity, but you stood there and said nothing."

"It was for Munshi Sahib to decide if the boy should stay." The tall groom got to his feet, and turned far-seeing eyes upon the other two men. "It was not for us to offer our opinions," he added, as he started away to take the lady's horse.

Dittoo clucked to himself as he hunched his way to Mariam Bibi's bedroom with a reviving cup of tea. Her munshi was a clever old gentleman, there was no doubt of that. But he was old, and old men made mistakes.

This was certainly a serious error. How would they manage, with a boy of ill repute in the house?

Nothing would upset Dittoo more than to see his unusual English lady hurt.

He had served her through many adventures over the past three years, but the first of these, her miraculous rescue of Saboor, had been the greatest.

He sighed, missing the child.

He would never forget the moment on a winter night in Lahore, when he entered her tent and found her sitting on her bed, a badly treated native baby in her arms.

In his twenty-five years of serving the British, Dittoo had never seen a European woman weep over one of his own people.

When it dawned on him that the child was Saboor, Maharajah Ranjit Singh's heavily guarded child hostage, whom the Maharajah believed had magical powers, his embarrassment at the lady's previous, unpredictable behavior had turned to admiration.

From that moment he had been convinced that she was a powerful sorceress, a modest one, to be sure, since she very rarely used her abilities, but a sorceress nonetheless.

He sniffed as he scuffed his shoes off outside her door. As for Yar Mohammad and his calm magnanimity, he would feel the boy's presence more than anyone. For all that he was a groom by trade, Yar

Mohammad had loved and served Munshi Sahib faithfully for two years, bringing his tea, washing his clothes, and seeing to his food.

He, of all people, must have noticed how the boy had clung to Munshi Sahib from the moment he entered the gate.

Dittoo would have been willing to bet that Yar Mohammad had just lost his position.

Chapter 9

September 20, 1841

All summer in Kabul had been a delight. The days had been pleasantly hot, the evenings balmy, and the air so clear that one could almost read by the light of the moon. The cantonment had reveled in the city's apricots, its cherries, its great, purple mulberries and milky nuts.

Now that summer was ending, the days were cooler, and the markets were beginning to fill with fresh grapes and melons.

Sir William Macnaghten had arranged an excursion to the tomb of Babur Shah, the cultivated founder of the Mughal Empire, whose memorial garden stood on the western slope of the Sher Darwaza south of the city. After leaving the cantonment, a large, variously mounted party of officers and ladies had followed the Kabul River upstream, past formal gardens and orchards, then between the Sher Darwaza and Asmai heights, where the river emerged from the hills onto the flat Kabul plain. There, the party had crossed the river near a little painted shrine with pennants waving, and followed an uphill dirt track to the garden. Wild roses and jasmine covered the mountainside, perfuming the air and lifting the spirits. The usual grumbling and irritation of such a trip were absent. No one had complained—not Lady Macnaghten, who, for all her elegance, was a poor horsewoman; not Aunt Claire, whose palanquin bearers had patiently dragged her up the steep slope in an open sedan chair; not even the gout-ridden General Elphinstone, who had also been carried up, for it was hoped that the mountain air would do him good.

Now, after strolling in the tomb's terraced garden, with its elegant little mosque and cascading water, the party picnicked at folding tables beneath spreading plane trees, while bees buzzed around them and doves cooed in the branches overhead.

Mariana yawned behind her hand. If only she were here with someone she loved. . . .

"I hear we have put down another revolt in Kandahar," Alexander Burnes said lazily, as he helped himself to the boiled mutton.

"We have indeed," Sir William replied. "Some people have been saying that Afghanistan cannot be settled at the point of a bayonet, but I could not disagree more." He signaled to a servant to pour the wine. "The situation in the south proves my point exactly. Since Shah Shuja came to the throne, his disappointed relatives have been pouting like spoiled children. They seem to think we should be giving *them* money, too. But it seems that as soon as we put one naughty boy in a corner, the rest become terrified."

Lady Macnaghten's nephew cleared his throat. "Of course," he put in hesitantly, "they are quite dangerous in their own—"

"*Dangerous?*" General Sale stared at Charles Mott. "What do you mean? The Afghans are great braggarts, but they are cowards at heart, every last man of them."

"Quite right," agreed his wife, as Mott shrank into his beautiful riding coat.

"Did you say the revolt was in *Kandahar*?" Lady Macnaghten leaned forward eagerly.

"I did," replied her husband.

At her significant glance, Aunt Claire nudged Mariana. "I hope your lieutenant is all right," she whispered.

"Could someone," General Elphinstone said faintly, "please take me away? I believe I must lie down."

Brigadier Shelton looked up from cutting his chicken with one hand. "Man's an invalid," he commented to no one in particular.

AN HOUR after the party had returned from its outing, three men stood at the foot of General Elphinstone's bed.

"I am done up, sir, done up in body and mind," the old man

announced mournfully. "As you have seen, one simple excursion has caused me a violent attack of gout and fever. I have no strength left, and my mental capacity is quite gone. Why, I can scarcely remember the names of my officers."

His one-armed second-in-command snorted audibly. "I hope he remembers *mine*," he muttered.

"I have written once more to Calcutta," the general added, "asking them to send me back to India. Perhaps this time the Governor-General will take pity on an old man and instruct General Nott to come up from Kandahar and replace me."

"I quite understand, sir." Sir William Macnaghten nodded as he drew a gold timepiece from his waistcoat pocket. "In my next communication with Lord Auckland, I shall add my own plea to yours. But let me reiterate, sir, that Afghanistan is at peace. We have no reason to anticipate any military action more than a foray or two, to keep the peace. In fact, it is so quiet that it has been suggested we send General Sale and his First Brigade back to India. And now, sir, we must leave you to rest."

"I cannot understand why Elphinstone is so bothered," Macnaghten confided to Brigadier Shelton as they descended the stairs. "He has practically nothing to do. Why does he not simply enjoy the lovely weather?"

"The man is a fool," snapped Brigadier Shelton. "A hopeless, doddering fool."

THE NEXT morning, Mariana sat in her room, Fitzgerald's latest letter in her hand.

Kandahar, he had written, *is a desert wasteland. If it were not for our recent military success, I should be very glad to be gone. The whole landscape is parched and hostile. The walled, irrigated gardens northwest of here provide us with fresh fruit and vegetables, but they, too, are dusty and full of stones. Sometimes I like to imagine that a lush paradise lies beyond the spine of mountains I see from my window, but even if such an Eden did exist I would take little pleasure in it. What would be the worth of cool breezes or the scent of mint and lavender underfoot to a man with no other companions but his fellow officers?*

Formal and distant at first, the lieutenant's letters had begun to show discomfiting signs of romantic longing. Mariana hoped no one else had seen this latest one arrive. Nothing would be more awful than to have Aunt Claire discover its existence and demand that it be read aloud.

She pictured Fitzgerald, powerful shoulders bent over a makeshift desk, choosing his words, imagining the moment when he saw her again. Whose fault was it that his letters had taken this new turn? Her own had given him no encouragement.

She folded the paper and shut it into her writing box. If Fitzgerald did love her, as her family in England and Aunt Claire had dreamed, it was dishonest to let him hope, but what else could she do?

She could not deny that his presence at Lady Macnaghten's party had given her reassurance. If she did marry him, she would somehow swallow her grief and make him happy. She would lay aside her memories of a gifted child and a graceful man with sharp-scented skin, and forget her dream of learning the Waliullah family's mystic secrets while her darling Saboor leaned against her knee and her own precious, dark-haired babies played at her feet.

If she did marry him, everyone but her would be relieved beyond measure.

She stood and walked to the window, imagining her mother in Sussex, speaking to a fellow parishioner after church. "Oh, yes," Mama would say, her voice, so like Aunt Claire's, carrying all the way across the churchyard. "My daughter, *Mrs. Fitzgerald,* is *very* happy in India."

To her mother, Fitzgerald must seem like the Archangel Gabriel.

Outside Mariana's window, a bowlegged water carrier crossed the garden, a full goatskin on his back, splashing the bare ground to quell the ever-present dust. Beyond the wall, past the Residence compound, the looming mountains, as always, stared her down.

She turned from the window, poured cold water into her basin, and splashed it onto her face. If Hassan did write to her after all, if he asked her to return to Lahore, her family would never understand the joy his invitation would give her.

A paper lay on her dressing table. She dried her face and glanced at it.

It was her translation of Jalaluddin Rumi, whose most famous verses she had quoted so dramatically in her letter to Hassan, thanking him for the gift of his gold medallion:

Listen to the reed flute, she had written, *hear it complain,*
Bewailing its separation:—
"Ever since I was torn from my reed bed,
My plaintive notes have caused men and women to moan.
Search out a man whose own breast has burst from severance,
That I may express to him the agony of my love-desire."

The agony of my love-desire. She winced at the memory.

She had only one, faint hope for that humiliating letter—that it had been lost on its way to Lahore.

She sighed as she put her towel away. She needed distraction now, but never had her life felt so empty of adventure. Fitzgerald's letters complained of the dullness of Kandahar, but her life in Kabul was not much better.

Each morning, accompanied by Ghulam Ali and the silent Yar Mohammad, she rode out of the Residence compound and turned toward the great, fortified Bala Hisar, whose outstretched protecting wall climbed uphill and over the steep Sher Darwaza, and reached down to encircle the irregularly shaped walled city at its feet. Each day, instead of crossing the Kabul River and entering the city, she turned and rode toward the harsh mountains she had crossed the previous March.

"You must not enter Kabul proper without a European escort," her uncle had warned her once again. "While I am certain the Afghans will treat you decently, I cannot afford to take that risk."

A year earlier, Mariana would have ignored her uncle's instructions. On her very first day, she would have passed without hesitation through the nearest gate and into the fascinating fortified city that stood at the crossroads of the world. There, mingling with people from the far corners of Asia, she would have wandered its narrow lanes, its gardens and caravanserais, and admired its bazaars and their merchandise from China, Russia, Arabia, and India.

But this was different. This country had a faintly menacing flavor.

Each day she rode past the tempting city gates, with their throngs of laden porters and shouting sellers of grapes and watermelons. Each day she followed the dusty road along the river, past fruit gardens and the high, frowning bastions of the Bala Hisar, then between rows of poplar balsam trees toward the bare mountains.

After lunch, she wrote to her mother and sister of the picnics, amateur theatricals, and dinner parties she had attended with her aunt and uncle. To her father, she copied Fitzgerald's accounts of skirmishes with insurgents in Kandahar, and described the conversations she had overheard about fighting in the north.

To Fitzgerald, she wrote about nothing.

We have enjoyed one pleasant night after another, she had written yesterday. *Last evening, we dined under a full moon in Lady Macnaghten's garden. Brightly colored Indian cloth lanterns glowed like jewels from every tree. It was quite lovely.*

The garden *had* been lovely to look at, but the dinner conversation had revolved tediously around Sir William's recent appointment as Governor of Bombay, presumably to repay him for his work in Afghanistan. He and Lady Macnaghten were to leave within two months. Macnaghten's successor, Alexander Burnes, his face reddened from the wine, had prattled endlessly about the smoked salmon and cigars he ordered weekly from India for his parties in the city.

Burnes's neighbor, Captain Johnson, who had also drunk too much, had talked on about the wonders of living in Kabul without replying properly to any of Mariana's questions about the city.

"I can scarcely bear to leave town," the captain had announced to the table at large, his pale face animated after she asked him to describe the city bazaars. "Now that I keep the cash for Shah Shuja's soldiers in my house, I hardly need to go anywhere.

"To me," he had added rapturously, exchanging a glance with Alexander Burnes, "the beauties of the countryside are nothing compared to the pleasures of the city."

As they walked home afterward, Uncle Adrian had shaken his head. "Johnson may enjoy living in the city, but he is a fool to keep Shah Shuja's cash there."

In a moment the brass gong would sound, announcing lunch. Mariana straightened her back and returned to her desk. She snapped open her writing box and withdrew a letter she had written a week before.

It was probably full of mistakes, for she had not asked her teacher to correct it, but the time had come to send it on its way, and then to take the consequences.

I hope you have recovered fully from your wounds, she had written. *I ask your forgiveness for my past mistakes. Nothing would make me happier than to know that there is still a place for me at Qamar Haveli.*

I long to see you and your family once again, and to embrace my dear Saboor.

She had not had the courage to write more. With her first letter greeted by silence, she probably should not have written at all.

If it were meant for an English person, this letter would travel by official courier. Moving swiftly by relay in a pack of official dispatches, it would reach Lahore within ten days. But this letter, whose graceful, right-to-left Urdu script was intended only for native eyes, must be carried on foot.

She took in a long breath. It was now or not at all. She put her head round the door and shouted for Dittoo.

"Call Ghulam Ali," she ordered.

She emptied her cash box onto her bed, then, fearing the pile of coins would not be enough, she added to it two gold rings that had once belonged to her grandmother.

"Make certain you give it into Hassan Sahib's own hands," she said a few moments later.

"I do not need the rings," the courier declared brusquely, waving a sunburned hand. "I know how this work is done. Will you need a reply to your letter?" he added, almost kindly, his pink eyelids narrowing in the bright light from her window.

She felt herself blush. "Yes, if possible."

She watched him tuck the letter into his clothes and leave her.

A moment later, the gong rang.

What would happen now, she wondered, as she shut her door and marched down the tiled corridor toward the dining room.

Only Munshi Sahib could tell her. From the poetry he chose for her lessons, it was clear her teacher often read her mind. If he read hers so easily, then surely he could read Hassan's, for what barrier was distance to a soul in flight, especially that of her munshi, the great interpreter of dreams, and also, it seemed, of thoughts?

But she had never found the courage to ask him if Hassan had read her first letter, if he longed for her as he waited for sleep, if he loved her still.

"And now, Bibi," her teacher said, two hours later, in his instructive voice, "read me your translation from yesterday."

Before she began to read, Mariana looked warily toward the dining room window.

Her munshi's visits had lost some of their luster in recent months, for he no longer came alone from his small room near the servants' quarters. Instead, he was accompanied on that short, daily journey by the disturbing young Afghan asylum-seeker, whose three days of asylum had since lengthened to five months.

Each day they approached the bungalow together, the boy clinging to the old man like a well-meaning limpet, gripping his ancient elbow, frowning with concern as he pointed out loose stones along the pathway.

In the beginning, Mariana had waited impatiently for Nur Rahman's three days to end. Unnerved by the pollution on his face, wondering how the munshi could bear his presence, she had looked away whenever the boy hurried past her in the garden or on the avenue, carrying plates of fruit or pots of hot tea to the old man's room.

Her servants had appeared to feel the same. Dittoo had pretended the boy did not exist. Ghulam Ali had spat onto the ground at Nur Rahman's approach. Tall Yar Mohammad, whose former place at Munshi Sahib's side had been usurped, watched the boy with unreadable eyes.

On his third afternoon, when he accompanied Munshi Sahib to her lesson, Mariana had thought Nur Rahman had come to say good-bye.

"I hope all will be well with you after you leave here," she had offered when he greeted her as usual, a hand over his heart.

"I am sure you will find your way," she added, when he raised his head and stared into her face, his fringed eyes filled with curiosity and hope.

Her teacher had raised a wrinkled hand. "There is no need for farewells, Bibi," he had said gently. "Nur Rahman will be staying here."

"But Munshi Sahib," she had protested, horrified at this change of plan, "how can he stay? My aunt is bound to notice him. When she does, she will have him thrown onto the road—" She shifted from Farsi to Urdu and lowered her voice. "I do not want him here."

"He will look after me," her teacher had decreed. "He will sleep outside my door," he added serenely, as if that somehow made all the difference.

Today, as always, the two had arrived together. As always, the boy stayed behind, watching as the munshi entered by the front door, as befitting his station as a learned native, and stopped to remove his shoes before entering the dining room.

Munshi Sahib's real name was Mohammad Shafiuddin. Long ago in Bangalore, he had taught native languages to Mariana's uncle and a number of other young British officers. When Uncle Adrian had rediscovered him twenty years later, walking peacefully along the Mall in Simla, a thousand miles north of the city where they had been teacher and student, he had engaged the old man on the spot to teach Mariana Urdu and Persian, the court languages of northern India.

Uncle Adrian had not known then, and still did not know, that Munshi Sahib was a dear friend of Shaikh Waliullah.

"*I rocked to and fro,*" Mariana recited slowly, her forefinger following the words on the paper, "*that the child, my heart, might become still.*

"*A child sleeps when one sways the cradle.
Give my heart-babe milk, relieve us from its weeping,
O thou, that helpest every moment a hundred helpless like me.
The heart's home, first to last, is Thy City of Union:
How long wilt Thou keep in exile this forlorn heart?*"

How well those lines described her feelings. . . .

Her teacher nodded. "Very good. You have captured the soul's pain at its separation from the divine."

Mariana smoothed the paper on the table's surface, searching for the proper words to ask him, but nothing came.

If her teacher recognized how desperately she wanted to know Hassan's feelings, he gave no sign of it. Instead, he rocked on his heels beside her, his hands still behind his back, his gaze far away.

She gathered her courage. "Munshi Sahib," she began as she had done several times before, then faltered, tongue-tied once again, when he turned his mild gaze upon her.

Why was this so difficult? Why did the subject of her feelings cover her with such shame and confusion? What prevented her from asking him such a simple question?

"And now, Bibi," he said, taking a paper from his clothes and laying it on the table, "here is tomorrow's poem."

She glanced distractedly at the page, covered with lines of Persian handwriting. She must discover the truth about Hassan from someone else.

Another mystic would know—someone as advanced as Munshi

Sahib or Shaikh Waliullah would know at once what Hassan was thinking. She would have no reason to feel shame in front of a stranger whom she would never see again....

"I wonder, Munshi Sahib," she said casually, fingering the new page, "if there are any Followers of the Path like yourself here in Kabul."

"Yes, of course there are, Bibi." He pointed to the paper. "And now, this poem concerns—"

"And are they as wise as you?" *Please let them be even wiser.* She looked up into his face, hoping.

He withdrew his hand. "There have been learned men in Kabul for more than a thousand years, Bibi," he replied. "Maulana Jalaluddin Rumi himself was born to the north of here more than six hundred years ago. He would have remained here all his life had Balkh not been laid waste by Genghis Khan."

"But do they understand men's hearts as you do, Munshi Sahib?" she persisted.

"Ah, Bibi," he sighed, "no man can encompass all that is to be known. The wisest among us can hold no more than a mustard seed's weight of knowledge in his heart. But nevertheless, each Follower of the Path has his own particular understanding, and each person's understanding has value."

"Who are these men?"

Her teacher looked over her head, his eyes far away. "If you will give me time, I will find many practitioners hereabouts, but as of now, I know only one, for he came here long ago, from India."

"He is a Follower of the Path?"

The old man nodded. "He is called Haji Khan. As a young man, he traveled from his home in Bengal to Arabia, to perform the great pilgrimage that is required of all Muslims. On his third day in Mecca, he dreamed that he must travel to Kabul and remain there for the rest of his life. He was obliged to forget his family in Bengal. He was not permitted to work. His only duties were to pray, and to remember God."

Mariana stared. "But however did he survive in a strange city, knowing no one?"

"People saw who and what he was. They brought him food. Someone gave him a room to live in, and brought him warm clothes and fuel when winter came. The people gave him the title of Haji, for he had been no ordinary pilgrim, and they added Khan to his name out of respect. He has lived in the same room near the Char Chatta Bazaar for twenty-six years."

Mariana nodded seriously. "Will you take me," she said carefully, "to meet Haji Khan?"

Her teacher nodded. "That can be arranged."

But the walled city was forbidden to her. *You must not go there,* her uncle had decreed.

"But does he ever leave the city?" she asked him sharply. "Does he ever visit another place?"

Coughing erupted outside the drawing room window. In Nur Rahman's opinion, the coughing announced, her lesson was over.

Munshi Sahib smiled at the sound. "We will speak of Haji Khan another time. And now," he asked, "may I have your permission to depart?"

There was no point in trying to make him stay. Mariana nodded disappointedly, then watched her teacher step into the passageway and push his bare feet into a pair of worn leather slippers.

"Come, dear Father," she heard Nur Rahman say, as they rounded the corner of the bungalow. "You must rest now, before the *asr* prayer. You spend so much of the night on your prayer mat...."

Chapter 10

"I want an exact copy of this gown," Mariana announced, holding up her favorite sprigged cotton to the man who squatted on a sheet of cloth in the verandah, a pair of scissors beside him. "And make sure, Ravi, that you do not cut the sleeves too tight this time. I can hardly get into the pink muslin you made for me last month."

"Yes, Memsahib." The tailor gestured with a long finger at the bolt of white cotton in front of him, "And are you adding any decoration? Any lace?"

As Mariana was about to reply, Nur Rahman flitted around the side of the house, humming a strange-sounding melody to himself. He paused in front of the verandah, his eyes on the cloth.

Seeing him there, she remembered something she had noticed the previous day—a woman walking behind a man with a loaded donkey, covered from head to foot in a billowing white cloak that fell over her shoulders and back from a fitted cap, while a long veil in front dropped to her waist, pierced by a latticework peephole.

Of course.

She could not travel openly to the city, but with stealth, many things were possible.

She bent and handed her sprigged cotton gown to the tailor. "No lace," she said hastily, then hurried down the front step and into the garden, gesturing for Nur Rahman to wait.

"That cloth could be used for an Afghan woman's *chaderi,* could it not?" she inquired.

He nodded.

She glanced over her shoulder. "If I have one made for myself," she half whispered, "will you take me into the city?"

His eyes widened. "Oh, no, Khanum, never! If I am discovered in Kabul, I will be killed."

Of course he would be killed. That was what his panah had been about.

She felt her shoulders droop. She should have known that if she wanted to enter Kabul, she would have to go alone.

But she *would* do it, even if it meant searching among the alley-ways of the city, perhaps without success, for Haji Khan.

As she turned away from the boy, he brightened. "But, Khanum," he whispered, "if you will make another chaderi for me, I will take you there."

He sighed dramatically, his arms spread out. "In spite of its danger for me, I have missed my Kabul. It will do my heart good to see it again, even if I must do so as a woman."

THE NEXT morning, weighed down by the woolen riding habit she wore beneath her newly stitched chaderi, Mariana struggled to balance a bundle of twigs on her head as she hurried after Nur Rahman, avoiding the loaded pack animals of a nomad kafila that took up most of the roadway.

She peered through her latticework peephole. In front of her, Nur Rahman covered the ground swiftly, his white skirts billowing around his legs.

Her own yards of cotton had trapped the morning's heat, causing her hair to plaster itself to her neck and face. Her twigs dug painfully into her scalp; her arm ached from holding them steady. In the half-mile they had covered, she had dropped them twice, once into the path of an oncoming donkey, once among a herd of goats.

"You *must* carry something," the boy had insisted as he retied her kindling into a neat bundle for the second time. "Without a good reason, why would a woman like you be walking along the road?

And you should hold your chaderi closed in front, so people do not see those heavy black clothes you are wearing."

For all its present discomfort, this visit to the city had not been difficult to manage. Mariana had ridden out after breakfast as usual, accompanied by Yar Mohammad and a young under-groom substituting for the absent Ghulam Ali, but instead of taking her usual route toward the mountains, she had stopped at a mulberry garden a mile from the city, where Nur Rahman had been waiting as planned. There she had dismounted, handed her veiled top hat to the young groom, unfolded her chaderi, and ordered both men to wait for her return.

Yar Mohammad's weather-beaten face had bunched in dismay as she dropped the yards of white fabric over her shoulders. "If you wish to see the city, Memsahib," he had said in his resonant voice, "you should do so with honor, from the back of your mare. And you should not," he had added, gesturing with his chin toward Nur Rahman, "be trusting such a young person to guard your safety."

Now, perspiration pricked Mariana's upper lip. Grit cracked between her teeth. Yar Mohammad had been correct. Walking along the road with a load of kindling on her head was certainly less dignified than riding a horse, and she missed the safe company of her groom.

A dignified-looking male goat with tall, curved horns crossed a nearby field, followed at a distance by a jostling herd of she-goats, while a boy with a stick rounded up the stragglers. Mariana watched them without interest as she struggled along. The city across the river, with its high-walled fortress, had looked so near when they started walking. . . .

"We must stop and rest," she croaked.

"Not yet," the boy replied over his shoulder.

She sighed irritably inside her chaderi. How had Nur Rahman come to be in charge of this expedition? If they had not been in the open, with strangers listening on all sides, she would have given him a lesson in the proper comportment required of a servant. But then, he was not exactly a servant. In fact, he was no servant at all.

"Are you certain that you know Haji Khan's house?" she asked him a little later, as they sat side by side beneath a dusty tree.

"Of course I know where he lives." The boy's eyes glowed behind his veil. "I know *everything* about Kabul."

"Have you ever seen him?"

"No, but everyone knows he is a great man of Kabul. Even the Amir's family used to visit him at his house."

"They did not call him to their palace in the Bala Hisar?"

Nur Rahman lifted his chin. "Haji Khan is too great a man to go here and there at people's beck and call. Have you brought money?"

"A little."

"We must give him something—attar, honey from the Safed Koh, or a bag of walnuts. He lives," he added, "on the offerings of people such as yourself."

As they prepared to continue their journey, a long file of camels with bulging loads passed by, each animal swaying from side to side, in the manner of a kafila on the move. Uzbeks in striped silk *chapan*s strode alongside their swaying charges, frowning as they marched, as if walking itself were a serious occupation. Like everyone else on the road, they gave no sign of having noticed Mariana and her companion.

"Why are you walking like an old lady?" Nur Rahman demanded a quarter of an hour later, as they crossed a narrow pedestrian bridge leading directly over the Kabul River and into the city. "Everyone is looking. They can see your big foreign boots."

"I did not ask to cross this horrible bridge," Mariana snapped as she advanced wide-legged across the trembling planks, her twigs clutched in cloth-covered arms. She jerked her head. "Why have we not taken the brick one over there?"

"You complained so much," he replied reasonably, "that I took the shorter route."

By the time they entered the city, Mariana was too hot and irritated to speak. In front of her, Nur Rahman flitted along the wall of an enormous walled garden; he hurried from twisting street to street, his twigs balanced gracefully, moving easily past the doorways of houses and through the city's various bazaars, where goods were displayed in colorful heaps.

The crowds were dense. Slight men in embroidered caps walked shoulder to shoulder with wild-haired country folk and noble-faced old men in elaborate turbans. Donkeys, horses, and camels passed by, loaded with riders or goods. A few women passed, some holding brightly colored shawls over their faces, some in chaderis, all following a few paces behind their men. Two tall men in dark blue strode past, the skins of snow leopards thrown over their shoulders.

For all Mariana's annoyance, it was fortunate that Nur Rahman had agreed to come with her. Without him, she would have needed Theseus's ball of string to find her way about this labyrinthine city.

After passing through the wood market with its sounds of rhythmic chopping, they turned into a long, straight bazaar full of armorers, saddlers, and bookbinders, and a shop selling tiny bottles of heavily scented oil. There they stopped. At Nur Rahman's direction, Mariana bought the most expensive one. A trace of it perfumed the back of her hand, where the shopkeeper had put a single drop. Its complicated sweetness made her think of Hassan.

They turned a sharp corner, passed through a medieval-looking doorway with great metal studs, and entered a lane so constricted that the sunlight did not reach the dusty cobblestones, although it was only eleven in the morning. If she reached out, Mariana could have touched the walls on both sides of the alley. She held her skirts aside from a burbling waste gutter that ran at the alley's edge.

"We are in the *mohalla* of Bagh Ali Mardan Khan." Nur Rahman's voice lifted with happiness. "This is where I used to live. Haji Khan's house is close by here."

Mariana peered right and left through her peephole. The buildings were made of unbaked mud bricks between tall wooden uprights. Many had elegant balconies, held up by wooden posts, and elaborately carved doors. All had latticework window shutters that moved up and down. The upper windows stood open in the heat. A shadowy figure appeared in a doorway, then drew back inside. A battered-looking, long-haired cat slunk along one wall. Mariana smelled sewage, charcoal smoke, and burning fat.

A moment later, Nur Rahman stopped short. "This is the house." He pointed to a high wooden door with a heavy lintel.

He hammered on it, balancing his twigs with one hand.

For a time, no one came. Fearing someone would appear asking questions, Mariana glanced behind her. "Perhaps we should have—"

Nur Rahman's only response was to hammer more energetically.

The door swung inward. An old man wearing broken shoes looked them up and down. "Peace," he offered, a hand over his heart.

"Peace," Mariana replied, craning to see inside. The man stepped back and let them into a small, cobbled courtyard. A cow stood tethered to a tree in one corner. A nightingale in a wicker birdcage swung from a branch above its head. It was not a rich man's courtyard, but it offered peace, along with the smell of cow dung.

To her left, under a vine-covered portico, a door stood open.

Beside it, a pile of discarded shoes indicated the presence of a number of men. A few long-barreled jezails with curved, decorated wooden stocks leaned against a corner. Two or three fierce-looking knives lay on the portico floor.

A rasping voice came from within. "What you have not understood, Hashmat Jan," the voice decreed in Persian, "is that Paradise is for the *soul,* not the *body.*"

"True." A different, warmer voice intoned a few verses of rhythmic Arabic, then shifted to Persian. "In *Sura Ha Mim,* it is written:

"Therein shall ye have
All that your souls
Shall desire; therein
Shall ye have all
That ye ask for!"

"I already know what I desire," put in a third, young-sounding voice. "I have been promised virgins and wine—"

"Virgins! Wine! You, Hashmat, are a fool," rasped the first voice.

"Haji Khan," the doorkeeper announced, "guests have come!"

"Oh, you who stand outside," said the voice, "enter."

Mariana put down her twigs and pulled off her riding boots. She had intended to tell Nur Rahman to wait outside while she met privately with Haji Khan, but such a meeting was clearly impossible. Judging from all those shoes and weapons, the room was full to bursting with Afghan men.

She would never be able to ask her question now.

She stepped over the threshold on stocking feet, and found herself in a windowless chamber, whose only illumination came from the open doorway behind her, and from a small, filigreed copper lamp at the back of the room.

The lamp shone weakly onto the faces of a dozen turbaned men who sat shoulder to shoulder upon a floor covered with layers of tribal rugs. Some of the men looked like the fierce, ragged men she had seen walking on the road. Others, who wore clean, starched clothing, looked like Afghan versions of Hassan's family members. One or two of the group seemed to carry a special authority. Perhaps they, too, were Followers of the Path.

She hesitated in the doorway. The gatekeeper had failed to say she was a woman. Was she really welcome among all these men?

Certain she was not, she glanced quickly about her, taking in as much as she could before she was asked to leave.

Embroidered hangings of every conceivable hue, some new, some rotting with age, covered the walls of the room. One or two of them were decorated with great wheel-like patterns. Others were thickly covered in triangles of bright silk stitching. Still others had been sewn with small, irregularly shaped mirrors that gleamed in the lamplight.

A heavy, sweet scent, akin to the one she had bought in the market, hung in the air, eclipsing the smell of the courtyard.

At the back of the room, a sparsely bearded man sat cross-legged upon a string bed. His face was soft-featured, not sharply boned like those of the men who crowded around him. A smoking chillum stood beside him on the floor.

Where his pupils should have been, his eyes were white.

He beckoned to her. "Come closer," he ordered.

The men moved aside without speaking to let her pass. The blind man pointed to a straw stool beside him.

The room was very hot. Not knowing what to do with her tiny gift, she laid it hesitantly on a square of cloth beside him. She groped for her handkerchief and mopped her face under her veil.

"May peace be upon you, Haji Khan." Nur Rahman's pleading voice came from the doorway. "May I pay my respects?"

"Pay them from where you are standing. You have no need of me. But you, Khanum," the blind man turned to Mariana, "you have something to ask me."

For all the harsh sound of his voice, the man wore a benign expression. He tilted his head, as if he could imagine her face by listening to her breathe. Behind her the Afghans shifted and murmured. The pipe beside her gave off a bitter smoke.

She opened her mouth to speak, then closed it again. Confusion, not embarrassment, stopped her from asking, in that male and public company, whether Hassan still loved her, and if he did not, whether she should marry Fitzgerald. Those questions, so urgent when she had embarked on this adventure, now shriveled to nothing before the sightless Bengali in his odd, perfumed chamber.

Prompted by Haji Khan and his surroundings, another more pressing question arose in their place. Powerful and inarticulate, it tugged at her, begging to be asked.

She had no idea what it was.

Haji Khan closed his eyes. "You are not yet ready, Khanum," he said, moving his head to and fro, "to know the answer to your question. But do not worry. It will come to you of its own accord, at the proper time."

Your question. Which one? She opened her mouth to ask, and saw that he had turned away from her.

Behind him on the wall hung an open cupboard, divided into small compartments, each one containing many small rolls of paper. He felt among them, his fingers fluttering, then pulled out a paper and laid it next to Mariana's little bottle of perfume.

"Read this eleven times every morning, and every evening," he said as he drew back his hand. "Your answer will come in due course."

But which answer was that? "Haji Sahib," she asked quickly, "please tell me—"

"You may visit me again," he added, as if she had not spoken.

Had she been dismissed? Mariana took the little paper and glanced behind her. Nur Rahman beckoned urgently from the doorway.

But they had only just arrived. . . .

She stood and made her disappointed way to the door.

"And now, Hashmat," she heard him say as she pulled on her boots, "you must stop this nonsense of yours. Whatever you may believe about killing those who are not Muslims, there is no quick route to the Garden, especially not through murder of innocent people, who may very well believe in Allah, although not in the same way as you. Victory is not a camel to be bought with a single transaction. It comes only after a long struggle against our own vain desires.

"If you want to go to Paradise," he added firmly, "then offer your prayers and give charity to those in need."

"What did Haji Khan mean by saying I have no need of him?" Nur Rahman blurted out after the outer door of the house had closed heavily behind them. He hunched his shoulders inside his chaderi. "I am as good as anyone else."

"He probably meant that you already have Munshi Sahib."

"But you have him, too."

"Not in the same way." Now that she could not see his face, Mariana felt herself warming toward the boy. "He is my language teacher, but you serve him day and night. As you care for his comfort, perhaps he will care for your soul."

"Do you think so?" Nur Rahman's voice brightened. "More than anything," he went on confidentially, "I want to go to Paradise after I die. I have heard that it is easy, that all I have to do is kill an Englishman, but now Haji Khan has said that is not true."

"Kill an *Englishman*?" Mariana stared at him from beneath her twigs.

"I myself would not do it. I would not even kill one of your Hindu servants, because you have offered me panah, and I have eaten your salt. But others will, because the English are all infidels, like the Hindus."

They had turned from Haji Khan's narrow lane into a wider street lined with shops and lean-tos selling fruit and vegetables. "Come," he added over his shoulder. "I will show you the bazaar. It is very beautiful."

"Wait, Nur Rahman!" She hurried after him, her riding boots thudding on the packed earth. "*Who* has been saying that we are infidels, that men will go to Paradise for killing us?"

"The chiefs who have allied themselves with Wazir Akbar Khan, the son of our Amir. Everyone knows that Abdullah Khan is one, and Aminullah Khan is another."

She frowned. "How do you know this?"

"Afghan people come and go from the cantonment every day. I have heard these things from traders, from Hazara laborers, from everyone.

"The British," Nur Rahman added, "have replaced our Amir Dost Mohammad with Shah Shuja, whom no one respects. He plunders the great chiefs of their lands and their money, and the British uphold his rule with a huge army that buys up all our food, so our own people go hungry. And they have no shame. They have—"

"Be careful!" Mariana caught the boy's arm and pushed him against a wall as a group of boisterous men rounded a corner ahead of them in the narrow street. Muskets resting carelessly on their shoulders, they strode past Mariana and Nur Rahman, talking loudly among themselves, their arms swinging.

There was something actively dangerous about them. "Who were they?" she whispered when they had gone.

"They are relatives of Shah Shuja. These people are full of themselves now. See that man over there?" he added, gesturing toward a dignified-looking gentleman who had pressed himself into a nearby doorway. "He was protecting himself just now."

He pointed ahead of them. "Look," he added, changing the subject. "That is the Char Chatta Bazaar."

In front of Mariana, the street opened out into a teeming marketplace. A little way past baskets of ripe, fly-covered grapes and heaps of pale melons, a heavy stone archway led into a vast covered arcade. This must be the central market of Kabul.

Mariana and Nur Rahman dodged donkey carts and more fruit, then passed under the archway and into the great, echoing bazaar, whose broad, cobbled floor was lined with small shops. Birds swooped under the high vaulted ceiling. The inner walls of the market held glittering traces of mirrored plasterwork. Far ahead of them, a sunlit area opened up. Mariana saw trees, followed by a second heavy archway, as if the market's architecture had been interrupted to let in light and air.

The shops stood side by side on either side of the passageway; each one raised several steps above the cobblestones. Crowds of men from all parts of Asia surged past, while cooks fried tidbits of spiced meat in great iron pans, and merchants hawked goods directly from the backs of donkeys. Mariana could not take her eyes from the wares on display: gold and silver, turban silks and weaponry, brass samovars and Chinese porcelains. Next to a jeweler's shop, a knife-seller's wares had been spread out, temptingly, on a cloth.

The jeweler's wooden cases held crude carved silver and lapis necklaces and cufflike bracelets. As she reached out, steadying herself to step up into the tiny shop, a smooth voice spoke into her ear. "What a lovely, white hand," it said.

Nur Rahman stiffened beside her.

Startled, Mariana jerked her hand back and hid it beneath her chaderi.

The man had spoken in accented Persian. His tone had been suggestive. Mariana turned and found herself face-to-face with a rotund, smiling, clean-shaven man in a bulky muslin turban and the long, loose clothing of a Pashtun. A showily carved dagger handle protruded from the striped silk sash around his waist. He smiled, his brown eyes dancing with anticipation.

It was Sir Alexander Burnes, the British Resident.

Behind him, also in Afghan dress, his lanky friend Captain Johnson leaned casually against a stone pillar. He, too, offered Mariana an encouraging smile.

"A hand as graceful and white as yours," Burnes continued, bending confidentially toward her, peering past the latticework in front of her eyes, "is not often seen in Kabul. I am sure that if you will show me your face, I will find it every bit as lovely."

The beauties of the countryside, Johnson had said, *are nothing compared to the pleasures of the city.*

"My house is not far off. I can arrange for you to be taken there with utmost discretion," Burnes added, his voice becoming oilier by the second.

Fury overtook Mariana's surprise. *"Do not,"* she said tightly, *"come near me."*

Burnes's eyes widened. He stepped backward, smiling uncertainly, his hands raised before him. "I beg forgiveness, Khanum," he said. "Perhaps I have made a mistake."

The passing throng had noticed their exchange. Men glanced at her, derisive smiles on their faces.

If she accused Burnes publicly, he might be killed in front of her. "Have you no shame?" she whispered in furious Farsi. "Have you no decency?"

"Forgive me," the Englishman repeated, his hands still raised. Behind him, Johnson melted into the crowd.

"I," she said distinctly, "have never been so insulted in *all my life*."

Astonishment dawned on Burnes's face then, for she had spoken that last sentence in English.

NUR RAHMAN leaned toward the English lady as they hurried from one crooked lane to another on their return journey. "I could not speak openly to you of such things, Khanum," he offered confidentially, "but this is what the British officers have been doing.

"Shah Shuja gives them whatever they want," he went on. "He is their slave. Only a month ago, he had a man hanged for killing his wife. She, a woman of high family, had committed *gunah* with one of your Englishmen. It is these things that cause the greatest hatred."

Seeing her twitch, the boy shrugged. "People have been bringing these stories to the cantonment for months."

Many women of noble family, it was whispered, had succumbed to the Englishmen. No one knew why. Several had been killed for betraying their families, but others had managed to evade being caught. Nur Rahman sighed aloud, unable to help admiring those who had taken such a deadly risk. Surely, for a brave man or woman, nothing could match the exhilaration of chancing one's life. Even he, in his flimsy disguise, was doing so.

The English lady must have been in a great hurry to leave the city, for heavy black clothes, chaderi and all, she now strode beside him as rapidly as any Afghan.

Perhaps she had heard what the narrow-faced Pashtun had said in the market.

"Now that the men of Kabul are prevented from defending their honor," the man had observed, "we are seeing how their women behave themselves."

Nur Rahman felt sorry for the lady. By the time he had run to her for asylum, time had already been growing short for her people. It grew even shorter now.

The price of flour was now so high that the people of the city were going hungry in their own houses. It would not be long before those who suffered, and those who could be persuaded to join them, would take their revenge. Soon, the braggarts who roamed the streets of Kabul with such confidence would pay for their pride.

That was the cycle of life—one was victim, then avenger, then victim.

What would happen then to the woman who had spared his life?

They were curious people, these foreigners. The men dressed in dusty black wool clothing, even in the heat of summer. They wore their stiff hats outdoors, but took them off when they went inside. What an odd thing to do—with bared heads, how could they show one another respect? Their women's dress was even stranger—all of them, even the old ladies, revealed their shapes embarrassingly with their tight, uncomfortable-looking garments. This one, too, wrapped her slim figure with heavy, close-fitting things, even when she rode toward the mountains each day, sitting sideways on her mare.

As she walked beside him, Nur Rahman could see a black hem trailing below the loose folds of her chaderi. He turned his head and glanced behind him through his peephole. People were looking at her. They had seen how oddly she was dressed, but luckily, no

Englishwoman had ever been seen in the city, so they were unlikely to guess what she was. And among this polyglot population, nothing seemed strange.

He sighed, picturing the foreign ladies in their evening clothes. Those indecently cut gowns were the best of all. Each day after sunset he made a point of waiting at a corner of the English lady's bungalow, in case the family had been invited out to dinner. It would never do to miss a lamplit glimpse of bare chests and shoulders as she and her aunt passed out through the front door.

He had also observed how the old woman and her husband spoke to their servants, and what food they offered them. Although the husband said little, maintaining a quiet, worried air, the fat woman spoke stiffly, through pursed lips, to their collection of serving-men and under-serving-men, palanquin bearers, sweepers, gardeners, and water-carriers. She even did the same when she addressed the tall, dignified groom. She barely spoke at all to the albino with his blistered skin and pink eyes.

Nur Rahman had also been shocked to discover that while he, his wonderful old man, and all the household servants ate cooked lentils and vegetables, rice and bread, the English people ate meat, prepared for them daily by a peculiar-looking cook in a loincloth.

Such behavior was unfathomable to Nur Rahman. How could those English have kept the meat only for themselves? Was this an Indian custom? How could they have failed to offer all their food to their servants, especially to Nur Rahman's dear Shafi Khan, for whom he would readily give his life?

Even Painda Gul, may he roast for eternity in the fires of Hell, had shared his meals, morsel for morsel, with Nur Rahman.

Nur Rahman had not mentioned his distress to the old man. Instead, a few months ago, he had simply waited for his opportunity, and stolen four small mutton chops from a butcher in the bazaar. He had cooked his ill-gotten treasure with a few cloves and black peppercorns and a stick of cinnamon bark slipped from the Englishman's kitchen. When they were done, he had offered them triumphantly to the old man.

Munshi Sahib had looked, unsmiling, at the plate, then at Nur Rahman's flushed face. "My dear child," he had said, "you have not gained this food with your right hand."

The smell of the meat had filled Nur Rahman's senses and brought water to his mouth, but the old man's words had cut him to the heart. He should have known that the great Shafi Khan would never put stolen meat into his mouth.

"We must not let any food go to waste," the old man had said. "Take it outside and feed it to the poor. They are innocent. Eating it will do them no harm."

Nur Rahman had wept as he held out his fragrant offering to a ragged child. Penniless, he could find no remedy for the niggardliness of the English people, no delicacy to be cooked for his beloved benefactor, who had counseled the Englishwoman to save his life, who now allowed Nur Rahman to sleep outside his door, and to prepare his morning tea.

Later, the old man had chided him gently, saying that food for the body was no more than that, and that the best food of all was food for the soul.

Food for the soul. Nur Rahman stole a glance at the Englishwoman. What, he wondered, was written on the small roll of paper that lay hidden in her clothes? Did it contain the secrets of Paradise? He would give anything to know what he must do to gain the Garden, where all sins were forgiven.

As much as he loved his gentle old man, he could not help wishing that the famous Haji Khan had given *him* a little roll of paper.

Chapter 11

"The reason you cannot understand these verses, Bibi," Mariana's munshi explained the following day, "is that they are written in Arabic."

"And I must recite them in Arabic?"

He shook his head. "Only the prayers must be recited in the original Arabic. These lines may be read in your own language, although of course Arabic is better."

When he first entered the dining room for her lesson, she had hesitated to tell her teacher of her secret visit to Haji Khan, fearing what he would say. In the end she had realized that it would be wiser to tell the truth.

When she had, he had offered her no reproach, only a silent, appraising look.

She stared at the little page, now unrolled on the dining table, its corners weighed down by her inkstand and a candlestick from the sideboard, its surface covered with unintelligible handwriting. What did it say, this talisman from Haji Khan's trove of papers?

Line by line, her teacher translated Haji Khan's paper into English. Line by line, she copied out his dictated words, growing more and more disappointed as she worked.

Shower thy blessings upon our leader and master Muhammad:
Thy worshiper, thine apostle, thy Messenger, the Unlettered
* Prophet,*
His spiritual descendants, his consorts, his progeny, all:
In number as many as the numerous things created,
As deep as the fulfillment of the soul's longing,
As brilliant as the embellishment of the high heavens,
As powerful as the Affirmation of Faith.

Haji Khan's verses did not describe the durability of love in the face of obstacles, or explain the necessity of abandoning a lost cause. They did not hint at the urgent, veiled question that had pestered her as she sat beside him in his dark, perfumed room.

Baffled, she pointed to the paper. "What does this mean, Munshi Sahib?"

"It is a *durood,* Bibi, an invocation of Allah's blessings upon the Prophet Muhammad. In offering a durood, the reciter brings Allah's blessings upon himself. Some duroods also protect the reciter from the promptings of evil, or from those who might do him harm."

"That is interesting, Munshi Sahib, but why has Haji Khan given it to me?"

"I cannot say." He frowned. "Did he give you any instructions?"

"He told me to recite what is written on this paper eleven times, morning and evening."

"Then I suggest you do it."

"Impossible, Munshi Sahib. I cannot do such a thing."

Her teacher shrugged. "If that is because you are Christian, I remind you that Christians, like Jews and Muslims, are *ahl-e-kitab,* People of the Book. They recognize the same prophets, the same laws. Haji Khan is known to have traveled very far along the Path to Peace," he added. "If he has suggested that you recite this durood, he has done so for a reason, although what it is, I cannot say."

"He is also blind in both eyes," she pointed out. "The cupboard behind him was full of identical rolls of paper. He could easily have given me the wrong one."

Her teacher did not reply. Instead, he reached into one of the pockets of his long snowy shirt and withdrew a string of carved wooden beads. A silk tassel hung from a single large bead on the string. "These are for you, Bibi," he said, as he laid them carefully on the table. "If you choose to do what Haji Khan suggests, you will need to count your recitations."

In her bedroom an hour later she stared into space, Haji Khan's paper in her hand.

The answer will come to you of its own accord, at the proper time, he had told her. He had also invited her to return.

For all that he had said little to her, he had been a compelling presence, sitting white-eyed before his guests in that close little room. He had known at once that it was she, and not Nur Rahman, who had a question to ask.

And yet these verses offered her nothing.

If he *had* meant to give her this durood, why had he done it? What did he think would happen if she did as he had told her?

She had longed to learn mystical secrets from the moment she had met the Shaikh and his powerful sister, but it had never occurred to her that to do so she might have to stop being a Christian. That she could not do. It was one thing to study Oriental mysticism, but it was quite another to forsake the Church of England.

She could not imagine what her vicar father would say if he learned of the durood, or even of the beads that now lay hidden in the pocket of her gown.

But as alien as those verses had sounded upon her lips, and as strange as Munshi Sahib's beads had felt in her fingers, she was certain that together they offered her a doorway into some beautiful, unknown place.

The doorway beckoned. It was her choice to enter it, or pass it by.

"IT IS perfectly apparent to me," Sir William Macnaghten said quietly the next afternoon as he sat in Babur Shah's memorial garden, "that if London wishes to save money, they should cut expenditures somewhere else."

The English party had returned to Babur's tomb to enjoy one more outing before the weather turned cold. When Macnaghten and several political officers moved away from the others to a quiet grove of trees, Mariana had followed them and seated herself nearby, her back against a tree, straining to hear their conversation.

"This entire region is open to us," Sir William went on. "With only a few more men we can take Bokhara in the north *and* Herat in the west."

"Sir William," Mariana's uncle replied cautiously, "have you considered our lines of supply? They are dangerously long already, and easily severed by insurgents in all those narrow passes."

"We should perhaps take the Afghan point of view into account," Charles Mott added, with uncharacteristic confidence, "especially that of the chiefs of the country and the religious leaders—"

"But," Sir William went on, ignoring both remarks, "the government has insisted that I cut back expenses, and I have done so.

"General Sale's First Brigade will return to India next month. They will take the short road east, through Jalalabad. I have also cut the annual stipend for the Eastern Ghilzais by half. If the saving from these measures proves insufficient, then Shah Shuja will have to give up some of his little luxuries."

Mariana held her breath, waiting for her uncle's response.

"You have done *that*?" When Adrian Lamb replied, his voice was filled with dismay. "You have cut the payment to the Ghilzai tribes who control all the passes between here and Jalalabad?"

"Oh, Uncle William," wailed Charles Mott. "I really wonder—"

"I have done it," Macnaghten said decisively. "Of course they kicked up a row about the deductions from their pay. One of them tried to protest, but Sir Alexander handled him very well. It will do them no good to complain," he added. "And if they lift so much as a finger against us, they will be trounced for their pains, the rascals."

"By General Sale, on his way to India?"

"Precisely. After all, he will be traveling through their country."

Mariana heard her uncle clear his throat. "I am sure you are aware, Sir William," he said cautiously, "that Akbar Khan has come down from Tashkurgan in the north. He is said to be traveling toward Hazajarat, west of here. Are you certain he is not conniving against us with Ghilzai chiefs such as Abdullah Khan and Aminullah Khan? Those two men give all the appearance of being both dangerous and very much against us. I fear there may be a pattern of revolt, all instigated by Akbar, if we do anything to—"

"*Mr. Lamb,*" Sir William snapped, "I am tired of your incessant croaking. We are in no danger at all. With the exception of one or two little uprisings, this country is in a state of perfect tranquility."

The ensuing silence from Mariana's uncle spoke volumes.

"Why has Sir Alexander declined to come today?" Uncle Adrian inquired as the three men passed by Mariana on their way to the table where the lunch was being laid.

"He said he has urgent business in the city," replied Sir William.

Urgent business indeed. Still leaning against her comfortable tree trunk, Mariana pictured the voluble, excessive Burnes in the bazaar, ridiculous in his Afghan disguise, starting back from her in surprise, the leer wiped from his face.

Repugnant as that moment had been, Nur Rahman's later remarks had been more upsetting. How could Burnes, with all his experience in Central Asia, have risked the rage of powerful Afghans by soliciting their women in the marketplace, and successfully, too, if Nur Rahman were to be believed? And what of his lackey, the cowardly Johnson, the man now responsible for Shah Shuja's treasure?

If an Afghan's honor requires revenge, Munshi Sahib had told her, *he will exact it, whatever the price.*

As she rejoined the others, Mariana glanced around her at Sir William's guests and his pretty wife, who offered him a private little smile as he reached across her for the wine bottle.

Burnes and Johnson were a danger to them all. She should report them, but how would she ever explain her own presence in the Char Chatta Bazaar, disguised as an Afghan woman?

Since their arrival, Uncle Adrian had gathered a number of paid informers from various parts of the country. Mariana had seen them often—men young and old, wearing the dress of various tribes and regions. They always entered the garden by the front gate, then spoke quietly to her uncle on the verandah.

Surely they had told him about Burnes's activities. But, she realized, just as surely, he had discounted their stories. After all, an informer is paid to provide interesting news.

"I shall never tire of this view." Lady Macnaghten sighed from her folding chair at the table. "Kabul has proved to be everything I had hoped for, although I must admit I am quite surfeited with grapes. I find myself pining for a nice, sour English gooseberry."

Aunt Claire nodded beneath her parasol. "And I do not care if I never see another melon. Mariana, tell Adil to bring me a glass of water."

"But," General Elphinstone added, grimacing as he lifted his swollen leg onto a straw stool, "nothing can compare to the brilliance of the light and freshness of the breeze, especially here on this mountainside."

Lady Macnaghten laid a hand on her husband's arm and pointed toward the Persian inscription over the mosque's marble entrance. "You must translate that verse for us again, William," she said happily. "I find it so very affecting."

He cleared his throat. "*Only this mosque of beauty,*" he recited in a sonorous tone, "*this temple of nobility, constructed for the prayer of saints and the epiphany of cherubs, was fit to stand in so venerable a sanctuary as this highway of archangels, this theatre of heaven, the light garden of the God-forgiven angel king.*"

"Ah," General Elphinstone sighed, "how well they were able to express themselves in those days! It is difficult to imagine the Afghan savages of today being capable of such eloquence."

Savages. Mariana gazed down at the winding Kabul River and the orchard-filled Chahardeh valley beyond, imagining the starched, neatly bearded men she had seen in Haji Khan's room. She had not spoken to them, of course, but she had no doubt that for all the weaponry and reputed violence of the Afghans, Kabul had its own poets and scholars, scientists, doctors, and learned men.

Why was it so difficult for her people to accept that simple fact?

"It is no wonder that the Emperor Babur fell in love with this country," Uncle Adrian observed. "If he were as good a king as people say, then he deserved to rule this beautiful land."

She nodded her agreement. With its clear, crystalline light, so different from the damp luminosity of England and the dusty haze of India, Afghanistan was indeed beautiful. What a pity her own people had forced upon it that sour, nervous Shah Shuja and his swaggering followers.

The snow on the distant mountain peaks turned from pink to violet as the afternoon progressed. As the valley below the garden took on hues of ochre and gold, Mariana wished Hassan and Saboor could see it with her.

She sighed. Perhaps her second letter would reach Hassan safely.

She pictured Ghulam Ali trudging along the road from Kabul, with its rocky outcroppings and rushing streams full of rounded pebbles, his loose cotton clothing stained from travel. Was he at this moment crossing a mountain meadow perfumed with aromatic grass, or climbing a hillside covered with wild lavender and thistles?

When would he cross into India?

His unusual appearance might prevent him from being recognized immediately as a servant of the British. That might be a good thing. He still carried his long-bladed Khyber knife, did he not?

If anything happened to the courier who had helped her rescue Hassan the night he was wounded, and who had later hurried after her from Lahore, Hassan's carefully wrapped gold medallion hidden in his pocket, she would never forgive herself.

The Qur'anic verse carved into the little medallion possessed a beauty that tugged at Mariana, as did Haji Khan's durood.

The fulfillment of the soul's longing. Did verses like these have the power to inspire dreams or answer the questions of the soul? Could they touch a heart with poetic alchemy, and change it forever?

She did not know, but as she sat in Babur Shah's garden among her own people, she made up her mind to try reciting the durood, but with one small change to protect her Christianity.

THE SUN was low in the sky when Sir William's guests and their armed guard assembled for the return journey.

Lady Macnaghten put a booted foot onto her groom's proffered knee, and climbed awkwardly into her sidesaddle. "What a lovely day," she fluted as she adjusted her riding veil. "I expect to be happily exhausted tomorrow."

"It is a good thing," observed her husband, "that Kabul is such a quiet station. In these times of peace we may tire ourselves with abandon."

"What a pity Sir Alexander was unable to join us," she said. "He would so much have enjoyed the view."

"Come along, Mariana," her uncle called, as the rest of the party descended the hill toward the garden's elegant gateway. "Yar Mohammad has brought your mare."

"Be careful crossing the bridge," he warned a little later. "People are coming the other way. And remember not to look at them."

A tall, heavily bearded rider approached from the opposite bank, followed by three dogs and six or seven horsemen. She glanced at the tall rider as he came near, and drew in her breath. On his leather-clad wrist, hooded and silent, rode a pure white hawk.

She lowered her gaze, feeling the man's eyes upon her.

Several rabbits and a score of large, red-legged partridges hung from the horses' saddles. From the corner of her eye she saw the white hawk open its wings partway, and hunch its shoulders. There was no hint of gray anywhere on its wings or body. Its leather hood had been embroidered with silver thread.

"That is a *tujhun*," her uncle said quietly. "A Siberian goshawk. They are great hunters and very rare."

"Why did that man look so familiar?" Mariana asked, after the hunting party had clattered past them on the bridge, talking among themselves, their long-haired hounds trotting alongside them.

"That, my dear," her uncle said, glancing over his shoulder at the departing horsemen, "was Abdullah Khan himself, the Achakzai chief who knocked down those tents at the race meeting. Do you remember him throwing down his tent peg as if he were challenging Shah Shuja to a duel? I was told he had returned to the Pishin valley after that, but my information was clearly wrong.

"I do not like seeing him here in Kabul," he added. "I do not like the derisive look I saw on his face as he passed us, or the way his men talked among themselves and pointed in our direction."

He frowned. "All this reminds me that I must discover the whereabouts of that doddering old Aminullah Khan. For all I know, he is here as well."

The day was fading rapidly. The little shrine beside the river was now alive with people, their lanterns casting shadows as they moved about among the trees. Mariana imagined the wicked old tribesman lurking in the dark with his men, like the villain in a fairy tale.

"We must catch up with the others," her uncle said sharply. "I do not like to be out at dusk without an escort.

"It is rumored," he murmured as they neared the Residence compound, "that Abdullah Khan killed his elder brother by burying him in the ground, tying a rope to his neck, and then riding circles around him until his head was torn from his shoulders. That story may or may not be true, but it illustrates the man's reputation."

That night, Mariana lay whispering in the dark, as Munshi Sahib's beads clicked between her fingers.

It was acceptable, he had told her, to recite Haji Khan's durood in

English. He had not, however, authorized the small alteration she had made.

"Shower thy blessings," she whispered, hoping for a glimpse through the blind man's doorway, "upon *their* leader and master Muhammad. . . ."

Chapter 12

Y ou have *cut* the annual payment to the Eastern Ghilzai chiefs by *half*?" Shah Shuja dropped his bunch of grapes and regarded Sir William with dignified horror. "You have done this without so much as asking my advice?"

Behind him, elegant and self-possessed, his double row of ministers murmured among one another, turbaned heads together, their eyes upon the two black-clad Englishmen in front of him.

"Sire," the Envoy replied, "we had no option. Our government in Calcutta has been insisting for months that we cut our—"

"Ah, Macnaghten, you took no time to think." The Shah pushed the fruit bowl away from him and turned a tired eye upon his guests.

Of the other officers, both civil and military, who stood behind Burnes and Macnaghten, only three spoke Farsi. Of those, only Mariana's uncle and his assistant watched Shah Shuja's reaction with any interest.

When Macnaghten threw them a fiercely defensive glance, Charles Mott shuffled his feet. Adrian Lamb did not drop his gaze.

"Did you consider your agreement with the Ghilzais before you cut their payment?" the Shah went on in his high, unpleasant voice. "Did you weigh the loss of your honor in breaking your promise?"

"Honor?" Macnaghten gave a lighthearted shrug. "I hardly think *that* matters in this country, Sire, where no one—"

"Honor matters very much in this country, Macnaghten. I have warned you before of the danger of taking gold from some chiefs while giving it to others. Even if you have not done exactly that," the Shah added, "the appearance of it has created enemies for yourselves and for me. Now, you have compounded your mistake."

Macnaghten smiled broadly, his hands open in front of him. "But Sire," he argued, "all we have done is make things fairer. The other chiefs still must pay, but the Ghilzais are getting *less*. Is that not a good thing?

"These people are such children," he muttered to Burnes beneath his breath, his smile still in place.

"You have returned me to my throne, Macnaghten." Shah Shuja sighed. "But you have snatched the sovereignty of my country from my hands. Believing that your big guns will keep you safe, you interfere with us, and force your British ways upon us. In your pride, you have turned all the chiefs against me."

Behind him, his ministers nodded their agreement.

Alexander Burnes stiffened in his chair. "There is no need, Sire, to speak to us in this manner. We have harmed no one. Your enemies are free and unblinded. Why—"

"Have you not understood the saying that 'the enemy of my enemy is my friend'?" The corners of the Shah's mouth turned down. "In taxing them severely, you have injured chiefs to the north and south of Kabul. In breaking your promise to them, you have injured the Eastern Ghilzai chiefs. And do not forget that Akbar Khan, son of Dost Mohammad, who has sworn to regain his father's throne, waits with his men at Bamian, to the west. All will now unite against you. Whether you accept it or not, you are now encircled by your enemies."

"Really, Sire, that is the most—"

The Shah held up a silencing hand. "Once they have identified a common foe, our people form alliances against him, but not before each separate faction has proved itself with exploits against that foe, for Afghans do not rally under one leader, but under a confederation of leaders. What you regard as a few small uprisings may well be those exploits, which will lead to greater and greater attacks by larger and larger numbers of men.

"Your British officers have been openly insulted in the bazaar when they have tried to order tools and weapons from our artisans. Two of them have been stabbed in the marketplaces of Kabul. Several of your Indian soldiers have been killed when they strayed from your cantonment. Do you think these incidents are unrelated?"

Macnaghten smiled again. "But Sire, if we have so many enemies, then why do people flock to join in our horse races and our entertainments? Why do they smile and joke with us as if we were brothers? Why do they offer us gifts and friendship?"

"Yes," Burnes joined in, "and why do they call me 'Eskandar' so happily? Why do they use my Christian name?"

Shah Shuja leaned back against his silken bolster. "That is no Christian name. Eskandar, or Alexander, is a very ancient name indeed. But let me tell you something else: it is not the habit of my people to reveal their feelings. They will smile at you until the very moment when you feel the bite of their knives.

"Mark my words, Macnaghten," he added, "there will be reprisals against you for this cutting of payments to the Ghilzais."

Macnaghten bowed. "As you say, Sire. And now, with your permission, I must return to my duties."

The Shah shook his head. "Ah, Macnaghten," he said wearily, "how little you understand my Afghanistan."

THAT SAME afternoon, in the simpler atmosphere of Qamar Haveli, Safiya Sultana leaned back against a cotton-encased bolster and chewed meditatively on a slice of melon.

Her life boasted many pleasures. For the moment at least, everyone in the house was in good health. Hassan, now fully recovered and preparing to leave for Peshawar, rode daily with Saboor. Their excursions to the countryside, either sedately on horse and pony, or galloping full-tilt from village to village on Hassan's beautiful new mare, gave the child real joy. Safiya never tired of watching Saboor charge across the room, his clothes flying, and throw his arms about his father whenever Hassan appeared in the sitting room doorway.

They made a good pair, father and son, experienced courtier and child mystic.

Of course they were not far apart in understanding. Like all the men in the Waliullah household, Hassan had been a member of his father's brotherhood since he was eighteen. He had offered the same prayers and performed the same daily recitations as everyone else, and had gained much from both. Safiya had watched proudly as he became a man of honor, respected in the walled city, and trusted by Maharajah Ranjit Singh.

She had always believed that Hassan's gifts of charm and persuasiveness would serve him well in his life.

It was only his self-consciousness and his perfectionism that worried her.

Of course Hassan had never shown any interest in becoming a spiritual leader. He had none of his son's mysterious prescience, or his enthusiasm for sitting in the courtyard for hours at a time with Waliullah and his guests.

Those traits could belong only to the person who would be the next Shaikh of the Karakoyia brotherhood.

Dear little Saboor. May his bright energy last a hundred years.

Although he was only four, he already displayed a keen desire to learn. Every morning, in the large sitting room, he bounced in his place on the sheeted floor, ready with a hundred questions, when Safiya regaled her family ladies and their children with instructive stories. He spent his afternoons in the courtyard with his grandfather, learning to recite from the Qur'an, his round eyes growing wiser day by day.

Other members of the household were also in good condition. Safiya's young cousin had been delivered of a strong baby girl, whose cries now echoed from room to room in the upstairs ladies' quarters. Waliullah's elderly gap-toothed sister-in-law, who had collapsed suddenly from the heat one summer afternoon, had since recovered, and was back to gossiping as much as ever.

The harvest of Kandahari pomegranates promised to be good, and the young guava trees had survived the summer rains.

Safiya had much to be thankful for.

A jumping, shouting game outside the sitting room had become too noisy. "Go downstairs this instant," she snapped at Saboor and half a dozen of his grinning cousins.

When silence fell in the verandah, she thought the children had all gone away, but when Safiya glanced idly through the doorway, she saw that Saboor was still there, watching her silently, half-hidden by the door curtains.

She pointed to the tray of fruit in front of her. "Come, child," she said, patting the floor beside her when he hesitated. "I will cut you a slice of melon."

"What is wrong?" she asked, when he sat down and leaned silently against her. "You were playing so happily a moment ago."

The child gazed into her face for a moment, then got to his knees, pushed a few loose strands of iron-gray hair aside, and cupped a hand over her ear.

"Please, Bhaji," he whispered wetly, his breath tickling her ear. "*Please* make Abba go to where An-nah is, and bring her home."

She laid a plump arm about his shoulders. So that was it. The boy still missed the English girl. And why should he not? Mariam had become mother to him after his own poor little mother died. She had protected and loved him for two full years.

"I will do what I can, my darling," she rumbled, knowing well how little influence she had over Hassan. "I will do what I can."

A question struck her as the little boy clattered down the stairs to rejoin his game. Why was he missing Mariam now, after so many months? He had been upset, of course, after she left in January, but in the long time that followed, he had seemed happily reconciled to her absence.

What could have happened to make him long for her now?

Chapter 13

W̶e hear that General Sale was wounded in the Khurd-Kabul pass, this time in the leg," Charles Mott volunteered from his seat beside the British officers' cricket field. "Otherwise, the First Brigade has done wonderfully well."

A second man, a captain of the 13th Foot, did not take his eyes from the game. "Of course," he put in, "it was a pity about that night attack on Colonel Monteith's encampment, with so many of our men killed. Thirty-five, if I remember correctly."

"Monteith should have punished the Afghan traitors in his camp who let the attackers past the sentries," observed another officer, "but in any case, the pass is now cleared, and that is what matters."

"We hear," Charles Mott added, "that within a few days, the whole distance between Kabul and Jalalabad will be open to our own caravans, and of course to you, Sir William, as well, when you return to India."

Sir William Macnaghten stopped talking to the wan-looking General Elphinstone, and offered his nephew by marriage a satisfied nod.

"Yes, indeed, Charles," he said.

Conversations in the cantonment had centered for weeks upon Sir William's new posting as Governor of Bombay. Lady Macnaghten, who had only recently finished decorating the Residence in Kabul, was already deeply concerned about her future, far grander house.

"I cannot imagine how I shall survive it," she had confided gaily to Mariana.

In front of Mariana, his arms windmilling, a curly-haired lieutenant galloped down the cricket pitch. Behind him, the two brown Bibi Mahro hills rose sharply against a hard, blue sky. An equally brown village climbed the slope of the nearer hill. What, Mariana wondered, did the occupants of that village make of the British and their game?

She smiled absently at someone's remark about the young bowler's peculiar style, but her mind was not upon the cricket. A glass of pomegranate juice in her hand, she sat still, imagining what she would say to Harry Fitzgerald when they met.

From the look of it, that meeting would take place any moment. Not only had he returned to Kabul the previous day, he was here, at the cricket game. She frowned, aware of his blond presence as he strolled to and fro among the spectators, greeting old friends and cheering on the bowler.

Now that General Sale and the Eastern Ghilzais were fighting on the road to Peshawar, it would be some time before Ghulam Ali could make his way back to Kabul.

She would not know Hassan's feelings until he returned.

Word of Fitzgerald's arrival had, of course, come from Lady Macnaghten. *You are to be present tomorrow afternoon at the cricket field near the Darwaza Sirdar,* she had instructed Mariana in the previous day's hand-delivered letter. *Do not worry about your appearance. Vijaya will be coming to you before lunch.*

Mariana had made a point of not mentioning Fitzgerald to her family, but silence had done her no good. For weeks, as his return to Kabul approached, Aunt Claire had repeatedly cautioned her to keep her eyes lowered and remain silent about her past.

"And you must," she had added, raising a plump finger for emphasis, "be discreet in what you say. You have, my dear Mariana, the very dangerous habit of speaking your mind. That liberty, I remind you, is reserved for *married ladies only.*"

Lady Macnaghten had been no less involved. Undistracted by the effort of choosing silk for the Bombay Government House dining room, she had peered critically at Mariana's face and fingernails, and instructed her to burn her favorite gray afternoon gown.

"You simply cannot wear that dreary color again," she had insisted;

"I have some lovely lemon silk that will be perfect for you. And the tiniest bit of cochineal powder will do wonders for your cheeks.

"You must use *all* means available to enhance your appearance," she continued, ignoring Mariana's shocked stare at the suggestion that she paint her face. "Cochineal is a wonderful native invention. I am told on great authority that in the morning, after all those tiny red insects have been set free, the muslin bag is inspected very carefully. If even one of the little creatures has died in the night, the whole of it is thrown away.

"You always look pretty when you take the trouble," she concluded. "The same cannot be said of everyone. Do make use of your good looks before it is too late. *No one will ever know,*" she added with a wicked little smile.

The crack of a bat was followed by shouting. Mariana turned, looking for Fitzgerald, and saw him leaning against a tree in his buckskin breeches and blue jacket, his smooth head bent as he listened to something his companion was saying. Would he hold his head at the same angle when she told him she could neither accept nor refuse his proposal, and that he must wait for an indeterminate length of time for her reply?

Would he actually ask her to marry him?

He started in her direction. As he approached, still talking to his friend, she turned hastily to the cricket, begging him silently not to sit down in the unfortunately empty chair beside her.

"May I join you, Miss Givens?"

He was bowing above her. His friend had disappeared. "Of course you may, Lieutenant," she replied helplessly.

The folding chair groaned as he sat down. "It is a pleasure to see people enjoying themselves," he offered, smiling a little stiffly. "Kandahar may have wonderful melons, but otherwise, it is a great, stony wasteland."

She kept her eyes on the game, uncomfortably aware of his bulk and the creaking of his chair.

People were looking at them. Beneath her parasol, Aunt Claire made a fluttering gesture, signaling either encouragement or warning. Lady Macnaghten frowned and patted her hair significantly.

"Have you enjoyed the Kabul summer?" he asked.

"In a way, yes." Mariana offered him a cautious smile. "The weather has been glorious and the fruit lovely. After two years in India, I had quite forgotten what cherries taste like."

"I must say I am very happy to be—" His voice trailed off.

He was staring into space, his square, freckled hands tight on the arms of his chair.

The last thing she wanted was a clumsy, fearful suitor. Suddenly repelled by the musty scent of his blue woolen jacket, she searched about her for reinforcements, but found the rest of the party, even her aunt, otherwise occupied. Even Charles Mott was deep in conversation with Fitzgerald's friend.

She took in a calming breath. "I hear there was fighting on the road to Kabul," she ventured.

"There was." He turned to her, his face intense. "Miss Givens," he said abruptly, "what have you been told about our battle in the Zurmat valley?"

She blinked in surprise. "I have heard," she replied, "that someone called Colonel Herring had been killed near Kandahar, that a force had been sent to avenge his death, and that the attackers seemed very brave at first, but melted away after a few artillery shots."

"They did melt away. And when they went into the hills, we blew up their forts. But for all our apparent victory, we did not kill any of them, nor have they surrendered to us."

She frowned. "Everyone here believes the Afghans are cowards who cannot withstand our artillery fire."

"I do not think that is the case." He leaned closer to her and dropped his voice. "They have no heavy guns of their own, which means they are unused to being fired upon. They withdraw when they first encounter our artillery, but I believe they do so only to discuss their next move."

Mariana studied him. His eyes, as green as hers, were unafraid. No longer clenched, his hands now rested on his knees. They were covered with dry lines, as if they had been well used. He had not been thinking of her at all.

"This has already happened, in the Kohdaman valley," he added. "I can see clearly that the Afghan fighting style is very different from ours. Their warriors appear, then retreat, then appear again, and each time they come back, *there are more of them.*

"We, of course, march out openly, in our red and blue uniforms. We fight in an orderly fashion, in columns and squares. They go into battle in ordinary clothes the same color as the dust and the rocks. Their movements are impossible to predict. They come unexpectedly, from nowhere, do what damage they can, then vanish like ghosts, or they snipe at us, invisibly, from behind rocks. They have no fear of our guns, whatever our people may say, and no chivalry. They descend upon our wounded like vultures. Sometimes they even cut off—I am sorry," he said hastily, seeing the look on her face. "This is no proper conversation for a lady."

He dropped his eyes. "I have no one to speak to about this. Whenever I have tried to discuss it, I am called a croaker. I am only telling you because we talked about military matters so often before—"

Her revulsion gone, she resisted an impulse to lay a hand on his arm. It had been months since an English person had spoken seriously to her.

Perhaps, for now, he would be her friend.

"I am certain that we can beat the Afghans," he continued, interrupting her thoughts, "but to do so, we must outwit them. I fear we have dangerously underestimated them.

"I am very worried, Miss Givens," he added, "very worried."

"I am so sorry," she whispered.

Turning to her, he stared for an instant at the front of her gown, as if he were gazing at the flesh beneath her bodice. "I could not bear," he said huskily, "to know you were in any danger."

"Thank you, Lieutenant," was all she could manage.

A moment later, Harry Fitzgerald excused himself, and was gone.

Twenty feet away, Aunt Claire regarded her with a small, fashionable, and unmistakably triumphant smile.

"I AM so pleased," cooed Lady Macnaghten as she rode beside Mariana on the way back. "I thought you made a handsome pair, you and your lieutenant. What were you speaking of with such concentration?"

"I hardly remember," Mariana replied vaguely.

"And you were looking quite nice, but a curl of your hair had come loose. The whole time you were speaking with Fitzgerald, it hung irritatingly down over your left ear.

"And now," she continued, shifting uncomfortably in her sidesaddle, "you must pursue your advantage. Be ready at all times for him to call on you. And for goodness sake, there is no need to show *all* your teeth when you smile."

October 19, 1841

In the five days since Harry Fitzgerald's return, he had called on Mariana three times. Three features had characterized each of those visits: Aunt Claire's simpering idiocy, Fitzgerald's patient good manners, and Mariana's growing irritation.

While her aunt's efforts to safeguard Mariana's good name had protected her from any upsetting declaration he might have made, her breathless reminiscences about her childhood in Sussex were agony to listen to.

"My aunt, Claire Woodrow," she burbled over sherry one afternoon, as Mariana fidgeted beside her, "my father's elder sister after whom I was named, came to live in Weddington when I was small. Her husband had recently *died,* you see...."

Saved from the work of conversing, Fitzgerald had offered no more than a series of bland smiles. When he stood up to leave, Mariana followed him, her lemon silk skirts rustling, then turned and faced her aunt after the front door had closed behind him.

"I do believe," her aunt sighed, "he is the *handsomest*—"

"Handsome he may be," Mariana said pointedly, "but must we talk of ourselves *all* the time he is here?"

Aunt Claire drew back, her chins trembling. "But what on earth should we talk of?"

"*Him.*" Mariana sighed. "You wish me to marry Fitzgerald, but we know nothing about him."

Her own vetting, she knew, was a cold, unloving exercise that, in the end, would cause someone hurt. It pained her to hear the lilt in her aunt's voice, and the little humming noises she made as she busied herself about the bungalow.

While Aunt Claire sang to herself, Mariana waited for Ghulam Ali.

Where was he now? Was he on his way back from India, preparing to travel safely through the passes after Jalalabad, now that General Sale had cleared the way? Was Hassan's reply to her hidden in his clothes, or had Hassan sent back no reply but only silence, the bitterest answer of all?

If only she had sent Ghulam Ali sooner, he would have returned safely and she would already know....

Until she knew the truth of Hassan's feelings, she would remain as she was, trapped between hopefulness and resignation.

THAT EVENING, as she tightened her stays in preparation for another of Lady Macnaghten's dinner parties, Mariana steeled herself to learn more about Harry Fitzgerald.

She knew that he was the younger of two brothers, both serving in India, who had lost their father when they were very small, and that a kindly uncle had later purchased commissions for them in the Indian army. When Aunt Claire had actually asked him a question about himself, Mariana had also learned that his mother had been ill for some years. When he spoke of her, his expression had softened, revealing, Mariana hoped, a capacity for tender feelings.

She had known since they first met that he was a thinking officer, as ardent a student of military strategy as she had been, and loyal to the men in his battery. He had suffered without complaint when false gossip had damaged his reputation. These were good signs, but they told Mariana nothing of how he would treat her if they were married. Would the Bengal Horse Artillery mean more to him than she or her children? Would he forget her existence once she was his?

It was not uncommon for Indian army officers to be posted to remote corners of the country. In some cases, their wives had been the only European women in small stations. Left alone with no one to talk to while their husbands campaigned for months on end, some of them had lost their minds. Who knew how many might have been saved if their husbands had thought to send them to friends or relatives.

She would not ask for Fitzgerald's love, because she could not offer her own, but she must know he would not be as cruel as that.

One woman who had endured that experience had been the dauntless Lady Sale, who seemed none the worse for it. The woman must be made of iron.

Mariana sighed as she dropped her best rose-colored evening gown over her head, then struggled with its tiny covered buttons. Whatever Fitzgerald was, if she understood him in advance, she would be better able to bear her fate.

The party, an extravagant affair featuring roast boar from a recent hunt, was a compromise, for it followed several attempts by Lady Macnaghten to organize a dance. Her latest effort had been abandoned at the last moment due to disturbances in the Kohdaman valley which had kept Sir William and the army too occupied to participate.

Everyone would be in attendance this evening save for Lady Sale, who never went out when her husband was away, and General Elphinstone, who had been confined to his bed since the cricket match.

"Why, good evening, Miss Givens." Charles Mott bowed before her, his hair fashionably mussed into the appearance of a dish mop, his coat so wasp-waisted that it was a wonder he could breathe.

As she replied to his greeting, a man who had been standing with his back to her spun about and frowned in her direction. Lady Macnaghten caught his look as she rustled past.

"I am sure, Sir Alexander," she fluted, gesturing with her fan, "that you remember Miss Mariana Givens."

Burnes bowed. Mariana inclined her head, hoping he would be gone when she looked up, but he was not. Instead, he stood in front of her, his Clan Campbell tartan as resplendent as Charles Mott's dandified clothes. His round face held no shame, only keen interest. "I take it," he said smoothly, "that Miss Givens has learned to speak a little Persian."

"I would not know about that." Her interest waning, Lady Macnaghten swept off to greet another guest.

Burnes leaned closer and dropped his voice. "I also take it that Miss Givens enjoys an occasional jaunt into the wicked city of

Kabul. I find that most interesting. Of course I was shocked when I first heard—"

Before he could finish, or Mariana could think how to punish him, Aunt Claire appeared and clutched her above the elbow. "*He* is here," she stage-whispered, pointing with urgent indiscretion toward the drawing room doorway.

Five minutes later, a hand on Fitzgerald's arm, Mariana stood waiting to go in to dinner.

This was no time to think about Burnes. Dining at Fitzgerald's side would offer her the investigative opportunity she sought, although she had already noted how little attention he paid to her best gown, her carefully arranged curls, or even the hint of rosy cochineal powder Vijaya had applied to her cheeks. Instead, he glanced at her pleated bodice with such unnerving hunger that she had taken a hurried step backward.

Servants crowded the edges of the dining room. A liveried serving-man in a starched turban pulled out her chair. She sat down before Lady Macnaghten's gleaming silver and drew in her skirts, grateful that she was not sitting next to Alexander Burnes.

If she had been, she would have feigned a sudden, piercing headache.

From the moment they sat down, Fitzgerald began to talk, freely, in an undertone, about the military situation in Kabul. "The city smiths are making weapons by the dozen," he murmured, as Lady Macnaghten laughed gaily at the table's end, "but not for us. They refuse our requests in an insulting, ill-mannered way. I understand they spat at the feet of one of our officers. And I wonder about these—

"What is the matter with Burnes?" he added, as Mariana stirred her mulligatawny soup. "He has been staring at you all evening. I beg your pardon for the indelicacy, but has he begun calling upon you in my absence?"

"No," Mariana answered emphatically. "He has not."

Dinner proceeded with all the usual clatter, conversation, and excess of wine. Lady Macnaghten, her cheeks suspiciously rosy, flirted her fan at one end of the table; her husband smiled at the other. Burnes drank even more than usual.

"—spreading a rumor that we are planning to seize the tribal chiefs and send them to *London*!" Mariana heard him say. "Of course I put that ruffian Abdullah Khan in his place. I called him a dog, and threatened to crop his ears. It did him no end of good. As for the aged Aminullah Khan, if I ever meet him, I shall wait for the right moment, then put out my foot and trip him up!

"I shall enjoy seeing the palsied old creature crawling about as he tries to get up again!" he added, over the laughter of his fellow guests.

As three servants burst through the door, carrying the roast boar on a great wooden plank, an apple in its jaws, Burnes leaned across the table toward Mariana.

"What," he asked loudly between the silver birds, "did you say your name is?"

"My name," she said tartly, "is Mariana Givens."

"Ah, yes, Miss Givens." He smiled loosely. "We have something in common, you and I."

For an angry instant she felt trapped. Then Harry Fitzgerald put a calming hand on her arm and leaned heavily over his plate. "I do not believe, Sir Alexander," he said in a level tone, "that the lady understands what you mean."

Buoyed by his support, Mariana offered Burnes a level green gaze. "Nor," she said evenly, "do I *care*."

His pale face stricken, Charles Mott looked despairingly from Fitzgerald's hand to Mariana's face.

Sir William Macnaghten coughed noisily at the table's end. "The boar has arrived!" he announced.

Burnes subsided into his seat. Fitzgerald turned to Mariana. "I do not like that man," he said, "but you have nothing to fear from him as long as I am here."

He smiled at her in a way she had almost forgotten, beautifully, crookedly, his chin raised. "And I hope that will be a very long time."

"Why on earth were you so short with the Resident?" her aunt inquired on the way home. "Whatever has *he* done to deserve such rude treatment?"

Chapter 13

October 20, 1841

I t had taken Ghulam Ali longer than it should have to reach the Punjab. Parched and filthy from the dust of the road, the courier had emerged from the Khyber Pass and into the hilly Peshawar valley a little more than four weeks after he had tucked the English lady's letter into his clothes and bidden her good-bye.

His heart lifted at the knowledge that he was now in his home country, but with that lifting came new anxiety. He had serious work before him.

At the beginning of his journey, aware of the dangers of solitary travel, he had fallen in with a large Tajik wedding party on its way to Jalalabad. Jovial and celebrating, the family had moved unhurriedly through the first several passes between Kabul and their destination, bringing with them forty camel-loads of bride gifts and trade goods, and scores of horses and donkeys. Small children in brightly embroidered clothes had ridden in baskets tied to the backs of donkeys. Live chickens had hung upside down, tied uncomfortably by their legs to the backs of the loaded camels.

Ghulam Ali had enjoyed the family's company, especially after they killed a sheep at Butkhak and enjoyed roast meat and music until the stars overhead began to fade. He had been grateful for the good humor of their chief, a man with a thick beard and curly mustache, for the route to Jalalabad had not improved since he had taken it to Kabul six months earlier with the English party. The six-mile-long Khurd-Kabul gorge had not lost its forbiddingly steep sides, the icy stream that rushed along its floor, or the narrow, stony pathway that crossed the little river no fewer than twenty-three times. The perpendicular basalt walls of the Jagdalak Pass had been unchanged; at its narrowest, the Jagdalak, with its right-angle turns and frighteningly narrow bottlenecks, had still been only six feet wide.

He had enjoyed himself with the Tajiks, but after taking three leisurely weeks to cover half the hundred-and-forty-mile distance to Peshawar, he had tired of their slow progress. When he met a group of Eastern Ghilzai nomads outside the city of Jalalabad, he had fallen in with them, grateful to learn that they expected to cross the Khyber Pass within ten days.

Had the Tajiks offered him the news that he learned from his new Ghilzai hosts, Ghulam Ali would never have taken time to savor their smoky kababs or enjoy the beauty of their music and the sight of the men stamping their feet as they danced in the firelight. He would instead have abandoned them, and hurried on alone, toward India.

The Ghilzais, who were driving a great, bleating flock of fat-tailed sheep down to the Punjab, had been sinewy and rough-featured, with untrimmed beards and hair that fell to their shoulders beneath carelessly tied turbans. Like all tribesmen, they had been conspicuously armed.

Ghulam Ali had joined their party as they prepared to travel across the flat desert between Jalalabad and the Khyber Pass. They were prodding their charges with long sticks while a dozen camels stood waiting, already loaded with black woolen tents and cooking vessels.

He had kept his distance at first, staying out of their way, waiting to be included. They, honoring the Pashtoon law of hospitality, had made room for him beside their cooking fire at the noon halt.

One of them, a handsome, lanky fellow, had gestured for Ghulam Ali to join him as he kneaded dough beside a cooking fire. "Where are you traveling?" he had inquired in accented Punjabi, after learning that Ghulam Ali was from Lahore.

"My cousin is getting married in Lahore," the courier had lied, not revealing his real purpose, for everyone knew that couriers carried cash.

The man's name was Qadeer. The men in his group came from two families. They were the first of their tribe to start the annual migration to India, for it was autumn, and time for the Ghilzai nomads to travel from their summer quarters in the high, brutal mountains of Central Asia to the hot, fertile Indian plains, through passes that brought some of them to Peshawar and the Punjab beyond, and others to the great towns of the Dera Jat, in the south.

Qadeer and his fellow tribesmen had, as always, gone ahead, driving the sheep. The rest of their families, their camels, donkeys, women, and children would join them after a month. Other groups would do the same at their own pace. The last of the Ghilzai nomads would leave Kabul by early December.

"The last families go only as far as Peshawar," Qadeer said. "They like the cold weather, but we continue on as far as Lahore. That is where I learned to speak your language. We take what we need on the way."

He offered Ghulam Ali a satisfied smile. "I stole a lovely horse in Sargodha two years ago. It is a good life."

Ghulam Ali kept to himself, sleeping near their fire, eating the food Qadeer pressed on him with fierce hospitality.

On the third evening, one of the other men folded himself down next to Ghulam Ali, his ragged shawl trailing in the dust. He said something in Pushto and smiled harshly into Ghulam Ali's face.

Qadeer tipped his head toward his friend. "Shah Gul here wants to know whether you are really going to a family wedding," he said matter-of-factly, his hands moving with gentle precision as he wedged a four-legged iron plate over the fire and adjusted the kettle among the coals.

"He thinks you are a servant of the British feranghis."

"I am not with the foreigners." Ghulam Ali raised his chin and lied for the second time. "I came with a kafila bringing indigo and cotton cloth from India. Now I am going home."

"That is good," Qadeer replied. "If you had been a servant of the feranghis, I would have killed you after you left us."

Killed? Ghulam Ali swallowed.

"The British should not have come," Qadeer added, as he dropped a flat round of dough onto the hot metal plate. "And now that they have cheated us, their time here is finished. The night of long knives has begun."

Cheated? Long knives? Ghulam Ali's mind reeled. How could this be? Why, the English lady and her family had gone picnicking in the hills only the day before he left, with their cotton umbrellas and hampers of food. . . .

Shah Gul spoke at length, his raptor's face expressionless.

"You are fortunate to have come through when you did," Qadeer explained. "My people killed thirty-five British soldiers at Butkhak a few days ago. We plundered a rich caravan from India at Tezeen a few days ago, and killed everyone in it." He spat into the fire. "It was carrying goods for the British, their cursed *sharab* and other things. No one will dare to use the passes near Kabul now. When it is time, we will be ready—here in the east, to the west, to the north, and the south. As soon as we settle our flocks we are going back." Smiling, he patted the knives whose handles protruded from his sash.

He gestured with a long arm at the plain with its other camps, flocks, and black tents. "All our warriors are gathering."

Ghulam Ali was unable to think of a suitable reply.

Later, his stomach full of flat bread and yoghurt, pomegranates and tea, he stretched out on the ground, needing sleep, his small bundle of belongings beneath his head, his shawl spread over him for warmth, but his eyes did not close. The long-bladed Khyber knife he had carried since he was a child had seemed weapon enough when he embarked upon this journey, but it would be useless if the tribesmen attacked him together. He would be dead, or worse, dying slowly of many cuts, before he had time to draw it from its sheath.

As he listened to the stirring of the flock and the quiet voices of the men who guarded them, he reached into his clothes and touched the Englishwoman's letter with careful fingers.

The next day, one of the ewes went lame. Qadeer carried her across his shoulders as they crossed the stony Lowyah Dakkah plain.

"So," Ghulam Ali said carefully, "a rebellion has begun against Shah Shuja and the British?"

Qadeer gave a curious, giggling laugh. "Of course it has, my friend," he had replied as he strode along, the ewe wrapped around his neck like a great, shaggy collar. "Wazir Akbar Khan is no coward like his father, Dost Mohammad, who threw down his arms before the British and ran away to India. The Amir's eldest son is a man of courage and honor. All will happen quickly, now that the *shabna-mas*, the night letters, have gone to every part of the country and the people are ready."

That night they reached the old fort at Haft Chah, the last stop before the Khyber Pass. There, while the camp was asleep Ghulam Ali slipped away from the Ghilzais, and ran.

In the end, he crossed the Khyber with a group of heavily guarded Hindu merchants bound for Peshawar with a cargo of dried fruit, musk, and caged Persian cats. The merchants and their long file of shaggy, jingling donkeys were part of a steady stream of men and animals following that narrow, stony track through the foothills of the Suleiman Koh range.

The Khyber Pass had been in use for countless centuries. Aryan invaders had traveled it long before history began. Barefoot Buddhist monks had crossed it two thousand years before, followed by hordes of Huns and the armies of Babur, Nadir Shah, and Ahmad Shah Durrani.

It was not a high pass, for its summit stood only three thousand five hundred feet above sea level, but it was long and dangerous. Sometimes crossing flat valleys, sometimes clinging with hairpin turns to the harsh slopes of the Suleiman Koh, or passing through narrow defiles, the pass stretched for thirty-three miles through territory occupied by Afridi tribesmen, who lived, as the Ghilzais did, by plunder.

The Afridis had no special enmity for the servants of English people, but even so, Ghulam Ali had been glad of the hard-eyed men hired by the Hindu traders, who strode beside the donkeys, long-barreled muskets slung over their shoulders, their eyes scanning the hills on either side of the road.

He strode toward the city of Peshawar with his caravan, the tail of his turban across his face to keep out the ever-present dust, past mud forts and watchtowers, past black nomad tents and flocks of sheep, goats, and cows that grazed between scrubby tamarisk trees.

As he walked, he thought about his first encounter with the Englishwoman.

He had delivered a letter to her in Calcutta, a year earlier. The letter had been from Hassan Ali Khan. Ghulam Ali had, of course, never learned what news or instructions that letter had contained, but shortly afterward the lady, her uncle, and her aunt had packed their belongings and begun the long journey across the width of India, from Bengal to the Punjab, bringing with them Hassan's small, gifted son Saboor, who seemed to be under her protection.

Ghulam Ali had accompanied them on that journey.

There had been no Englishwomen in the Punjab. Ghulam Ali had never before seen the like of Hassan's wife, with her steady, green gaze and oddly revealing clothing. Horrified that the Waliullah family had been saddled with such an unseemly female, he had avoided her as much as possible on that journey.

But she had won him over in the end, for she had somehow understood that he had suffered in his life. Tormented since childhood for his strange paleness and pink eyes, he had never known friendship. She, who did not distinguish between rich and poor, accepted man and outcast, had respected his humanity and given him hope. Together they had saved Hassan Ali Khan from certain death.

Best of all, in her talkative, hunched-over servant, Dittoo, Ghulam Ali had found a man he could trust. Later, he had added Yar Mohammad to that short list.

Ahead of him a concentrated haze stood in the distant sky. They were nearing the Gateway to India, the old high-walled city of Peshawar.

An hour later, the Hindu traders led their animals through the shouting congestion at the city's Kabul Gate, whose name needed no explanation. To their left, in the street of goldsmiths, stood Mahabat Khan's grand mosque, from whose topless minarets the Maharajah's enemies were thrown daily to their deaths. Before them ran the broad Qissa Khwani, the Street of Storytellers, home of Peshawar's tea shops and caravanserais, where all the news of the world was told.

Like all caravanserais, the one they stopped at was no more than a great open square, its perimeter lined with gaping, three-sided sheds with bare rooms above, where a traveler might find shelter. Its huge courtyard was already filled with shouting men, grunting animals, and great heaps of bales and bundles. Ghulam Ali yawned. With luck he would find an empty corner in an upstairs room. With no luck he would sleep with the donkeys.

Abandoning his merchants and their charges, he set off to drink at the courtyard well. After that he would buy something to eat and a moment to himself to consider his situation.

The Englishwoman's letter must be important, for she had sent it all the way from Kabul. But whatever news that letter contained, it was nothing compared to the critical information that he, Ghulam Ali, must now deliver. As soon as he had filled his stomach he would hurry to the market, find a scribe, and dictate his own letter, telling Hassan of the dangers threatening his wife and her family.

He would then hurry to the hilltop citadel of Ghor Khatri at the center of the city, where the Maharajah's appointed governor had built his palace, and find an official relay runner going to Lahore. He would then bribe the man to put the lady's letter and his own into the pouch, for delivery to Hassan.

A good *qasid* could get it to Lahore in three days.

Then, without stopping to enjoy the city's fruits or its *chappli* kababs of ground mutton cooked in its own fat, he would find a way to return to Kabul, where he would offer what aid he could to the lady and her family.

Since the British army had already fought with the Ghilzais in the passes near Kabul, she must know of the coming rebellion. He hoped she was not too frightened.

If Allah willed, Hassan Ali Khan would arrive to rescue them before it was too late....

As he drank from the dipper at the well, Ghulam Ali sensed eyes upon him. Three tattered-looking men watched him from a makeshift tea shop. Knife handles protruded from the coarse sashes wound around their waists. Jezails leaned against the wall behind them. They spoke together, then glanced at him again.

They were dressed like the Ghilzais he had left behind on the Jalalabad plain. From the way they looked at him, they knew who he was. Cursing his white skin and yellow beard, he returned the dipper to its place and left the well, forcing himself not to hurry.

I would have killed you after you left us. He had been a fool to leave the Ghilzais, but if he had stayed, he would never have succeeded in keeping up his lie, for they had watched his every move, had seen him sweat at each of their questions, each of their glances.

In the end it had made no difference. Leaving them so abruptly and without good-byes, he had given himself away.

Desperate to escape, he hurried between piles of baggage, herds of goats, and dozens of kneeling camels. All that mattered now was that he preserve his life long enough to help the English lady.

At the entrance to the caravanserai, he pushed through the crowded gateway and onto the main street.

He stepped onto the road and turned toward the street of goldsmiths. Surely he would find a scribe near the mosque. There was danger in each hurried step he took, but he had no choice. Surely, the Ghilzais would not bother to follow him into a place of prayer....

Chapter 16

After spending an hour in the mosque, dictating his letter to an eager young scribe, Ghulam Ali hurried up a dusty hill, toward the massive gate of the Ghor Khatri, the great walled caravanserai that was now the residence of the governor.

"I have business inside," he barked impatiently to the uniformed guards at the gate. "I am a courier for the Assistant Foreign Minister."

A Sikh infantry officer in a steel helmet and chain mail vest looked him unhurriedly up and down. "You say you are Hassan Ali Khan Sahib's courier?"

"I am." Ghulam Ali hunched his shoulders against the man's inspection.

"He's gone out."

"Gone *out*? Is he here in *Peshawar*?"

The officer snorted. "How are you his courier, if you do not know where he is?"

"Where has he gone?" Ghulam Ali demanded. "When is he coming back?"

The officer waved an uninterested hand. "How should I know? They go to the chaikhanas and the Englishman's house. Hassan Ali Khan has his own—"

He stopped speaking, for Ghulam Ali had already turned on his heel and started down the hill, toward the crowded warren of alleys below the Ghor Khatri.

His throat was dry with fear, but he did not stop at the ancient Shabaz Well whose waters were icy cold, even in summer. Instead, he hurried through colorful bazaars and cobbled lanes, past mean little doorways and great houses with lovely carved balconies, past merchants and rich men, beggars and thieves, gamblers, cutthroats and starving dogs, until he arrived once again in the Street of Storytellers.

There, he stopped short.

The Qissa Khwani was broad enough to accommodate five passing kafilas at once. Lines of pack animals carrying bales of goods took up its dusty width, all accompanied by hordes of armed men. Up and down the street, a hundred tea shops beckoned, their canvas awnings sheltering travelers from the sun, each customer with a pot of tea before him. Ghulam Ali took in the smells of animals and cooking meat, of burning incense and sewage.

He had no idea where to find Hassan in this busy thoroughfare.

Certain he would know where to look, he had allowed instinct to drive him this far. Now, confused by the crowd, he stood at the side of the road, uncertain, hungry, and afraid for his life.

Why should Hassan have come here after he left the Citadel? Why should a man of his station spend his time in this busy, dirty street, when he could be visiting some dignitary in his house, leaning on silk cushions, eating white grapes, and drinking water perfumed with roses?

Ghulam Ali frowned. Had the officer on guard started to say that Hassan had his own accommodation in the city?

He looked about him nervously. Fearing to stand out in the open, he climbed two stone steps into a small, crudely built tea shop, and looked for a place to sit. He had enough money left to sit on a chaikhana's small, carpeted platform and drink a pot of sweet tea while he made up his mind what to do. Later, he would satisfy his hunger with a princely meal of bread and kababs bought from a street vendor.

He settled himself near the tea shop's great, hissing samovar, signaled to a small boy for his tea, and recognized a horseman's familiar back, passing on the street outside.

There was no mistaking Hassan Ali Khan as he rode past the shop accompanied by half a dozen servants on foot. Who else sat with such grace, or wore such clothes—a yellow *durahi* turban, a striped sash about his waist, and elegantly embroidered slippers? It was only his horse that Ghulam Ali did not recognize, a startlingly beautiful gray Turkmen mare.

Before Ghulam Ali had time to rise from the tea shop carpet, Hassan reined in his mare, dismounted, and signaled to one of his servants to look after her. A moment later, his back still to Ghulam Ali, he opened his arms to greet someone.

It was the tall, pale-eyed Afghan trader who had rescued him from the Hazuri Bagh, then carried him to the house near the Delhi Gate where Ghulam Ali and the English lady had found him in the middle of the night, bloody and ill.

The two men embraced three times, chest to chest and bearded cheek to cheek, first on one side, then the other, then back again, in the manner of men whose hearts can never be separated.

Giddy with relief, forgetting his fear, Ghulam Ali lurched to his tired feet and stumbled down the tea shop steps.

"Her name is Ghyr Khush," Hassan was saying as Ghulam Ali approached. "It means 'gray bird' in Turki. Yusuf bought her a few days before he died."

Seeing the deep grief on his face, Ghulam Ali lowered his eyes. "*As-salaam-o-alaikum*, peace be upon you," he offered to each man in turn.

The Afghan responded somberly, but Hassan's face brightened. "And peace upon you, Ghulam Ali," he returned, smiling. "It is good to see someone from home. You have been traveling hard, I see."

Ghulam Ali nodded, aware of his dusty beard and filthy, unwashed clothes. "I have brought a letter to you from Kabul. But there is other news. I must—"

"Give me the letter." Hassan held out his hand.

The Afghan hitched his two long-barreled jezails higher on his shoulder. Hassan hesitated for an instant, then without even glancing at it, pushed the paper into one of his pockets. As he did so, Ghulam Ali heard a faint crackling, as if another letter already occupied the same place.

"You need food." Hassan took a silver coin from his purse. "Eat, keep whatever is left." He pointed an upturned hand toward a nearby tea shop. "When you are finished, come to that chaikhana and tell me your news."

"Yusuf's father insisted I take the mare," he said with a sigh as Ghulam Ali left them. "Ah, Zulmai, how I miss him!"

A *kababchi* sat outdoors, frying his wares in a great iron pan. As Ghulam Ali started toward the fragrant promise of food, he remembered to be afraid, then changed his mind, straightened his shoulders and lengthened his stride. For the first time since he left the caravanserai, he did not bother to look behind him for pursuing Ghilzais.

As he sat on an upturned stone, wolfing down a thick oblong nan and several chappli kababs, he studied Hassan's mare, and thought of his friend Yar Mohammad.

The groom, a true lover of horses, should have been here to see Ghyr Khush, as she stood quietly, surrounded by Hassan's protecting servants. Long and slim of line, with a high-set, nearly vertical neck, a narrow breast, and clean, slender legs, she attracted appreciative glances from every man who passed by, and rightly so, for she was an Akhal Tekke: a breed that had been favored by kings for as long as anyone remembered.

Yar Mohammad, who had dreamed all his life of caring for an Akhal Tekke, had described the horses to Ghulam Ali, his hands moving in arcs and arabesques as he spoke. They were beautiful to look at, but their proud elegance was only one of their features. Bred for the desert, Akhal Tekkes could withstand extremes of heat and cold, and were capable of going without water and with very little food for as long as four days at a stretch. To carry three men to safety across shifting sands after sustaining a battle wound was nothing to an Akhal Tekke, for their stamina was unsurpassed by any other breed of horse. They jumped like cats, and their speed had been likened to that of a falcon on the wing.

Ghulam Ali smiled, picturing his friend's face when he saw the mare for the first time, and realized that this perfect silver-gray animal belonged to the very family he served.

When he had eaten, Ghulam Ali crossed the road, dodging men and animals, entered the chaikhana, and squatted down a respectful distance from Hassan and Zulmai, who were deep in conversation on a carpeted platform, gesturing over pots of tea. A smoking chillum stood between them.

Only his left hand, with its missing finger, indicated that Hassan had suffered harm in the Hazuri Bagh. He appeared as calm and elegant as always, his broken nose prominent in his open, fair-skinned face, but Ghulam Ali, a perceptive interpreter of the moods of others, thought otherwise.

Something in Hassan's posture revealed that he was angry.

He frowned at Ghulam Ali. "When you were in Kabul," he asked, "did you hear that the British were cutting their payment to the Eastern Ghilzais?"

"Yes, Sahib." Ghulam Ali nodded eagerly. "That is what I have come to tell you. The British have cheated them, and they are very angry. They have begun stopping caravans in the passes near Kabul. They are saying that a 'night of long knives' is to begin soon."

Zulmai nodded. "So it is true."

Hassan leaned forward. "Were you in danger on the road?"

A silver taweez, a powerful talisman, doubtless the work of Safiya Sultana, swung from his neck on a thick black thread. He would soon need all its power of protection, thought Ghulam Ali.

"I was in danger." Ghulam Ali nodded. "By Allah's grace I reached Jalalabad before the passes were closed, but some Ghilzais here know I am a servant of British people. I fear they will—"

Zulmai waved a careless hand. "You have nothing to fear now. They will also block the road south between Kabul and Kandahar," he added, turning to Hassan.

"So," Hassan said grimly, "with the roads to India cut, the British are trapped in Kabul."

British. Hassan's shoulders seemed to tense when he spoke the word. That was it, Ghulam Ali thought. Hassan was angry with the British. Of course he was. The British were fools.

Ghulam Ali dropped his eyes, remembering the English lady's joy when he gave her the little packet he had carried from Lahore and given to her on the road to Kabul. He thought of her blushes when she handed him the letter that now lay in Hassan's pocket.

Surely Hassan was not angry with her....

It was difficult to tell. He scowled silently into the street, his elbows resting on his knees.

"If the shorter route between Jalalabad and Kabul is closed," he asked at last, "then what of the other routes? What of the Lataband Pass?"

Zulmai stirred his tea thoughtfully. "The Lataband will not be safe. It will be full of Ghilzai kafilas with women and children on their way to India. For all that they will be avoiding the fighting, their men will be happy to take whatever you have. That is their way.

If I were going to Kabul, I would take the route from Thal through the Kurram valley and the Paiwar and Shuturgarden passes, and I would bring an armed guard."

"And what is that road like?"

Zulmai opened his hands. "It is like all roads: good in dry weather, and difficult when it rains. It is steeper than the one you would have taken through Jalalabad, and of course to get to it, you must first travel south to Kohat."

Ghulam Ali scratched his head beneath his turban. What a harsh country this was!

As if he had read the courier's thoughts, Zulmai the Afghan put back his head and smiled, showing white teeth. "Hafiz would remind us," he said, "not to grieve, for even if the road of life is rough, and the end of it cannot be seen, there is no road that does not lead to the Goal."

Hassan's face warmed. "You and your poets," he said.

"And you and yours."

Zulmai lost his smile. "So you *are* traveling to Kabul?"

Hassan spread his hands. "Now that Ghulam Ali has confirmed our fears, I must see to the safety of my uncle-in-law and other family members."

Other family members. That, Ghulam Ali knew, was the closest Hassan would come to mentioning the English lady.

Hassan showed no feeling when he spoke.

"And you will go by the Kurram River valley?" Zulmai persisted.

"Since you suggest it." Hassan's face became still, as if, in his imagination, he was already traveling.

"You are not going without me."

Hassan stared at the Afghan. "But you cannot possibly go back to Kabul at this time of year. What of your kafila? What of your trade goods, your horses, your rubies and saffron?"

"Habibullah is here. He can do the necessary while I am gone. He knows what will happen to him if he steals from me. And that reminds me." Zulmai took a leather pouch from among his clothes. "I have brought you something." Without waiting for a reply, he withdrew a small glass vial from the pouch. "Musk," he said as he handed it to Hassan.

"We must find a large kafila to join," he added, as Hassan removed the vial's stopper causing the air around them to fill with dark sweetness.

"But that will take too long," Hassan objected sharply. "There is no time to waste."

"To travel any other way would be madness." Zulmai jerked his chin toward Hassan's Turkmen mare. "Think of your Gray Bird. Think of what your friend Yusuf would tell you. '*Yar,*' he would say to you, 'if you try to take her north without a strong guard, you will be dead within a day.' "

Hassan replaced the stopper on the vial, and laid a hand over his heart. "My friend," he said soberly, "if you choose to come with me, I will be most grateful." Then he turned his head and glanced at the street, his expression bleak and worried.

Ghulam Ali sighed as he watched Hassan embrace Zulmai for the second time. As difficult as the return journey to Kabul would be for all of them, he, at least, would not be alone.

THAT SAME morning, as Safiya Sultana wheezed her way up the kitchen stairs, a thought struck her.

How could she have forgotten that when she was the same age as Saboor, she, too, had lost her appetite?

Over the past week, the child's usual enthusiasm for eating had waned. He had chewed and swallowed his favorite foods dutifully, but without seeming to taste them, his eyes half closed, as if he were looking at something he did not want to see.

Some persistent worry had clearly robbed him of his appetite, she decided, as she sat waiting for the afternoon meal. Whatever it was, it had also caused the thin cough that did not leave him, even now, as he leaned against her, staring into space.

"Are you missing your An-nah?" she asked, surveying his broad, worried face.

He nodded. "I always think of Kabul, where she is."

"And what do you know of that place?" Taken by surprise, Safiya looked closely at him. "Who has told you stories of Afghanistan?"

"No one has told me, Bhaji. I have seen it in my dreams."

"And what stories do your dreams tell you?" she asked gently.

"They do not tell stories." He shook his head somberly. "In my dreams I see tall mountains and sharp rocks. When I see them, I feel sad."

When he looked into her face, she saw him suddenly not as a child, but as the man he would become.

"I feel sad that An-nah is far away, where the mountains are high and the rocks are very sharp. It looks so cold there."

He gave a small, unhappy cough.

"He is beginning to have visions," she told her brother that evening, when they were alone in her chamber. "He sees the mountains of Afghanistan. He says the very sight of them brings him sorrow."

"Poor child." The Shaikh sighed. "He has been given the burden of seeing into the future."

"But he only sees what Allah Most Gracious allows."

"That is true. And since it is, his visions are important. Whatever Saboor is seeing, I hope it does not portend ill for this family."

Chapter 11

The next morning, Mariana marched out onto the verandah where the tailor squatted, his scissors beside him.

"Ravi," she announced, pointing to a bolt of cotton that lay, half-unrolled, on the verandah floor, "I want you to make me a proper Afghan shalwar kameez. Have it ready by this evening."

It was time for her to return to the city, but without the encumbrance of a heavy, woolen riding habit beneath her chaderi.

You may visit me again, Haji Khan had told her. More than a month had gone by since their first strange meeting. He must be wondering if she had received the answer he had promised her.

Of course she had not. Eleven times each morning and eleven times each night for weeks and weeks she had recited her amended version of his durood. Nothing had happened. Furthermore, she was still unsure which question those verses were meant to address. Was it her paralyzing choice between Hassan and Fitzgerald, or the other, mysterious query that had arisen in her heart as she sat in his crowded, stifling room?

Had Haji Khan even given her the correct roll of paper?

He certainly had never asked her what she wanted to know.

Before she could even consider what that second question might be, she must discover the truth about her future. When she thought about Fitzgerald, a wave of pleasure washed over her at the prospect of seeing him again, followed instantly by confusion and guilt.

How could she—a married woman—find Fitzgerald attractive? But how could she not? He *was* attractive.

The only solution to her doubts was to revisit Haji Khan.

She would start off early the following morning, before Aunt Claire or Uncle Adrian appeared for breakfast, leaving word that she had gone for an early ride. As soon as she arrived in Haji Khan's presence, she would screw up her courage and tell him plainly of her dilemma, ignoring as best she could his crowd of listening followers.

The time had come to stop waiting for Ghulam Ali's return. She must know now whether her future was with elegant, perfumed Hassan or blunt, protective Fitzgerald; among Hassan's strangely compelling family or among her own people.

When she had finished ordering her native clothing, she sent for Yar Mohammad.

"I will be leaving the house at seven tomorrow morning," she informed him. "Please be ready to take me to the mulberry garden. From there I will be going into the city with Nur Rahman."

"This time, Bibi," he replied, his bony face set, "you will ride your mare, and *I* will accompany you."

EARLY THE next morning, before Aunt Claire or Uncle Adrian had emerged from their room for breakfast, Mariana slipped from the house. Beneath her chaderi she wore the long shirt, baggy, gathered trousers, and enveloping shawl of an Afghan woman. Her feet were encased in embroidered slippers, purchased from the cantonment's Indian bazaar. Her hair hung down her back in a single, curly plait.

The morning was cold. She shivered as she made her way to the stables, unwilling to be seen mounting her mare at the front door. There she found Nur Rahman standing in front of Yar Mohammad, retying his turban.

"You look better now," he announced. "Remember to point to your mouth if anyone talks to you. They will think you are deaf, or that someone has cut out your tongue."

The boy turned to Mariana. "I will have to tell him the way," he confided. "He has no idea where we are going."

What an odd group they were, she thought as they started off—a woman in Afghan clothes riding on an English sidesaddle, accompanied by a hill man from northern India and an Afghan boy dressed as a woman.

The road was busy as they approached the city, with groups of intent-looking men interspersed with the usual Uzbek and Tajik traders, wizened Hazara laborers with impossibly large loads on their backs, and boys with poles over their shoulders, carrying dripping cloth cones of yoghurt to the marketplace. Many of them glanced at Mariana, and frowned in surprise. One or two tried to engage Yar Mohammad in conversation, but lost interest when he did as Nur Rahman had told him.

After a short detour, to purchase a bottle of Bukhara honey, they arrived at Haji Khan's door.

"Guests have come," the old gatekeeper announced, as he had before.

"Enter." Haji Khan's rasping voice was unchanged. This time, Mariana noted, only one jezail, and no knives, had been left on the verandah.

The blind man raised his head as Mariana and Nur Rahman stepped inside and greeted him, leaving Yar Mohammad to tend the mare.

He held up a hand. "Where," he inquired, "is our third guest?"

"Oh," said Nur Rahman airily, "he is outside with the—"

"Send for him," Haji Khan snapped. "Such a man is not to be left standing in the courtyard."

Such a man. From the way Haji Khan spoke, Yar Mohammad was worth more than Mariana and Nur Rahman together.

As before, a filigreed copper lamp illuminated the far end of the blind man's windowless room, now unoccupied save for Haji Khan and a small, mild-looking person, presumably the owner of the jezail, who ran dark eyes over Mariana and her companions, greeted them, then fell into contemplative silence.

Mariana arranged herself on the straw stool, the honey ready in her hand, and looked about her. The room, with its wall hangings, was unchanged. The heavy perfume in the air smelled vaguely familiar.

Whatever it was, it seemed to have a power of its own, for she felt her breathing deepen.

"Well, Khanum," Haji Khan inquired, as she laid her offering beside him, "what have you to tell me? What have you learned?"

"Haji Khan, I have learned nothing." Mariana cleared her throat nervously. The confidence she had felt when she started off earlier had drained away when she stepped over his threshold. Once again, her concerns, so pressing at home, now seemed petty and unimportant.

"Did you recite the durood I have given you?"

"Not as it is written," she said, too loudly, then dropped her voice. "I am Christian, you see."

She heard the Afghan visitor shift on the floor behind her.

"You, Khanum," Haji Khan snapped, "are a *very* foolish woman. Islam is meant for all the people who roam the face of the earth. It acknowledges one God. It shares its laws and its faith with Jews and Christians. Why do you not know this?

"Have I asked you," he added irritably, "to recite the *Shahada,* the attestation of faith? Have I asked you to recite *La illaha illa Allah, Muhammad Rasul Allah*?"

"No," she said in a small voice.

"Then I have not asked you to embrace Islam. You have more to decide than who is to be your husband," he went on. "If you recite the durood exactly as it is written, you will receive the answers you seek. If you do not, you will have wasted my time. In any case, I have no more to say about it."

"Haji Khan," Nur Rahman called eagerly from the doorway, "speak to us of Paradise."

The blind man did not reply. Instead, he lifted his head, as if searching for someone. "Third visitor," he commanded, "speak to us. Tell us of the key to Paradise."

Yar Mohammad's resonant voice came from a shadowy corner of the room. "It is peace," he said.

"And what is the key to life?"

"It is *ishq*, the Essence of Love," Yar Mohammad responded, without hesitating. "When a man has peace and love in his heart, he will travel far toward the Goal."

Mariana breathed in. She should have known he was more than a simple groom.

Haji Khan sighed gustily. "It is so good to hear these words. Truly, brother, your *murshid* is a great man. Or, I should say, your two murshids, for you, unlike most men, have the good fortune to have more than one great teacher. Yes," he continued. "You are blessed with guidance from both Shaikh Waliullah Karakoyia of Lahore, and Shafiuddin Khan, the great interpreter of dreams. It has given me signal pleasure to sit so many times with my friend Shafi over these past months."

Shafiuddin Khan? But that was Munshi Sahib's real name. No one had told Mariana of those visits. How many times had he come?

"And now," Haji Khan said, "I only lack the joy of meeting Shaikh Waliullah."

"But what *is* the Goal Yar Mohammad speaks of?" Nur Rahman's voice came from the back of the room.

"It is to see the face of the Beloved," Yar Mohammad and Haji Khan responded in unison.

Nur Rahman sighed rapturously. "In the Garden?"

"Yes," responded Haji Khan.

The room around Mariana, with its embroidered hangings and heavy, scented air, seemed to alter. In her imagination, it was no longer a dark and windowless chamber, but a gateway, leading to another world. It almost seemed that, past the string bed where blind Haji Khan sat motionless in the light of his copper lamp, a door had opened. Beyond it lay a vista shrouded in fog, its only visible feature a path leading away to another, more beautiful world.

Gate and path beckoned to her.

Mariana's unasked question returned. It tugged urgently at her, demanding to be asked.

"What must *I* do," she blurted out, "to attain the Garden, and see the face of the Beloved?"

The image disappeared. Light-headed, she imagined Papa in his vicar's robes, and her mother dressed for church, both their faces filled with horror.

But why should she not call God the Beloved? Why should she not aspire to Paradise? Everyone knew Eden had been a garden. Besides, this was *her* life, *her* adventure.

Haji Khan's rasping voice brought her back to reality. "Only do as I have said. Recite—"

"Listen!" The silent guest spoke for the first time. Mariana turned and saw him sitting bolt upright, his face alert, a hand raised for silence.

Outside, faint shouting arose. It grew louder, as if a large, triumphant crowd were approaching.

Something in the quiet man's face frightened Mariana.

"What is it?" she asked. "What is wrong?"

"I fear, Khanum," Haji Khan said gently, "that your Mr. Alexander Burnes is in grave trouble. You have chosen," he added, "a difficult day to enter the city."

"But why? What has he done?"

Before the words had left Mariana's throat, her hand was over her mouth. All the hints that Burnes, Macnaghten, and the others had ignored came rushing back to her—the closing of the passes to India; the fighting in the north; Akbar Khan's movements around the country; the fighting that Fitzgerald had met with on the road from Kandahar.

Each time they come back, Fitzgerald had said, *there are more of them.*

The Kabulis must know of Burnes's drinking, of the women he lured into his house. Who knew what else he had done to cause hatred to spread like poison through the city?

Living here, within reach, he was an easy target.

"What will they do to him?" she asked, and immediately regretted her question.

No one replied.

The quiet man got to his feet and stepped outside. Mariana heard the heavy outer door creak, and then a sudden torrent of noise as if a river of rage were streaming past them in the street.

The door creaked again, then thudded shut. The guest reappeared and stepped over the threshold. "These visitors should be escorted from the city as soon as it is safe," he said, gesturing toward Mariana and the others.

Haji Khan nodded and turned his white eyes to Yar Mohammad. "Leave the horse here," he ordered, "and follow Nadir. He will take you to safety."

Yar Mohammad unfolded himself from the floor.

Mariana hesitated for a moment before Haji Khan's string bed. "I will do it," she half-whispered. "I will recite the durood properly."

He nodded. "Go," he commanded.

She, Yar Mohammad, Nur Rahman, and the man called Nadir stood in the courtyard, listening to the crowd rush by outside. As it passed, voices rose above the general din. Their tone caused a chill to run down Mariana's spine.

"Aminullah Khan says there is a great treasure to be looted from the house across the street," crowed one male voice.

"We will take it," shouted another, "but not until we have finished the infidel Eskander Burnes."

Aminullah Khan. The sick old man Burnes had laughed about only ten days ago...

After the sound had faded in the crooked street, the guest stepped outside, followed by Yar Mohammad, then Mariana and Nur Rahman. As the elderly guard swung the heavy doors shut behind them, Haji Khan's caged nightingale gave out a series of lovely, bubbling cries.

The quiet stranger walked in front with a rapid, rolling stride, his jezail slung across one shoulder. He did not look back. Yar Mohammad walked beside him, the long knife he had taken from his clothes ready in his hand. Mariana followed them, together with Nur Rahman, who for once seemed to have nothing to say.

Burnes's house must have been nearby, for Mariana heard the shouts of the gathering mob echoing behind her as she crept along the margin of the narrow street, her stiff new slippers with their upward-pointing toes biting into her feet. Groups of men strode past her, hurrying to join the others, faces intent, weapons resting on their shoulders.

The city bazaars were eerily silent as they passed. No wood sellers chopped their wares in the Chob Faroshi as they passed. No tinsmiths filled the air with rhythmic hammering. Even the Char Chatta shops were shuttered. As she tried to ignore the blisters growing on her feet, Mariana calculated how long it would take them to reach the cantonment.

Tonight she would recite the words on Haji Khan's little roll of paper. She had given him her word.

"I HAVE done nothing to harm you! *Nothing!*" Alexander Burnes shouted to the crowd. Below him, between the posts that held up his carved balcony, heavy thudding indicated that the mob was now forcing the door to his house. "Do not shoot," he cautioned the guards who stood, muskets loaded, on the rooftop.

Beside him, his assistant surveyed the crowd with a practiced eye. "There were three hundred an hour ago," said Major William Broadfoot. "Now I would say there are ten times that many. They are packed into the road here, and I suspect there are more, out of sight around the corners."

Burnes had begun to perspire. "What of the back of the house?"

His companion shrugged.

"William," Burnes said somberly, "I should have listened to the warnings. I am to be sacrificed to these savages, but you have no part in this."

"It is my duty, sir," Broadfoot assured him. "Do not worry. Reinforcements will be here soon. It is already two hours since we sent your letter to the cantonment."

Before he could say more, the first shots ricocheted off the wall behind them. He pushed Burnes through the open shutters. "Get inside, sir," he ordered, then turned his attention, and his musket, to the crowd. "Open fire!" he called to the guard on the roof.

He killed six Afghans before he dropped to the balcony floor, shot mercifully through the heart.

One by one, the six guards fell.

The mob burst into the wide courtyard, and set the stables, then the house, ablaze. Inside the burning house, Burnes put on his Afghan costume with shaking hands.

"Hurry," said the Kashmiri who had come to suggest he escape by the back door.

"I *am* hurrying," Burnes panted as he wound on his lucky turban, the one he had always worn on his woman-hunting forays.

They opened the back door only enough to let them squeeze outside and into the crowd that stood shoulder to shoulder, shifting impatiently. The crowd smelled of sweat, unwashed clothing, and lust for blood.

The door shut behind them.

Someone turned and looked into Burnes's face. He dropped his head, hoping...

"He is here, I have him!" The Kashmiri raised his voice. "Here is Eskandar Burnes!"

Before Sir Alexander Burnes, British Resident at Kabul, had time to protest the Kashmiri's betrayal, before he had time to pray, the mob had fallen upon him.

There was no room for jezails in the narrow street, so they used knives: heavy pointed churas with long, straight blades for thrusting; ivory-handled *kukri* knives with downward-curving blades, heavy enough to slash a man in half; beautifully weighted Persian daggers with decorated hilts, Indian *katar*s for tiger hunting, with wedge-shaped blades and strange handles, damascened *khanjar*s and *jambiya*s, whose upward-curving blades were sharpened on both edges.

When at last the crowd turned away, satisfied with its work, Sir Alexander Burnes, British Resident at Kabul, was no more than a scattered collection of body parts and blood-soaked rags.

"The British will come, now," spectators muttered as the jubilant crowd marched, shouting, through the city. "They will come with their great, damaging guns. *They will come.*"

Chapter 18

They must get clear of the city, Mariana told herself as she toiled painfully past the wall of a large formal garden. Word of the attack on Burnes must have reached the cantonment hours ago. The British rescue party would already be on the march, bent on saving him, or avenging his death.

They would kill any armed man they encountered inside the city gates: the quiet stranger who strode ahead of Mariana, his jezail slung across his back, and Yar Mohammad, too, whose long knife was visible among his clothes. She and Nur Rahman would not be safe, either. Mariana had seen the indiscriminate violence of soldiers before.

The rescue force, with its destructive guns and eager, red-coated soldiers, would exact bloody retribution from anyone they found near Burnes's house, and would also do terrible damage to the whole surrounding neighborhood, whose houses would be full of frightened women and children.

God forbid they should harm Haji Khan's house or injure him. . . .

It was clear that the mob would not be stopped in time. Mariana had seen that truth on Haji Khan's blind face, and in the impassive demeanor of the man who now led her to safety. She had seen it in the triumphant smiles on the men who had passed them in the city, on their way to join the attack.

At this very moment, Burnes was either dead or dying.

What would happen next?

When an Afghan is insulted, or even imagines an insult, he will kill to preserve his honor, Munshi Sahib had told her. The British, for their own reasons, had looked the other way over the recent affronts they had suffered, but now they must act.

When in Rome, do as the Romans do.

May God save me, her munshi had quoted, *from the vengeance of the Afghan.* May God now save the innocent of this city from the punishment of the British and their army.

What did the silent man in front of her think of the British? Perhaps he believed them inferior to himself and his kind. Perhaps he saw their refusal to punish without proof of guilt as indecision, their efforts at diplomacy as lack of self-respect. If he himself were a Ghilzai, he might have reason to believe the British lacked honor. After all, Macnaghten had broken his word over their payments.

And the British, too, had their stubborn pride.

Mere children, Macnaghten had called the Afghans.

Cowards, the military officers had sneered, *who run from our guns.*

I called him a dog and threatened to crop his ears, Burnes had crowed.

Now, roused to anger, the British would retaliate against the city with horrible force.

Remembering the satisfaction on Lady Sale's face at the thought of Afghan men roasting alive on the burning timbers at Ghazni, Mariana ducked her head and forced her blistered feet onward.

AT NINE-THIRTY A.M., two hours after Burnes's desperate note had arrived at the Envoy's house, Sir William Macnaghten sat, bristling with irritation, at one end of his dining table. Senior officers had taken the remaining dining chairs. Lesser officers stood against the walls.

"To send a regiment into the city, and then to arrest Abdullah Khan and the other ringleaders," Macnaghten said briskly, "would be pure insanity and utterly unfeasible. I suggest we tell Brigadier Shelton to break his camp at Sia Sang, take half his men to Shah Shuja at the Bala Hisar, and send the rest here, to the cantonment."

"But how will that help Burnes?" asked a mustachioed colonel.

Harry Fitzgerald and several other officers nodded their agreement. "Surely," Fitzgerald put in, "something ought to be done about the leaders of—"

"I don't care where Shelton goes, as long as he does not come here." General Elphinstone grimaced as he lifted his swollen leg onto an empty chair. "I cannot bear the man. Has anyone," he added, "told Shah Shuja of this?"

Macnaghten shrugged. "The Shah already knows of it. He says he warned us this would happen if we did not listen to his advice. Hardly a useful remark at this juncture."

"But what can be done for *Burnes*?" General Sale's son-in-law asked urgently.

"Do not ask me, Sturt." General Elphinstone let out a heavy sigh. "I am sure I have no idea."

Several young officers exchanged glances. "But we cannot simply abandon him," Sturt insisted.

"Unlike your father-in-law, Sturt," Macnaghten snapped, "we do not take unnecessary risks with our men. When Burnes chose to live in the city, he understood the danger. He knew how difficult it would be to control a mob of Afghans in a confined space."

"May I," General Elphinstone asked plaintively, "trouble someone for a cup of coffee?"

At the table's far end, Mariana's uncle conferred briefly with his assistant, then cleared his throat. "Sir William," he said carefully, "I believe we *must* act decisively."

Officers nodded around the table.

"To allow *any* attack on Burnes's house to go unchallenged would be extremely dangerous. We have powerful enemies in this country. I have been told several times that the tribes in the south, the Kohistanis in the north, and the Ghilzais in the east are all in league against us. They are beginning to see us as weak. If we do not put down a mob attack on one of our senior officers, they will think we are incapable of defending ourselves."

"*Incapable?*" Macnaghten gaped at him.

"We have put up with too much already." Mariana's uncle raised his voice over the murmuring. "We have done nothing to avenge the spitting at our officers in the bazaar," he added, while beside him Charles Mott looked from face to face, collecting nods of agreement. "We have ignored the stabbings of Lieutenant Hale and Captain Jennings, and the shooting of our sepoys on the road. Any Afghan would have taken murderous revenge at such insults, yet we have let them all pass without so much as a whiff of grapeshot."

Macnaghten's face reddened. "But we do not know who *did* these things. Are you suggesting we punish men without evidence of their guilt?"

"There was also the surprise nighttime raid on my encampment at Butkhak," the mustachioed colonel put in. "Shah Shuja's personal guard, seconded to my force, let four hundred Ghilzais into my camp. We lost thirty-five of our men. Apparently everyone saw Abdullah Khan's henchmen ride out of the city late that afternoon, and head in our direction. The same men," he added bitterly, "were seen afterward, riding back to town through Brigadier Shelton's camp at Sia Sang. Nothing was done then, either."

"Then what of *you,* Monteith," Macnaghten snapped. "If you knew who let in the attackers, why did *you* not shoot them on the spot? Do not blame us for your failures."

Charles Mott leaned forward. "Pride and revenge are two facts of Afghan life," he said, his long face earnest beneath its fashionable mop of hair. "We have not taken—"

Macnaghten brought his open hand down hard on the dining table, setting off a series of winces around the room. "Are you suggesting that the riot is *our* fault? I am tired of this croaking, this litany of—"

"I thought I asked for coffee," General Elphinstone put in irritably.

An aide left the room, banging the door shut behind him.

Adrian Lamb's bare head shone with perspiration. "We must act immediately to punish the city mob, Sir William. If we fail to do so, we will be seen as cowards. I fear that within days, we ourselves will be attacked in force."

"*Cowards?*" Macnaghten stabbed his pen into a bottle of ink and began to write noisily, the nib of his pen scratching the paper. "Brigadier Shelton," he read aloud as he wrote, "will leave his encampment at Sia Sang and take half his men to the Bala Hisar. He will send the rest of them here, to the cantonment. Then, if possible, he will send a rescue party into the city."

"If *possible?*" Captain Sturt stared. "But surely—"

"*If possible.*" Macnaghten jerked himself abruptly to his feet. "Shelton goes to the Bala Hisar. That is all."

AN HOUR later, a sobbing Mariana stood before her uncle on bloody, bare feet, still wearing her Afghan disguise. "But *why*?" she shouted. "*Why* did they send no rescue force to the city! *Why* did they do *nothing* to save Sir Alexander from that murderous mob? And now that he must be dead, *why* do they not avenge him?"

"I am too angry to speak about it," Uncle Adrian replied stonily. "You have flagrantly disobeyed me, and I shall not easily forgive you. Your aunt has been in bed ever since she discovered you had vanished without a word. She thought you had been kidnapped by Afghans.

"You are not to tell *anyone* what you know of Sir Alexander's fate," he added fiercely. "It is rumored that he is still alive, and you are *not* to dash that hope. *Do you hear me?*"

He turned on his heel and left her, but not before she had seen the anguish on his face.

Moments later, Aunt Claire reached from her bed, flung her arms about Mariana, kissed her damply, then collapsed onto her pillows.

"You must never vanish like that again," she wheezed, punctuating her words with rhythmic yanks on Mariana's tangled hair. "Look at you in your horrible native clothes. You are a *cruel* girl. I could kill you, I really could!"

Mariana withdrew to her room as quickly as she was able, and sent for Dittoo.

"Such a commotion in the house," he confided, as he emptied a kettle of hot water into a basin at Mariana's feet, "such shouting and tearing of clothes! Memsahib even called your Munshi Sahib to come," he added, as he shook salt into the water, "and tell her what had happened to you."

"She called *Munshi Sahib*? What did he say?" Mariana winced as she lowered a bloody foot into the water.

"He said he believed you had gone to speak to someone in the city, and that he was certain you would return before long. He also said that it was very unlikely that you had been kidnapped."

The lunch gong sounded. Mariana changed wearily into an afternoon gown and brushed out her hair, gritting her teeth at the pain in her scalp.

Her aunt did not appear at the table. Mariana could not touch the boiled mutton or the milk pudding, even though gentle old Adil offered them many times. Neither she nor her uncle spoke.

They were all in peril now. A goat, Fitzgerald had observed, could climb the Residence compound wall. . . .

"AT TWO o'clock this afternoon," Fitzgerald confided to Mariana's uncle, after ousting Mariana and her munshi politely but urgently from the dining room, "Shah Shuja sent a party of his guard into the city to rescue Burnes. A detachment of his infantry entered the Shor Bazaar from the Bala Hisar with two of our guns."

Her ear to the closed door, Mariana heard the hope in her uncle's voice. "And what happened then?"

"A large mob was waiting for them. Every rooftop and balcony along the way was crowded with gunmen, as were many of the upper windows. The force held out for some thirty minutes before they broke and retreated, with two hundred killed or wounded."

"Ah." Uncle Adrian's voice sobered.

"Of course," Fitzgerald added, "half the Shah's infantry were unreliable Afghans, and the rest were only half-trained and shockingly officered. His gunners had no experience at all. We had not taken nearly enough trouble to train his army."

"Were they able to reach Burnes's house?"

"I am afraid they were not." Fitzgerald's voice, level and calm, seemed at odds with the severity of his news. "From the moment they entered the city, they were hemmed in on all sides, perfect targets for the marksmen on the rooftops.

"Of course they were closely formed into infantry squares," he added without emotion.

Infantry squares? Mariana frowned. Why had they used the square formation during street firing? A solid block of soldiers had served Lord Wellington well enough against the French cavalry at Waterloo, but surely this had been a very different sort of battle.

"And the six-pounders," Fitzgerald went on, "were no use at all in that cramped space. Even properly trained gunners could not have aimed them at the rooftops at such short range. They were fired only once, into some houses in front, where the road turned, but that was all. Worse, both guns were abandoned, with only one of them spiked and disabled. The other one is in enemy hands—"

His voice trailed away.

"Has Brigadier Shelton gone to the Bala Hisar yet?" Uncle Adrian asked.

remains of Burnes's poor, dismembered body, and gathered them one by one, onto the cloth.

"I will see to your burial, my dear, foolish Eskandar," Sharif vowed in a whisper as he and his men carried their reeking burden away into the darkness.

Chapter 19

November 6, 1841

We must pack at once." By the light of her candle, Aunt Claire's face was gray with fright. "A messenger has come from the cantonment with orders to evacuate the Residence compound."

Mariana sat up, blinking. "What time is it?" she asked.

"It's nearly five-thirty in the morning. We are to leave the Residence compound by nine o'clock. They are saying we are not safe here."

Two braids hung down beneath Aunt Claire's lace nightcap. Mariana had not realized how thin her aunt's hair had become.

"The Macnaghtens are to stay with Lady Sale," Aunt Claire added over her shoulder as she shuffled away, the lamp swaying in her hand. "We are to occupy officers' quarters."

Half an hour later, Dittoo backed through Mariana's door with her coffee tray. He was close to tears. "What has happened, Bibi?" he cried, the coffee things clattering as he put the tray down with trembling hands. "Why must we leave our house?"

"I don't know, Dittoo," she replied. "I can only say that we must do it."

"But they are saying that your Munshi Sahib and the rest of us must live in tents." His voice broke. "I want to go home to India, Bibi. It is so cold here—"

"I will see that you all have warm quilts," she interrupted hastily, fearing her own feelings might show. "And now, go downstairs and help with the kitchen things. And do not forget to pack the sheets and towels," she called after him.

When he was gone, she sat on the edge of her bed and dropped her head into her hands.

What had become of her people, the bravest, most sensible people on earth? How had they failed to recognize the terrible danger of interfering with people they did not understand? Now, faced with the violent consequences of their actions, why were they so weak-kneed?

And why could they not see that innocents like Dittoo and her poor, terrified aunt would be forced to pay the unfair price of their folly?

She forced herself to her feet and began to pack.

They would all be lucky, she thought, as she tucked Haji Khan's paper securely into her bodice, if that price were no more than the misery of living in a barracks, or a tent in the snow.

"Captain Sturt was stabbed in the face yesterday, by a courtier at the Bala Hisar," her uncle told her two hours later, as they stood waiting for their horses. "His tongue and face were paralyzed. For hours he could neither swallow nor speak. Lady Sale and her daughter have nursed him all night. Thank God, he is now expected to recover."

Uncle Adrian looked puffy-eyed, as if he, too, had not slept. "It seems that the Afghans are gathering in large numbers. The road between here and the city is full of armed villagers on their way to join the uprising. Please say nothing about this to your aunt. I cannot wait for General Sale and the First Brigade to arrive."

The horses had come. Yar Mohammad led Mariana's mare to the mounting steps, his demeanor as calm and watchful as always. He must have worn that same expression as he led her safely from Haji Khan's house, his long kukri knife ready in his hand.

He had been her faithful protector for two years: a bony-faced mountain villager who never seemed to hurry, but whose quick action had once saved her when she was bitten by a snake, and who had guarded her from the child thief who had come all those months ago to steal Saboor.

Every time Mariana looked at Yar Mohammad, or at blunt, faithful Ghulam Ali, she thought of Lahore, and Saboor, and of Hassan Ali Khan.

She ducked her head to hide the tears gathering in her eyes. *Please let nothing ill happen to them now....*

Followed by a train of laden donkeys, they pushed their way through the gate in the rampart wall that divided the Residence compound from the military cantonment.

Looking about her, Mariana saw that everything had changed.

When she had last seen it, the open parade ground had been occupied by groups of red-coated soldiers practicing intricate drills. It was now home to rows of tents, piles of cannonballs, and sprawling heaps of baggage. The sounds of thudding hammers and rasping saws came from what remained of the parade ground's open space.

A white blur of distant tents had appeared along the cantonment's southern rampart. The native bazaar, it seemed, had been brought inside the cantonment's protective walls.

An excited crowd of Indian men, women, and children milled about near the barracks. As Mariana watched, several British officers appeared and herded them out of the way.

Near the gate, red-coated infantrymen climbed ladders to the parapet, to stand guard behind its toothlike fortifications.

When one of them pointed south, toward the city, Mariana noticed a rent beneath the arm of his coat.

Were all the soldiers as unkempt as that man? She frowned as half a dozen native lancers rode past her. They were indeed, she concluded, observing their patched trousers and threadbare coats. They must not have been issued new uniforms for a year at least.

Accompanied by heavily bearded Indian gunners, a team of horses pulled an artillery piece toward the main gate, its long barrel pointing backward, while a mounted British officer barked orders beside them.

No one had taken any notice of Mariana and her family.

"Why are we stopping? Why are they putting me down?" cried Aunt Claire from her palanquin when Mariana and her uncle reined in their horses, looking for someone to show them their new quarters.

"I think," Uncle Adrian said, pointing toward a walled compound just visible past the tents and baggage, "it would be wise to go to Lady Sale's house for now, until things are calmer here."

Half an hour later, they, Lady Sale, and a subdued Lady Macnaghten sat on high-backed chairs in the Sales' spartan drawing room, while bustling footfalls overhead told them of the continuing effort to care for the wounded Captain Sturt.

Attending all night to her son-in-law had done nothing to reduce Lady Sale's accustomed forcefulness. "This insurrection has been mismanaged from the beginning," she said bluntly, as she took a glass of sherry from a tray. "We have only the supineness of our own command, and their silly fantasy of our security to blame for these attacks."

"Exactly." Mariana opened her hands, delighted to find someone who agreed with her. "And I cannot imagine why we have not avenged Sir Alexander's murder. After all, it was four days ago. If we were Afghans—"

"*Murder? Four days ago?*" Lady Sale's rangy body came to immediate, stiff attention. "How *dare* you say such a horrible thing? And who are *you* to claim knowledge of Sir Alexander's fate?"

Mariana shrank into her chair, her heart thudding. Although the room was cold, she felt hot moisture seeping down her back. She did not dare look at her uncle.

"But we all know he has taken refuge with friends in the city!" Lady Macnaghten's hand trembled as she reached for her sherry. Her hair, Mariana now noticed, was the tiniest bit untidy, and her gown less than perfectly ironed. "We all know he has only a minor leg wound."

"Miss Givens is only guessing," Uncle Adrian assured her. "My niece is a *very* foolish young lady," he added, glaring at Mariana.

"And a disrespectful one at that," Lady Sale added nastily. "She has no right to remark upon the policies of Her Majesty's appointed officials. If there is anything I cannot abide," she sniffed, "it is a *croaker.*

"We have no more than three days' worth of food within the cantonment walls," she went on, exempting herself from any such charge. "All the rest of our stores are in the commissariat fort. If we lose it, we shall have lost more than the vital food and medical stores inside it. The insurgents will also have gained control of the Kohistan Road, and cut our contact with the city."

"The city?" Aunt Claire frowned. "But why should we want contact with Kabul? Is it not full of Afghans?"

Lady Sale stared at her. "The city, my dear lady," she said loudly and slowly, as if to an imbecile, "is where *everything is.*"

"I am sure," Lady Macnaghten put in with forced brightness, "we shall all manage somehow. My husband is very skilled at talking to the Afghans. He speaks Persian, you know...."

Her voice faded. Mariana tried to catch her eye, but she looked away.

Uncle Adrian cleared his throat. "Let us talk of something else," he said firmly. "I understand, Lady Sale, that Captain Sturt is now able to speak. You must be very relieved."

"I am indeed." Lady Sale offered him a narrow-lipped smile. "He appeared to have been dreadfully wounded at first, but he is now sitting up and asking for soup."

UNCLE ADRIAN and his family had been assigned the shared quarters of three junior officers: three cupboardlike bedrooms and an ill-furnished sitting room with a fireplace and two windows looking toward the infantry barracks. As soon as they arrived at the low, ugly building, Mariana shut herself into her room, a tiny, ice-cold chamber that seemed, from articles that still remained, to have belonged to a Lieutenant Cowperthwaite.

She would listen to her aunt's complaints later.

Where was Fitzgerald? She opened her large trunk and surveyed its contents, hoping he was not out in the open, being shot at by Afghans. But he must be, for he had not sent them so much as a single message.

It was no use wondering what had become of Hassan.

"It is all *your* fault that we have not been invited to dine with Lady Sale," Aunt Claire trumpeted accusingly from her palanquin that evening, as they wove their way across the dark parade ground on their way to dinner.

She was, of course, correct. And as a worried-looking subaltern showed them to a makeshift table in a corner of the British cavalry officers' mess, Mariana saw that as disagreeable as dinner at Lady Sale's might have been, this one promised to be even worse.

They were not alone. Sharing their table were two silent officers' wives and their seven collective children, all of whom seemed too dispirited to eat. But worse than their lackluster companions, and Mariana's feeling of being an interloper in that martial setting, was the general atmosphere of the dining room.

The officers at their long table were festively enough dressed, in elaborate mess kits covered in gold braid and epaulettes, and the room was candlelit and full of regimental silver, but the conversation was subdued, and the faces around the table, young and old, fresh and weather-beaten, looked sullen and angry.

The food, when it came, consisted of soggy rice and stringy boiled chicken. As she pushed it about her plate, Mariana listened to the sounds around her—the hushed voices of the children, the scrape of knives and forks against china, and an occasional, barked order for more wine.

There was no laughter, no joy in that room.

It was no wonder, Mariana thought, that the officers preferred drinking to talking. It was widely known that two thousand gunmen could be seen waiting on the nearby hills, but for all that and for all the reports of a steady stream of armed villagers heading for the city, no orders had come from General Elphinstone to launch a proper attack.

"May I trouble you for the salt?" whispered one of the wives.

Mariana could offer the woman only a half-smile.

"Only time will tell what lies ahead," her uncle said glumly, as they braved the cold walk back to their quarters, with Aunt Claire's palanquin bearers puffing behind them.

Half an hour later, someone knocked at Mariana's door.

"It is Charles Mott, Miss Givens," said a muffled voice. "May I speak to you for a moment?"

He wore no coat. He shivered in the narrow passageway, his top hat in his hands. "I apologize for intruding at this late hour," he said rapidly, "but I fear greatly for your safety. I know that Mr. Lamb will never desert his post, but I feel I must tell you that there is a way for you and Mrs. Lamb to get away from here before it is too late."

"Too late?" She frowned into his earnest face.

"Yes." He glanced over his shoulder. "I cannot go into it, but you must go to one of the Afghan chiefs and ask him for asylum for yourself and your aunt.

"Asylum is an unwritten law of the Pushtuns," he added. "You will be perfectly safe in their custody. Of course Mr. Lamb would never avail himself—"

"Panah?" she interrupted. "You want me to ask for panah?"

He nodded. "You have heard of it. I should have known. Please do it, Miss Givens. It is your only hope. I could not," he added, his face filled with painful longing, "bear it, if anything were to happen to—"

"Thank you for your advice, Mr. Mott," Mariana said hastily. "I shall keep it in mind."

He must be mad, she thought, as she prepared for sleep. No circumstances, no matter how dire, would force her to seek protection from her enemies.

SHE WAS startled awake at dawn by the thudding of artillery. As she sat up on Lieutenant Cowperthwaite's string bed, her quilt to her chin, Dittoo appeared with her coffee tray. "The tents are very cold, Bibi," he offered from between chattering teeth, "and there is only enough coffee for one more day."

Hoping the sound of the guns indicated some positive action, she gulped her cooling coffee, buttoned herself into her warmest gown, pushed her curls into the first bonnet she found, and opened her door.

There was no one in the corridor. She pushed open the heavy outer door and stepped onto the beaten earth outside.

Between rows of tents, fires crackled and smoked, each one surrounded by a cluster of native soldiers with shawls thrown over their uniforms. Hollow coughing echoed from row to row.

No Europeans were visible save Lady Sale, who had emerged, booted and bonneted, from her compound across from the officers' quarters, a riding crop in her hand.

"What are *you* doing here?" she inquired coldly, when Mariana went up to greet her. "You should be attending to your aunt."

Mariana raised her chin. "I wish to know what is going on. I want to see the fighting."

"You cannot see it from here." Lady Sale pointed upward. "I have already tried to get a view from my rooftop, with no success. I can hear the artillery plainly enough from there, but the battle itself is out of sight."

She raked Mariana up and down with narrowed eyes. "Yesterday, with great authority, you announced that Sir Alexander Burnes had been murdered four days before. You must tell me where you got that information. Do not attempt to lie to me. If you do, I shall know it at once."

Mariana stiffened. "I cannot say."

"I do not like you," Lady Sale said flatly, "but I can see that you are an unusual young woman. I will not repeat what you tell me."

She was imperious and rude, but she did not look like a gossip.

"Very well," Mariana replied. "I was in Kabul when Burnes was killed. The mob rushed past us, shouting that Aminullah Khan had ordered an attack on his house. It was clear to me, and everyone else, that he would be dead within the hour."

Lady Sale raised an impatient hand. "What an utterly preposterous—"

"I was dressed," Mariana added evenly, "as an Afghan woman."

Lady Sale's hand froze in mid-gesture.

"And that," Mariana concluded, "is all I am willing to say."

Refusing to drop her eyes, she returned Lady Sale's stare.

In the end, it was Lady Sale who looked away.

"Well, then," she said briskly, after a moment's pause, "since you are standing here, you may as well come with me."

Without another word, she strode off at a rapid pace, past rows of tents, barracks, and horse lines, toward the south-facing side of the cantonment, home now to the shabby tents of thousands of former occupants of the Indian bazaar, who, like the soldiers, now squatted in groups, warming their hands over smoky cooking fires, babies on their laps.

After pushing her way by heaps of baggage and tethered animals and driving off a pursuing crowd of barefoot Indian children with menacing pokes of her riding crop, she pointed to the cantonment's outer rampart wall.

"We can see the native bazaar from here," she announced.

Beside the southwest corner bastion, a substantial crack in the wall afforded a clear view of a crooked lane in the now-deserted bazaar. Lady Sale put her eye to it. A moment later, she drew back, grim satisfaction on her face.

"As I suspected," she said, drawing back to let Mariana look, "it is full of the enemy. They have reached the very foot of our outer wall."

Mariana peered out. On either side of the lane, double-storied buildings had been thrown together to provide shops and housing for the blacksmiths, musicians, tailors, merchants, and other camp followers who had accompanied the army from India.

At first she saw nothing, but then a white-clad figure emerged from a low door, carrying something in its arms. The figure, that of a heavily armed man, flitted across the lane and out of sight behind another door, as a musket ball from the parapet above raised a little puff of dust by his flying feet.

"Since it cannot be seen from here," Lady Sale said matter-of-factly, "the present fighting must be taking place at the commissariat fort, which is out of sight through the trees. If they had taken the elementary step of keeping our food and medical stores inside the cantonment, none of this would have happened." She sighed. "All the wine and beer are there as well."

Drums beat the call to arms. A short while later, a body of red-coated European infantrymen, accompanied by a gun and six gunners, quick-marched past them on their way to the main gate.

How many of those men would return alive? Mariana shuddered.

As if in response to her question, a cart pulled in through the same gate. A score of wounded native soldiers had been flung into it, as if in the midst of battle. One of them sat against the side of the cart, sobbing hoarsely. Shiny blood covered one side of his uniform, staining his white cross belt.

When the cart turned, she saw that his left arm had been nearly severed at the shoulder.

"That reminds me," Lady Sale said briskly, "we shall be needing bandages. I shall expect you tomorrow morning. Bring every sheet and towel you can spare. We shall need all our strength to hold out until my husband returns."

As much as she disliked General Sale, Mariana could not wait to see that old, scar-faced veteran lead his reinforcements in through the cantonment gate.

"I KNOW everything!" Nur Rahman cried that afternoon, as Munshi Sahib removed his shoes outside Mariana's door. "There was a battle at a fort near the main road. I heard the story from a man who was there."

"But where?" Mariana demanded. "At which fort?"

Please, let it not be the commissariat fort....

"The one where the food stores are kept." He pointed toward the southwest. "Thousands of people have come, hungry for the wheat and beans and rice, and the tea and oil and sugar. They are carrying it all away."

Mariana dropped into her chair and ran a hand over her face. What would they do now? How would the babies from the bazaar or the small children from last evening survive a siege in freezing weather?

Her teacher entered and gestured for silence, but Nur Rahman was unstoppable. "All the nearby forts are full of gunmen," he went on excitedly, "and so is the King's Garden. They have blocked the road to—"

"Enough!" Munshi Sahib flapped an authoritative hand toward the doorway, and turned to Mariana. "With your kind permission, Bibi," he said gently, "Nur Rahman and I will take our leave. This is not a good day for a lesson."

"No." She reached out a pleading hand. "Please, stay with me."

He looked into her face, then nodded serenely, his qaraquli hat elegant on his narrow head. "I shall stay if you wish, Bibi," he agreed, "but today will be a holiday from the poetry of Sa'adi and Hafiz. Instead, I shall tell you a story, or rather the first part of a story, for it is too long to be told all at once."

Wondering what lesson he wanted to impart, Mariana moved to sit on her string bed. She gestured toward her single, straight-backed chair, but her teacher remained standing as he always did, rocking a little on his stocking feet, his hands folded together behind his back. With his plain shawl draped about his shoulders in the regal way of his people, he belonged to a different world from hers.

Suddenly Mariana envied him.

"In a kingdom very far from here," he began, his eyes roaming her small room as he spoke, as if he could see beyond its walls and into the far distance, "a king sat on the roof of his palace, and looked out over his country. He gazed over the rolling hills, the sparkling rivers, and the lush fruit gardens of his rich and varied land with joy and humility, for nowhere was there a happier or more prosperous kingdom."

A noisy sigh issued from the corridor. Looking out, Mariana saw that Nur Rahman was listening intently.

"The king's joy," Munshi Sahib continued, "came from the knowledge that he had brought his country to its present state of wealth and happiness. His humility came from the understanding that all his success was due to a simple bit of wisdom that he carried in his heart."

A distant door slammed. Dittoo came into view with Adil shuffling behind him, each one carrying a pile of folded towels. Mariana motioned for them to put them down and listen.

"The king had acquired this wisdom," her teacher went on, "when he was a little prince. One day, as he played in the palace garden, he had seen an old woman at the gate, with a gift of dried fruit for his father, the king. Seeing her basket of dried figs and apricots, almonds and pistachio nuts, the little prince had run excitedly to her, for like most children he was very fond of dried fruit.

"As he approached, the old woman turned to him, her face as luminous as the moon, her gaze as serene as the night sky.

" 'O prince,' she said, 'I bring a secret for your ears alone, if you promise to live by its wisdom for the rest of your days.'

" 'I promise, old mother,' the little prince cried, dancing with excitement as he stood before her."

Saboor would have done the same thing. Mariana pictured him running toward the radiant old woman, his curls bouncing, his eager feet thudding on the garden path.

"He forgot the dried fruit," the munshi continued, "for more than anything in the world, the little prince loved a secret.

" 'Here is my secret then,' the old woman said tenderly. 'It is yours alone until you choose to impart it to others.'

"Bending her radiant face close to his, so that only he could hear, she murmured, *True happiness lies only in the faithful heart.*' "

"True happiness," echoed Nur Rahman.

"Proud of his important secret," the munshi continued, "the little prince took care to remember it. He repeated it to himself before he slept that night, and for countless nights thereafter. For years, the old woman's words followed him into his dreams.

"By the time the little prince became king, the secret was so deeply engraved upon his heart that his thoughts, speech, and deeds were all colored by their wisdom. He was the most generous, kind, and noble king his people had ever known. Grateful for their good fortune, they followed their beloved king's example, and treated one another with honesty and kindness, and were rewarded with prosperity and happiness beyond imagining.

"Now the king had grown old. Sitting upon his palace roof, he thought about the future.

"He was at peace, for he knew that his beloved sons would rule the kingdom well. He had been careful to tell each little prince the old woman's wise words. Like their father, each of his sons had repeated the secret nightly for many years. Any one of them would make an estimable king.

"But it came to him that he had yet to share his knowledge with others beyond his family.

" 'Before I die,' he thought, 'I must offer this wisdom to other rulers, that they may, with the help of Allah Most Gracious, bring peace and happiness to their people.'

"He sent for his best messenger, a young boy whose name was Muballigh.

" 'My boy,' he said, after Muballigh entered his room and bowed deeply, 'I am old, and the time has come for me to send my last and most important message, not to the people of this kingdom, but to lands far and near.

" 'The message cannot be written, for it is carried in the heart. You, Muballigh, will carry it to the rulers of other countries. You will deliver it into the ear of each king, so that he alone may hear it. When you have delivered the message well, you may return home.' "

"*Hai,*" Dittoo sighed from the passageway, "such a difficult work!"

" 'Your journey will take long,' the king added. 'Perhaps by the time you return, I will be gone, and one of my sons will rule in my place. But I will have died happily, knowing that my best and most trusted messenger travels through the world offering to other rulers the key to all our happiness.'

"So saying, the old king motioned Muballigh forward. He bent close to the boy's ear.

" 'True happiness,' he whispered, 'lies only in the faithful heart.'

"With a serene smile, he sent Muballigh on his way."

The munshi unfolded his hands and straightened his shoulders. "And now, Bibi, with your kind permission, I will take your leave."

"Will you tell us the rest of the story tomorrow?" Nur Rahman and Dittoo asked in unison, before Mariana could reply.

"We shall see," the old man replied.

AFTER DINNER, Mariana sat on the edge of her bed, Haji Khan's rolled-up durood in her hand. She no longer looked at it as she repeated the words, but wrapping her fingers around the paper gave her a reassuring sense of the blind man's wise presence.

The oil lamp threw shadows against the wall of her room, but the shadows told her nothing of her future. She had seen no vision yet, nor had she received any knowledge, but then, this was only the seventh day.

The durood offered her something to cling to while life in the cantonment grew more perilous: a secret and significant action she could take. She would hold those verses in her heart and memory even as the Afghan insurgents closed in, knowing they could never be taken from her, even if all else were lost.

Perhaps, in the end, they would give her the answers she sought. Perhaps understanding would arrive tomorrow in a great, giddy rush. Oh, please, let the news be good. Let her learn that Hassan was coming to rescue her. . . .

But whatever her fate, one circumstance gave her relief: that her darling, round-eyed Saboor was not with her at this terrifying time. She felt deeply for the poor women she had met in the cavalry mess, who had clearly been desperately worried for their children. She pitied the poor children, too, so subdued, all their bright energy lost.

How was little Saboor? Was he well? Was he happy? Did he go out riding with his father every day?

Did he miss his An-nah as she missed him?

She sighed as she reached to turn down her lamp. Of one thing she was certain—unlike the children from last night, Saboor was safe at Qamar Haveli.

Chapter 20

Maharajah Sher Singh's mercenary Governor of Peshawar smiled charmingly at the man who sat before him on the carpeted floor.

"I understand, Hassan Ali Khan," he said in accented Urdu, "that your small son now sits each afternoon in the courtyard of your house in Lahore, receiving his grandfather's followers who come to call. Such hospitality; such opening of your family gates to strangers!"

He drew deeply on the pipe, producing a satisfying bubbling sound from its base. "You must be very proud of the child. How old is he now?"

"He is nearly four, Governor Sahib." Hassan inclined his head toward the curious figure in front of him.

Paolo Avitabile the Neapolitan blew out a plume of tobacco smoke and smiled again, offering a glimpse of graying teeth beneath his waxed mustachios. A heavily embroidered shirt peeped from beneath the lace-covered artillery jacket he had secured with a gold brocade sash. The egret feathers in his makeshift turban waved as he nodded his satisfaction.

"And your Turkmen mare that everyone is talking about—what a magnificent animal! Such a high, proud neck, such a sure, delicate step! If old Maharajah Ranjit Singh were still alive, she would be gracing his stable by now.

"I have called you here," the governor went on, "because I need a hundred shawls, fifty robes of state, and three dozen reasonably good horses, and you, my dear Hassan Ali Khan, are the perfect man to get them for me."

Hassan raised his chin. "And for what purpose are these things required?"

"Let us just say that I want them for political purposes."

"And how good are these *khelat*s to be?"

"Very good. We are paying for them from the Maharajah's treasury."

Hassan waved apologetic fingers. "Governor Sahib," he said, "I have come to placate the British about the five thousand Punjabi soldiers we have never sent to help them, and to deal with their complaints about the Afridis who rob their caravans. That is all I have come to do. When I have finished this work, I will leave for Kabul, where I have family business."

"Family business, you say? In Kabul, where the Englishwoman you married so hastily has gone?" Avitabile raised his eyebrows. "But they say you have divorced her."

He shrugged at Hassan's silence. "In any case, there is nothing to the work I am giving you. Everyone knows you are acquainted with good Afghan traders. Peshawar is full of horses. They are not as good as your Akhal Tekke, but they are good enough. Freshly made shawls pour into the city from Kashmir at this time of year. The whole business will take you less than three weeks."

"The horses and the shawls," Hassan replied patiently, "I can provide, but the khelats are a different matter. Proper robes of honor will take time—months, perhaps—to prepare. The cloth must be woven, the embroidery designs decided upon and executed. This is work for an experienced wardrobe master, not a diplomat."

Behind the governor's damask-covered platform, an array of Sikh officials stood listening, their fine jewels and Kashmir shawls scarcely less elaborate than those of the royal courtiers at the Lahore Citadel.

The Neapolitan's smile widened. "Nonsense." He gestured at Hassan's yellow handwoven *choga,* covered with intricate embroidery in faded red and celadon green. "Have copies made of the coat you are wearing."

"This coat," Hassan said evenly, "belonged to my great-grandfather. It may have taken a year to complete."

"The British," Avitabile went on smoothly, "have recently been trying to persuade the local chiefs to ally themselves with Afghanistan, and consequently with them. It is my duty to demonstrate to those chiefs the benefit of remaining with our Sikh government."

"I would have thought," Hassan returned, "that the minarets of Mahabat Khan's mosque were reminder enough. I understand that the ground below them is well dented from the impact of falling bodies."

A courtier gave a giggling laugh.

Avitabile did not join him. "We must seize this moment of confusion to reinforce the loyalty of the chiefs. I always prefer," he added pointedly, "to offer gifts and friendship first. I resort to punishment only if honest persuasion does not get me what I desire."

"And what does 'honest persuasion' mean in this case, Governor Sahib?"

The Neapolitan waved a beringed hand. "It means the time-honored method of keeping hostages. I already have members of all the families I intend to deal with under lock and key here at the Citadel."

"And of course there are the minarets," murmured another courtier.

Hassan opened his hands. "But the chiefs need only gold to persuade them. You must know there is an uprising in Afghanistan, and that the British are losing whatever control of the country they may have had."

"I," Avitabile purred, "am becoming tired of this conversation. You know as well as I do that if I offer those people gold, they will expect more and more. A khelat is a different matter. No one expects to be sent a new horse and robe of state each month. And speaking of khelats, I am sure another man can be found to procure them. Of course to search for him at this critical time would be a great inconvenience for me, but I might be persuaded to do so in exchange for something from you—your lovely horse, perhaps?"

Hassan pushed away his teacup. "I am sorry, Governor Sahib, but she was a gift. As for your khelats, I will do my best to arrange for them. And now, with your kind permission—"

"I quite understand your attachment to the horse," Avitabile replied, as Hassan stood to leave, "but please do not consider leaving for Kabul on your 'family business' before the work is done. And in your next letter to Lahore, please be sure to send my regards to your respected father, and a kiss to your little son. As I said earlier, you must be very proud of the child."

❧

LATER THAT morning, as Ghulam Ali squatted by the sitting-room door in Hassan's borrowed house, Zulmai the Afghan put down his teacup. "And you are certain," he asked Hassan, frowning, "that the governor has threatened to take your son hostage?"

Hassan Ali Khan gestured impatiently. "The man has no heart and an insatiable greed for power. I believe he is trying to build a kingdom of his own in Peshawar, by playing the British off against the Maharajah. He does not care about the khelats. I believe he wants me to stay here and help him with his dirty work."

Zulmai shook his head. "Avitabile's cruelty is well-known, even in Kabul," he agreed. "Since this is so, even his most subtle threats should not be ignored."

"For all I know," Hassan said, "he has already sent qasids to Lahore, ordering his henchmen to storm into Qamar Haveli and snatch away my son. After all, hostage-taking is one of his games."

Zulmai nodded. "Then you must send a message to your father, telling him of the danger to the child."

"I have already tried to engage one of the governor's qasids, but his relay-runners, like his hostages, are now under lock and key. Only he has access to them."

"I will carry your warning myself," Ghulam Ali put in abruptly from his place by the door.

"No." Hassan shook his head. "You will never get there in time. Only official relay-runners can do the work swiftly enough. But here is what you will do, Ghulam Ali," he declared, brightening, "you will post yourself outside the Citadel's main gate and stop the first qasid you see, whether he comes out through the gate or arrives there from somewhere else. You will then bring him to me, at knifepoint, if necessary. He will start my warning on its journey to Lahore.

"Until I know that my Saboor is safe," he added bitterly, "I must remain here, buying time, producing shawls and fripperies for that foreign son of shame."

He turned and stared out past the sitting room's filigreed shutters.

After laying a hand over his heart to express his feelings, Ghulam Ali set out on his mission. What, he wondered, as he wrapped his shawl about him and started for the Citadel, would happen to the Englishwoman and her family, now that Hassan Ali's rescue mission had been delayed? And what of his friends, the honest, bumbling

Dittoo and the dignified Yar Mohammad? What of the frail old munshi, and that fool, the dancing boy? May Allah Most Gracious keep them safe....

TWO HOURS later, a slight, dark-skinned runner with a mop of dusty hair trotted uphill toward the Citadel's main entrance, a short spear in one hand, a whip in the other. The dozen small bells tied to his whip jingled with each step he took.

His head raised, his eyes on the crowded Citadel entrance, he did not see a sunburned man with a yellow beard lurch to his feet. By the time sandals pounded on the dust behind him and a long, pointed Khyber knife dug into his ribs, neither his spear nor his swift running feet could save him.

"Turn around." His assailant's eyes were pink. He pushed the blade against the runner's slight body for emphasis. "Come with me."

By the time the little man stumbled into the sitting room of a fine city house, his face was streaked with tears.

"I must deliver my message to the governor," he wept, throwing himself at the feet of a bearded, elegantly dressed man. "If I do not, I will be thrown to my death like so many others. I have ten children, Sahib, ten small ones. Sahib, I beg you to let me do my duty."

"No one is asking you to die." The man picked up a paper that lay beside him on the carpet and wrote something diagonally across its back. "I am only asking you to send an important letter to Lahore. This man," he added, handing the paper to the terrifying yellow-beard, "will escort you back to the Citadel. When you arrive there, you will turn over whatever letter you were already carrying to the guards at the gate. When they ask why you are not taking it inside yourself, you will tell them you are feeling very ill, and that there was cholera in the village where you ate your evening meal. They will send you away at once.

"As soon as you are out of sight of the guards, Ghulam Ali here will give you this letter," he added, pointing to the paper in the yellow-beard's hands. "It is to be delivered into the hands of Shaikh Waliullah Karakoyia of Lahore's walled city, whose house is inside the Delhi Gate. Is that clear?"

The little runner wiped his nose on his sleeve. "Yes, Huzoor," he mumbled.

"What is your name?" the elegant man inquired.

"It is Hari."

The elegant man reached into his pocket. "Well, then, Hari, you must eat and drink before you leave."

He held out a small gold coin.

The little runner stared.

"The letter concerns my small son," the man added softly. "Since you have children of your own—"

Hari had already pocketed the coin. He put his hands together in front of him. "Your letter will reach Lahore in three days," he decreed in the tone of a man who knew his work.

The man nodded. "Inshallah, if God is willing," he murmured.

Three hours later, Hari the runner was trotting once again, bells jingling, along the Sarak-e-Azam, the ancient road leading from Kabul, through Peshawar and Lahore, and ultimately to Bengal, a distance of nearly two thousand miles. A mile outside Peshawar, he stopped at a ramshackle hut beneath a thorn tree and shook his whip. When another man as small and dark-skinned as himself emerged from the hut, Hari held out Hassan Ali's letter.

"This is for Lahore, brother," he puffed.

His fellow runner nodded, took the folded paper, and without saying more, set off at an even trot along the old road, his own bell-encrusted whip jingling with every step.

As Hari sat beside a dung fire that night, enjoying his supper of a chappati and a raw onion, he estimated that the letter would take a little more than two days and three nights to reach its destination.

That, he decided, as he bit down on the gentleman's gold coin, making certain it was genuine, would be good enough time. And the coin, which was indeed real, would be fair payment for the fright he had been given, and his extra exertion in running twice in one day.

No. He smiled to himself as he hid his new riches among his clothes. It was much more than fair.

THE FOLLOWING morning, in a gracious Peshawari sitting room, the British Political Agent to the Punjab cleared his throat. "As you well know, sir," he said evenly, in British-accented Urdu, "the Tripartite Treaty, which was signed more than *two years ago* by Lord Auckland, the Governor-General of India, by Maharajah Ranjit Singh of the Punjab, and by Shah Shuja-ul-Mulk, the King of Afghanistan, *particularly* provides for a five-thousand-strong Punjabi force to be kept ready at Peshawar, in the event they were needed for our Afghan Campaign. We have yet to see a *single* member of that force."

Major Wade had months ago abandoned his efforts to convince that Neapolitan pirate of a governor to comply with the treaty. Since then he had taken his case to every Punjabi official he could find in Peshawar, but with equally unsatisfactory results. This time would clearly be no different. The young diplomat in front of him barely looked up while he was speaking.

The man glanced briefly at the copy of the treaty the major had brought. "I know what it says," he said wearily. "I was present at the signing."

The major blinked. "Then you are aware of the seriousness of the promises it contains."

"I am."

With the exception of the mercenary governor, the Punjabi officials Wade had met in Peshawar had been Sikhs, with large turbans, carefully wrapped beards, and steel bangles on their wrists. Like them, this man was well dressed, in a loose-robed, native sort of way, but his trimmed beard and chin-length hair indicated that he was Muslim.

He was handsome, for a native. It was a pity, really, about the damage to his left hand. Major Wade, who was bad at such things, had already forgotten the name of the man's father, but there had been something about it—was it Wasif or Wazir or Wahidullah?— that tugged at his memory.

Wade glanced about him, noting the sitting room's beamed ceiling and carved inside balcony. No fewer than five servants hovered along the walls. He gave a mental shrug. This young man might be rich. He might even have influence with the Maharajah's court, but none of that was likely to help the British cause.

Whoever he was, he was no more cooperative than the previous officials had been.

Now that unsubstantiated rumors of a crisis in Kabul had begun to filter in, time was of the essence. The promised reinforcements, so important to the success of the initial British campaign, might now be equally vital to its rescue. Wade slapped his uniform gloves against his thigh, waiting for his host to say something more, but the young man only stared distractedly out of the window, his injured hand moving at his side, as if he were feeling something in an invisible pocket among his clothes.

Paper crackled faintly.

"I will take my leave then," Wade said, a little sharply, "but I will come again tomorrow, hoping for a better answer from your government."

Persistence, he had been told, was the only way to get anything done in India, but his ability to say the same words over and over had worn thin months before. Without waiting for the proper politenesses, he stood, and made for the door.

The young man leapt to his feet. "Forgive me," he said simply. "As I am sure you already know, it will be difficult for me to produce your soldiers. But," he added, half smiling as a servant held aside the door curtain, "you are most welcome to ask for them as many times as you like."

As they crossed a neat courtyard together on their way to the front gate, the man's name came back to Wade. *Waliullah,* that was it. And now he remembered what it was about that name. Two years earlier, an English girl had ruined her reputation with a native whose father's name was Waliullah.

This could well be the same young man. He was certainly good-looking enough to attract a silly girl.

As he waited for his horse, Wade searched his memory. The fool had married him, had she not? But she had since divorced him, or so the gossip ran, and gone to Kabul to find herself a proper husband.

It must have been difficult for this young fellow to give up the honor of having a European wife. After all, whoever the girl was, she had white skin.

Perhaps he still pined for her. If she were in Kabul, he might be worrying about her, trapped up there. After all, he had stared out of the window, his knuckles to his mouth. . . .

Well, it was all to the good that they were divorced. It was pure insanity for any Englishwoman to entangle herself with the natives. People should stick to their own kind.

After he mounted his horse, Wade memorized the young man's face as he smiled his farewell.

The way these Punjabi officials came and went it was possible he would never see the fellow again. That was a pity. He would have liked to learn more about this interesting young man.

Chapter 21

"Repeating the king's words to himself," the old munshi recounted several days later, his singsong storytelling voice roughened by recent illness, "Muballigh the messenger took the nearest road leading out of the kingdom."

Nur Rahman was not the only person who listened to Munshi Sahib from the corridor, for the young English lady had summoned Dittoo, Adil, and Yar Mohammad to join him. The men looked hungry and chilled to the bone as they squatted beside Nur Rahman, but still they listened eagerly, their heads tilted toward the doorway.

"Muballigh walked for many days," Munshi Sahib continued, "past fruit gardens, emerald-green rice paddies, and golden wheat fields—until he reached the border of his own land. It was easy to see where the boundary lay, for beyond it, instead of the rich fields of his country, a great, tangled forest of thornbushes stretched away as far as he could see.

"A narrow path led away through the bushes. Fearful of what lay ahead but remembering his beloved king's instructions, Muballigh stepped cautiously onto it.

"The path was difficult to follow. Great, pointed thorns tore at his clothes. The bushes grew taller, and towered above his head. The path twisted and turned, so that he could see only a little way before or behind him."

Nur Rahman shivered, feeling the messenger's fear and isolation as if they were his own. With only Painda Gul's bitter companionship, he, too, had been cut off from his home. Never in all those years had he had a confidant, a friend. . . .

"To give himself courage, Muballigh began to repeat the secret message aloud. 'Happiness lies only in the faithful heart,' he murmured to himself as he struggled along the path, 'in the faithful heart.'

"A clearing opened in front of him. No sooner had he sat down to rest than a whirring sound came from above his head and a large bird with great, ragged wings dropped from the sky and landed clumsily before him.

"The bird cocked its head and, looking Muballigh up and down, 'Tell me,' it asked, 'which spell you have been chanting as you travel through this forest.'

" 'I would gladly tell you, O Bird,' replied Muballigh politely, 'but I am forbidden to do so. My message is for the king of this country, and no one else.'

"The bird spread its ragged wings. 'If you tell me your secret,' it said temptingly, 'I will carry you over this miserable forest to the king's palace.'

" 'Alas,' Muballigh said sadly, 'I would like nothing more, but I cannot break my promise to my king.'

" 'As you wish.' So saying, the bird flapped away, leaving Muballigh alone among the thornbushes."

"*I* would have revealed the secret," Dittoo whispered loudly, "if only to have the bird's company for a little while."

"I, too, would have told," agreed Nur Rahman.

"And I," murmured Adil.

Only Yar Mohammad said nothing.

"Night had fallen," Munshi Sahib went on, "and Muballigh could travel no farther. He wrapped himself in his cloak and lay down to dream of his own peaceful land, where no cruel thorn trees barred the way.

"The next day he struggled again along the path. When at last he emerged from the forest, his clothes torn, his face and hands scratched and bleeding, he saw before him a great, dusty city.

"No fields or peaceful villages dotted the land, for the forest had encroached nearly to the city's high, brick walls. The city gates, open and unguarded, swung in the breeze.

"When Muballigh entered the city, he found its streets deserted. He wandered past closed-up shops and deserted-looking houses, searching in vain for someone to direct him to the palace, until he came to a large, tumbledown building that might once have been the residence of a king.

"He beat upon its great, peeling door until it creaked open a little way and a ragged man looked out.

" 'Peace be upon you,' offered Muballigh. 'I have come to deliver an important message to the ears of the king.'

"The doorkeeper shrugged, then led him across a dusty courtyard and into a small, unadorned room where a disheveled man sat on a reed stool. Had the servant not bowed deeply before him, Muballigh would never have known that he stood before a king."

Munshi Sahib stopped speaking and coughed, a hollow, worrying sound.

His audience exchanged glances.

"He suffers from cold at night," Nur Rahman whispered. "He has only one thin *rezai,* and it is not enough. Of course he never complains."

"I will bring him another one this evening," murmured Yar Mohammad.

The quilt Yar Mohammad was offering, Nur Rahman knew, was the only one he had.

"The king's clothes were poor," Munshi Sahib went on, "and his beard reached to his waist.

" 'What do you want?' he demanded.

" 'I have come,' replied Muballigh, 'with a message from my own king, whose country lies beyond the forest of thorns.'

" 'Impart your secret quickly then,' snapped the king. 'I have better things to do than listen to useless messages.'

"Muballigh bent toward him. 'True happiness,' he murmured tenderly, 'lies only in the faithful heart.'

" 'Is that all you have to say, O Foolish Messenger?' scoffed the king. 'How little you know! There is no happiness or faith in this kingdom, only treachery of a king's brother, who has stolen everything the king held dear.'

"Tears rolled down his cheeks. 'Leave me,' he wept, 'and take your useless secrets with you.'

"Muballigh did as he was told. Directed by the ragged door-keeper, he found a dusty road that led out of the city, across a barren plain. As he followed it, a rushing sound came from above his head, and the ragged bird stood before him once again.

" 'O Messenger,' it asked, 'will you return home, now that your secret message has been wasted on the King of Despair?'

" 'No, Bird,' Muballigh replied sadly. 'That I may only do when the message has been well received.'

"The bird spread its wings. 'If you wish me to carry you over this waterless plain to the next kingdom, you need only tell me your secret.'

"When Muballigh shook his head, the bird flapped away, leaving him alone again.

"And that," the munshi concluded hoarsely, "will be enough for today."

AFTER HER munshi and Nur Rahman departed, Mariana stared out of her window.

Caught up with Haji Khan's durood, she had so far given little thought to her munshi's story, but today, aware of how raptly the four men outside her door were listening, she had attended.

But perhaps her teacher was offering all five of them a lesson. After all, he never spoke without a purpose.

Happiness lies only in the faithful heart, he had said. But surely that was not all he had to say. In this dangerous time, it seemed perfectly childish to insist that faith and joy were the same.

All the faith in the world could not provide happiness to this besieged cantonment surrounded by hostile tribesmen, with food enough for only two days, the camels dying, the wounded lying in agony, and the native camp followers falling ill in droves.

And that sad truth did not apply only to the present. Belief in God had not spared her grieving parents after illness had carried off her two small brothers and her baby sister. Faith might have saved them from madness or despair, but it had certainly not brought them happiness.

She shivered. In just over a year, Saboor would be the same age her precious brother Ambrose had been when he died of typhoid, all shrunken and bald, his flaccid little hand in hers.

She had loved him so, her small, admiring brother who never

criticized her, who never told her she was clumsy, or that she talked too loudly. Ambrose had listened, enthralled, to her stories about frogs and fairies. He had smacked his lips when she brought him ripe peaches to eat. . . .

Tears spilled over her cheeks. This cantonment was not home. Why was she not with the people she had loved the most, Ambrose, her father, Saboor, Hassan?

She wiped her face, remembering Munshi Sahib standing in her tent that afternoon at Butkhak, one day's march from Kabul. His hands folded behind his back, his face intent, he had recited from the Qur'an.

"*Thou shalt surely,*" he had quoted, "*travel from stage to stage.*"

She had certainly done that—traveling from England to Calcutta, then Lahore, and now Kabul, from girlhood to wherever she was now.

What would happen to her at this cold, cheerless stage?

She turned from the window and its harsh, never-changing mountain view. Months earlier, Munshi Sahib had offered her that Qur'anic quotation as an antidote to her dream of a funeral procession. Now he was relating the story of the king's messenger. Since he never spoke idly, those two offerings must contain messages for her, although what they were she could not guess.

NUR RAHMAN sighed as he cleaned Munshi Sahib's oil lamp. How, he wondered, would his dear teacher survive a siege during the bitter Kabul winter?

Villagers from nearby Bibi Mahro had come that morning with enough grain to last the camp for two days, but who knew if or when they would return. If they did not come again very soon, sixteen thousand people would be put on half rations, then quarter rations, while the British sent their men into the countryside on the risky mission of buying food.

For this lovely old man to go without a full stomach in summer would be difficult enough, but in winter it could be deadly. He was already suffering from the cold. . . .

As he reached sadly for the lamp oil, Nur Rahman remembered something Munshi Sahib had said that afternoon.

Wrapped in his cloak, he had said, telling his story. *A dusty city.*

Those words rang in the boy's imagination. He smiled. Why had he not seen that he, of all the members of this household, might travel unnoticed among the horde of armed men that now filled the dusty Kohistan Road? How had he failed to recognize that, shuffling behind the disguised Yar Mohammad, he could pass the King's Garden where the besiegers had begun to gather, then cross the Pul-e-Khishti and enter the roiling, bloodthirsty city?

Tomorrow he would put on his white chaderi. Safely, a few paces behind the tall groom, he would go to the city. There, in the leather bazaar, he would buy his teacher a *poshteen,* a long sheepskin cloak to keep out the cold.

But that was not all he would do. He would bring medicinal fruit for Munshi Sahib's cough, and live chickens for the English lady and her family. Later, he would bring more poshteens, one for everyone in the household—even for himself. He would go again and again, for sweet red Kabuli carrots, for onions, for turnips and hot bread, fresh from the bakers, for live goats. It did not matter that the commissariat fort had fallen, and that all the British food stores were stolen.

He had no money, of course, but he had only to ask the English lady. If she and her family ran short of money, he would barter. Their house was full of imported goods that would bring a price in the city.

Later, if necessary, he would steal. After all, he had stolen before. But before it came to that, he would see to the old man's comfort.

He began to sing for the first time in days, a mournful, minor air that filled him with joy. For all that he was trapped in the endangered British cantonment, he had never felt so purposeful, or so happy.

When Yar Mohammad arrived, a worn, cotton-stuffed quilt under one arm, Nur Rahman took him aside.

"As you have given Shafi Sahib your rezai," the dancing boy said quietly, holding out his own tattered quilt, "please take this."

When Yar Mohammad shook his head, the boy smiled crookedly. "I took an unused one from the English lady's family this afternoon. As I am sure you do not approve of borrowing, I will use it myself. And there is something I must ask of you."

Chapter 22

"We hear wonderful things of Paradise," the youngish man with a pockmarked face offered that same afternoon, from the crowd surrounding Shaikh Waliullah's platform.

"And much of what you have been told is nonsense." The Shaikh surveyed his visitors, then returned his penetrating gaze to the man who had spoken. "I suppose, Rahmat, you have been led to believe that Paradise consists of an endless supply of wine and virgins?"

It was a pleasant afternoon. Bright sun illuminated the courtyard wall and fell upon those members of the crowd who had come too late to sit beneath the painted portico where the Shaikh sat, his wrinkled face amused.

Rahmat dropped his eyes. The Shaikh bent toward him, his starched headdress nodding. "Do not be ashamed," he said kindly. "These mistakes are common among our people. But from now on, you must not listen to what ignorant mullahs tell you. Remember, instead, the saying of our Prophet Muhammad, upon whom be peace, who said: 'Paradise is what the eye has not seen, nor the ear heard, nor has ever flashed across the mind of man.' "

He raised an instructive hand. "Keep in mind," he added, lifting his voice, "that the descriptions of Paradise, even those in the Qur'an, are only by way of example. For how else can the indescribable be described? As to those virgins—

"*The Companions of Paradise,*" he intoned, "*are not what you have been told.*

"*They are the cupbearers of the Infinite.
They will give you to drink from the fountain of Salsabil;
They will lead you to the treasure-gardens of the Beloved,
And offer you the greeting of 'Peace.'*

"That poem offers us something in the way of description," he decreed. "In any case it is better than all that nonsense about drink and women. And now, Saboor," he added, turning to the little boy who shared his platform, "you must go upstairs. Bhaji will want to give you your milk—"

"Look, Lalaji!" The child pointed toward the gate.

A Hindu in a loincloth and an unclean turban had entered the Shaikh's courtyard. He cut an odd figure among the Shaikh's guests with his short spear in one hand, and his jingling whip in the other.

"I am looking for Shaikh Waliullah Sahib," the stranger announced.

THE FOLLOWING morning, several hours before a group of armed strangers arrived at Qamar Haveli and asked politely after the Shaikh's little grandson, a commodious old palanquin was already on its way north to Sialkot. It traveled with an armed escort and a full complement of twelve jogging bearers, four of them carrying the oblong box's long poles on their shoulders, and the rest awaiting their respective turns. A donkey minced along behind, pulling a cart full of bundles, rolled-up quilts, and baskets of pomegranates and blood oranges. Several servants perched on top of the load.

"Stones to my left," droned the *sirdar* bearer from his position in front, relaying the conditions of the road to the three men who trotted blindly behind him. "Hole in the road to my right. Bullock cart coming toward us. I am moving to my left."

Neither of the sirdar palanquin's occupants was happy.

"But I do not *want* to visit my cousins in Sialkot," Saboor wailed as he sat beside Safiya Sultana in the cramped box, his high voice drowning out the bearers' voices. "I want to stay at *home*!"

"Quiet, Saboor," snapped his great-aunt. "Stop shouting into my ear."

Although she did not say so, Safiya Sultana, too, wished she were still at Qamar Haveli. Leaving her home, even for a short time, inevitably plunged her into aching homesickness. Today she had felt the first pang before they were out of the walled city.

She shifted uncomfortably on the palanquin's pillows, hoping that while she was gone, the cousin she had chosen would care properly for the health of the large Waliullah family and all its servants. Humaira must see to the coughs and fevers among the children and inspect the hand of the cook who had cut himself. Of course she must also go up and down the kitchen stairs each morning, to measure out the spices and fruits to be eaten that day and later to count the hundred-odd rounds of hot bread for each meal. But would she properly supervise the washing of the clothes?

Safiya sighed. Until she returned there would be no one to tell the children her special instructive stories, or to help the women who arrived unannounced from all parts of the walled city complaining of illnesses, of infertility, or of cruel treatment by their husbands or mothers-in-law.

No one, not even her twin brother, could perform the *uml*s, the secrets of the Karakoyia Brotherhood, that she knew. Wali, who enjoyed speedy results, had done the necessary recitations to be able to cure snakebite and scorpion sting by mystical means, and he also knew how to cool fire, but those umls solved only practical problems. Safiya's specialties were the more subtle cures, like the powerful one that quelled envy, one of the greatest evils of family life.

And what would they do if someone went missing? She had never taught her brother how to find a lost person...

She had planned to send Saboor to her niece in Sialkot with one of the family men, but had given up that idea when Saboor had flatly refused to travel without her.

Her presence, however, had not improved his mood.

"Azim and I were playing a new game in the courtyard," he pouted. "Poor Lalaji will have to meet all his guests without me, and—"

"Enough!" she grunted. "Leave me be, Saboor. Open the side and look at the passing sights, but do not lean out. And you must close the panel again if there's too much dust."

The sun had beaten down on the moving palanquin's roof since morning, turning it into a long, pillow-filled oven. Safiya mopped her face. With God's permission they would arrive at her cousin's house in Gujranwala by late afternoon.

She did not look forward to this visit. The last time she had stayed in that large household, her cousin Khalida had looked after her well enough, offering her fine food, excellent fruit, and a comfortable bed, but she had unkindly neglected a maidservant who was clearly suffering from fever, and had gossiped about other family members until Safiya thought her head would burst.

"And as to the girl my dear nephew Shamoun is engaged to," Khalida had cried in her high, penetrating voice, "she let her *dupatta* fall from her shoulders to her lap right in front of me. I saw the shape of her breasts with my own eyes. Have you ever heard of such immodesty? Why, the girl might as well be from the lowest of families. If I were the boy's mother, I would have broken the engagement at once."

Safiya sighed. They would have to remain at Khalida's house for at least a fortnight, as it would be unthinkable to stay there only a day or two. But at least in that disorganized household, Saboor would be protected from the Governor of Peshawar's long reach.

As soon as I learn that Saboor is safe, Hassan had written, *I will arrange my departure for Kabul.*

She sighed. That statement had pacified Saboor for the time being.

The child shifted against her, his face to the open side panel. She patted his back, hoping Hassan's plan to rescue his wife had been prompted by more than simple duty.

Hassan's letter had also made it clear that the whole of Afghanistan had now taken up arms against the British, and that one of their senior officers had been murdered.

God willing, Hassan would not meet with ill fortune on this perilous journey. If he had not forgiven himself for Yusuf Bhatti's death, his danger would increase.

Self-loathing would make a dangerous companion now.

She laid her head back, allowed her eyes to become heavy, and abandoned herself to other thoughts.

It had been two years since the family had learned to their surprise that the future of the Karakoyia Brotherhood rested on Saboor's small shoulders. Until that moment, it had not occurred to any of them that such a thing might happen. It was uncommon for a Sufi Shaikh to be succeeded by one of his relatives, and that unusual circumstance had already occurred nearly thirty years before, when her twin brother had been made Shaikh after the death of their grandfather, the great Shaikh Abd Dhul-Jalali Wal-Ikram.

Perhaps, with Allah's help, Saboor would grow to be as wise as her grandfather had been.

Saboor's father was another matter. For all his courtly manner, Hassan was a sensible man, and a good manager. As practicality was always in short supply among the dreamers and storytellers of Qamar Haveli, the management of the family's farmlands and fruit gardens had fallen entirely to him.

Safiya had no idea how she would do without her nephew. The thought of her brother trying to manage the family accounts made her shudder.

She opened her eyes. The next Shaikh of the Karakoyia Brotherhood was tugging at her sleeve. "I cannot see anything," he complained. "All I can see is running legs."

"Shut the panel, then," she told him, and closed her eyes again.

She had not always been close to Hassan. Fearing the strong bond between her husband and his twin sister, Hassan's mother for years had kept her little son from his clever, unglamorous aunt. Even after he learned to walk, Mahmuda had kept him to herself, insisting that he remain by her side night and day.

Safiya, of course, had not been blameless, for she had failed to see Mahmuda's desperate loneliness, separated as she was from her own generous, artistic family. Spartan in her own approach to life, Safiya had not understood the taste for lovely things that had been Mahmuda's legacy to Hassan, and perhaps even to Saboor.

It was a pity that Mahmuda had died when Hassan was only nineteen.

Safiya's opportunity to approach her nephew had come when he was four. Called away to attend to her father in his last illness, and suffering herself from recurring fevers, Mahmuda had been prevailed upon to leave her son behind.

After his mother's departure, Hassan had crouched alone in a corner of the sitting room, then wept himself to sleep.

The next morning, Safiya had called the family children together, and announced that she would tell them a story. Pretending not to notice Hassan in his corner, she had launched animatedly into a tale her grandmother had often told her.

The story had taken four mornings to tell. On the second morning,

Hassan had crept shyly toward his cousins. On the third morning, he had sat shoulder to shoulder with them, his mouth open, his eyes fixed on Safiya.

He had come to her on the fourth evening.

"Bhaji," he had whispered, lifting her hair away from her ear, as Saboor so often did now, "may I sleep with you tonight?"

A cloud of dust rushed into the palanquin, filling Safiya's lungs. She started up, wheezing. "I told you to close the panel, Saboor," she snapped, flapping her hands in front of her face. "Close it this instant!"

"But what shall we do now, Bhaji?" he asked, after he had banged the panel shut. "What shall we do?"

She smiled into his mournful little face. "Come, Saboor," she intoned, patting the mattress beside her. "Come here and listen to the story of the King's Messenger. It is a long story, and so I cannot tell it all today.

"In a kingdom very far from here..."

A HASTILY dispatched messenger had arrived in time to warn Khalida of her guests' impending arrival. Waiting men had hurried to push open the tall, double doors of her spacious house and admit the palanquin and its escort into a broad courtyard containing a fountain and several dusty trees. When Safiya and Saboor were shown into the ladies' quarters, Khalida had offered them shrill cries of welcome.

After lunch two days later, as she and Saboor rested against a pair of bolsters in Khalida's sitting room and the other family ladies snored around them, Safiya began the third part of the story.

"Muballigh," she began, whispering in order not to disturb the sleeping ladies, "left the bitter king's sorrowful country behind him and set off to find another king to receive his message.

"In time, the landscape changed from barrenness to plenty, and Muballigh knew he had arrived in a new country.

"Here were fields of ripening crops and orchards heavy with fruit. Animals grazed the land and people worked in the fields.

"But as he approached them, he was surprised to find that the people he had seen were not cheerful peasants. They looked more like slaves, toiling joylessly on the rich land, carrying huge loads on their backs, bending unsmiling to their work.

"When Muballigh entered a village, he found no children playing. No veiled housewives gossiped at the village well, but through the windows of the houses he saw richly dressed men and women lolling on cushions, laughing, eating, and drinking.

"A dirty-faced child passed him, carrying a tray of sweetmeats. When Muballigh asked her how to find the king's palace, she did not reply, but only pointed a thin hand toward a distant, gleaming city before hurrying away."

"But why was the girl's face dirty?" asked Saboor. "Why was her hand thin if she had sweets on her tray?"

"She was poor," his great-aunt whispered. "She had to work. But you must listen to the rest of the story.

"The city was both rich and beautiful. The carved gate to the palace had been polished until it glowed, and the gateway itself was inlaid with precious stones.

"A sumptuously dressed gatekeeper looked Muballigh up and down.

" 'I have come to see the king,' said Muballigh. 'I bring a message for his ears alone.'

"The gatekeeper clapped his hands. When a poor old man appeared, he pointed to a grand, nearby building. 'Take this person to the palace,' he ordered.

" 'The Vizier,' he said loftily, turning to Muballigh, 'will decide whether or not you will be allowed into the king's presence.'

"Muballigh followed the old man across inlaid courtyards and down painted corridors until he came to the king's Vizier, who lounged on a priceless carpet, surrounded by attendants.

" 'Who are you?' he demanded, curling his lip at Muballigh's travel-worn clothes. 'How dare you enter the king's antechamber?'

" 'I bring a message from my king,' Muballigh replied patiently, 'who rules the land beyond the Kingdom of Despair. The message is for your king's ears alone.'

" 'Very well.' The Vizier toyed with a thick rope of pearls around his neck. 'If your message proves to be as important as you believe it is, then you will escape with your life. But if it is as trivial as your appearance indicates, then before evening your head will adorn a spike on the palace wall.' "

"Why was he going to kill poor Muballigh?" Saboor demanded in a stage whisper. "He was only doing what his king asked him to—"

"Quiet." His great-aunt held a finger to her lips. "Like Muballigh's message, this story is for your ears alone." She glanced about the sitting room, taking in a group of soporific old ladies with thin quilts over their legs, and some children playing with a tangle of colored threads. "If the others learn that I am telling it, I shall have to start from the beginning.

"Muballigh was frightened by the Vizier's threat," she continued, "but he bravely followed the slave into an inner room. There, lying on a pile of brocade cushions, was the king. He was fat as a baby, and covered from head to foot in jewels. Slaves fanned him with enormous feather fans, musicians played, and young female slaves danced before him.

" 'I have no need of messages,' he announced, when Muballigh told him why he had come. 'But for all I know, yours might amuse me. Speak.'

"Muballigh leaned over him. *'True happiness lies only in the faithful heart,'* he murmured in his tenderest voice.

"The king threw back his head and laughed aloud. 'I have never heard anything so funny,' he gasped, wiping his eyes. 'Happiness lies in the, what did you say, the faithful heart?'

"He slapped the nearest eunuch on the back, then collapsed onto his cushions. 'I'll tell you where happiness lies,' he choked out. 'It is here, in this very room.

" 'What,' he crowed, gesturing about the sumptuous chamber, 'could make a man happier than to have defeated his enemy? Do you see these slaves who fan me? They are the sons of my brother, the King of Despair. These dancing girls are his daughters. My lands are tilled and tended by his people so that my own subjects do no work. All this wealth and happiness comes from one thing alone, my cleverness at defeating my enemy.

" 'Go your way, young man,' he added, mirthfully, 'and give your useless message to someone foolish enough to believe it. Throw him out,' he ordered the guards, 'but spare his life, for he has told me a fine joke.'

"Before he knew it Muballigh found himself lying in a heap outside the palace gate."

"Poor Muballigh," whispered Saboor.

"Sorely disappointed," Safiya continued, "he took the road leading to the next kingdom, but soon, too discouraged to travel any farther, he sat down and dropped his head into his hands. At once, a voice came from a tall dead tree nearby.

" 'Now that you have wasted your message on the King of Greed,' said the bird, 'will you return to your home?'

" 'No, Bird,' Muballigh said sadly.

" 'If you wish for my help,' it added, 'you need only tell me the secret you carry.'

"When Muballigh did not reply, it flapped its great wings and flew away. Soon it was only a speck in the sky almost too small to see.

"And that is all for today." Tired of speaking, Safiya sighed and leaned gratefully against her bolster. An instant later, she sat up, frowning.

Small, miserable sounds were coming from the child.

"Now what is the matter, Saboor?" she inquired.

"I want to go ho-o-o-me."

She drew him to her and stroked his face. "We will go home soon. Very soon."

"I want An-nah." His tears dotted Safiya Sultana's *kameez*. "Why is everything so sad, Bhaji? Why is poor Muballigh all alone? Why does Abba not bring An-nah home from Kabul?"

"T'ch," Safiya clucked. "Your Abba is leaving soon for Kabul. Inshallah, he will bring your An-nah home safely."

But the child would not be comforted. "And why," he sobbed, "is Muballigh alone? The bird keeps going away, and—"

Safiya sighed. "*Hai*, Saboor, it is only a story. But since you will not stop weeping, I suppose I shall have to tell you the rest of it."

Chapter 23

"I t will not be long now."
Zulmai the merchant hitched his jezail on his shoulder and surveyed the heap of tents, piles of furniture, oil lamps, and other supplies lying before him on the dusty ground. "I expect to have twenty more *yabu*s and a dozen mules within fifteen days. By that time that caravan I spoke of will be at Kohat, ready to leave."

"Fifteen days?" Hassan gestured impatiently at the busy caravanserai that boiled around them. "Why should it take so long to find pack animals? I see camels and ponies everywhere. Why can we not buy camels, and join some other caravan that is leaving earlier?"

"Those kafilas are not taking our route," Zulmai answered patiently, "and we cannot use camels, for a camel will not climb. As for the delay, everyone is traveling at this season. The mules and yabus in the market are thin and overworked. Fresh ones will not arrive for another ten days. But do you really want that many?" he added doubtfully. "Surely you do not need all these extra tents and—"

"I want them all," Hassan Ali Khan said decisively. "Who knows what we will find when we reach Kabul? There may be women and children who need our help."

Ghulam Ali looked up from the bale of rezais he was tying. This heap of baggage, with its thick carpets, heavy bolsters, and satin quilts, was easily as lavish as that of the Tajik wedding party he had joined on his way to Jalalabad, but it was fitting that Hassan should travel in luxury. After all, he was a rich man on his way to Kabul to collect his wife and bring her home.

If Hassan Ali Khan were traveling with his own family instead of an Afghan merchant, if his beautiful Akhal Tekke horse were white, not gray, and if his wife were a veiled stranger instead of the woman who had braved the violent streets of Lahore to save his life, this might be a wedding procession, and Hassan the groom on his way to take possession of his bride.

Of course when they arrived, there would be no one to put flower garlands about Hassan's neck as they did in the Punjab, or greet him with hospitality and respect.

"We will carry all our food," Hassan went on. "I want to avoid the villages on our route. There is no point in risking shortages along the way, and I want us to draw as little attention as possible."

Zulmai nodded a greeting to a man leading a shaggy camel. "As you wish, although you will be far from invisible with that horse." He raised his voice over the commotion around them. "There is always the risk of thieves and raiders."

Hassan shrugged. "That is why we are joining all those other people, and bringing our own guard."

"Does Governor Avitabile know you are leaving for Kabul?" Zulmai asked.

"If he does not, he will find out soon enough. His spies are everywhere. I am sure that even now we are being watched."

"And you do not think he will take revenge on you for insulting him and defying his orders?"

Hassan smiled. "My friend, Avitabile is not an Afghan. When he learns we have outplayed him by removing Saboor from danger, he will move on to his next game, his next victim."

Zulmai nodded. "So now," he said thoughtfully, "we have only to rescue your family in Kabul."

Hassan nodded absently, his fingers seeking something hidden in his clothes.

TWO DAYS later, Mariana's munshi took his usual place beside her chair and clasped his hands behind his back.

"Muballigh," he told his small audience, "followed the road out of the Kingdom of Greed, past gardens and fields, all tended by slaves from the Kingdom of Despair."

His voice still sounded hoarse after three days of illness, but it was not the state of her teacher's health that caused Mariana to fidget distractedly while he spoke.

During the night, someone had blocked the irrigation canal outside the rampart walls that had supplied the cantonment with water for more than two years.

After discovering that the tank was dry when he tried to make her morning coffee, Dittoo had fought his way through a crowd of several hundred people to a small irrigation channel outside the walls of the Residence compound, where he had managed to scoop up a few precious buckets full—enough for coffee and to boil the rice for everyone's lunch, but not enough for any other purpose. This morning Mariana had barely even washed her face. Had anyone, she wondered, thought of a survival strategy for the British force until General Sale arrived to relieve them?

Munshi Sahib cleared his throat. "After many days of traveling," he continued, gesturing with fingers whose nails were uncharacteristically dirty, "Muballigh came to a third kingdom. This kingdom was easy to identify, for unlike the previous two, it was both rich and poor, and its people were both happy and sad. As he traveled through it, Muballigh saw rich gardens, heavy with ripening fruit, and meager, poorly kept ones. In some villages, women laughed around the well; in others, beggars crouched hungrily in the doorways.

"As he gazed upon this new country's rolling hills and bright rivers, Muballigh longed more than ever to return home, and to see the face of his wise old king."

A tragic, familiar-sounding sigh floated in from the corridor. Mariana understood Dittoo's feelings. He, and probably Yar Mohammad, must ache to be in a safe, familiar place far from Kabul. But unlike them, she could not say where she belonged, or even where she would be welcome. The servants could describe every stone and brick of their ancestral villages, but for all that Mariana felt desperately homesick, she could not call anywhere her real home.

She could not long for Sussex and spinsterhood, or for some nameless Indian cantonment where she would live with Harry Fitzgerald. All she wanted was the tantalizing, unreachable Qamar Haveli. It was not home, but it was the only place she longed for. . . .

"Muballigh," the munshi continued, his voice roughening, "followed the road leading to the king's palace. As he trudged along, he saw an old man resting beneath a tree. Beside him lay a basket filled with raisins, almonds, pistachios, and other dried fruit."

"The old man motioned for Muballigh to approach him. 'I see, messenger,' he said weakly, 'that you are on your way to meet the king. I was going to see him myself, to give him this basket of dried fruit, but I can carry it no farther. Do me the kindness of delivering it to him. I cannot pay you for this work, but you may eat as much of it as you like.'

"Happy to oblige, Muballigh lifted the old man's basket onto his head and continued his journey. When at last he reached the palace gate, he found a smart-looking man standing guard.

"The guard returned Muballigh's greeting. 'I see,' he added, 'that you are dressed as a messenger, but you are carrying a basket like a peasant. Which are you, if I might ask, and what is your business here?'

" 'I am indeed a messenger,' replied Muballigh. 'I bring words for the king's ears alone. This dried fruit is a gift from an old peasant I met upon the road.'

" 'The king is not here,' said the guard, 'and so your message must wait. But if you leave the basket with me, I will see that his family receives it.' "

Munshi Sahib looked tired and wan, but he seemed determined to continue his story. His health should have improved, thanks to the resourceful Nur Rahman, who had ventured into the city three days ago with Yar Mohammad, a purse full of Mariana's rupees, and a borrowed donkey, to buy a sheepskin cloak for the old man, and a dozen quinces to stem his cough.

"Yar Mohammad looked exactly like an Afghan," he had told Mariana excitedly. "As before, he pretended to be speechless, so no one was surprised at my bargaining for the cloak and the fruit. We were very careful with the money," he added, then smiled, his heart-shaped face alight. "We have brought you potatoes and onions, and pomegranates from Jalalabad."

If they went on another of those adventures, Mariana promised herself, she would ask for sweet red carrots and small, dried apricots with their seeds still in.

"As Muballigh handed over the old man's gift," Munshi Sahib was saying, "a little boy came running from inside the palace.

" 'Oh, Guard,' he cried excitedly, seeing what was in the basket, 'is all this dried fruit for me?'

"The guard smiled. 'It is, O Prince,' he said affectionately, 'for you and all your family.'

" 'But since I am the eldest son,' the little prince added hopefully, 'may I have some now?'

"As he looked down at the child, Muballigh knew what he must do.

" 'Peace be upon you, little prince,' he said, tenderly. 'I have a secret message for your ears alone. I will tell it to you if you will promise to live by its wisdom for the rest of your days.'

" 'Oh, yes,' the child replied eagerly, for more than almonds and figs, he loved a secret.

" 'Then here it is,' said Muballigh. 'Remember that the secret is yours alone until you choose to impart its wisdom to others.'

"His face radiant from having carried the secret for so long, Muballigh leant over the little prince. *'True happiness,'* he whispered, *'lies only in the faithful heart.'* "

Faith. Mariana saw it every day in her munshi, who showed no sign of disturbance, even in this dangerous time. Were Haji Khan in her teacher's place, she was certain, he would be no different. She envied them both.

"The little prince looked into Muballigh's serene face, his eyes shining. Then, forgetting the basket of fruit, he ran back into the palace.

"His work done, Muballigh turned away from the gate. As he readied himself to travel to the next kingdom, a rushing sound came from above his head.

"In an instant the great bird stood before him. 'O Muballigh,' it said, 'you have delivered the message well. The prince will, indeed, find true happiness.'

" 'But how do you know my name?' Muballigh asked in surprise. 'And how have you come to know the secret message?'

"The bird cocked its ugly head. 'That message has never been a secret,' it said, 'and it never will be, although it flourishes best when sealed in an innocent heart. The wise cherish it, and disclose it only to those whom it will truly benefit. The unwise, as you have seen, treat the message as useless and the messenger as a fool.

" 'Come, then,' added the bird, turning its back and spreading its ragged wings. 'Come, faithful messenger, for you have earned true happiness for yourself. It is time for you to return home.' "

Home. Snuffling sounds came from the corridor. Mariana glanced through the doorway. Nur Rahman and Dittoo were weeping.

Munshi Sahib rocked back on his heels, staggered briefly, and then, before she had time to cry out, or Nur Rahman could rush to his side, he collapsed gently onto Mariana's carpet.

November 20, 1841

After Munshi Sahib's collapse, Nur Rahman had bundled him into several padded rezais, sat him on the borrowed donkey, and taken him away to Haji Khan's house in the city.

For three days, he had not returned. Each morning Mariana sent for Yar Mohammad and asked him for news, but he had only shaken his head, his eyes hollow with worry.

But her old teacher's illness was not the greatest difficulty Mariana had to face.

"We are not to be relieved," her uncle announced as they perched on two of the sitting room's three chairs after breakfast. "General Sale is not returning from Jalalabad."

"He is not coming? But why?" Mariana stared at her uncle.

"Macnaghten has asked him to return eleven separate times," he said heavily, "but as Envoy he has no military authority. No one can get poor old Elphinstone to make any decision at all. Sale has therefore decided for himself." He ran a hand over his bald head. "Sale is right. It seems that immediately after he fought his way through the Khurd-Kabul and Jagdalak defiles, the same tribesmen reappeared and closed them again, more tightly than before. It is a miracle that any messages have gotten through."

His nose was scarlet from the cold, although he sat close to the fire. "Of course you and I remember those deep passes well," he went on. "As Sale went through, the Ghilzai defenders ranged themselves high up on the corridor walls and poured fire down upon the column. It was only with great difficulty that Sale was able to crown the heights and dislodge them."

"They never told us that part of it. They said the passes were clear, and—"

"Ah, Mariana." Her uncle sighed. "It was sheer folly on all our parts to imagine the tribesmen would not return in even greater numbers. After all, that is their way."

Mariana shivered, remembering the steep, claustrophobic defile at Jagdalak. "But Sale's sappers must have blasted open the worst of the bottlenecks," she offered.

"I am sure they did, my dear, but that would not have helped much."

"Does he not worry about Lady Sale and his daughter?"

"He is a military man, my dear." Her uncle shook his head. "He must do what is right for the army, whatever the consequences. I am sure he is very worried about his family."

"Then what of General Nott at Kandahar? Will he get through to us with reinforcements?"

"He has said he will try. All we can do now is wait.

"That one-armed fool, Brigadier Shelton, thinks Sale is too frightened to return," he said, sighing again. "He has already said so, publicly, to Lady Sale.

"I wish he were still in a tent at Sia Sang," he added, "or anywhere but here. Since his return from the Bala Hisar, he has taken to rolling himself into a quilt during councils of war, and pretending to fall asleep."

Mariana shook her head.

"If Shelton is as good in the field as he thinks he is," her uncle went on, as he took a large thermometer from its leather case, "he should prove it now. It is forty degrees in this room," he said, studying the instrument, "but only because we have such a large fire. This morning it was just above freezing."

Outside the sitting room's single window, the sky was a heavy gray. Shriveled, brown stubble covered the ground. Mariana hugged herself inside her many shawls.

"Perhaps," she suggested, as her uncle put the thermometer away, "it would be better if we did not know how cold it is."

He hoisted himself to his feet and reached for his greatcoat. "I must go and see Sir William now," he said. "Would you mind looking in on your aunt while I am gone?"

Aunt Claire had been ill with fever since the weather turned cold. Wrapped to her eyes in shawls, a newly purchased *poshteen* spread over her lap, she did not smile when Mariana appeared in her doorway.

"I would give anything for a nice, hot cup of soup," she said faintly.

Mariana smiled as encouragingly as she could.

"I wish Lieutenant Fitzgerald would come," her aunt added, as Mariana patted her arm. "I always feel better when he is here."

A little later, Mariana stood in the open doorway of their quarters, looking pensively out over the parade ground, her icy hands tucked beneath her arms. Fitzgerald had not come to see them for three days, which meant he was even busier than usual with the cantonment's defenses. The last time he came, he had barely been able to keep his eyes open.

She had been unsurprised by his exhaustion. To defend a poorly built perimeter more than a mile long with insufficient men and guns would have been difficult anywhere. Here, with every foot of the cantonment wall exposed to attack, the job was too great for any one man.

Perhaps she would feel less cold in his burly, comforting presence, but whatever she might wish, his poor exhausted men needed him more than she did.

She had seen them standing guard on the ramparts during the bitter evenings, Englishmen and Indians, many with no more covering than the same woolen uniforms they had worn throughout the summer. At night, their painful coughing echoed over the parade ground.

Like Munshi Sahib, many of them now had pneumonia, but her teacher at least had a sheepskin cloak and a heavy quilt, and boiled quinces and Nur Rahman.

The others had barely any water, and not enough to eat....

She turned and stared past the parade ground and over the cantonment wall, toward a pair of low hills northwest of the cantonment. At least there was the food from Bibi Mahro.

Every third day, a file of camels entered the cantonment gate, laden with wheat from the flat-roofed village built into the side of one of those hills. The farmers of Bibi Mahro could not supply all the cantonment's needs, but they brought enough to provide the soldiers with half their daily bread ration.

It was all the cantonment could count upon.

Fodder was scarcer than wheat, and the animals were beginning to starve. Each day the bony carcasses of half a dozen camels and horses were dragged outside to be abandoned in the sun near the gates. Each night the pile of carcasses froze. Each day it thawed enough to rot a little more. Each day the air grew thicker with the sweet, nauseating smell of putrefying flesh.

At least Mariana's own food had improved. Thanks to Nur Rahman, she and her family had breakfasted that morning on bread from a Kabuli baker, warmed by Dittoo over a cooking fire. There had also been butter, although the cook had complained that it had been half butter and half goat hair when it arrived from the city.

Tea, chickens, sugar, even grapes and cabbages, appeared daily in the panniers of Nur Rahman's borrowed donkey, to be shared with the Macnaghtens and Lady Sale. When there was extra, Mariana shared it among the seven other ladies and their pallid children, but there was little she could do for the runny-nosed native children who swarmed barefoot outside the officers' quarters, begging for food, reminding her of herself, crouched in terrible need outside the gate of Qamar Haveli.

"Forgive me," she said, when they held out their little hands, "I am so sorry, so sorry."

Needing something else to think about, she set off to discover how Lady Macnaghten was bearing the current difficulties. Adding one more shawl to the three she already wore, she made her way across the frozen lawn to Lady Sale's house.

"Oh, it is you," someone said moistly, when Mariana arrived in the drawing room.

The speaker sat huddled beside the fire. From the sound of her voice, Lady Macnaghten had been weeping. Lady Sale was nowhere to be seen.

"It is foolish, really." Lady Macnaghten raised her head and regarded Mariana with tear-filled eyes. "It is just that Vijaya is ill, and I have no idea how to pin up my hair. My lips are so chapped from the cold that I can hardly move them. I envy your youth," she added mournfully. "A fresh-faced girl like you needs no assistance. I have criticized your appearance in the past, but it was only for your own good. You are a lovely girl, really."

Lovely? Before Mariana could collect herself to reply, Lady Macnaghten plunged on. "So many horrible things are happening all around us. In the past three days Captain MacCrea, Colonel Mackrell, and Captain Westmacott have all been cut to pieces by the Afghans. So many others have been wounded—their poor hands and feet, their arms and legs cut off with those terrible Afghan swords and knives. I saw Mr. Haughton yesterday, such a handsome man, with no right hand.

"It breaks my heart to see how our brave officers are suffering," she wailed. "Each day they fall, trying to protect us. I want to do something useful, but I cannot even pin up my own hair."

She tore off her pretty lace cap, freeing two black braids to drop down her back. "Look at me!" she cried. "I cannot even leave this house."

Something useful. Mariana stood silently in the drawing room doorway. Beyond rolling a few bandages, she herself had done nothing.

It had been up to vain, selfish Lady Macnaghten to point out this shameful fact.

But for all Mariana's remorse, she had no more idea what to do than the beautiful woman who sat before her, painful tears coursing down her cheeks.

"MOVE THE entire force to the Bala Hisar?" That same afternoon, General Elphinstone blew out a breath through puckered lips as he sat, hunched over the dining table in his house. "I cannot see that as a solution."

"Sir, such a move will offer us great advantages." General Sale's son-in-law leaned forward, the stab wounds to his face still raw and disfiguring. "Our troops will be free to attack the city and nearby forts, instead of constantly standing guard on our ramparts in this freezing weather. Food will be easy to procure from the city, and the insurgents will be unable to drive us out, for the fortress itself commands the entire surrounding area."

"Hear, hear," put in Harry Fitzgerald and half a dozen young officers.

"Hah!" Brigadier Shelton barked from where he lay on the carpet.

"Have either of you considered the difficulty of removing our sick and wounded to the Bala Hisar?"

He threw back his rezai and raised himself onto his one elbow. "Have you thought for a moment of the livestock we should have to leave behind us, or the disastrous fighting we should face on our way?"

"Yes, yes," General Elphinstone put in eagerly, his elderly face flushing at this unexpected agreement by his hated second-in-command. "*Have* you?"

Sturt's ruined face hardened. "It is no more than two miles to the Bala Hisar," he replied evenly. "We can cover our march by placing guns on the Sia Sang hills to sweep the plain. The sick and wounded will travel on camels or in covered litters."

"As for our livestock," Fitzgerald put in, "since there is no forage to be had, they will have to be shot in any case. The horse artillery will suffer and the cavalry will lose their mounts, but neither of them will be needed once we are at the Bala Hisar."

"Quite right," chorused several other voices.

The general coughed heavily as he lifted a bandaged leg to an empty chair. "But what of the sacrifice of valuable government property? What of the houses? And what of the enemy's triumph, seeing us march from our own cantonment?"

"There will be no triumph, sir," put in a young man with wildly curling hair. "With our horses shot and our guns spiked, there will be nothing remaining of value to them. Of course, with all the camp followers and baggage, there are bound to be deaths, but the long-run military advantage is too great to dismiss."

The old general shook his head, his jowls wobbling. "I do not know."

"We shall do nothing of the kind," Shelton snapped from his pillows. "We shall stay exactly where we are."

As they left General Elphinstone's house together, Fitzgerald turned to Sturt. "All this reminds me of the fate of the Athenians at Syracuse," he murmured.

"Like them," he went on, when Sturt grunted his agreement, "we embarked on a military folly, believing we had every advantage over our enemies. Now we, too, are far from home, cut off, and fighting for our lives."

"The Athenians, at least, had great generals," Sturt said bitterly.

"But even so, they died to a man. Let us pray we do not suffer their fate." He frowned. "Have you any idea what is wrong with our senior officers? Can *you* fathom their inability to act?"

Sturt shrugged. "They are cowards," he replied. "That is all there is to it."

"I CANNOT bear," Aunt Claire announced from her bed two days later, "to hear of any more battles lost to the Afghans."

As her aunt sighed over her tea tray, Mariana sat beside her in thoughtful silence. Harry Fitzgerald had sent a note saying he would call before dinner. What fresh bad news, she wondered, would he have to tell them?

At six o'clock, Dittoo knocked on Mariana's door. "The big British officer is here," he said breathlessly. "He is asking only for you, Bibi. There is new wood on the fire."

Without bothering to splash water onto her face, Mariana rushed to the sitting room, where she found Fitzgerald striding up and down among the furniture, unshaven, his forage cap in a callused hand, looking as if he had come directly from his troops.

The musty smell of his uniform filled the little room.

"You must know by now," he said, before she had sat down, "that General Sale is not returning from Jalalabad. I have been told today that General Nott is not coming, either. He says he cannot risk the long, dangerous road from Kandahar."

His hair stood up on his head, and his boots were stained with mud, but he did not seem to notice. "This morning," he added, "the village of Bibi Mahro came under attack by a large body of men from Kabul. They have positioned themselves on the hill above it, and are firing down into it. It will only be a matter of time before they get inside."

"And it is our only remaining source of food."

"Exactly," he agreed.

"Then," she offered, "surely there is nothing for us to do but go to the Bala—"

"We cannot," he interrupted. "General Elphinstone and Brigadier Shelton have both refused to let us move from here."

"But how are we to feed ourselves?"

With money enough, or with goods to barter, Nur Rahman could supply twenty, perhaps thirty people with his ruse and his donkey, but what of the thousands of others, British and native, grown-ups and babies?

He turned to face her, his back to the window. "One quarter of the British force is to attack Bibi Mahro before dawn tomorrow, under Brigadier Shelton."

"And you are to fight?" she asked carefully.

"I am," he said. "The plan is to take one gun of the horse artillery."

"Only one gun? But why, when we have *seven* guns in the cantonment? Everyone knows an overused gun becomes too hot to fire. Without artillery, you might easily lose the—"

She pressed her lips together, afraid to say more.

His heavy shoulders moved up and down against the light. "General Elphinstone is convinced that we have insufficient powder for the guns, although gunpowder is the one thing we *do* have."

Fitzgerald had gone into battle many times before. So far, he had not even been wounded. Why, then, did a sudden wave of fear rush down her back? As he moved toward her and stood over her chair, she vowed not to flinch from what he had to say.

"Miss Givens," he leaned toward her, his face earnest, "I have no reason to believe I will not return after tomorrow's battle, but if I do not, I should like to die happy. This is not the best time to ask, but before I leave tomorrow, there is something I must know."

In spite of her vow, she jerked back in her chair. *Not now,* she wanted to cry out. *You must not ask me now, before I know the truth about Hassan, before I have finished Haji Khan's durood....*

"I want your promise that you will marry me."

Unable to escape his exhausted presence, she forced herself to offer him a smile, not her broad, genuine one, but another, smaller, feebler, and without joy.

"This is quite unexpected, Lieutenant," she said formally. "I must have a little time to make up my mind. You shall have my reply after the battle is over.

"But whatever happens tomorrow," she added hastily, horrified by the terrible disappointment on his face, "please know that you will be foremost in my thoughts."

He controlled his face, and bowed. "Very well, Miss Givens," he replied curtly. "I shall wait for your answer."

Without another word, he turned his back, and left her.

That evening, as she and her uncle sat at the small table in the cramped sitting room, Mariana could barely touch Nur Rahman's mutton and quince stew.

The time she had banked on had suddenly fled. Without knowing the truth, she must make her choice.

Whatever she did would cause damage.

She glared across the table at her oblivious uncle. Why had he and Aunt Claire made her pretend she was divorced?

She dropped her eyes. Worse, why had *she* lied to *them* about the night she had spent with Hassan, breathing in his perfume and the burnt scent of his skin?

I allowed nothing, she had told them, but she had allowed everything. How many thousand times had she relived that long, transforming night?

None of this was Fitzgerald's fault. How could she blame him for needing her answer before he went off, perhaps to die on the Bibi Mahro hills?

He could not have approached her before. After all, she had hurt him two years earlier, when she had announced her engagement to Hassan in front of him and scores of his fellow officers, all of whom knew how much he wanted to marry her.

She should be grateful. She *was* grateful. In spite of the pain she had caused him, and in spite of the disgrace and ostracism her native liaison had caused, he had still found it in his heart to forgive her.

He must have thought all along that she had come to Kabul to marry him.

He had made her a generous offer, and she had treated him like a merchant selling a bolt of cotton.

But he had given her no warning. Had she been prepared, she might have offered him a less hurtful reply, or at least a more truthful one.

And what of his own feelings? He had not said he loved her. Perhaps he did not. Perhaps, like her, he only wanted to imagine a peaceful future far from this cold, mountainous land, in a house with a garden, and fair-haired children playing at his feet.

She had sent him into battle without the one thing that would have given him hope. . . .

"You must eat something, my dear," Uncle Adrian said kindly. "We must all preserve our strength."

She looked up at her kind, unperceiving uncle. "I will try, Uncle

Adrian," she murmured, raising a forkful of rice and meat to her mouth. "I will try."

Later, after reciting the durood, she lay listening to the night sounds of the cantonment. Over the coughing of the troops, someone was singing a mysterious, rhythmic Indian air, full of trills and mournful wobbling sounds.

It was, Mariana thought, the song of a broken heart.

Chapter 25

November 23, 1841

"Since that young man of yours is in charge of the gun," Lady Sale announced, as she steered Mariana past her now defunct vegetable garden, "you had better come to the roof with me and have a look at the fighting."

Sorely regretting her shortcut past Lady Sale's house on her way to ask Nur Rahman for raisins, Mariana trailed reluctantly along a narrow space between the house and its outer wall.

The last thing she wanted to see from Lady Sale's flat roof, with its perfect view of the Bibi Mahro hills and the village below, was Harry Fitzgerald being killed or wounded.

Lady Sale stepped past the bloody feathers of a recently killed chicken, negotiated a pile of loose stones beneath her kitchen window, and took hold of a bamboo ladder that leaned conveniently against the wall. Without hesitating, she gripped the uprights with gloved hands, and began to climb.

Halfway up, she looked down, her field glasses swinging from her neck. "Stop dawdling, child," she snapped. "They've been up there since three in the morning. For all we know, the battle is nearly over."

Escape was impossible. Mariana stiffened her spine, and stepped onto the ladder.

They had sent a little over a thousand British and Indian fighting men to face a seemingly inexhaustible supply of Afghan fighters with better knowledge of the terrain.

She would not think of Fitzgerald and his gun, she decided, as she scrambled onto the roof. She did not know how she would bear her remorse if he died....

"Take shelter behind one of the chimneys," Lady Sale ordered. "Stray balls come whizzing past."

It was just after dawn, and the snow on the mountains had turned from purple to pink and gold. Mariana crouched behind her brick fortification, straining to see what was happening.

"Shelton took seventeen companies, a hundred sappers, a few troops of cavalry, and your young man's gun at two o'clock this morning," Lady Sale announced, her field glasses to her eyes. "He has set himself up on the hill immediately over the village, but he has already made his first mistake. He should have surprised the enemy while it was still dark, instead of wasting all this time."

"I should have thought," Mariana offered, "that the brigadier's first mistake was to bring only one gun. Surely he knows there is a standing order forbidding—"

"That, missy," Lady Sale barked from her post, "is no concern of yours. I, who am a general's wife, may comment upon our military operations. *You,* an unmarried woman with designs on an officer too low in rank to marry, may *not.*"

Mariana felt her face color. "I have read the rules," she insisted stubbornly. "It is true about the guns."

"Of course it is true," replied Lady Sale, "but it is for *me,* not you, to say so! Where," she asked after a pause, "have you learned about standing orders?"

"My father is interested in military history. I have read it since I was a child."

Lady Sale sniffed. "All well and good, but you should learn to behave yourself. Ah," she added, the field glasses once more to her eyes. "A party has started down from the top of the hill, no doubt to storm the village. Perhaps they will at last do something—but wait, they have missed the main gate, and gone past it, to one side. What fools! They are right in the line of fire from inside the walls. There," she cried, "several have already fallen!"

Where was Fitzgerald? "Lady Sale," Mariana began. "Can you tell me—"

Lady Sale took the glasses from her eyes and glared toward the hills. "What a stupid, senseless thing to do. They have missed their opportunity to take possession of the village! What *is* the matter with them all?"

A whistling sound came from nearby. "Musketry," she shouted, retreating behind her chimney. "By the way," she added, after the ball thudded into the edge of the roof, "your young man is doing quite well with his gun. He has managed to get it onto the very top of the hill and now he is firing down into the village. I can make out the smoke."

Your young man. Please, please, Mariana prayed, let Fitzgerald live until she could think of the right thing to say....

At nine o'clock they were still at their posts. The sun beat down on the flat roof, warming Mariana in spite of the cold wind.

Her throat felt dry. "Should we not go down," she suggested, "and have some water?"

"What for?" Lady Sale waved a gloved hand toward the battle. "Those men up there have had no water all morning. We, at least," she added, as a second musket ball thudded into the bricks, "are safe."

No more than a mile from Mariana's vantage point, the two Bibi Mahro hills stood side by side, separated by a deep gorge leading to a valley beyond. On top of the right-hand hill, plainly visible above the collection of flat-roofed houses that climbed its lower slope, two groups of red-coated infantry had formed their usual dense squares. Nearby, Mariana could make out a troop of irregular Indian cavalry, distinguished by their flowing, native dress. Puffs of smoke issued from nearby, presumably from the gun.

Someone sat astride a horse on the summit of the hill, his jacket a tiny smudge of color against the distant mountains. Was it Fitzgerald?

"I understand you blotted your copybook in Lahore, two years ago," Lady Sale said bluntly.

Mariana did not reply.

"A serious mistake," Lady Sale decreed. "One never recovers from a scandal like that. How on earth did you allow yourself to be duped into marrying a *native*?

"I should think you would have had more sense," she added, before Mariana could think of a reply. "Moreover, it is very unwise of you to pin your hopes on a lieutenant, who is much too young for you. With all your knowledge of military matters, you must know that a lieutenant may *not* marry, a captain *may* marry, and a colonel *must* marry.

"Have you seen those horsemen on the plain?" she asked, mercifully changing the subject.

A distant swarm of Afghan riders appeared below the hills and milled about as if waiting for a signal.

"Look," Mariana cried, pointing to the slope. "I think men are leaving the village!"

"They are indeed," Lady Sale agreed, her glasses trained upon the hill. "They are running away, while our storming party is pinned down and unable to enter and secure it. Fools! But at least the Irregular Horse has ridden downhill to intercept the deserters."

To Mariana's left, on the Kohistan Road, a thick stream of men on foot and horseback made its way toward them. "More armed men are coming from the city," Mariana cried. "They are heading toward the second hill! Why have we not sent a sortie from here to cut them off?"

The men from the city numbered several thousand. Moving rapidly for men on foot, they traveled in groups toward the hills, triangular pennants aloft. They had no artillery, and save for a single, gesticulating figure at their head, they appeared to be leaderless. Nonetheless they made a terrifying sight.

Twenty minutes later, Mariana watched the first of the column begin to climb the left-hand hill, clearly making for the gorge that separated them from the British force.

The Afghan horsemen had already chased off the British irregular cavalry.

"A silly, stupid failure," opined Lady Sale.

Fitzgerald's gun shot steadily at the column from the city. Puff after puff of smoke issued from his position, making it hard to see what was happening to the infantry squares nearby.

Mariana did not need to be told that the Afghan jezail, with its longer range and greater accuracy, was a better weapon than the British musket. If the enemy came within a quarter mile of the redcoated British and Indian squares on the hill, their fire would be both damaging and unreturned.

"We Afghans never use more than two balls to kill a man," Nur Rahman had boasted once. "We only waste ammunition at a wedding or over a good joke."

An hour later, the climbing column of Afghans had the British squares in their sights. Hidden behind hillocks and outcroppings, they picked off the closely packed infantrymen, one by one.

"The first square has collapsed," observed Lady Sale, as if she were commenting upon the weather.

"Why do the brigadier's men not get down?" Mariana asked desperately. "Why are they trying to hold those squares? Surely Shelton is expecting long-range weapons fire, not a cavalry charge. And I thought we sent a hundred sappers out with the force. Why have they not created a breastwork?"

How long, Mariana wondered, would the squares stand against hot enemy fire? How long would Fitzgerald's gun continue to serve them before it overheated? How long...

"Lady Sale," she murmured, "I do not believe I can watch any longer."

"Do not be a goose," Lady Sale snapped. "Those are *our* soldiers. Who is there to cheer them on but us?"

"But they are surrounded by the enemy. I cannot bear to see them lose."

"*Croaker!*" Lady Sale turned on Mariana, her high-boned face twisting with fury. "How dare you say we might lose? How dare you suggest that our Christian army is inferior to a pack of infidel savages?"

Her back to Mariana, she raised her glasses to her eyes in a sweeping gesture of British loyalty and confidence.

For two more hours, they watched the infantry squares suffer deadly losses. They saw the cavalry fail to charge. They saw the enemy, now at least ten thousand strong, overrun the unresisting British and Indian troops, and throw further reinforcements into Bibi Mahro village.

They saw the enemy capture Fitzgerald's gun, already overheated and spiked, and drive away his team of horses.

They cheered when Shelton's force somehow rallied, and drove the enemy from the gorge below, then stood in silence when, an hour later, a fresh body of Afghans arrived and rushed upon his one remaining square, slaughtering men and officers until all discipline broke. In the ensuing rout, men and officers, infantry and cavalry, all scrambled downhill toward the cantonment, killed as they ran by enemy horsemen who rode among them, hacking up the wounded where they fell, swinging swords that gleamed in the November sunlight.

As the mingled tide of panicked soldiers and pursuing Afghans neared the cantonment, a sudden burst of cannon fire came from within, followed by a brave, suicidal charge by a few native cavalrymen under a British officer, who was beheaded before Mariana's eyes with one sweep of an Afghan sword.

In moments, pursuers and pursued would all be inside the gate. No one could stop the insurgents now.

Mariana darted toward Lady Sale's betraying bamboo ladder, to fling it away. There would be time enough later, while the enemy swarmed over the cantonment, to think how to get down from the roof—

"Wait!" Lady Sale called from her post. "They are going away."

Only yards from the open gate, the horsemen had paused, then, unexpectedly, had spun about. By the time Mariana rushed back to look, they were already riding off the way they had come, bloody swords above their heads, their shrill cries of triumph echoing across the plain.

As they prepared to make their way to the ground, Lady Sale extended a gloved hand. "I am sorry to say," she said somberly, "that your Lieutenant Fitzgerald has been shot. I saw him fall before the retreat began."

Numb with shock, Mariana stepped onto the waiting ladder.

Ten minutes later, still accompanied by Lady Sale, she shivered in a corner of the cantonment gateway, watching the remnants of Brigadier Shelton's force stream inside.

The air, already fouled by the rotting flesh of the dead animals outside the wall, now smelled of gunpowder and blood. The air was full of the panting breath of the filthy, exhausted survivors, the unsteady tramp of their boots, and the hoarse, unheeded cries of British officers attempting to rally their men, both Indian and British, as they poured through the gate.

Most of them still had their weapons. All wore torn, bloody uniforms. Many were missing their forage caps. Dark-skinned or white, some dropped, panting, to the ground as soon as they entered, too spent to move, while others wandered about, open-mouthed and staring, as if they did not recognize their surroundings.

"We must go and look for Fitzgerald. I will not leave you until you have learned the truth," Lady Sale had said firmly, as she escorted Mariana through her garden, a steadying hand beneath her elbow.

Unsurprisingly, there had been no sign of him.

"If he does not appear soon," Lady Sale said into Mariana's ear, "we must assume the worst."

As she spoke, a final group of survivors straggled through the gate. Among them were three tattered natives, dragging a dusty, wounded European between them.

His chest was caked with blood. His ankle dripped crimson. It was only after the men had dropped him to the ground and thrown themselves down, groaning, beside him, that Mariana recognized Harry Fitzgerald.

With a cry, she started toward him.

"Stop." Lady Sale gripped her by the arm. "This is no time for you to act the heroine. You cannot do anything for him now. People will come and take him to hospital with the other wounded."

As two young Englishmen rushed up and bent over him, Fitzgerald raised his dusty head as if he were looking for someone. "Tell Shelton," he croaked, "that we may have killed Abdullah Khan."

"You may have *killed* him?" they cried eagerly.

His head dropped back. "We knocked him from his horse with a shot of artillery."

Several young officers rushed forward. Mariana watched them carry him away, his blood dripping into the dust.

On the night she had found Hassan in the house with the yellow door, blood had formed a little pool beneath the string bed where he lay. . . .

"You may send your young man a message," Lady Sale declared as she steered Mariana across the parade ground, "and you may visit him, but not until he is better. I cannot imagine," she added, "how his men got him all the way here from the top of the hill. He must be a very popular officer."

Lost in her own thoughts, Mariana did not reply.

Chapter 26

December 16, 1841

After many delays, Zulmai's dozen mules and twenty tough mountain ponies had arrived at last, and Hassan's rescue party, with its servants, coolies, and guards and its load of tents, quilts, food, and sundries, had taken the road south from Peshawar to Kohat, to join its protecting Hindu caravan.

Following a scarcely visible track between the uneven out-croppings of the Safed Koh range, the caravan's seventy-odd travel-ers and forty-eight pack animals had crossed the stony Kohat Pass with its half-ruined watchtowers and gun factories, their kafila guarded by ragged men Hassan and Zulmai had recruited from various forts along the way.

They found the mud-walled caravanserai at Kohat full of traders from Taxila and Bannu, and even from Sadda, halfway up the Kurram valley, but empty of any sign of a caravan traveling to Kabul. Inquiries brought nothing but shaken heads from fellow travelers.

Now, four days after their arrival, Ghulam Ali stepped up into Hassan's shedlike room along one wall of the caravanserai.

It had rained since they arrived. Outside, in the great open court, windswept sleet had turned the ground to ankle-deep slush.

A new brass samovar bubbled merrily beside Hassan's sodden

doorway, filling the already damp room with steam and wood smoke. Carpets from Hassan's baggage covered the brick floor. A *charpai* leaned up against one wall.

"There is news," Hassan announced, setting down his teacup. "Akbar Khan has reached Kabul."

Zulmai nodded. "The people there love Akbar Khan as much as they hate the British. Now the insurgency will begin in earnest."

"We will leave here tomorrow, kafila or no kafila." Hassan raised his voice over the squealing of the yabus outside.

He shivered in spite of the blanket he wore about his head and shoulders. At first, he had seemed worn down by impatience. Now his gaze was heavy with worry.

Anticipating the misery of the journey, Ghulam Ali hunched his shoulders. Zulmai put down his chillum and blew a plume of smoke into the air.

"It is already winter," Hassan pointed out. "Hardship will be our companion whatever the weather. As for your Hindu caravan, Zulmai," he added with a sour smile, "it is either too late to be of use, or else it does not exist."

Ghulam Ali raised his chin. "And what of thieves on the way?" he asked, roughly, to conceal his fears.

Zulmai smiled, then recited something in Persian, a hand waving for emphasis.

"*The greatness of the wayfarer's goal,*" he translated for Ghulam Ali, "*can be seen in the steep windings of the track, and the high passes, and the bandits lying in wait.*

"That is from Rumi," he added.

The greatness of the goal. Ghulam Ali glanced at Hassan, and saw him look quickly away.

"Do not fret," Zulmai added. "The people here are all Bangashes. They have no quarrel with us, or the British. The Ghilzais are on the other side of the Paiwar Kotal."

The next morning they set off on the narrow caravan track leading southwest to Thal where they would turn again, this time to the northwest, and follow the Kurram River valley past the Safed Koh mountain range and into the heart of Ghilzai country.

Hassan and Zulmai rode in front, Hassan in a new, embroidered poshteen, with a musket at his side, talking quietly to his lovely Ghyr Khush, and Zulmai, heavily armed, a thin shawl flung over his shoulders and his feet bare inside heavy shoes with upward pointing toes.

Behind them followed the laden animals with their drivers, Ghulam Ali, two dozen coolies, and a crowd of servants, all in sheepskin and leather boots, while the hungry-looking Bangash guards, some too young for beards, strode alongside, jezails hanging from their shoulders, their black eyes rimmed with kohl beneath turbans or tight-fitting skullcaps.

"A turban is an Afghan's honor," Ghulam Ali had been told on the road to Jalalabad, "and his weapons are his jewelry."

THREE DAYS later, Lady Sale stopped Mariana as they passed each other in the parade ground.

"Dr. Brydon tells me you may as well visit Fitzgerald," she said abruptly. "If you promise not to faint, I shall take you to see him. Come for tea this afternoon."

When she heard the news, Mariana's aunt let out a little cry of delight from within her muffling shawls. "Ah, my dear," she cooed hoarsely, "you *must* go to him at once."

Tea at Lady Sale's was a curious affair. Lady Sale was now a guest in her own sparsely furnished drawing room, having gone to stay in her daughter's house when the Macnaghtens arrived from the Residence compound. The tea the ladies drank, and the sugar they stirred into it, were both courtesy of Nur Rahman.

Mariana wrapped her fingers around the warm cup, appreciating the fleeting comfort it offered her.

Since the battle of Bibi Mahro, the weather, and everyone's condition, had grown worse. While the temperature dropped and snow blanketed the ground, soldiers in ragged uniforms shivered weakly on the ramparts, knowing they would remain cold after they came off duty because General Elphinstone, inexplicably, had forbidden the lighting of fires.

Seven hundred of the men were already ill.

The bark and all the twigs from the cantonment's trees had gone to feed the animals. Horses and mules gnawed desperately on tent pegs. Camels lamented as camels do, then lay down and died.

By now, the newly dead pack animals were being used for food. The cantonment butchers gave the best of their meat to the British officers and their families, and the remainder to those native troops whose religion allowed them to eat it.

Only the picked bones of the starved donkeys and camels now

found their way onto the rotting pile outside the gate, whose stink permeated every corner of the cantonment.

Lady Sale finished her tea and laid down her cup. "We must pay our hospital visit before dark," she decreed.

"I shall join you." Lady Macnaghten adjusted several embroidered shawls about her shoulders as she spoke.

Her appearance had changed in the weeks since Vijaya's illness. A hint of gray had appeared at her temples. Her dewy skin had become chapped, and her frilly gown looked as if she had slept in it.

She drew herself up, as if expecting refusal. "It is my wish," she added soulfully, "to succor the poor, wounded officers in any way I can. I have thought of offering them each a daily cup of tea. I am sure your Afghan boy will provide enough for that purpose, Miss Givens."

"If that is what you wish, I shall be glad to escort you." Lady Sale's plain face filled with disapproval. "But I must warn you that this will not be a social call. I do not know that tea will do the officers much good."

"Of course it will." Lady Macnaghten stood, her skirts rustling. "Everyone likes a nice cup of tea," she said plaintively.

"If you do not mind," Aunt Claire quavered from her chair, "I believe I shall return to our quarters."

Mariana looked up at the sound of male throat-clearing to see Sir William Macnaghten standing in the drawing room doorway.

He, too, had changed. His hair, a glossy black when she first arrived in Kabul, was now entirely gray, as were his imposing eyebrows. Behind wire-rimmed spectacles, his eyes seemed large and dark as if he were terribly afraid of something.

They all must look different now.

He glanced at his wife. "I shall be working in the dining room this afternoon," he said. "I hope it will not inconvenience—"

"Not at all, dear William!" Lady Macnaghten offered him a loving smile. "We are on our way to call upon the wounded officers."

He did not reply, but his bleak look told Mariana more than she wished to know.

"Do not say anything to excite Fitzgerald," Lady Sale warned her a little while later, as they crossed the frozen ground to the cavalry officers' mess, now the officers' hospital. "You must simply let him know you are there. As for the other officers," she added, "try not to look at them too closely. Some have been very badly injured."

As she stood in the hospital doorway, Mariana understood Lady Sale's warning.

What had made her think it would boast an orderly row of occupied beds? Why had she imagined the patients dressed in nightclothes and propped up on pillows, like every sick person she had seen before?

Wrapped in bloody bandages and heaped with quilts, thirty-two officers lay crowded haphazardly into the dining room and its adjacent sitting room. They occupied string beds, sideboards, even the long mess table that now stood out of the way, beneath the windows. Some of the wounded even sat slumped on chairs, apparently due to a shortage of places to lie down.

A dozen native sepoys squatted on the floor between the beds, attending to the injured. One of them held an uneaten plate of mushy lentils hopefully in front of a wan-looking officer with a bandaged head, who stared into space, drool running from the corner of his mouth.

Covered chamber pots stood in corners and beneath the beds. The reek of stale, urine-soaked clothing and blood added itself to the pervasive stink of rotting carcasses from outside the gate.

Realizing she was being watched, Mariana forced herself to take her hand from her nose.

Some of the wounded turned and stared at the ladies in the doorway, but most seemed too preoccupied to notice them. One young man lay, snoring loudly, near the door, his mouth wide open, his eyes shut. Another sat up, gazing into space, a cushion beneath his chin propping up his heavily bandaged head and neck.

"That is Lieutenant Haughton," whispered Lady Sale. "He has lost a hand, and the muscles on one side of his neck have been severed, so that he cannot hold up his head. He is not expected to survive."

A man in a filthy army uniform with a stubble of beard bent over a boyish officer, whose face seemed to be wet with tears. He looked up, nodded briefly, and went back to his work.

"That is Dr. Brydon," murmured Lady Sale.

Mariana swallowed. If this was the condition of wounded British officers, what must be the fate of the native soldiers, who had no servants and no doctor?

Fighting a desire to run from the scene, she took hold of Lady Macnaghten's trembling elbow and followed Lady Sale over the threshold.

Heavy, labored breathing filled the room. The terrible sighs of the injured added themselves to the stench, giving the room a hellish atmosphere.

A red-headed man twisted from side to side on a pair of rough planks that had been stretched between two chairs, his breath hissing between clenched teeth. He had no pillow. One of his legs protruded from his quilts, revealing a shot to the upper leg, covered with a blackened bandage.

Hassan's wound had been almost the same as this man's, but when Mariana had last seen him, he had been lying in his own house, cared for by his family, including Safiya Sultana, who had fed him opium for his pain.

These brave souls had no such luxury. All the medicines for the entire cantonment had been stored in the lost and looted commissariat fort.

Where was Fitzgerald?

As if she had read Mariana's thoughts, Lady Sale pointed to a corner of the room. "He is there," she said.

Fitzgerald lay on a string bed. A red beard Mariana had not seen before covered his lower face. He was perspiring heavily in spite of the cold. His face and hands were as dirty as they had been when his men carried him inside the gate, but someone had at least put a clean bandage on his wounded shoulder. Mariana glanced toward his feet, and saw them both outlined beneath his blankets. At least they had not cut off his foot.

"Miss Givens," he whispered. "How good of you to come."

His lips, she noticed, were cracked and bloody.

Lady Sale appeared at her side. "A ball from an Afghan jezail smashed his shoulder at close range," she said in an undertone. "Dr. Brydon says the bones have been so badly broken that he will never move his left arm properly again. But he has also been shot through the lung. That is the more dangerous wound. Do not let him see that you are worried."

Mariana smiled down at him as warmly as she could manage.

"He is young and strong enough to survive," Lady Sale went on quietly, "but if his fever does not abate within the next few days, we must be prepared for the worst."

Mariana bent over Fitzgerald, her hands at her sides. "Are you in great pain?" she asked, and instantly feared she had said the wrong thing.

"No." He gasped, then grimaced as he tried unsuccessfully to move his bad shoulder. "There are others here far worse off than I."

She reached down and laid a hand on his uninjured shoulder. "I am certain you will be much better soon," she offered brightly, forcing herself to look into his eyes, "but I will not tire you now."

As she turned to rejoin the other ladies, Fitzgerald's brave front slipped. For an instant, Mariana glimpsed raw longing on his face.

As she arrived at Lady Sale's side, the snoring by the door reached a crescendo, and then stopped abruptly, leaving an empty echo of itself among the sighs of the wounded.

She glanced at the doctor in time to see him signal to one of the servants. In a flash, the man dragged the sleeping patient's quilts away, revealing a pair of bloody, bandaged legs, cut off above the knee. A moment later, he spread the quilts over someone else.

"What is he *doing*?" Mariana whispered. "Why has he taken away the poor man's—"

"That officer is dead," Lady Sale replied harshly. "Did you not hear him stop breathing?

"I shall return in a moment," she added over her shoulder, as she started away to greet a tall officer with two bandaged arms.

A rustling thud came from behind Mariana. Lady Macnaghten had fallen, unconscious, to the floor.

SIR WILLIAM'S meeting had begun soon after the ladies had left the house.

"What?" he now exclaimed from his seat at the head of Lady Sale's dining table. "Are you telling me that the fighters who drove us from the field at Bibi Mahro were no more than tradesmen and artisans from the city!"

"I fear," Mariana's uncle replied gently, "that is exactly who they were."

"So our brave army ran from *the citizens of Kabul*?"

"They did. The only good news is that Abdullah Khan has since died of his wounds."

Macnaghten mopped his face. "And the Afghans who are now offering us terms are those same ordinary men?"

"No, Sir William. They are the tribal chiefs who still owe their allegiance to Dost Mohammad. They are acting on the orders of Akbar Khan."

"Dost Mohammad's son? But I thought he had vanished into the north over a year ago."

"He has returned, sir, and sworn to avenge his father's humiliation."

"I wish our enemies had identified themselves from the beginning," Macnaghten said irritably. "When we came, everyone behaved as if we were rescuing them from a tyrant."

Lamb cleared his throat. "Not all of them, Sir William. Akbar Khan never accepted us.

"Aminullah Khan and Abdullah Khan never accepted Shah Shuja, either," he added gently. "Of course Afghans do not always tell the truth, especially to people they do not know or trust."

Macnaghten sighed. "And now they have joined forces with Akbar?"

Lamb nodded to his assistant. "Will you explain Akbar Khan's terms to the Envoy, Charles?"

Lady Macnaghten's nephew cleared his throat. "As I understand it, sir," he said, "Akbar has asked us to leave Kabul, and return to India. He will not harm us, he says, but we *must* go, and we must leave some of our people here as hostages, to be released when his father has been returned to the throne."

Macnaghten frowned. "And what of Shah Shuja?"

"He is to remain here."

"But we brought him all the way from India! We cannot simply leave him behind, to be blinded, or murdered, or both, and all this in order to save our own skins!"

Mariana's uncle shrugged. "That is what Akbar is asking for, sir."

"Think of British honor, man!"

A bony-looking subaltern put his head around the door. "A number of the enemy have come from the city, Sir William," he announced. "They are a hundred yards away, demolishing our bridge across the river."

"And what has been our response?"

The subaltern stood straight, his cheeks flushing. "We have not responded, sir. Our officers are only watching them, from behind our parapet."

"*Not responded?*" Macnaghten shouted. "Go at once, Andrews, and tell them they *must* respond. Tell them that if they do not, I shall have a court of inquiry set up in this dining room *tomorrow morning.*"

After the subaltern had bowed and left, Macnaghten turned wearily to Mariana's uncle. "How has this happened, Lamb? How is it that I find myself responsible for *every* decision we make? Why are the senior military officers so hopelessly incapable?

"We have an army four thousand strong and not a *single* decent senior officer," he added. "Shelton made a perfect hash of the battle at Bibi Mahro. Monteith allowed gunmen to enter his camp at night and slaughter his men. All of them failed to save the commissariat fort, or even poor Burnes, for that matter. Even now, they do not lift a hand to defend us. The list goes on and on. I tell you, Lamb, I am living in a nightmare."

Mariana's uncle nodded silent agreement.

"I still think we ought to move to the Bala Hisar," Charles Mott put in from his end of the table.

Macnaghten nodded. "It offers our best chance to defend ourselves and survive the winter. With luck Elphinstone will be persuaded to agree with the rest of us. Sturt has gone to him this afternoon. If the old boy does agree, then we can ignore that fool Shelton and all *his* croaking, and make arrangements to leave here."

He sighed. "Until Sturt returns, all we can do is wait."

Without another word, he turned away from his visitors and stared fixedly out the window.

FORTY YARDS away, in his own house, General Elphinstone regarded Captain Sturt distractedly from beneath the knitted nightcap that he had pulled down almost to his eyes.

"My dear fellow," he said, his jowls wobbling as he shook his head, "I am far too ill to have the slightest idea what we should do."

At the foot of the bed, Captain Sturt shifted his weight. "I understand your difficulty, sir," he said carefully, "but I must ask you to reconsider your—"

"But one thing I *do* believe," interrupted the general, "is that we must *not* leave here and move into the Bala Hisar."

He wore a heavy woolen dressing gown with a tasseled waist cord. A fur-lined robe lay on his knees. He peered into Sturt's scarred face like an old dog that hopes he is still loved.

"Sir," Sturt attempted, "the men will all starve if we—"

Elphinstone raised a trembling hand. "Our honor will be forever forfeit if we abandon our cantonment," he intoned. "Can you not see that, my dear Sturt? Besides, we shall never arrive there without dreadful losses. You have already seen what these Afghans are capable of. Think of your wife and mother-in-law, Sturt!"

"Sir," the younger man protested through clenched teeth, "we are less than *two miles* from the Bala Hisar. That is no distance at—"

"I am far too exhausted to speak about it anymore." The general reached, wincing, into the pocket of his dressing gown. "Here you are, my dear fellow," he said, holding out a folded paper. "Take this letter to Sir William. It contains all my thoughts on our present situation."

The three men in Lady Sale's dining room looked up when Captain Sturt entered.

"It is no use," he said bitterly, handing the letter to Macnaghten. "General Elphinstone would not let me finish a single sentence."

" 'Winter is advancing,' " Macnaghten read aloud. " 'We find ourselves in a state of siege, with every man in Afghanistan arming against us. We have little food and no forage left, and our water and communications have been cut off. Our animals are starving, and great numbers of our troops are sick or wounded. We have no strength left to attack even armed civilians, and none to defend ourselves. Worse, we have no hope of relief from any quarter.' "

He raised his head. "All this is true," he said sourly, "but it is largely his fault."

" 'As no further military action can be taken,' " he continued, his eyes on the letter, " 'you *must* come to an agreement with the enemy for our withdrawal to India. Honorable terms are better for our government than our being destroyed here.'

"*Honorable terms? Withdraw to India!*" Macnaghten refolded the letter and threw it onto the table. "That is exactly what Elphinstone and Shelton have both wanted all along."

He raised his head and looked cheerlessly at his three companions. "Gentlemen," he said, "our army, even our most senior officers, have given in to fear. I have done all I can to encourage this flaccid force to do its duty, but I can no longer hope for a single successful military action on our part. I must now follow a course that will bring utter ruin and disgrace upon us. Tomorrow morning I shall ask for an audience with Akbar Khan.

"I can tell you this, Lamb," he added sorrowfully, "all our reputations are forfeit now. History will not treat us kindly."

The front door banged open. Voices cried out for assistance. Sir

William arrived in the passage in time to see his deathly pale wife being carried into the house.

THAT NIGHT as she prepared for bed, Mariana did not wish to recite the durood. All she wanted was to draw the covers over her head and shut out Fitzgerald's begging eyes and the horrors she had seen, but Munshi Sahib had told her that self-discipline was the key to proper living.

"Weakness," he had said mildly, "comes from lack of attention. A man who rushes here and there, ignoring his duty and his promises, forgetting the needs of others and obeying the selfish demands of his own heart, will never find peace."

Munshi Sahib had found peace. She saw it in every gesture he made, every word he uttered. In the teeth of this murderous time, in the cold, with almost no water and little to eat, he had never failed to maintain his usual, unruffled calm.

Had he or Haji Khan, she wondered, ever given in to passion or panic? Had Shaikh Waliullah or Safiya Sultana? Had Hassan?

She knew the durood by heart, so there was no need to keep her lamp burning. She blew it out, and lay down.

"You must always recite a durood while sitting," Munshi Sahib had told her. "Otherwise, you may fall asleep before you have finished."

But she was too cold and tired to sit up. She tucked her quilts around her, and began to recite.

Her eyes began to close at the seventh repetition. At the ninth, she felt her breathing deepen.

Only two more . . .

As she began the eleventh repetition, a picture unfolded in her mind's eye of a desert landscape. It lay, wide open, before her, its rolling surface as white as snow. Ahead of her, a full moon hung in the eastern sky, its silver light falling upon the ground, illuminating the path she was to take.

She must go forward, toward the beckoning moon, for joy lay somewhere ahead.

She was not alone. Camel bells chinked beside and behind her, revealing the presence of invisible others, but in her waking dream she did not turn her head to look at them.

Following the moon's path, she walked straight ahead, her feet sinking into the sand. Joy filled her heart, and lightened her steps.

Yes, she thought drowsily as she drifted into sleep, that was the message of Haji Khan's durood: for those who practiced these recitations, even the worst of times could not entirely erase hope, or the beauty of dreams.

What a pity that Munshi Sahib, the great interpreter of visions, had been taken away to the city....

Chapter 21

December 23, 1841

As he followed Yar Mohammad and the borrowed donkey along the frozen Kohistan Road, Nur Rahman glanced nervously through his peephole at the crowd of horsemen and foot travelers around him.

On previous occasions, he had hummed to himself as he hurried toward the city to rejoin his dear old Munshi Sahib, whose health was improving a little each day. But on this morning, the atmosphere on the road had changed. His plan to fetch chickens, turnips, and round red pumpkins faded, engulfed by a steady stream of men who poured out of the city and over the Pul-e-Khishti bridge, all of them traveling north.

What news had sent them from their homes on this cold day, their faces hard and intent, speaking little as they moved, alone or in groups, in the direction of the British cantonment?

Nur Rahman wished he were already at Haji Khan's house, boiling water in the samovar for Munshi Sahib's tea, instead of on the open highway.

"I do not like your boots," he said tensely to his shrouded companion. "People will see that they are foreign."

"Never mind them," the English lady replied sharply. "Tell Yar

Mohammad not to walk so quickly. I can hardly see out of this chaderi as it is. I am certain to fall on this slippery road."

For the past four days, every time he had seen the Englishwoman, she had pestered him to take her to visit Munshi Sahib and Haji Khan. For four days he had fended her off, using every excuse he could find, but she had won in the end. Now, forced to bring her to the city, he sweated beneath his disguise.

The air was clear. A bitter wind rattled the branches of the trees along the road. Travelers of all nationalities were, of course, to be seen, but the people Nur Rahman feared were his fellow Pashtuns, who streamed past him by the hundreds.

For months, Nur Rahman had been afraid of discovery by Painda Gul's Pashtun relatives, but in the presence of these warriors, he felt a shiver of real terror. Who knew what horrors their long knives might inflict on him if they discovered he had been buying food and carrying it to their enemies?

A tall man with a skullcap and a long beard turned to his companions as they strode by. "Why has Sirdar Akbar Khan waited so long to make his move?" he asked in Pushto.

A second man shrugged. "He wished to test the infidel Englishman's honor one final time."

A third spat onto the ice at his feet. "What need is there for tests? These English are all liars. I say Macnaghten should have been killed months ago."

Nur Rahman turned to the Englishwoman. She, who spoke only Farsi, could not have understood those words. "Hurry," he whispered urgently, reaching out a damp hand. "We must *hurry*."

NO ONE had even glanced at them, but still Mariana bent her head and pulled her chaderi closer over her chest. There was no point in adding to Nur Rahman's agitation.

She had lengthened her steps when he urged her to walk faster, but for all his anxiety, and in spite of the armed men who strode past them or clattered by on horses, she felt safer on the Kohistan Road than she did within the ramparts of the British garrison.

Here, only a thousand yards from the cantonment, with its frightened population and starving animals, the landscape looked calm and prosperous, and the people robust and healthy. Judging from the bounty that Nur Rahman brought from the city on his borrowed donkey, the markets must be full of lovely, fresh food.

Cold rose through the thin soles of her boots, causing her feet to ache, but no amount of discomfort could reduce her excitement.

She had wanted for so long to make this short, thrilling journey....

After breakfast, claiming a headache, she had pretended to go and lie down, and then had escaped the house. Poor Aunt Claire, who was none too well herself, was unlikely to investigate that story, and in any case, Mariana would return well before lunch. Then she would need only to tiptoe silently past Aunt Claire's bedroom, hide her chaderi, and climb into bed.

Her heart lifted. Soon she would buy fresh food for her family. Even better, she would meet her long-absent Munshi Sahib and Haji Khan *at the same time*.

She had never realized that the two men were such good friends.

She breathed in the clean air, grateful for Nur Rahman's regular visits to the beleaguered cantonment, for the two wise men who would soon offer her their guidance, and for her beautiful, saving dream. That otherworldly vision had offered her something she badly needed in this time of deprivation and suffering: hope of a future far from the bleak cantonment, a road to take, and peace at the end of the journey.

Haji Khan, it seemed, had chosen the correct roll of paper, after all.

Each night, before she slept, she relived her dream, imagining rolling desert, silence broken only by the chink of camel bells, and a lamplike moon hanging in the eastern sky.

It seemed impossible that she had not yet described it to Munshi Sahib. What a great moment it would be, when she presented her vision to him and Haji Khan together!

Of course Nur Rahman had already told her that the old man might still be too unwell to speak to her. "His breathing is not good," he had said, as they set off from the cantonment, Yar Mohammad leading the donkey, Mariana and Nur Rahman following behind. "He needs me at his side every moment, to give him hot drinks and put heated bricks by his feet."

Haji Khan, too, was a powerful man. Given the choice, even if her munshi were not there, Mariana would be a daily visitor to that dark, perfumed chamber near the Char Chatta Bazaar. Everything about the room—the respectful silence of Haji Khan's followers, his caged songbird, even the intricate embroidery of his wall hangings—suggested secrets to be uncovered, languages to be studied, and a way of living to be tried.

Everything about him and his house reminded her of Hassan.

She fingered the gold medallion under her bodice. He must have had his reasons for sending it to her, but whatever they were, they had not prevented him from abandoning her in a time of desperate need.

She should never have wasted her time hoping, or writing those letters. . . .

She frowned at the passing crowd. It was true that armed men filled the road to the cantonment, but how enticingly Kabul beckoned from beyond the river, its smoke rising lazily on the breeze, its markets full of root vegetables, pomegranates, and carefully preserved grapes. . . .

A body of Pashtun horsemen clattered toward them. Their leader, an elderly gray-bearded man with a wolflike face, sat loosely on a bay stallion, one hand holding his horse's reins, the other resting on his knee.

He might have felt Mariana's gaze, for he turned in his saddle and glanced thoughtfully at her, his eyes resting on her riding boots. A moment later, he spoke softly to his horse and trotted on.

"Hurry, Khanum," Nur Rahman urged.

Perhaps, she thought as she quickened her steps, something would come of Sir William's latest negotiations with Akbar Khan. From her uncle's vague references the previous evening, it seemed that a new offer had come from that quarter. With luck, all would be settled by the evening, and within a week or two they would be on their way back to India.

AS MARIANA was making her way toward the city, her uncle stood in Lady Sale's dining room, watching Sir William Macnaghten gather up his papers.

"I am concerned about this meeting of yours, sir," he said carefully. "I am suspicious of Akbar Khan's sudden change of heart."

Macnaghten looked as if he had not slept for a week. "You may be right, Lamb," he said wearily, "but in these past ten days I have come to my wits' end."

"I cannot fathom," pressed Adrian Lamb, "why, after flatly refusing to give us either amnesty or provisions for our departure, he has suddenly offered us so many concessions. And, if I may be direct, sir, *you* have intrigued against *him* in the past few days. Is it possible, sir, that—"

Macnaghten gestured impatiently. "My dear Lamb, what else should I do in this situation? The only way to gain advantage now is to sow dissension between the tribes. Besides, I have done no more than offer cash payments to the Durranis and Ghilzais in exchange for abandonment of Akbar's cause."

"But we have no hand to play, sir." Adrian Lamb's voice rose. "Why has Akbar offered to supply us with food until next spring? Why has he promised to rule Afghanistan *together* with Shah Shuja, his enemy? Even more puzzling, why has he offered to kill Aminullah Khan, his ally and friend, the man who arranged for Burnes's murder? I fear that Akbar may not think it beneath his honor to trick you. After all, these people have very different ideas of—"

Macnaghten raised a silencing hand. "Perhaps the chiefs I approached have taken the bait, and joined us. Perhaps that is why he has proposed such favorable terms." He smiled. "Although I found it quite disgusting, I was pleased to be offered Aminullah Khan's head on a platter. I refused, of course, but I must say it would have given me great pleasure to see that palsied old ruffian dead." He sighed. "I suppose arresting him will have to be sufficient for now."

Adrian put out a pleading hand "Akbar Khan's offer amounts to a betrayal of the Afghan people, sir. *They* clearly do not want Shah Shuja to remain on the throne. I cannot believe they will accept Akbar as a paid employee of *our* government. And why should they tolerate our presence here for the rest of the winter?"

"He has made us an offer," Macnaghten said patiently, "and now I must investigate it. For us to remain here for a few months, fully provisioned, then leave in the spring with our heads high, would be the best possible ending to this story.

"Do you remember, Lamb," he added wistfully, "how great our dreams were for this country?"

Adrian Lamb nodded. "I remember, sir."

"I shall take Lawrence, Trevor, and Mackenzie with me," Macnaghten continued, as they walked to his waiting horse. "And of course I shall have a cavalry escort, and Shelton's two regiments are ready to storm Aminullah Khan's fort and arrest him.

"I shall enjoy that," he added as he mounted his horse. "Well, good-bye, then, Lamb. With luck, you shall see me again in an hour or two. And if I should not return," he added quietly, "look after my wife, will you?"

WHEN MACNAGHTEN and the three captains met by the cantonment gate, there was no sign of a cavalry escort, only a few Residency guards hugging themselves against the cold.

Macnaghten frowned. "Where is everyone else? Where are Shelton's regiments?"

"They are not yet ready, sir," replied Captain Mackenzie. "The cavalry also did not parade in time, but they should be here soon."

"Soon is not good enough. I cannot afford to be late."

Macnaghten spurred his horse unkindly, and started for the open gate, causing the other officers to trot hastily after him. "This," he said darkly, "is the same slackness I have had to endure since the very start of the outbreak."

"And are you certain, sir," asked one of the three accompanying captains, "that there is no risk of treachery from Akbar Khan?"

"Of *course* there is risk, Lawrence," Macnaghten snapped, "but what can I do? The general will not fight, nor will the brigadier. No help is to be expected from any quarter. For six weeks our enemies have visited every possible inconvenience and deprivation upon us. They have been playing with us, and have not fulfilled any of their promises, but nevertheless, I must take this final chance.

"I would rather risk a hundred deaths, Lawrence," he declared, "than suffer the disgrace we all must endure if we retreat from Afghanistan with dishonor."

A large carpet had been spread over the snow on sloping ground out of the wind. An unclean crowd of silent tribesmen stood ranged about it in a half circle. Among them six or seven chiefs on horseback spoke to one another.

"Akbar Khan seemed quite pleased with the pair of pistols I sent him last week," Macnaghten remarked, as he and the three other officers approached the waiting Afghans. "Let us hope they have given him reason to be kindly disposed toward us."

After formal greetings had been exchanged, all the men dismounted, and a smiling Macnaghten was handed onto the carpet.

Behind him, one of the captains had refused to sit down. Instead, he crouched on one knee, watching tensely as the chiefs and the host of other, wilder onlookers crowded closer and closer.

"Sit down, Lawrence," hissed Captain Trevor, "and take your hand from your sword. You are making it appear that we don't trust them."

Ignoring this exchange, Sirdar Akbar Khan, the handsome eldest son of Dost Mohammad, leaned comfortably on a large bolster and gazed with lustrous brown eyes upon the Englishman beside him.

"I must ask you, Macnaghten," he said gently, "if you are quite ready to carry into effect the proposition we have offered you."

The Envoy smiled easily. "Why not?"

The sirdar smiled approvingly in return. "Come, then," he said, moving to rise, "I must take you to Aminullah Khan's fort."

"But why?" Macnaghten stiffened against his bolster. "I am not yet ready to arrest him. My regiments have not arrived."

The sirdar, his beautiful eyes on the Envoy's, did not reply. The tribesmen edged closer.

"It is a trap, sir!" Lawrence reached for his sword.

Understanding, Macnaghten scrambled to his feet.

His horse waited at the edge of the crowd. He started toward it, but Akbar Khan came up behind him and caught him by both arms.

"I cannot allow you to return to your cantonment," he said politely.

"Trevor, Lawrence, Mackenzie!" The Envoy's frightened voice barely carried as far as the trio of officers behind him, but it was too late.

Akbar's face had changed. "*Begeer! Begeer!* Seize them!" he cried, his features distorted, his voice tight and shrill.

In an instant the crowd of tattered onlookers shed its silence.

With a high triumphant yell, the mob closed in on the four Englishmen. Many hands gripped Sir William Macnaghten, and held him motionless. Jostling tribesmen snatched away the British officers' weapons, and pinned their arms behind their backs.

Caught in the storm, all but one of Macnaghten's native escort pushed their way through the struggling crowd and bolted, headlong, from the scene. The remaining man, a mustachioed Rajput sepoy, lunged toward Macnaghten, but before he had reached the Envoy's side, a sword sliced through the back of his neck. He dropped, gurgling, to his knees, his half-severed head lolling to one side, but a single dreadful wound was not enough to satisfy the Sirdar's warriors. Knives raised, they fell on him. While he still breathed, they hacked his limbs, one by one, from his body.

Macnaghten sagged against his captors, his face gray with shock, his spectacles askew. His top hat lay on its side at his feet. He opened his mouth to speak, but whatever he said was lost in the din around him.

Someone shouted orders. The three British captains were frog-marched to a group of waiting horses, and forced to mount pillion behind three of the chiefs.

Thwarted by the loss of their quarry, the mob surged toward the horses, swords and knives in hand. "Do not spare the accursed!" they screamed, slicing with their knives at the three captains, who now clung to the chiefs for protection. "Kill the infidels! Shed their blood! Do not let them escape!"

As they worked to free themselves and their captives from the crowd, the three chiefs turned upon their own people. "Leave them," they shouted, laying about them with heavy swords, causing several men to stagger backward, spurting blood. "Leave our hostages to us!"

The three horses surged to a gallop. A moment later, Captain Trevor lost his grip on his captor and fell, shoulder-first, onto the icy ground. In an instant, a dozen members of the pursuing mob stood over his prone body, long knives rising and falling.

Behind them, Akbar Khan and a stocky, richly dressed man man-handled Macnaghten down the slope toward the river, so forcefully that the Envoy's feet dragged behind him like those of a condemned man.

He was indeed condemned. As Akbar's chiefs galloped away with the two surviving captains, Macnaghten's last, helpless cry followed them across the snow.

"*Az barae Khuda!* For God's sake!" he screamed hoarsely, as the yelling crowd closed in.

"SOMETHING IS wrong," Nur Rahman said sharply. He turned and stared nervously behind him. "Something has happened there," he added, pointing north, along the road. "I can feel it."

Mariana frowned. The last of the stream of tribesmen had passed them only a moment earlier, thin shawls billowing in the icy breeze. Beyond the river and its brick bridge, the busy city beckoned.

In no time, the three of them would be in the labyrinthine alleys of Kabul, with its cobbled streets and tempting markets, on their way to Haji Khan's house.

"What do you mean?" she said irritably, turning to look. "Why must you always—"

Nur Rahman gasped aloud. "They are coming back," he cried, pointing. "Look! The fighters are returning!"

A hand to her eyes, Mariana peered into the distance, but all she saw was a thick, advancing crowd of men, whose raised voices proclaimed important, unintelligible news.

They seemed to take up the whole road. Their shouting echoed across the flat valley.

Other travelers had also seen them. An old man on a mule paused uncertainly, as if waiting for instructions. A pair of Uighur tribesmen with goatee beards were already coaxing their horses into the knee-deep snow at the side of the road.

"I see them coming," Mariana agreed, "but what have they to do with us?"

Yar Mohammad, too, had stopped. He, too, looked back, a hand on the donkey's neck.

Nur Rahman looked rapidly from side to side, as if he were seeking an escape route. "We must not enter the city," he said decisively. "There is no telling what will happen there once the crowd returns. And we must not turn back to the cantonment, for they have blocked the way."

"No!" Mariana protested. "We must go on. The city is right here, in front of us, and Haji Khan's house is not far from the gate. We'll be there long before the crowd arrives. I need a chicken for my aunt's soup," she added plaintively, "and you yourself said that Munshi Sahib needs your company."

She sighed impatiently. What was the matter with the boy? Did he have some mad reason to prevent her from seeing her munshi?

Aunt Claire had especially wished for grapes. . . .

"Hurry," Nur Rahman shouted. "There is no time!"

Ignoring the stares of their fellow travelers, he lifted the skirts of his chaderi and sprinted forward, toward Yar Mohammad and the donkey. The animal's reins in one hand, and Yar Mohammad's sleeve in the other, he tugged them both into the snow, gesturing for Mariana to follow.

The man on the mule, the Uighurs, and a family whose half-dozen women and children had been stuffed onto four camels, had also left the road. All of them waited, their eyes on the advancing crowd.

"Turn away," Nur Rahman ordered sharply. "Do not look."

Snow had packed itself into the tops of Mariana's boots and drenched her thin cotton trousers and the hem of her chaderi. Fearful of the real terror in Nur Rahman's voice, she turned from the road, her hands to her ears.

The crowd was upon them. Its collective voice resembled the din made by the river of men that had passed Haji Khan's door on the morning of Alexander Burnes's death.

Was this new mob as murderous as that one? Unable to stop herself, Mariana turned to look.

Packed shoulder to shoulder, a column of several thousand men advanced toward them, filling the roadway, shouting unintelligibly and firing weapons into the air.

She glanced at Nur Rahman, and saw that his chaderi was trembling, as if his whole body were shaking. The old man steered his mule farther off the road. Only Yar Mohammad showed no sign of worry. He stood straight, his bony face impassive, the donkey's reins dangling from his fingers, as the mob flowed toward them, faces contorted with a kind of joy, light gleaming on the blades of their long knives.

Mariana searched about her, but there was nowhere to hide, only an expanse of dirty snow, and leafless trees full of whistling wind.

What was that, impaled on a long stick above the heads of the mob? Was it really a top hat, its brim half torn off? And what was that that followed the hat, also on a stick? It looked like a cannonball, only—

By the time Mariana understood what it was, there was no time to turn away, or even to lift the face-covering flap of her chaderi. There was only time to bend over and vomit helplessly into the unclean snow at her feet.

"But," Adrian Lamb argued later that afternoon, "General Elphinstone is telling everyone that Sir William and his companions have been removed to the city for further negotiations."

The ashen-faced subaltern who stood before Mariana's uncle was no more than a boy. He shook his head. "No, sir," he said mournfully, "Akbar and Aminullah Khan have murdered Sir William and Captain Trevor, and have taken Lawrence and Mackenzie away. They have already paraded Sir William's head and limbs in the city. His torso is now hanging from a meat hook in the Char Chatta Bazaar. I heard this from an irregular native cavalryman whose brother-in-law saw it all.

"They are massing at the Pul-e-Khishti now, waiting for our counter-attack," he added.

Adrian Lamb exchanged a glance with his assistant, and then got to his feet. "Thank you, Harris," he said grimly, "I am glad you came to me at once. And now, if anyone needs me, I shall be conferring with General Elphinstone and Brigadier Shelton."

Twenty minutes later he and Brigadier Shelton stood over the bed where General Elphinstone lay bundled and shivering. Faint shouts and thudding of musket fire floated in through the closed bedroom shutters.

"Are you telling me," Adrian Lamb inquired tightly, shifting his gaze from the general to his second-in-command, "that there is to be *no* retaliatory attack upon the city, even now, after Sir William's revolting, disgraceful murder?"

"We are," barked Shelton.

"And we are to sit on our heels and do nothing, even with our troops sufficiently enraged to storm and carry the city of Kabul and arrest Akbar and Aminullah?"

"We are hopelessly outnumbered," the general wheezed from his bed. "It is only by sheerest luck that we have so far managed to escape a devastating attack by thousands of yelling tribesmen.

"Surely," he added, pointing a trembling finger toward the window, "you can hear the horrible din they are raising even now outside the city walls. I understand they are massed near the Pul-e-Khishti, screaming and firing into the air. They may storm our gates at any moment."

Mariana's uncle let out a bitter sigh. "I have it on good authority," he said evenly, "that the noise we are hearing is in preparation for an expected attack by *us* on *them*."

The general coughed weakly.

The brigadier hunched his bony shoulders. "May I ask, Lamb, who gave *you*, a mere intelligence man, the right to come into this room and criticize the chief military officers of this cantonment?"

"No one *gave* me the right, Brigadier," Adrian Lamb said grimly. "It was there for the taking."

IT WAS Christmas.

Mariana tried not to fidget as she sat beside her aunt's bed. "Of course you are getting better, Aunt Claire," she insisted, for the third time that afternoon.

"I do not know, my dear," her aunt replied faintly. "Sometimes I wonder if I shall ever see England again."

Unable to argue, Mariana could only reach out and pat her wrinkled hand.

Since her frightening but safe return to the cantonment, she had paid three condolence visits to Lady Sale's house, but had not yet seen the newly widowed Lady Macnaghten, who was still secluded in her bedroom. That morning, while sounds of painful grief emanated from the far end of the house, Mariana had sat in the icy drawing room with Lady Sale and a few other officers' wives, help-less to offer comfort, wondering about her own future.

Swathed in shawls and straight of back, Lady Sale had talked of the weather, her voice raised over Lady Macnaghten's muffled sob-bing, as if she could drive the shock and sorrow from the house by simple force of personality.

With Sir William dead, Eldred Pottinger, the most sensible of the civil officers, had been made temporary Envoy, but as everyone re-marked, his appointment would do no good as long as the senior army officers were unable to act.

If only General Sale were here with his 1st Brigade, and not ninety miles away in Jalalabad, everything would be different. Mariana ran a hand over her face. Against her pillows, Aunt Claire yawned and closed her eyes.

Their own household was also suffering. Besides Aunt Claire, who seemed to have collapsed from cold and anxiety, several of the servants, including Uncle Adrian's old Adil, had ugly-sounding coughs. They had enough food in the house, thanks to Nur Rahman's forays to the city bazaars, but there was barely any water, and it was diffi-cult, even with a roaring fire, to bring the temperature more than eight degrees above freezing in any of the rooms.

None of Mariana's clothes had been washed for weeks. She could not remember when she had last bathed.

While Aunt Claire snored gently, Mariana stared into space, her thoughts racing.

If Hassan had come to Kabul instead of divorcing or abandon-ing her, she and her family would be in Lahore by now. If Harry Fitzgerald were not exhausted from doing his duty while wounded, he would at least try to save them. He had said as much himself.

But the harsh truth was that no help was on the way, and time was running out.

If they were to escape from here, they must rely upon themselves.

Excluding Uncle Adrian, who would certainly insist upon remain-ing at his post, the household with all its servants numbered twenty-two souls. How could such a large group of foreigners slip past the Ghilzai tribesmen who now dominated the roads, the hills, and all the surrounding forts?

Except for the sweepers who hastily threw the picked bones of the dead animals outside, no one dared venture beyond the cantonment gates. Anyone in uniform who stepped more than a few yards from the gate was brought down instantly by a well-aimed musket shot.

Even the unarmed and scarecrow-thin camp followers who wandered unwisely outside the walls were robbed, beaten, and left to die.

Akbar Khan's sharp-shooting allies, it seemed, were watching them day and night.

Besides Charles Mott's mad proposal that she ask an enemy chief for asylum, she could think of only one plan. Undisturbed by the fighting around the cantonment, the kafilas of the nomadic Pashtoon tribes were still passing by on their way to Butkhak and the passes to India, bringing their trading goods, their herds, and their camels.

According to Nur Rahman, many were traveling by the Lataband Pass, where people made wishes and tied rags to the bushes for luck.

Not all of those nomads would be Ghilzais.

If Mariana could manage disguises for everyone in the household, including the toothless sweeperess and the cross-eyed woman who polished Aunt Claire's silver, it might be possible to persuade a family of nomads to carry them to the Punjab.

But could she really wave down a moving caravan in full view of passing travelers, then bargain with its leader through the hole in her chaderi, revealing her identity as she did so? And even if she did persuade a kafila of non-Ghilzais to take them, how could she buy a safe passage for so many people, with all her money spent on Nur Rahman's forays to the city?

Uncle Adrian kept no hoard of gold coins. Aunt Claire's pearls would scarcely be enough.

Mariana bent and laid her forehead on the edge of her aunt's bed. Perhaps Charles's plan was not as mad as she had thought. After all, she herself had given asylum to Nur Rahman. But to throw her family on the mercy of an enemy seemed far too desperate a gamble.

Every morning for weeks she had awoken with the same tightening in her middle, the same heavy feeling in her temples. Fear and loss surrounded her, draining her strength. She could not remember feeling so tired.

Three years ago, she had relished danger. She had embarked on one adventure after another, full of hope—that she was doing the right thing, that she would be seen as a hero. Each of her actions— her rescue of Saboor from the neglectful old Maharajah, her mistaken marriage to Hassan, even that mad mission to fetch Hassan home, wounded, from the house with the yellow door—had all begun in the hope of recognition and a bright future.

But even her most daring and successful adventures had been marred by complications and bad results—pursuit by soldiers, courtiers, and child thieves; ostracism by her own people; fear and mistrust; and, in the end, her loss of Hassan.

Now, after so many failures, how could she face this new, elemental danger? Exhausted, dirty, and cold, with a houseful of unhealthy people, how could she trust herself? How could she even imagine success?

All she wanted was rest, and someone to tell her what to do.

There was no space in her whirling head for the question that had tugged at her in Haji Khan's house. All that now remained of those visits to the city were a little roll of paper and a single lovely vision of an unknown desert and a full, beckoning moon.

She pushed herself to her feet, and bent down to kiss Aunt Claire's wrinkled cheek. It was nearly time for dinner, but there was something she must do first.

She had not seen Fitzgerald since her visit to the hospital. In the five days since his release, he had used every ounce of his energy to shore up the cantonment defenses. There had been no time for social calls.

Of course she had sent him a regular share of Nur Rahman's bounty, but all the same, she felt she had neglected him.

Now it was Christmas Day.

There was just enough time before dinner to deliver a few nuts and raisins to his quarters. If she dropped them off herself, that might pass for attentiveness. . . .

A short while later she made her way through the snowy darkness to the long building that housed the surviving junior officers, then stood waiting, her breath white in the moonlight, for Fitzgerald's orderly to answer her knock.

Instead, his own voice came from within.

"It is Mariana Givens," she said through the door.

The bolt moved.

"Come in, Miss Givens." Fitzgerald bowed a little stiffly, and stood aside to let her in, as an Indian manservant slipped past her and out of the room.

For a lady to enter an officer's private quarters without another lady's chaperoning presence would be a grave breach of proper behavior, and an unnecessary encouragement to the officer in question.

Mariana stepped inside. "I have brought you something," she began, then stopped short inside the doorway.

Well aware that her own unwashed appearance left much to be desired, she still had not expected what she saw.

Fitzgerald had become a shadow in the days since she had last seen him, a shuffling caricature of himself. His handsome gunner's uniform now hung in loose folds on his frame. His hair fell, ragged and uncut, below his ears. The bones stood out in his face.

His left arm had been strapped to his chest with a filthy bandage. A pair of woolen shawls lay on his shoulders.

But most of all, it was his eyes, hollow and intense, that caught her attention.

"A Christmas visit." He smiled and waved his good hand toward a cane chair near the fire. "How good of you to come.

"We have moved all the guns for the fourth time," he volunteered, as she handed him her gift and sat down. "The Afghans had become too used to our artillery positions. We mean to surprise them tomorrow morning."

Mariana nodded, not trusting her voice.

He looked like a man on the verge of madness or death.

An open book lay upside down on a small table next to her. As he dragged a second chair toward the little fire, she picked it up, and found it open to "Hohenlinden" by Robert Campbell. She glanced at the last stanza.

Ah! Few shall part where many meet!
The snow shall be their winding-sheet;
And every turf beneath their feet
Shall be a soldier's sepulchre.

Hungry, cold, and in pain, alone in his quarters, Fitzgerald had been trying to entertain himself, and this was what he had been reading.

Tears flooded her eyes.

What would happen to them all?

The long, black-clad funeral procession that she had seen at Butkhak so many months before rose again in her mind's eye—the vision that Munshi Sahib, the great interpreter of dreams, had never explained.

When she begged him to tell her its meaning, he had only quoted the Qur'an.

She closed the book, and tried to smile at Fitzgerald.

As if he read her thoughts, Fitzgerald cleared his throat and bent forward in his chair. "Miss Givens," he said hoarsely, wincing a little as he tried to reach toward her, "I know you cannot stay long, but since you are here, I have something to ask you."

She knew what was coming. She waited for it, her hands clasped around the book in her lap.

"I wonder if you recall a promise you made to me before the battle of Bibi Mahro."

His hollow gaze was candid, but it held something else she could hardly bear to see: hope.

"I believe," he added, offering her a ghost of his old crooked, knowing smile, "that the battle ended some weeks ago."

He leaned forward and peered attentively into her face.

He knew she did not love him.

She dropped her eyes. What good would a refusal do either of them? Except for a bag of nuts and raisins, she had nothing to offer this good man.

She raised her chin and regarded her ragged lieutenant. "Yes," she replied. "I will marry you."

"Thank you." Fitzgerald nodded seriously, as if she had done him a service, then held out his good hand for her to take.

She smiled grimly as she trudged back to her quarters, thinking of the two people who would most have enjoyed that moment.

Unfortunately neither Aunt Claire nor Lady Macnaghten was able to celebrate it.

Chapter 29

December 26, 1841

The following morning, as Mariana huddled alone before the sitting room fire, wondering whether she should tell Aunt Claire of her engagement or keep it to herself, someone knocked on the door.

"Your Munshi Sahib has come," called Dittoo's muffled voice.

Mariana jumped to her feet.

A moment later, supported by a solicitous Nur Rahman, the old man stood in front of her, wrapped incongruously in a yellow satin rezai, his golden qaraquli hat pulled low on his forehead.

He seemed to have grown smaller since she had seen him last.

She pointed to the straight-backed chair she had been sitting on. "Please sit down, Munshi Sahib."

Why on earth, she wondered, as he shuffled over to the fire and lowered himself onto the chair, had he left his bed in this weather to come all the way from the city to visit her?

He looked like a wizened king, with his golden rezai, and the boy crouched at his feet, pressing his legs rhythmically with both hands. His shallow coughing filled the little room.

It was the first time he had sat down in Mariana's presence.

"I have come, Bibi," he wheezed, "to learn whether Haji Khan's durood has borne fruit. Have you seen, heard, or smelled anything unusual while you were reciting?"

She nodded, remembering her vision for the first time in days.

"And may I know what you have seen?"

Looking into his calm, rheumy eyes, she forgot her fears and misery. She even forgot her horrid breakfast of black tea and dried mulberries.

Leaving out no detail, she described the rolling desert landscape of her dream, the camel bells signaling the presence of other travelers, the fresh breeze and the heavy, fecund moon that had seemed to promise her every happiness.

She told him of the peace she felt even now, as she spoke of it.

"But what does it mean, Munshi Sahib?" she asked, leaning toward him, her kingly little interpreter of dreams. "Does it contain the answer to the question I brought to Haji Khan three months ago?"

He regarded her for a moment, then signaled to Nur Rahman that he wanted to rise.

"It means, Bibi," he said mildly, as he prepared to leave her, "that you should not have made the promise that you made yesterday."

His words fell on her like a blow. "Why?" she breathed.

"You will see for yourself," he replied.

Then, wrapped in his golden quilt, he made his dignified way to the door.

A HUNDRED miles away, Hassan and Zulmai stopped to water their animals at the silver river that wound toward them between flat, stony banks.

Ghulam Ali bowed his muffled head against the wind and turned to signal to the animal drivers that straggled behind them.

Each morning for the past ten days, before the sun appeared over the tops of the mountains, the travelers had offered their prayers on the cold ground and taken a few swallows of water before folding their tents and starting off.

Each day they had made between eight and ten miles.

Today, having traversed four miles of rough terrain along a vague track, every member of the kafila, including Ghulam Ali, was yawning and famished.

A little distance away, Hassan, dressed in embroidered sheepskins and an Afghan-style turban, clucked solicitously as he guided his silver mare down a shale slope to the river's edge, while the two dozen

Turi tribesmen they had recruited from local villages stepped forward to fetch water for their tea.

They had come a long way from Peshawar, but even so, they had covered only half of the distance to Kabul, and the worst part of their journey still lay ahead.

Hurrying had been impossible. Throughout the long, uncomfortable journey from Kohat to Thal, as they struggled over bare, uneven ground cut by deep ravines, Hassan had worn a concentrated look, as if he had put everything but this one, vital journey out of his mind.

Near Hangu they had met a rich caravan from the north, bringing horses with thick coats, and a hundred big Bukhara camels loaded with Russian fabric, dried apricots, and pistachio nuts.

The leader of the caravan had shrugged when Hassan asked him for news of Shah Shuja and the British.

"The British are finished," he said. "Their main water supply was cut off long ago. Akbar Khan and his men have stopped them from buying food from the villages. For weeks now, anyone who strays more than a few yards from their cantonment has been shot.

"Many of their officers have been killed, including their two leaders. As for Shah Shuja," the man added, "it is only a matter of time before he, too, dies."

Hassan's fist had opened and closed on his knee. "Have the British talked of leaving Kabul?"

The leader smiled. "Talk is all they do. These British do not fight. They cower, starving, behind their walls, sending message after message to Sirdar Akbar Khan. But he will not easily let them go after they knocked his father from the throne."

At Thal, Hassan and Zulmai had turned northwest, and started up the long, fertile Kurrum River valley, passing nomad family groups bringing their flocks down from the north, their camels festooned with cooking pots, live chickens, and tent hangings.

Now, as they let the animals drink, a group of such nomads walked by with their swaying camels, whose ankle bells chinked with every step.

"Ho," called the headman, "where are you going?"

"To Kabul," Hassan replied.

"What takes you to Kabul in this bitter weather," he asked, "when the scent of blood is in the air?"

"Family business," Hassan replied shortly.

The headman looked him over. "For all your Afghan dress," he observed, "I see that you are Indian. Keep in mind that death awaits the infidel British and their Indian lackeys."

When Hassan did not answer him, the headman shrugged and continued on his way.

The valley floor in front of them rose and fell in waves, with steep ascents and sudden descents. The road ahead had been cut into steep, curving hillsides in places. In others it ran along the gray shingle of the riverbed, with its ribbon of silver water. At Shinak Kili, distant mountains, now rose-colored, now magenta, frowned from the distance, and groups of villages beckoned, their haze of smoke promising warmth and company.

Ahead of them, a narrow, camel-neck of a road wound its way to the Shuturgarden Pass and the last leg of their journey.

Two days later, hunched against the cold, they followed a frozen riverbed through the high, winding Shuturgarden's most dangerous defile, a claustrophobic six-mile stretch between smooth rock walls so high that sunlight did not reach the stony riverbed below.

Of the pack animals, the stubborn, scrambling yabus fared best on the icy, uneven track. The mules were not as lucky.

"Undo its load!" Hassan shouted, as Ghulam Ali and three other men ran, their shoes slipping, to haul a downed mule to its feet. "See if it has broken its bones!"

The animal had caught a forefoot between the stones, and fallen onto its side, crushing some of the chickens tied to its back. As Ghulam Ali struggled with stiff fingers to release its load, several dead chickens, open boxes of tea leaves, and a stream of cooking oil lay in a messy heap at his feet.

With a wheezing cry, the mule got up, and stood on three legs, a twisted forefoot dangling off the ground.

"Shoot it," Zulmai ordered. "We will eat the dead chickens tonight. The rest of the load, except for the live birds, must be left behind."

This was the rule of the kafila. For each dead pack animal, a load would be abandoned. With each fallen hill pony or mule, something they needed would be lost: quilts, perhaps, or tents, rice, fodder, or tea.

The men would protect their own mounts to the last, and their weapons to the death.

Half the mules were gone. Five had already been shot, and a

stealthy night raid by Ali Khel tribesmen two days before had cost the kafila twelve more, together with most of Hassan's elaborate furnishings.

"I suppose," Hassan offered ruefully that evening, as he and Zulmai ate chicken beside the fire in their tent, "that my stolen furnishings are serving some Afghan family well."

"It is lucky you did not keep your jewels and perfumes with those things," Zulmai replied. "Some tribesman would be wearing them all by now. In any case," he added as he wiped his fingers on the tail of his shirt, "most of your wealth is in that horse of yours."

Later, Hassan tilted his chin toward the ragged escort they had acquired the day before. "These new guards of ours," he murmured, "they are Ghilzais, are they not?"

Zulmai nodded.

"Then they will know what is happening in Kabul."

"Yes, they will. Many of their people will have gone there to fight the British. Shall I ask them for news?"

Hassan shook his head. "They cannot tell me of my family, and I cannot bear to hear them boast of their success."

"WHY ARE you so worried, Saboor?" Safiya Sultana demanded that afternoon, as they rode home from Sialkot in her family's roomy old palanquin. "Your Abba has already gone to fetch Mariam from Kabul. Why are you so afraid?"

She peered into her great-nephew's tear-filled eyes. "Have you had another dream, *jan?*" she asked, over the steady "hah-hah" of the palanquin bearers. "Have you seen something that has frightened you?"

But the child could only make the same sound that he had made for the past hour of their journey home from Sialkot: a small, helpless "o-o-oh" that seemed to come from the depths of his heart.

"I do not know what to do with him," Safiya Sultana confided to her brother after their arrival at Qamar Haveli. "I fear he has seen something too disturbing to speak aloud."

The Shaikh gave her a sharp look. "Allah forbid, is it possible that Mariam has died?"

"I do not believe so. If that were true, Saboor would be suffering even more than he is now."

"Send him to me after he has eaten," the Shaikh offered. "I will give him a verse to recite."

Safiya brightened. "A verse?"

"I am thinking of a small portion of the Qur'an, from Sura Inshirah, *Expansion:*

"So, verily,
With every difficulty
There is relief:
Verily, with every difficulty
There is relief."

His sister nodded.

Later that afternoon, as she sat before a tray of goat's liver, spiced *dal,* and two thick rounds of potato-stuffed bread, Safiya Sultana considered the English girl's plight.

The news trickling down through the passes from Afghanistan worsened each day. The whole country, it seemed, had taken up arms against the British.

Safiya did not know much about Afghan war-making but she knew two things: first, that no Afghan would deliberately shoot a woman in battle, and second, that besieging a fort and starving out its inhabitants was one of their most commonplace strategies.

Her mouth full, she glanced uncomfortably at the loaded dishes before her. Starvation was a fate Safiya Sultana could not bear to imagine.

What then of Mariam? The poor girl must be in a terrible state in that besieged fort. If she were not rescued soon, she might well perish from hunger or cold, or untreated illness.

Safiya looked down at the child who coughed sadly beside her, wrapped in her old brown shawl. It was no surprise that his little face had thinned from anxiety.

It must be terrible to see life, with all its sorrows, as clearly as he did. . . .

She held out a bit of fried bread. "Eat one more bite," she commanded, "and then go downstairs and sit in the sun with your grandfather. He has a verse from the Qur'an Sharif for you to recite. And do not forget," she added, after he swallowed her offering and stood up, "that Inshallah, your Abba will soon be fetching An-nah home."

Saboor's anguished look told her she would have been wiser to say nothing.

As a little maidservant took away the tray, Safiya tried to picture Hassan as he traveled toward Kabul, but having never seen even the great Badshahi Mosque that adorned the western edge of her own walled city, she could not imagine his surroundings, or the circumstances of his journey.

She signaled the little maidservant to bring the ewer and carved copper basin, then held out her greasy right hand and nodded.

She sighed as the girl poured a thin stream of rose-scented water over her hand. As much as she wanted Hassan to forgive his wife and himself, in this emergency no one's feelings mattered.

Downstairs in the family courtyard, Shaikh Waliullah studied the child beside him.

"What have you dreamed, my darling?" he asked. "What have you seen that has frightened you?"

He took the little boy's chin in his hand, his light, pleasant voice at odds with the power of his gaze.

"Stories." Saboor squeezed his eyes shut.

"And are they sad, your stories?"

The soft face crumpled. "They are very sad," the child wailed. "I hate the stories, but they keep coming back."

"Can you tell me what they are?"

Tears smeared Saboor's face. He shook his head.

The old man took his grandchild into his arms, raised his eyes to an upstairs window of the ladies' quarters, and met his sister's worried gaze.

THAT EVENING, Zulmai put his head back and swallowed the last of his tea. "You are wrong, Hassan," he said decisively. "I saw it happen. Yusuf waited too long to kill the boy assassin. Before he pulled the trigger, the child got off a shot and alerted the guards, who fired at both of you." He spread his hands. "How is that your fault?"

"He thought I would shoot." Hassan sighed from his place on the other side of the fire. "But I could not."

Zulmai smiled. "Yusuf knew you would never do it. So did I. No," he concluded, "it was Yusuf's fate to hesitate at that moment, and then to die. My father used to say," he added casually, "that he who takes responsibility for God's work is arrogant, while he who blames it on another man is an idolater."

"I have not told you all of it," Hassan added. From the way he stared into the fire, Ghulam Ali understood that they would never hear the rest of his story.

It had to do with the English lady, then. Otherwise, Hassan would have told it all.

From his vantage point near the tent doorway, Ghulam Ali watched Hassan lift his maimed hand, as if to put it into a pocket in his clothes, then change his mind and drop it onto his knee. "We are traveling too slowly," he said abruptly.

Zulmai leaned over, reached into his saddlebag, and pulled out a brass water pipe. "We will smoke before we sleep," he announced, in the way of a friend who knows not to pry.

He filled the water container half full, then dropped tobacco into the shallow, perforated bowl that rested on its top. He scooped a burning ember from the fire onto a perforated brass dish, and laid that over the tobacco.

The coal glowed as he sucked, his fist clenched around the mouthpiece of the pipe. The water gurgled gently as the smoke entered it, then rose in bubbles to the surface, to make its journey through the mouthpiece.

"Ah." He sighed, blowing out a stream of smoke as he handed the pipe to Hassan. "That is good."

The next day, as they sat before their cooking fire at Khushi, the Place of Delight, he gestured expansively. "This place is beautiful in summer," he offered, ignoring the food freezing on his plate. "Everything is green and beautiful here, and the grapes are the sweetest you ever tasted. Khushi is a paradise in the desert."

"Beautiful it may be," Hassan replied shortly, "but it will not keep me here. I am going on alone. I can no longer bear to travel at this slow pace."

"Not alone, and not yet." Zulmai shook his head. "You will start after we cross the Logar River, and you will take two of our best-mounted guards. Your horse will easily carry you to Kabul from there, if you start before dawn and stop only to offer your prayers. We will meet in Kabul, at the Pul-e-Khishti bridge, three days after you leave."

Chapter 30

January 2, 1842

I *know* I agreed to do this," Mariana said wearily, two days later, her voice muffled by her chaderi. "It is just that I'm not—"

"There is no other way," Nur Rahman insisted. "You must do it now."

Together, they peered north along the Kohistan Road. In the distance, five figures on horseback picked their way toward them, down the nearer Bibi Mahro hill.

"I told you they would not stay in the village for long." Nur Rahman lifted the flap of his chaderi from his face. "The old man with the gray beard is the one you must ask for panah," he said. "He will be riding in front."

"Surely there is another solution," she murmured. "Surely, if we go back to the cantonment, we can think of a better plan."

The boy shook his head forcefully. "There is no better plan. You must act today, before it is too late."

Desperate to find a way out of Kabul, Mariana had asked Nur Rahman to disguise her family and servants and send them to India with a nomad kafila, but the boy had refused. They would be impossible to disguise, he had said flatly. None of them resembled Afghans in anything they did, or any gesture they made. Her uncle threw back his head and guffawed when he laughed, something Afghans never did, and her aunt's gestures were too careful, as if she were holding something back. The Indian servants moved slowly, bent forward as if in deep thought, unlike his people who walked swiftly, their backs straight, their eyes on the horizon.

Mariana, he had added tactlessly, had only escaped notice because Afghan men did not waste their glances on women.

Of all the members of that household, he had said firmly, only Munshi Sahib could be hidden in Kabul until the storm blew over. Even Yar Mohammad could not pretend to be speechless forever.

"You must ask a tribal chief for panah," he had announced.

She had agreed with him then, but now, trembling at the side of the road, she felt her courage fail.

The tribesmen were closer now, their leader riding the same bay animal Mariana had seen once before. They were terrifying to look at, swathed in heavy leather and wool, the shawls they had thrown over their turbans rendering their faces barely visible.

"But do you know this chief?" she asked for the third time that morning. "Are you certain he will—"

"I do not know him," Nur Rahman interrupted irritably, "but I can see that he is a man of consequence, with the means to protect you and your household in comfort. That is all that matters."

She did not move.

He gestured impatiently. "Do you think I would guide you wrong after you saved my life? Can you not understand that I am doing this for your sake, not mine? Do you not trust me?"

"Of course I trust you," she said doubtfully, her eyes searching his through the hole in her chaderi.

"The graybeard is Pashtun," he added. "Pashtuns are required to give asylum to anyone who asks properly. If you were holding the severed head of his only son in your hand, he would still accept your plea for protection.

"Step in front of him when he approaches. Take his stirrup in your hand, and ask for panah, as I did when I came to you. And remember, after you have laid hold of his stirrup, do *not* let go. And be honest. Tell him why you need his protection. Leave *nothing* out, or he will not help you."

She made a small noise inside her chaderi. "Perhaps I will do it," she murmured. "Perhaps."

The boy shrugged angrily.

She pushed back the long sleeves of her poshteen and blew on her fingers. She made a clumsy figure, with her chaderi thrown over her heavy sheepskin cloak.

Anonymous and menacing, the horsemen advanced rapidly, weapons rattling. While Nur Rahman twitched beside her, she closed her eyes, willing herself to decide, but felt only a sickening tightness in her middle.

"Go, Khanum," he said suddenly, and pushed her forcefully toward the riders.

Afraid to look up, weighed down by her sheepskin cloak, she stumbled to the middle of the road.

The group parted. Without seeming to register her presence, they began to ride around her.

The bay stallion with his harsh-faced rider had pulled to her right. Panting with fright and exertion, she lunged awkwardly toward him, and reached for his near stirrup.

The frozen ground felt slick beneath her feet. Her knuckles grazed a filthy boot. Her fingers found a leather strap and gripped it tightly.

The startled animal danced. Mariana stumbled, hampered by her chaderi, her boots slipping, her free hand flailing for balance.

The graybeard did not reach down to strike her, or to peel her fingers from his stirrup. Instead he spoke sharply to his mount, and the horse stood still.

"Panah," she croaked, unable to look at his pitiless face. "Panah."

The other horsemen had stopped, their eyes averted from her. Aware of their penetrating curiosity, Mariana stood still, listening to the blowing of the horses, and the clanking of weapons.

There were five riders including their chief, and only herself and—

Still holding the stirrup, she whirled about, searching the road. Where was Nur Rahman? Surely he had not run away....

He was still there, but only barely. Bent double, he had begun to edge away from the horses.

She was about to call out when the graybeard spoke.

"Panah?" His voice sounded strangely hollow. "You want asylum?"

He sat on his mount exactly as he had before: one hand on the reins, the other resting on his knee. His eyes, the same color as his beard, looked as cold as the sky.

"Yes." She nodded.

Other travelers passed them. Most pretended not to notice her, but several children on a camel pointed, shouting. From the corner of her eye, she watched Nur Rahman move carefully away, abandoning her.

Be honest, he had said. *If you were holding the severed head of his only son in your hand . . .*

Remembering his own plea for asylum months before, she reached up with her free hand and clutched the muddy hem of the old man's coat.

"I am British," she announced in her careful Farsi, her fingers tightening on the stirrup and the handful of sheepskin. "My people are under siege. We have committed mistakes since we came from India. I ask for protection for myself and for my family. I ask to be taken back safely to India."

"And," he inquired, "which mistakes have your people made?"

Leave nothing out, Nur Rahman had said, *or he will not help you*.

She swallowed. "Without asking the Afghan people's permission, we deposed Amir Dost Mohammad and put Shah Shuja on the throne in his place. We tried to force the Kabulis and others to do our bidding. We taxed the chiefs, we broke our promises, we—"

"Enough." The old man raised the hand from his knee. Mariana saw that it shook slightly. "You need say no more. How many are in your household?"

If she had won, Mariana felt no triumph. For better or worse, the British were her people, and she had betrayed them to save her own skin. She dropped her hands and stood in the road, her shoulders drooping.

"How many?" the chief repeated in his hollow voice.

"Between twenty-two and twenty-seven." She forced herself to think. She must leave room for Lady Macnaghten and Lady Sale and her pregnant daughter. And what of those wan, frightened families . . .

"Perhaps a few more," she added. "There are children."

He nodded. "You will come with me. Zarma Jan, take the other one."

Nur Rahman began to run.

Before she could protest, before she could argue that this was not what she had expected, that she must return to her people first, the old man leaned over, seized her upper arm, and hauled her onto his saddle. Terrified of falling, she swung one leg over the horse's back and threw her arms around his thickly clad body.

Scuffling behind her, followed by a squawk of protest, told her that Nur Rahman had not escaped.

The chief kicked his mount to a gallop.

Never in Mariana's life had she ridden astride. Too frightened to breathe, she clung to the old tribesman, her eyes shut against the whipping tail of his turban, her hands slipping dangerously on the rough leather of his coat.

They rode east toward the looming Bala Hisar, and thundered across a wooden bridge over the Kabul River. As they rode on and on, she felt, rather than saw, the Hindu Kush mountains looming in front of them.

At last the horse slowed, then stopped.

She opened her eyes. All five horses now stood still in front of a square, mud brick fort with heavy, octagonal watchtowers at its corners. An expanse of snow-covered fields stretched away from it, toward the steep hills. Wind rattled the leafless branches of nearby trees.

Shouts came from above. Men gestured over a curving parapet. A moment later the fort's double doors swung inward, and they rode into a large, odd-shaped courtyard with several full-sized buildings jutting into it.

As soon as the door had thudded shut behind them, the men dismounted. A group of small boys in skullcaps had gathered. They stared at her and Nur Rahman. The chief beckoned to one of them and sent him racing off with, Mariana supposed, the news of their arrival.

Before she could ask where they were, or whose fort it was, the men all strode away and vanished into a nearby building, leaving Mariana and Nur Rahman to find their own way off the horses.

Mariana scrambled to the ground, still breathing hard from the journey, but Nur Rahman did not move. He wept, hunched over, in the saddle.

"They will kill me," he blubbered. "They will cut me to pieces with their long knives."

"What do you mean?" Fear clutched at Mariana. "You promised me we'd be safe here."

"I said *you* would be safe." He wiped his face with a corner of his chaderi. "I will die horribly at the hands of the women of this house," he whispered, "when they discover that I, a man, have entered their quarters."

Attracted by their voices, the men on the roof now peered down into the courtyard, long-barreled jezails in their hands.

Of course the women would kill Nur Rahman. And God knew what the men would do. Mariana looked quickly about her. There was no way out now, but even if there were, the flat fields surrounding the fort would offer Nur Rahman no protective cover as he ran for his life.

She hurried to him. "Come," she urged. "Staying on that horse will only make things worse."

As he slid to the ground, two women in brown chaderis appeared in the doorway of a second building. They beckoned, two mud-colored ghosts, their thoughts impossible to divine.

Left with no choice, Mariana and Nur Rahman crossed the courtyard and followed the women into an inner building whose own courtyard boasted a tree and several tethered horses and goats.

Nur Rahman's whole body trembled. "Pashtun women have great power," he confided. "It is they who decide who should live and who should die."

Ahead of them, the women threw back their chaderis and pointed, smiling, to a corner room whose window overlooked the courtyard. The older of the two said something in Pushto.

Nur Rahman nodded for them both, then crept through the doorway behind Mariana.

The room was bare, save for a single string bed against one wall. They sat down on it together.

"I cannot bear to think of you dying to save my life," she said in a small voice.

"When I die," he whispered, "I hope to go to Paradise. It is my only dream, for in Paradise are all the things I have longed for in this life."

"What you have longed for?"

"Friends," he said simply. "I want to recline on beautiful carpets with loving companions, to eat the perfect fruits of the Garden and to drink from the fountain of Salsabil."

The perfect fruits of the Garden. No one had ever given Mariana such a vivid description of Heaven, not even her father, whom she had peppered with questions when she was twelve, after her little brother's sad death.

"Most of all," Nur Rahman added, "I long to see the face of the Beloved."

"The Beloved." Her God had always been the Heavenly Father. Saying Nur Rahman's words aloud, she found herself filled with longing.

Munshi Sahib had told her once that Christians and Muslims shared the same God. Of course her father would disagree.

From the wistfulness of his tone, the boy had never had a friend. What sort of life had he led?

"But I will never be accepted into the Garden," he added mournfully.

"What?" Mariana blinked. "Why?"

"I have committed many sins." His head lowered, he picked at his fingers. "My sins are numerous, and too grave to be forgiven."

No. This was too cruel. It was true that Nur Rahman looked distressingly unsavory, but what of his kindness toward Munshi Sahib? What of his efforts to save her family? What of his courage at this moment, as he sat uncomplaining in this room with its window onto the courtyard, waiting to die?

"I am certain," Mariana said decisively, "that God will forgive all your sins. Why would He not? You are young, almost a child. God always forgives children."

"He does?" The boy's voice brightened. "Do you think He will—"

He fell silent. A short, heavyset woman had entered, followed by a maidservant carrying two steaming cups of green tea on a tray. "Peace," she offered.

Before Mariana had time to digest the irony of that greeting, the woman said something else, and tipped her chin toward the door.

"Her name is Zahida. She is telling us to have tea in another room," translated Nur Rahman.

The second room was as cold as the first one, but it had thick carpets and bolsters on the floor. It smelled of burning charcoal. As Mariana sipped cardamom-flavored tea, the woman held out paper, a pen, and a bottle of ink.

"They are sending their men to escort your family here," Nur Rahman explained. "She wants you to write and tell them to be ready tomorrow morning."

The woman, who wore a silver nose ring, was old enough to be Mariana's mother. Mariana examined her through the peephole in her chaderi, wondering if she were friend or foe.

She spoke again.

"She wants us to take off our chaderis." Nur Rahman's eyes were wide behind his peephole.

"Tell her we will do it in a moment," Mariana replied.

Dear Uncle Adrian, she wrote, *a local chief has granted panah to our household. You, Aunt Claire, and all the servants are to come immediately to his fort escorted by a body of his own horsemen who are waiting outside the cantonment gate. Please act upon this offer at once.*

He would understand the word *panah,* and its significance.

I have asked our host to send us on to India, she added. *Please extend this offer to Lady Macnaghten, Lady Sale and her daughter, and anyone with small children.*

It is our one chance of escape from Kabul. Do not be afraid. The chief will not break the Pashtun Code.

Hoping she was telling the truth, she paused to glance at the boy beside her.

I am sending this letter with Nur Rahman, she added, *so you will know it is genuine.*

She signed the paper with a flourish. "My servant here," she said, as she handed it to the waiting woman, "will carry this letter to my family."

"May I ask," she added over Nur Rahman's squeak of relief, "to whom this fort belongs?"

The woman named Zahida stared in surprise. "You do not know?"

Something in her voice made Mariana's jaw tighten.

"You are under the protection," Zahida announced, "of Aminullah Khan."

Palsied old creature trying to get up. Deaf as a post. Mariana shrank against her bolster, remembering the slight tremor in his left hand. No one, not even Macnaghten, had known what the man looked like.

She had put her family at his mercy.

It was too late to escape, too late even to snatch her letter away from the woman who now signaled for Nur Rahman to follow her out.

"Do not worry, Khanum," he whispered before he left for the blessed, questionable safety of the cantonment. "Your family will be safe here."

A moment later, numb with fright, Mariana was alone.

Chapter 31

Zahida returned moments after Nur Rahman's departure. Planted in front of Mariana, she pointed across the small courtyard and repeated the same unintelligible phrase until Mariana understood to her great relief that she was being given an opportunity to visit the family latrine.

After crunching her way back across the courtyard snow, Mariana watched from her bolster as Zahida came and went from the room with the string bed, bringing a lamp, a small carpet, and a jug of water.

The third time she came, a pillow stuffed with cotton wool under one arm, she was followed by three excited girls who rushed into the sitting room, then stood still, staring at Mariana's tangle of unwashed brown curls and her pale, uncovered face, their noses wrinkling with distaste.

Zahida spoke sharply. The girls hurried away.

It took Mariana a moment to understand what was wrong. It was herself. She had gone many weeks without a bath.

Ignoring her reddening face, Zahida made a gesture indicating she would return, then disappeared up a flight of stairs to an upper floor of the building, whose rooms, like Mariana's, overlooked the courtyard.

When she came back, it was already dark. She carried a towel and clean clothes—a folded shalwar kameez, a long shirt and baggy trousers of the same coarse homespun as her own loose clothing, a long, broad veil of thin cotton to put over the head, and a brown woolen shawl. Motioning for Mariana to follow, she led her to a tiny windowless room where someone had left two brass pails of water, one steaming hot, the other cold. A teapot-shaped vessel stood between them. An oil lamp in the corner of the room sent a frail, shadowy light over the scene.

Zahida gestured eloquently, closed the door, and left a shivering Mariana to take her bath.

Later, when Mariana opened the door, well scrubbed and newly dressed, a girl led her to an upstairs room whose arched windows had been blocked with split bamboo blinds.

A pile of discarded shoes lay outside the door. Female voices came from inside. The smell of cooking meat from somewhere in the building brought water to Mariana's mouth.

"This is where we keep the *sandali*." The girl waited for Mariana to step nervously out of her shoes, then held aside the door curtain.

The middle-sized room was warm and thickly carpeted, its air close from the presence of a score of women and children who sat on mattresses around a large, square table, all of them craning to look at her. A great padded quilt, large enough to cover the table and all their legs, dominated the room.

Zahida came over and led Mariana toward an ancient lady with Aminullah Khan's fierce gray eyes.

As she had seen people do, Mariana laid a hand over her heart and wished the lady peace.

Obeying the old lady's commanding gesture, she sat down, her legs under the quilt, and was immediately greeted by delicious, comforting warmth. A brazier, or several of them, had been pushed beneath the table, their coals well burned and covered with ashes.

Sighing with pleasure, she forgot for a moment that she was among her enemies. She let a small boy pour water over her hands. She sipped green tea.

The old woman offered her a harsh smile.

As a small bowl of roasted almonds arrived in front of her, a bespectacled woman of indeterminate age approached, and signaled for the pregnant girl beside Mariana to move aside.

"I speak Dari," she said, as she sat down and leaned against the heavy bolster behind her. "I will translate for the others."

Mariana smiled. Happily, there would be nothing to translate but her thanks.

She was wrong.

"What is your story, Mairmuna?" the woman asked, pushing her spectacles up her nose. Her smile revealed perfect teeth. "Why have you asked us for asylum?"

Mariana swallowed, aware that all conversation in the room had ceased.

What should she tell these enemy women, whose menfolk had slaughtered Burnes and Macnaghten, and killed or wounded so many others? Had she not said more than enough to Aminullah Khan when she asked for panah? Did they expect her to admit to the desperate conditions in the cantonment? Were they looking for another apology?

Perspiration collected along her hairline. A nearby girl with fair skin gazed at her with enormous eyes.

If she said something wrong, if she mistakenly insulted them, would they kill her, or send her back to the cantonment?

"I am," she fumbled, buying time, "the only Englishwoman in Kabul who wears a chaderi. I have been into the city. There is no country," she added, remembering the Envoy's picnics in Babur Shah's garden, "as majestic in its beauty as Afghanistan. I have never known poetry more lovely than that of Rumi, of Sa'adi—"

The translator frowned. The women murmured.

Oh no! They were Pashtun! They would despise the classical Persian poets, would think them unmanly compared to their own bards, whose proud verses were as ferocious as they were....

"Of course," Mariana added lamely, "I have yet to read the works of the great Ahmad Shah Durrani."

"Yes," pursued her translator, "but why have you asked for asylum? What is your story?"

So this was the price of asylum: the truth. The place of honor at the table, the tea, the almonds, were only the beginning.

The old woman was watching her.

"I pray," Mariana replied, her stomach churning, "that I have committed no crime terrible enough to require protection from enemies, but I admit that my people have made mistakes that have angered Akbar Khan and caused bitterness among the tribes. It is from the consequences of those mistakes that I seek your protection."

The ancient lady spoke sharply.

Zahida's nose ring bobbed as she nodded seriously. "You wish to avoid the just punishment that your people's actions have provoked."

Just punishment? Mariana recoiled at the calm brutality of those words, but as she looked about the table she saw no trace of triumphant vengeance, only curiosity.

Could it be that these Ghilzai women only wanted information? Did they only seek the details of a story that would be told to their descendants for the next hundred years: of the British people who had tried to invade Afghanistan and betrayed their own honor, and of the Englishwoman who had come to their fort seeking protection from the just wrath of their tribe?

Could it be that they wanted no less than the full story of their victory?

Be honest or they will not help you.

Mariana began to speak. For the next five minutes, as the women leaned forward to catch every word, she described the British plan to protect their holdings in India by putting a king of their choice upon the throne of Afghanistan. She recognized the burden that the huge British force had imposed upon the region's food supply. Her eyes lowered, she acknowledged that taxing the tribal chiefs to pay Shah Shuja's expenses had insulted them, for they regarded themselves as the equals of their king.

When she was finished, the ladies nodded, but kept on looking at her, their faces expectant.

"All that is true," agreed the translator, "but what of the British fort? If you have come to us to escape the conditions there, you should tell us what they are."

Mariana's thoughts raced. Any information about the desperate state of the cantonment, the lack of water, the terrible food rationing, or the illnesses that raged among the men, would aid her enemies.

Every word she said would go straight to Aminullah Khan's ears.

She spoke instead of her own family: of her aunt's constant coughing and fevers, of her uncle's exhaustion, even of her munshi's illness. While insisting that they had plenty of food, she admitted her fear that her uncle and aunt, the only relatives she had in India, might not survive the winter.

She shrugged and shook her head when they asked her of Macnaghten's decision to halve the cash payment promised to the Eastern Ghilzais. She offered no hint of the collapse of the British command. She did not mention Alexander Burnes's shocking behavior with Afghan women.

She told them very little about herself. She did not even mention Hassan Ali Khan.

At length, a cloth was spread over the quilt on the table, and a file of maidservants entered, carrying dishes of rice with chicken buried inside and covered with raisins and slivered carrots, lamb cooked with dried Bukhara plums, stewed beans, grilled pumpkin, strained yoghurt, and great, heaping piles of bread.

There were no forks, knives, or spoons. Remembering Safiya Sultana's patient lessons, Mariana ate, messily, with the first two fingers and thumb of her right hand.

By the time she had finished eating, her eyelids had begun to droop. Before the young boy had finished his second round with the ewer and basin, she turned to the translator.

"Forgive me," she murmured, "for I must sleep."

Zahida nodded. "Sleep," she said. "We have arranged for your journey to India. You will be leaving the day after tomorrow."

Still dressed in her homespun clothes, Mariana wrapped herself tightly in her padded quilts, and laid her head on the cotton-stuffed pillow.

Tomorrow, God willing, Uncle Adrian would come with Aunt Claire, the servants, and perhaps some others from the cantonment. The next day they would be on their way to India.

It was nearly over.

If their caravan took the southern route, they would arrive in the Dera Jat, near the Indus River, a long way southeast of Lahore, but at least they would be out of this terrifying place. After that, she would somehow find a way to return to Lahore, and Qamar Haveli.

There she would learn if she was still Hassan's wife, as Munshi Sahib had seemed to imply.

The lamp flickered, sending shadows across the ceiling. She stared at them, wondering if he would tell Hassan that she had accepted Fitzgerald.

She squirmed inside her quilts at the thought.

Had Hassan read her first, romantic letter, sent so long ago, its words taken from Rumi's "Masnavi" and bent to her own purpose?

Had he ever received her second letter? Possibly not, for Ghulam Ali might easily have perished months ago in the passes, murdered by cousins of Aminullah Khan himself, her undelivered message still hidden in his clothes.

What a reckless fool she had been....

She sat up and blew out the lamp.

The women were still awake. Female voices drifted down the stairs, laughing, arguing, talking at once, most likely about her.

These people were her enemies, the enemies of the poor, beleaguered British, and they were happy.

Unable to think any longer, she rolled over on the creaking bed and fell asleep.

Chapter 32

January 3, 1842

Hassan and Zulmai had crossed the Logar River the previous day.

By the time Mariana rode into Aminullah Khan's fort, Hassan and his two-man escort had been nearing Kabul, bent low over their horses' necks, shawls wrapped over their heads and faces.

They had set off at sunrise, leaving Zulmai and the baggage behind, and ridden swiftly along the Logar's northward course, past the leafless fruit trees that crowded the river's bank, their branches shaking in the wind.

At noon, seven hours later, the elder of Hassan's guards had held up a hand.

"Our horses cannot go any longer without resting," he said respectfully, "but your Akhal Tekke will take you all the way to the city, if you choose to continue without us."

"I will go on alone. May you live," Hassan added politely by way of farewell. "May you not be tired!"

Ghyr Khush's ears twitched when he spoke to her, then she trotted on.

By midafternoon Hassan had reached the great caravanserai and animal market west of Kabul. A chaikhana stood by the gate, its samovar bubbling. He dismounted stiffly, and tethered his mare.

A little while later, the elderly tea shop proprietor put a second pot of tea in front of him, and pointed along the serai's high brick wall. "The best place to camp is on this side," he offered. "It is here that you should wait for your friend's arrival."

"I will take your advice," Hassan replied, "but first I have work to do. Can you tell me the whereabouts of the British fort?"

The old man regarded him seriously. "If I were you," he said, "I would avoid that accursed place. You, who are from India, should give it a wide berth."

Hassan thanked him, remounted his tired mare, and rode away through the tall caravanserai gate.

He found the road leading to the cantonment choked with heavily armed men and boys, who stared at him as he passed. As he approached the walled fort, a foul smell filled the air.

The main entrance was tightly closed. No sentries stood outside. He dismounted and hammered on the great doors, but there was no response. After riding all the way around the cantonment's outer wall, looking in vain for an open entrance, he stationed himself at a discreet distance from a promising-looking secondary gate. When at last it opened to let out a man leading a donkey, Hassan spoke urgently to his mare. Ghyr Khush sprang at once to a gallop, but they arrived too late.

Before the doors closed firmly in front of him, Hassan had looked briefly inside to see a dozen men staring out at him, raw fear on their faces.

"Shut the gate, shut the gate!" they had cried, as if their lives depended on it.

His luck was no better on the second day.

"Did you find what you were seeking?" the old tea seller asked, when Hassan returned to the caravanserai.

"Not yet, father," he replied politely, "but I will continue to try. Perhaps," he added, "you can give me information about someone who lives in the city."

MARIANA AWOKE to daylight, and the sound of household bustle outside her room.

Fearing she had overslept, she put her feet over the side of her bed, put on her slippers, draped herself in her shawls, and went outside.

Sunlight fell into the small courtyard in front of her, brightening the coats of the tethered animals and glinting in the icy ground. A servant woman in leather boots climbed the stairs, a water vessel on her head. Rosy-cheeked children darted through a doorway.

Something drew Mariana's glance upward. The fierce old woman from the previous night stood at an upstairs window, studying her.

She caught Mariana's eye, and disappeared inside.

Perhaps she was the matriarch of the family, who held the power to decide who should live and who should die. If so, what was she thinking?

A moment later, a young girl arrived and conducted Mariana to the upstairs room. There, luxuriating in the warmth from the brazier and closely observed by a pushing crowd of children, she drank hot green tea and ate sweet porridge with ground meat in it, and a piece of Afghan bread.

As she finished her food, male voices shouted from the rooftop.

Someone had arrived.

Mariana hurried into her chaderi, then, together with the flock of children, she rushed out into the main courtyard in time to see the heavy outer doors of the fort swing open. A moment later, her uncle rode inside, accompanied by a nervous-looking groom leading a second horse with a sidesaddle on its back.

They were alone. Uncle Adrian dismounted and stood uncertainly, his eyes roving the courtyard.

She dashed across the snow and flung her arms about his neck. "Uncle Adrian," she cried, "I am so glad you have come! But where is Aunt Claire?" she added, frowning toward the gate. "Where are the servants?"

He held her away from him, and peered through her latticework. "Oh, Mariana, it grieves me to see you in native costume." His voice trembled. "Tell me, have they hurt you?"

She stared in surprise. "No, not at all. I had a hot bath last night, and a lovely dinner. They have given me my own room. They have promised to send us to India in a day or two."

He released her shoulders. "You poor little fool." He sighed.

In spite of the cold, his face was slick with perspiration beneath his top hat. Newly clean herself, she now realized that he gave off an ugly, sweetish smell. His hands were grimy. His cough sounded dry.

"These Afghans will demand money for your release. If we do not pay them an enormous ransom, they will slaughter you like a lamb."

"Uncle Adrian," she said carefully, wondering if desperation had affected his judgment, "they have granted us asylum—"

He waved her to silence, and glanced over his shoulder. "Do not make another sound," he whispered. "I shall try to persuade them to turn you over to me."

Mariana drew herself up inside her chaderi. "I am *not* a prisoner, Uncle Adrian. I am a *guest*. These are Pashtuns. Have you forgotten the code of Pashtunwali?"

He blinked uncertainly.

"*Please,* Uncle Adrian," she begged, her chin beginning to wobble. "If you do not bring Aunt Claire and the servants, they will all die. It was for *their* sake that I took the chief's stirrup in my hand and begged for his protection. For *their* sake."

His gaze focused. "And which chief is that?" he asked, his voice sharpening, his eyes boring into hers. "From which of our enemies have you treacherously begged for asylum?"

She dropped her eyes to her snow-caked boots. "This fort belongs to Aminullah Khan," she whispered.

"But please, *please* listen to me," she added, now crying in earnest at the sight of his face. "Everything we learned about their code of conduct is true. Why should Aunt Claire or Lady Macnaghten or Lady Sale die because of the stupidity of our generals? Aunt Claire is my mother's only sister. You can go back and do your duty if you wish, but how can you let *her* die?"

His face was set. "It is a matter of honor."

He nodded to the groom. The man stepped forward, leading the saddled horses. He was going to take her away.

"No, Uncle Adrian," she sobbed, flinching from his reaching hand. "If you leave now, the asylum will be broken. They will shoot you in the back."

As she spoke, a door in a nearby building flew open, and Aminullah Khan started toward them. He limped slightly, and his left arm hung at his side, as if he did not use it very much, but from his manner, it was quite clear that he was master of the fort, and everyone in it.

He smiled as he drew near, the planes of his face losing none of their harshness. "Forgive me," he offered, a hand over his heart, ignoring Mariana who sniffed wetly at her uncle's side. "I have only now heard of your arrival. Please come inside where it is warmer. We will have tea."

He waved his good hand toward the same building where he had disappeared the previous afternoon. As he did so, other men came from inside, joined him, and offered their own greetings.

Exhausted, filthy, without even a knife, Uncle Adrian stood no chance against the ten heavily armed tribesmen who smiled encouragingly and pointed to the brick building and its open door.

Before he walked away with the men who had cut to pieces both his superior officers, he threw Mariana a single, anguished glance.

"Whatever they ask you, remember to tell them the truth," she called after him, *"the truth!"*

She wiped her nose on the sleeve of her chaderi, hunched her shoulders, and started toward the women's quarters.

Whatever happened now, her uncle would suffer.

Even if he reached India safely, his troubles would be far from over. The Governor-General would never understand why he had abandoned his post at such a critical time. No one would believe that he had become trapped in Aminullah's fort while trying to rescue his niece.

There would be a humiliating investigation, followed by demotion, perhaps even the loss of his pension.

She waited jumpily for two hours in the upstairs room before more shouting came from the rooftop. She rushed downstairs once more.

Uncle Adrian must have eaten something, for he looked less haggard than before, but she had never seen him so miserable. He stood beside Aminullah Khan, looking on wanly as his household servants filed through the gate and into the fort.

Already inside stood a carved palanquin, its twelve bearers crouched around it, muffled in their shawls.

They had come. Mariana looked eagerly from face to face among the crowd. All the servants were there: Yar Mohammad, standing protectively by Aunt Claire's palanquin, Dittoo, with his hair sticking messily from his turban, old Adil, the Bengali Mug cook with his knives in a leather bag, the cross-eyed silver-polisher and the sweeperess and her daughter. All huddled nervously together, along with a score of others.

"Adrian? Are you there?" Aunt Claire's plaintive voice called from the palanquin. "Where on earth *are* we?"

Mariana frowned, searching the courtyard. "But where are Lady

Macnaghten and Lady Sale?" she asked. "Where is Lady Sale's daughter?"

Surely they had been invited. Surely they would not have missed this chance to get out of Afghanistan. Lady Sale's daughter was expecting a child...

He shook his head. "When I saw there was no escape for either of us from this fort, I sent for your aunt and the servants, fearing to leave them alone at the cantonment. But how could I ask the other ladies to come? I had promised Sir William," he added bleakly, "to look after his wife."

AN HOUR later, Mariana stood guard outside the door of the bathing chamber, a fresh set of homespun clothes and Aunt Claire's musty gown and underthings bundled together in her arms.

Sounds of splashing came from within.

"Are you there, my dear?" her aunt asked tremulously for the third time. "I do not wish to find myself alone and naked, in a fort full of Afghans."

"When you are ready," Mariana said through the door, "I will hand you the clean things Zahida has brought for you."

Later, sounds of struggle came from inside, accompanied by heavy breathing. Mariana imagined her aunt pulling up the unfamiliar, baggy Afghan trousers and tying the drawstring around her ample middle, then pulling the loose camisole down over her head, followed by the long, matching homespun shirt.

"Come inside, Mariana," she cried a moment later, through a crack in the door. "Bring my real clothes. I will *not* leave this bathing room without my stays.

"Shut the door!" she ordered when Mariana entered, then stood before her, resplendent in the lamplight, her large breasts wobbling freely beneath the coarsely woven cotton shirt. "Never in my life," she wailed, "have I been dressed so indecently!"

"You may certainly wear your stays," Mariana replied cautiously, "but they have not been washed for more than a month. Besides, you are to wear these as well."

She held up a long, broad white veil and an equally generous shawl. "Both of them cover the chest."

Her aunt's chins quivered with indignation. "I cannot imagine what your uncle was thinking, to get us into this predicament. As long as I live, I shall never breathe a *word* of this experience."

Her uncle? Mariana shook out the veil. "Let me," she said hastily, "show you how to wear this."

Two hours later, in the upstairs sitting room, Mariana sighed with relief.

Aunt Claire had liked the dinner.

Mariana had braced herself for an open display of disgust at the spicy dishes that came in abundance from downstairs, with flat ovals of fresh tandoori bread. Instead, she watched fascinated as Aunt Claire, after only token objections at the lack of utensils, put away many cups of tea, several helpings of chicken *pulao,* carrots, yoghurt, and a dish of split peas.

The only thing she refused to do was speak to their hostesses.

"I will *not* converse with these savages," she decreed, waving dismissive fingers in the direction of the fierce old lady who watched her with hooded eyes from the other side of the table. "I will reluctantly wear their clothes and eat their food, but you must not expect me to take any notice of them."

She did, however, take great notice of the next course, a dish of sweet rice pudding sprinkled with pistachio nuts.

THE FOLLOWING morning, as her aunt snored beside her, Mariana was awoken by an insistent voice outside her door.

"Mairmuna!" called a young female voice. "Mairmuna."

Mariana dressed, and pulled aside the curtain. A child stood outside, pointing toward the main courtyard. Mariana nodded.

"Get up, Aunt Claire," she said urgently, shaking the bundle of rezais on the other bed. "We must prepare to leave for India."

Aunt Claire sat up blinking, the lace nightcap she had salvaged from the cantonment still squarely on her head. "Where is Adrian?" she asked sharply. "Where is your uncle? I do not like him going off and leaving us. Where is my tea?"

"We will see Uncle Adrian soon," Mariana replied, busying herself with her boots. "Where is your poshteen?"

An hour later, after a hasty breakfast, Zahida put on her chaderi and escorted Mariana and her aunt to the main courtyard.

All around them was confusion. Aminullah Khan stood near the fort's main entrance, conferring with his henchman. Other armed men milled about. Camels knelt side by side, their necks stretched out, groaning and complaining while men loaded sacks of Aunt Claire's household belongings onto their backs.

Two of the camels had been dressed in colorful hangings. They knelt, apart from the others, waiting to be mounted.

"We will get a new one when we reach India." Uncle Adrian gestured toward Aunt Claire's palanquin, now abandoned on its side in a corner. "The bearers cannot carry you through the snow. Half of them are ill already. You *will* ride a camel, and that is that.

"And put on the chaderi that woman has given you," he added. "It is only good manners to do so. After all, these desperadoes may be saving your life."

He reached up and put a cautious hand to the folds of his borrowed turban.

Dittoo appeared before Mariana. "Bibi," he cried, wringing his hands, "please forgive me. They would not let me bring your morning tea. They would not even tell me where to find you. Poor Adil has been so upset..."

Already wan and bony, he looked as if he was about to weep.

"It does not matter, Dittoo," she shouted above the din in the courtyard. "Afghans always keep men and women apart."

"But your tea, your clothes, the dusting! Memsahib's things!"

Aminullah Khan appeared, with his supporters. "Well, well," he said heartily, "I see that all is ready. After you join the camp I have arranged for you, I shall accompany you as far as the Sher Darwaza pass. After that, my people will escort you all the way to Dera Ghazi Khan..."

Mariana's uncle acknowledged Aminullah's remark with a careful nod.

An hour later, Aunt Claire let out a piercing scream as her camel lurched to its feet.

"*If* I survive this journey," she confided as she and Mariana swayed, side by side, toward the fort's main entrance, "I solemnly promise *never* to leave my bed again."

The double doors of the fort stood wide, revealing a cold, sunlit landscape beyond. Aminullah Khan rode out first on his bay stallion, followed by Mariana's uncle and a few of his men. Next came the two heavily guarded camels, the gaggle of Indian servants, on foot and with their own protecting tribesmen, and the line of baggage animals.

The kafila turned and followed a trampled path through the snow toward the Bala Hisar, the city, and the great caravanserai to the west of Kabul, where their escort waited.

As Mariana rode out through the gate, a small figure flew toward her across the snow. She raised the flap of her chaderi in order to see who it was, but she already knew.

"Munshi Sahib sent me," Nur Rahman panted as he jogged along beside her camel, his balled-up chaderi beneath his arm. "He told me there was something I had to do for you, Khanum. I wept and kissed his hands, but he insisted I leave him. I would do anything for him," he added, "and so I have come."

His fringed eyes darkened. "He told me that, Allah willing, I will receive a great reward." But when he said it, tears stood in his eyes.

AS HASSAN rode toward the city for the third time, a caravan came toward him, traveling in the opposite direction.

Strongly guarded, its pace set by camels, the kafila moved at a dignified speed, taking up the width of the road. Two of the camels carried heavily shrouded female figures.

His eyes carefully averted from the women, Hassan guided Ghyr Khush off the road. As he did so, one of them turned, saw him, and cried out.

Chapter 33

"Nur Rahman!" Her heart thundering, Mariana searched over her shoulder for the dancing boy among the file of servants and guards behind her. "Nur Rahman!" she shouted, not caring who was listening.

"Behind us," she gasped, when he arrived at her side. "A man on a gray horse!"

She reached under her chaderi and tore Hassan's gold medallion and chain from her neck. "Give him these," she ordered breathlessly, dropping them into his outstretched hand. "Tell him a lady wishes to see him."

"Which man?" the boy asked, his face bunching in confusion. "Who?"

"He is wearing a poshteen and a brown turban made from a shawl," she half shouted. "He is on a gray horse. His name is Hassan. *Hurry!*"

The boy nodded, pocketed the bauble, and ran.

Stiff with anxiety, Mariana swayed on her camel, hating the lengthening distance between her and Hassan, wishing she could use her sudden, fierce energy to speed Nur Rahman on his way as he raced back the way they had come, past the guards and the pack animals, along the narrow, trampled track leading to the city.

Had the boy understood her? Had she described Hassan sufficiently?

If there were more than one gray horse on the road, would Nur Rahman give the medallion to the wrong man?

What would she do if Hassan disappeared, unfound, into the city?

What if the man she had seen was not Hassan?

"Whatever is the matter, Mariana?" inquired her aunt from atop the other camel. "Why were you shouting at the top of your voice?"

NUR RAHMAN ran heavily, the cold air burning his lungs, his poshteen weighing on his shoulders.

Why, he wondered, had the English lady ordered him to stop a stranger on the road and offer him the fine gift that now lay in his pocket?

She might have gone mad, of course, but whatever illness had unexpectedly overtaken her mind, it was clear that at this moment she wanted desperately to meet that mysterious man on his gray horse.

But powerful as her desire might be, it was no greater than Nur Rahman's need to live. When the road cleared for a moment, he stopped, looked about him carefully, then took his blue chaderi from beneath his arm and threw it hastily over his head and shoulders.

He peered ahead of him, through his disguise. Whoever this stranger was, he had ridden away as soon as the lady saw him, for there were no gray horses anywhere nearby.

Of several riders in the distance, only one, who rode apart from the others, seemed to be on a pale-colored mount.

His eyes on that faraway figure, Nur Rahman trotted along the road, the chaderi catching at his legs, his breath rasping in his ears.

A group of horsemen rode toward him, obscuring his view. Moments after they passed, others came from behind and did the same.

When they moved away, Nur Rahman stared at the road ahead.

The rider had disappeared.

Afraid to turn back, Nur Rahman ran on, sweating beneath his chaderi, aware of people's curiosity at the sight of a woman alone, praying that no one would stop and question him, that no one would offer him help.

He stopped for tea near the Pul-e-Khishti and drank rapidly, hidden in a doorway. He would wait for the man here, he decided, for sooner or later, everyone in Kabul passed over the bridge.

"Oh, Allah," he whispered, "please let the lady's stranger return on his gray horse before it is too late."

Tomorrow she would march with Aminullah's kafila. He had promised Munshi Sahib not to leave her...

Two hours later, he still waited in his doorway, his feet numb, his eyes on the traffic crossing the bridge. On the right bank of the Kabul River, the sellers of silver ornaments had boarded up their shops. Oil lamps and fires lit the approaching night. Groups of armed men talked among themselves as they crossed the river and moved in groups toward the cantonment.

As the sunset call to prayer rang out, Nur Rahman looked up, and sucked in his breath. Twenty yards away, a man in a brown-shawl turban rode through the fading light, across the teeming bridge.

There was something about him...

But what was the color of his horse?

The crowd parted. A proud, silver-gray horse's head appeared, then vanished again.

Nur Rahman leapt to his feet and began to run.

He forced himself through the crowd, ignoring the surprised glances as he elbowed his way past loaded coolies and gangs of small boys, struggling all the while to keep his eye on his quarry.

Across the bridge at last, he peered eagerly into the crowd.

The man and his horse had vanished into the city.

Sagging with exhaustion and disappointment, Nur Rahman turned into the Char Chatta Bazaar and followed it to its end, ignoring the smell of kababs cooking over hot coals and the lamplight that changed the bazaar into a tunnel of mysteries as the afternoon faded.

After two more turns, he was deep in the labyrinth of the old city, hurrying past its closed-up shops, avoiding puddles of dirty, melted snow, grateful to have come so far without drawing attention.

He stopped at last, raised his closed fists, and pounded on a high wooden door with a heavy lintel. After the bolt groaned and the door creaked open, he stepped over the threshold and into Haji Khan's courtyard, then stood still.

Tethered to the courtyard's lone tree stood a silver-gray horse.

The boy gestured silently toward Haji Khan's room. The old gatekeeper nodded.

Haji Khan's chamber looked the same as it had when Nur

Rahman had left it that morning, down to the nightingale in its cage on a low table beside the blind man's platform.

The room was warmed by a small brazier of well-burnt coals that did little to dispel the chill. Nur Rahman could see his breath as he crouched beside the door.

A dozen men sat facing Haji Khan, their backs to him. Seven of them wore turbans. Munshi Sahib, of course, wore his golden qaraquli hat.

Only one man wore a brown turban fashioned from an expensive Kashmir shawl.

"After I found I could not enter the cantonment," he was saying, "I spoke to hawkers of food along the road. None of them had seen a lady of her description leave its gates."

He sounded worn and disappointed. Nur Rahman held his breath and leaned forward.

"They did not see her, my dear Hassan," Munshi Sahib replied gently, "because she was wearing a chaderi when she left the British fort. She is now under the protection of Aminullah Khan. It was only yesterday that we learned of her escape."

My dear Hassan? Nur Rahman craned to see the man's face. He seemed to know everyone....

"A brave, resourceful action." A white-bearded man nodded approvingly. "An action worthy of our own women."

The man called Hassan hunched his shoulders. "But has he taken her out of Kabul?" he asked tensely. "Does anyone know where she is?"

Nur Rahman could wait no longer. "May peace be upon you, Haji Khan," he interrupted.

Everyone turned to look at him. All but one man registered surprise at the sight of him in his chaderi. From his place on the carpet, Munshi Sahib lifted an encouraging hand.

The blind man raised his chin. "And peace upon you, my child," he returned. "On what errand have you come?"

"I am searching," Nur Rahman announced, already certain what the reply would be, "for the owner of the gray horse that is tethered outside."

The man in the brown turban frowned. "The horse is mine," he said.

The boy reached into his pocket and withdrew the gold medallion on its delicate chain. "In that case," he said, savoring the drama of the moment, "I have something to give you."

THAT EVENING, in General Elphinstone's drawing room, Brigadier Shelton glared at his Commander in Chief. "Of *course* we can trust Akbar Khan," he barked. "He has signed the treaty with us, hasn't he? He has promised us safe passage to Peshawar, hasn't he? What else could we possibly ask for?"

Charles Mott squared his shoulders. "And in return," he observed, "we have promised him all our treasure, and seven of our guns. I call that a very generous offer to the man who murdered my uncle."

"What right have you to call it anything," snapped Shelton, "when your own superior has *run away*?"

"He has *not* run away, Brigadier." Mott lifted his chin. "As I have already reported, he has been detained by the same chief who abducted his niece."

He dropped his gaze from Shelton's.

Shelton shrugged an armless shoulder. "I could not care less about either of them, Mr. Mott. In any case, Akbar has told us a dozen times that he had nothing to do with the Envoy's murder. He has wept over it for hours."

"He may have wept," General Elphinstone said weakly from his place beside the fire, "but nonetheless, I fear he has been false to us. One of our officers has been warned that ten thousand tribesmen are already waiting for our column at Khurd-Kabul, and another ten thousand at Surkhab."

"And all in spite of Akbar's promise of protection and plenty of food for the journey?" Shelton insisted, his voice rising.

"I call that a clever move, not a promise," Mott replied doggedly. "Now, if we attempt to protect ourselves or provide our own food, it will show our lack of faith in him. If we do nothing, we may find he has deceived us."

"A clever move, you call it?" sneered the brigadier.

"I do, since I am the intelligence officer in this room."

"There is another point to be made," Lady Sale's son-in-law put in, his scarred face contracting painfully as he spoke. "The entrance to the cantonment is too narrow for our force to move out with the proper speed. I suggest we throw down our eastern rampart and create a forty-foot breach in the wall."

"But," objected General Elphinstone, "if we open such a large breach, then who is to defend it?"

"No one *can* defend it!" shouted Shelton. "We cannot defend the smallest thing! Was I the only witness to the plundering of our camels and *dhoolie*s this morning, as they returned from leaving our wounded at the Bala Hisar? Did I alone see our drivers and bearers stripped of all their clothes and forced to run for their lives, naked, across the snow?"

The general sighed. "I do not know why no one ever fights these people off when they attack us. Have we no sentries, no proper guard?

"I have received another letter from Shah Shuja, begging us not to desert him," he added mournfully. "I wish I had any idea what to do now."

Chapter 34

They were to leave in the morning. Mariana stared into space as she sipped her third cup of tea. The sun had already set. It was too late.

After Nur Rahman pounded away toward the city, she and her family had continued their dignified journey toward the vast caravanserai and animal market west of Kabul where Aminullah's men waited to escort them to India.

Perched atop her camel, frantic with nerves, she had hardly noticed the sweet air she breathed, or the clear azure sky above the steep brown hills in front of them. After they passed inside the caravanserai's high gate, she had paid little attention to the huddled camps scattered over the caravanserai's hilly terrain.

A short distance from the main gate, they had found their quarters, a pair of thick, black goat-hair tents that squatted close to the ground, each one boasting half a dozen armed guards.

Other tents stood nearby. A lamb had been tied to one of them.

"The ladies will take one tent, the men will take the other," Aminullah Khan had announced from the back of his horse, gesturing toward the black tents. "I will entertain you until your departure in the morning. Then I will accompany you as far as the Sher Darwaza pass."

The morning. Mariana sighed, adjusting her hopes. Perhaps the horseman had not been Hassan after all. Perhaps he had only turned his head as Hassan would have done....

She looked about her in the gathering darkness. Held up by many poles and wrapped in layers of black goat-hair, the women's tent was comfortable enough, although it was too cold inside for them to remove their poshteens. It also was attractive, with its thickly woven floor coverings, its mattresses and bolsters, its piles of woven saddlebags, and its cheerful little fire in a circle of stones, although Aunt Claire had already complained bitterly about being stuffed into the same ice-cold tent with all the female servants.

Mariana imagined Uncle Adrian with Yar Mohammad and the Mug cook, not to mention Dittoo.

The smell of roasting meat drifted in from outside, along with male voices. Earlier, hearing frightened bleating, Mariana had put her head out of the tent in time to see a man holding the dying lamb up by its hind legs, while the blood from its slit throat drained into the snow.

Now, chopped into pieces and threaded onto skewers, it was to be their dinner.

She was dozing against a bolster when Nur Rahman put his head hesitantly into the tent.

"Tell that boy to come in or go out, but for goodness sake close the flap," Aunt Claire snapped from her cocoon of quilts, causing Mariana to start awake. "We have a howling draft as it is. Why is *he* in the women's tent? And why is he swathed in—"

Before her aunt could finish, Mariana was on her feet, beckoning him inside.

"I thought I would never find your horseman," he whispered excitedly. "But there he was, at Haji Khan's house, drinking tea with Munshi Sahib. He—"

"Where is he now?" Mariana demanded, her thoughts whirling. "Is he here?"

"Of course not." The boy waved a vague arm. "He is at his own camp. Aminullah Khan would have him killed if he tried to visit you here. Aminullah has taken responsibility for your honor."

His face filled with curiosity. "Who is this man? Why do you want to see him?"

"Wait there." Without replying, she hurried across the tent floor, found her chaderi, and put it on. "Take me to him."

A plaintive voice rose from the carpet as she tugged on her boots. "Mariana! Where on earth are you going?"

"I shall be back soon, Aunt Claire," Mariana called over her shoulder as she and Nur Rahman, identical in their chaderis, left the black tent and started off into the darkness.

"Stop. I must explain first." Nur Rahman whispered something unintelligible to the trio of guards who sat outside, then motioned for Mariana to follow him.

"We must look as if we are going to that tent over there," he said quietly, pointing. "They must think we have gone to find other women to shield us while we relieve ourselves outside. There is very little time," he added, "only enough to wish the man peace before we return."

Fires glowed in the distance. Tents clustered near them. The boy pointed. "That is his camp."

A faint glow inside the largest tent told them it was occupied.

Mariana tried to smooth her hair, but it was beyond help after being stuffed into the embroidered cap of her chaderi, with most of its pins gone. Her lips were chapped from the cold.

She ran a nervous hand over her face. Why, in all those months, had she not imagined what she would say to Hassan?

Her stomach lurched as she remembered Harry Fitzgerald.

Someone heard them arrive. "Who is there?" inquired a male voice.

"It is I, Nur Rahman," called the boy.

"Enter," the voice replied.

Mariana signaled for Nur Rahman to wait, took a deep breath, lifted the door flap, and entered.

A single oil lamp lit the comfortably arranged tent. Its flame guttered in the draft from the door. Remembering, she bent to remove her boots.

Hassan was already on his feet when she entered. "I have been waiting for you," he said sharply, stepping toward her across a thick Bokhara carpet. "Where is the lady who sent you to find me?"

He was thinner than she remembered. He looked worn, as if he had recently completed some long and difficult work.

"Speak," he snapped, gesturing impatiently.

"Oh!" she cried, her hand to her mouth, too flustered to take in that he thought she was Nur Rahman. "Oh, your beautiful hand!"

He stopped short. He bent, and gazed through her cutwork. "It is you," he said.

He wore an exquisite, unfamiliar scent. Unnerved by his presence, she could only nod.

Nur Rahman's head appeared in the doorway. "Quickly, Khanum," he urged, "we must return at once."

Hassan turned, frowning at the interruption. Mariana raised a hand. "A moment, Nur Rahman."

"No!" The boy shook his head violently. "There is no time. You have left Aminullah Khan's tents without a male escort. If you do not return at once you will cause him dishonor. They kill their own women for making such mistakes," he added desperately.

Hassan strode across the carpet and jerked the door curtain open, letting in both Nur Rahman and a blast of freezing air. "Where is his camp?" he asked curtly.

Nur Rahman pointed. "Inside the gate. Near the mosque."

"If it is that far away," Hassan said decisively, "then you have already been gone too long. You cannot return."

Not return? "But I must go back," Mariana protested. "My aunt and uncle will worry. They will—"

Ignoring her, he pointed outside. "Nur Rahman, you will sleep in that tent over there. My servant Ghulam Ali will give you food."

Ghulam Ali had survived the journey after all! He had found Hassan, and given him her second letter. . . .

Mariana breathed in, trying to grasp her situation. Hassan's carpeted tent was lovely, with its small quilt-covered table on one side, and its pile of silk bolsters. Nevertheless, she felt a sudden pang of homesickness for her aunt and uncle, for Dittoo and Yar Mohammad. How would they manage without her? They were her family.

"Go," Hassan snapped.

Nur Rahman did not reply. As he walked out of the tent, a single sob floated behind him.

He had only been trying to protect her. All this time he had treated her with respect, and no one had bothered to tell him the truth.

"Wait," she called, stumbling after him. "That man is my husband," she said to his back.

He stopped short. "Your *husband*? Why did you not tell this to Aminullah Khan?"

Already turning back, she did not reply.

She found Hassan bending over a saddlebag, his back to her.

"You must write to your uncle," he said briskly, as he took out paper, a quill pen, and a bottle of ink, and laid them aside. "Tell him

you are safe. Tell him that I have undertaken to escort you to Lahore."
He straightened, frowning. "And take off that dirty chaderi.

"I would have brought the rest of your family with me," he
added, as she pulled off the yards of enveloping cotton and raked her
fingers through her tumbled hair, "but it would be disrespectful for
them to leave Aminullah Khan."

He held out the paper and pen. "Write," he said, then strode from
the tent.

When he returned with Nur Rahman, she was folding her letter.
He took it from her and handed it to the boy. "Deliver this without
your disguise," he ordered. "Be careful."

Dearest Uncle Adrian, the letter said, *My husband Hassan has arrived from India. I am safe with him.*

*Sadly, we must now part. It was not my intention to desert you at
this difficult time, but by calling on Hassan I have somehow broken
a Pashtun rule, and now may not return to Aminullah's camp.
Furthermore, it would be most unwise for us to interfere with
Aminullah's arrangements for you and the servants.*

*Please forgive me, and give all my love to Aunt Claire. God will-
ing, we will meet again in India.*

After Nur Rahman had trotted away, Hassan turned to Mariana
and looked silently at her. Something in his tired face made her want
to close her eyes.

She must tell him how she felt now, before she lost her courage.
She must voice her remorse and hope before it was too late.

"I am *so*—" she began.

He silenced her with a raised hand, then took her arm and guided
her to the sandali with its pile of bolsters.

"You did not write," she said, as she stretched her legs beneath the
table, toward the warmth of the brazier.

He did not reply or look at her, but as the shawls across his chest
rose and fell, a wave of feeling seemed to come from him, as it had
once, long before. It crossed the space between them and washed
over her. Her breathing quickened.

"You asked Aminullah Khan for panah," he said softly, "and
brought those whom you love to safety."

She nodded.

What did he want from her? She would die if he did not . . .

His eyes flicked away from hers. He reached into his clothes and pulled out a worn, stained paper. It crinkled between his fingers. "Do you remember this?" he asked, smiling.

"I said too much," she whispered, her face heating. "I did not—"

Beneath his warm, compelling perfume lay the sharp scent of his skin. He put the letter down, and leaned toward her. *"Search out a man,"* he murmured as he reached to open the front of her sheepskin cloak, *"whose own breast has burst from severance, that I may express to him the agony of my love-desire."*

Love-desire. His eyes on her face, he reached inside her cloak, and, with his damaged hand, drew a slow circle on one of her breasts, then the other.

"And though in my grief I stripped off my feathers and broke my wings, even this could not drive from my head this rough passion of love."

His eyes were half closed. She took his damaged hand and kissed the stump of his missing finger.

"I love you," she breathed. "I have loved you from the moment I first saw you."

As soon as she said those words, she realized they were true.

Chapter 35

She awoke the next morning to see Hassan bending over her, fully dressed but for his boots. He held the gold medallion on its chain.

"I believe this is yours," he said, holding it out. "I must buy provisions, and a mount for your journey to Lahore," he added, as he padded to the doorway. "Ghulam Ali and Nur Rahman will look after you until I return, as will my own servants. I will be back, Inshallah, by late morning. When I return, we will prepare to depart."

After the tent flap fell shut behind him, she closed her eyes.

"Nur Rahman," she called, "I want tea!"

HASSAN AND Zulmai waited on their horses at the head of a file of eight unburdened mules. "There is no point in going to the city," Zulmai pointed out. "All the shops will be closed. The British retreat is to take place tomorrow. Everyone is preparing to see the show. We should go instead to one of the forts near the Sher Darwaza. Someone there will be willing to sell us food for our journey."

"Show?" Hassan frowned. "So there is to be shooting."

Zulmai shrugged. "Akbar Khan may have offered the British safe passage, but he will never control the Ghilzais who want revenge for being cheated of their payments. And in any case, the British army is four thousand strong. It is not a merchant kafila. Fighting is an army's life."

"And what is that large army's condition?"

"From what I hear, they are weak from hunger, but hungry or not, fighting is what they will do. Even if they have shown little courage in the past weeks, they will fight tomorrow."

"And they will have no chance at all."

"None," Zulmai agreed. "Gunmen are already waiting for them in the Khurd-Kabul pass, and in the Haft Kotal. As the army passes, more men will come, and lie in wait at Tezeen and Jagdalak. But now," he concluded, clucking to his horse and signaling to the mule drivers, "let us stop talking and go."

The fort he chose was on a slope overlooking the Kabul River. It was not as impressive as some of the strongholds they had passed on their way to Kabul, but it was substantial enough, with its corner towers and high, irregular walls. Hassan and Zulmai left the road and turned toward it, then stopped a respectful distance from the main entrance, their mules lined up behind them, and waited for someone to take notice of them.

Almost immediately men with jezails appeared on the parapet. Moments later, the tall doors were flung open, and a group of men galloped out.

Their leader was a thickly built man with a startling red beard.

"Peace," he offered politely, a hand over his heart.

His eyes drifted to Ghyr Khush, then to the unburdened pack mules.

Zulmai returned his greeting. "We are travelers on our way to India. If you have a horse and provisions to spare, we wish to buy them for our journey."

The red-bearded man gestured invitingly toward the fort's open doorway. "My name is Jamaluddin Khan." He smiled, displaying several broken teeth. "Welcome to my house.

"For how many people do you need these provisions?" he asked, after he had settled his guests in the male quarters of his fort.

"Forty," Hassan replied over the rim of his teacup.

The three men sat, shoeless, on the sheet-covered floor of a large, square room that looked onto the fort's main courtyard, where Ghyr Khush, Zulmai's mount, and all eight mules stood tethered to several trees. Teacups, bowls of dried apricots, mulberries, and pistachio nuts were in front of the sitting men. A samovar hissed outside the door.

"And for how many days?" Jamaluddin went on.

"Twenty-one."

Jamaluddin nodded. "That can easily be arranged. But first," he said, "you must tell me your stories."

He turned to Hassan. "What has brought you, an Indian, to Kabul at this dangerous time? How was your journey? How long have you been here? And you, my Tajik friend," he added, smiling at Zulmai, "how have you come to be sitting in my house with an Indian gentleman?

"When you have finished your stories," he concluded happily, snapping a pistachio shell for emphasis, "I will tell you mine."

Two hours later, empty cups and pistachio shells covered the floor. They were still talking.

Jamaluddin tipped his red beard toward the sitting-room window. "You have a lovely horse," he offered. "It is a long time since I have seen such a beautiful animal."

His face softened. "I had an Akhal Tekke stallion once. He was tall and proud, and he ran like the wind as it crosses the steppes. His name was Ak Belek, for he had a white stocking on one foreleg."

He sighed. "I have had many good horses since then, but I have never forgotten Ak Belek."

"Your compliments," Hassan replied carefully, "have warmed my heart. But may we now discuss our needs for our journey? Is it possible for you to provide us with rice, beans, tea, and other—"

"But why discuss business so soon?" cried Jamaluddin. "You have only just arrived. The goat was killed at noon. To cook it properly will take time."

He leaned forward confidentially. "You have no idea how few interesting visitors we have in wintertime. You, of course, are from India," he added, gesturing in Hassan's direction. "As I am sure you know, people think all Indians are spies for the British."

"That, of course, is true." Hassan inclined his head. "For that reason, I am pleased to be traveling with my friend Zulmai.

"When will he cease these formalities," he whispered, when Jamaluddin's attention was turned elsewhere, "and get to our business?"

"We would be wise," replied Zulmai, "to wait until after we have eaten."

"But that will be hours from now." Hassan hunched his shoulders expressively. "We have been away far too long already."

"Do not fear." Zulmai put out a calming hand. "Let him talk himself out. We will eat his food, and then we will be on our way with our mules fully loaded."

All afternoon the food came—soup, fried meat turnovers, kababs with ovals of tandoori bread. As the sun sank behind the mountains, Jamaluddin was still talking. "This is the best dish of all!" he cried, as he swept a skewer of cubed sheep's liver onto a waiting round of bread in front of Hassan. "You see," he explained, a finger raised, "each dish must be perfectly flavored, and each must be different.

"Kababs are like Akhal Tekke horses," he went on. "Each one must have its own character, but each must be of the highest quality, like your lovely mare. What did you say her name was?"

Although his eyes had turned dark, Hassan's well-trained negotiator's body gave no hint of tension. "Her name is Ghyr Khush," he replied.

HASSAN'S WIRY little servant had brought Mariana's lunch. It was very simple—boiled dal, rice, and bread.

"Hassan Sahib will bring better things to eat when he returns," he had assured her, stepping aside while another man carried the brazier outside to refill it with hot embers. "You will see what fine food he has, even when he travels!"

When he held the door covering aside to leave her, the air that rushed in had felt icier than ever. The visible sliver of distant sky looked heavy and forbidding.

Nur Rahman had visited a little later. "It will snow soon," he observed. "I hope Hassan Ali returns before long.

"Many of the kafilas are moving out," he added. "If they continue to leave here, the caravanserai will be empty by tonight."

Unsurprisingly, after delivering her letter to her uncle the previous evening, Nur Rahman had rushed to tell Mariana's servants where she had gone. Equally unsurprisingly, Dittoo and Yar Mohammad had arrived at Hassan's tents soon after his departure.

As she sat among the bolsters, finishing her morning tea, two different coughs outside her doorway had signaled their presence.

Yar Mohammad had saluted her gravely, then stood, tall, angular, and barefoot, just inside the doorway. He had worn no poshteen, only a mismatched pair of shawls that lay in graceful folds about his shoulders, giving him the dignity of a king.

Dittoo, bundled into his own sheepskin, had rushed inside and taken up a position across the sandali from Mariana. "I am here to serve you, Bibi," he announced, straightening his shoulders, and looked meaningfully at her empty teacup. "I see there is work to be done."

"I, too, Bibi, ask permission to travel with you to Lahore," Yar Mohammad had added.

When Saboor first came to her, it had been Dittoo who had pushed little balls of rice and dal into his open, hungry mouth. "*Accha bacha,* good boy," he had crooned, as if he were speaking to his own son.

She had always felt safe with Yar Mohammad.

If Dittoo came with her now, he would again have the pleasure of looking after little Saboor. Yar Mohammad would have the joy of caring for Ghyr Khush. . . .

She shook her head. "It is not possible," she said, aware that her tone held no authority, only sadness. "My uncle and aunt are old, and their journey to India will be difficult. If you come with me, then who will look after them?"

"But they have Adil," Dittoo wailed. "They do not need another servant."

"Adil, too, is old and weak. You must serve them in his place. God willing, with both of you to care for them, they will live to see India again. Once they are safe, you will return to my service.

"May God protect you both," she concluded.

The tall groom bowed his head, his rough turban concealing his expression. "And may Allah protect you, Bibi," he had returned, in his resonant voice.

Dittoo had wept.

Before he followed the sobbing Dittoo from Hassan's tent, Yar Mohammad had raised his head and looked once at Mariana, his bony face as calm as ever.

With luck, they would all have a safe journey. And whatever happened, at least they were out of that dreadful, stinking cantonment.

Mariana waited uneasily, all afternoon, for Hassan's return. Tense from wondering why he was taking so long, she relaxed hopefully with each approaching footfall, only to feel her body tighten again as the passerby moved on.

There was something unsafe about the camp.

Ghulam Ali called on her after sunset.

Still listening for Hassan's return, she half-heard the story of Ghulam Ali's narrow escape from the Ghilzai nomads on the road to Peshawar, and his joy at discovering Hassan at the tea shop. She nodded at his report of the return journey's high winds, thieves, and lost mules, and his loving description of Hassan Ali's silver-gray mare.

"Yar Mohammad will be the envy of Lahore," he had declared, his rough voice full of pride. "Everyone will know that he spends his days with the great horse Ghyr Khush."

At last, she had blurted out the question she had been longing to ask. "Are my aunt and uncle still here? Are Yar Mohammad and Dittoo here?"

"No, Bibi." Ghulam Ali's white eyebrows rose. "They left just after sunrise this morning."

Then they were alone. Mariana tugged her poshteen over her shoulders, went to the doorway, and moved the curtain aside.

A raw wind whipped her hair. It was snowing.

"It is good that they have left," Ghulam Ali declared, "for tomorrow the British will march for Jalalabad."

Tomorrow. She looked out into the falling snow, imagining the British with their ragged army and starving camp followers, struggling down the narrow, dangerous road to Jalalabad and India.

But what would happen to her tomorrow? What if Hassan never returned?

A distant line of pack animals trudged away toward the caravanserai's gate. Nur Rahman had been correct. Of all the tents that had been there when she arrived, only three were still visible, huddled together a hundred yards away.

A man emerged from one of them, muffled in shawls. He stopped by the doorway and stared at her.

She backed hastily inside, took off her cloak, and pulled the sandali quilt to her chin. There was nothing to do now, but wait.

"IT HAS begun to snow." Jamaluddin Khan pointed to the courtyard, where white flakes fell lightly on the backs of the tethered animals. "I am pleased to see that you keep your Ghyr Khush covered with a felt blanket. That is the correct way. And since you cover her in this cold weather, I am sure you also cover her in hot weather, to keep her lean, and her sinews tight and strong."

"Of course," Zulmai replied, speaking for his friend. "But since it is late, and snow is falling, perhaps we should make our transaction. We would like to return to our camp tonight."

"Tonight? But no! It is too late to arrange for your provisions. And where is the sense in going out in this weather? You will certainly lose your way."

He spread his arms. "You must accept my hospitality tonight!"

"He desires my horse," Hassan whispered. "That is why he is not letting us go."

"I agree." Zulmai offered Hassan a hollow look. "I should have warned you not to bring her."

Hassan shrugged. "It is only a pity that I did not see it until now."

He turned to his host. "In exchange for your kind hospitality, Jamaluddin Khan," he said formally, "and for your offer of provisions for forty men for twenty-one days, I am presenting you with my mare, Ghyr Khush."

"Ghyr Khush?" Jamaluddin cried, with theatrical dismay. "No, no! I could never accept such a fine gift, such a beautiful gift!"

Hassan held up his hand. "You have offered us shelter from the bitter cold. You have killed a goat for our entertainment. We are brothers now."

He smiled without bitterness. "My wealth, Jamaluddin Khan, is your wealth."

"Ah." Jamaluddin sighed happily. "In that case, my brother, I accept. Tomorrow morning I will furnish you with the two best mounts this house has to offer, and also its finest food: live chickens and goats; almonds, pistachios, dried figs, and dates from my stores; rice, flour, and beans; sugar, tea, salt, and spices."

His eyes turned dreamy. "And as for Ghyr Khush, I will never raise my voice to her. I will let her gallop over open spaces as she was born to gallop. I will feed her with my own hands: eggs, mutton fat, barley, and *quatlame,* the food of her homeland. I will cover her in all weathers with layers of fine, felt blanket, and I will love her as I once loved my beautiful Ak Belek."

Chapter 36

Arguments had raged in the cantonment for days about how much artillery should be taken on the march, and how to get the army across the many rivers on the road to Jalalabad. In the Khurd-Kabul pass alone, it was rumored, the narrow road would cross the stream no less than thirty times.

"The six remaining guns," General Elphinstone finally declared, "belong to the Crown. On no account must they be left behind. We are abandoning too much valuable property as it is."

His arm strapped across his chest with a filthy bandage, Harry Fitzgerald shook his head as he received his instructions. "The artillery bullocks and horses are already half starved," he objected. "They will not be able to pull the guns through those steep defiles. And what if Afghan snipers—"

"Do as you are told," he was ordered. "Or, at least, begin to do it, since all orders are being countermanded within the hour."

"Guns, property!" Fitzgerald muttered later that afternoon, as he inspected his bony, shivering artillery horses. "Have they even *thought* of these animals? Have they even considered tents, or food for the men?"

"THE RETREAT is now set for tomorrow," Lady Sale announced that evening to her daughter, Charles Mott, and Lady Macnaghten, as they sat on her stiff-backed chairs around a fire that did little to warm the room.

Lady Macnaghten nodded. "I have made up my mind what I am taking with me," she said decisively.

Her voice, a full tone lower than it had been before her husband's death, held no hint of coquettishness. The three shawls she wore together over her head did not flatter her. "I cannot ask the coolies or the servants to carry many of my household belongings, and so I shall bring only my bed, my warm clothes, shawls, and rezais, and all the dried fruit from the Residence pantry. Thank goodness the servants have winter boots."

Her voice trailed away.

Charles Mott laid a hand on her arm. "I shall remain at your side, Aunt," he said gravely, "and see to your safety."

"We shall all stick together," Lady Sale agreed.

Lady Macnaghten smiled. "Indeed we shall. And we shall reach Jalalabad quite safely. I am sure of it."

"She is a gallant woman," Lady Sale observed to her daughter, after Lady Macnaghten had climbed the stairs to her room followed by her nephew, a candle flickering in his hand. "I would never have expected it of her. And that foppish, fool nephew of hers has somehow developed a spine."

She stood and held her hands to the fire. "I wonder what became of Miss Givens. I cannot believe Mott's claim that an Afghan chief abducted her, and then demanded her entire family, including the servants, as hostages. I think she and her uncle have plotted an escape to India."

"If they have," her daughter said bluntly, "then they are cowards."

"Perhaps they are," mused Lady Sale, "but they are clever cowards. There is more to that Givens girl than meets the eye. And now," she added briskly, "we must go to bed, for tomorrow we shall march."

MORNING ARRIVED in Mariana's tent without sun, or any sign of Hassan Ali Khan.

When Nur Rahman held out a cup of morning tea, Mariana

returned his greeting distractedly, her breath white in the tent's freezing air. When he did not leave immediately, but sat down by her doorway, his knife ready at his belt, she understood that he, too, was worried.

"All our drivers have taken their animals, and left," he volunteered.

"The pack animals are gone? But why?"

He shrugged. "Hassan Ali Khan is supposed to supply all their food. It finished last night. When he had not returned this morning, they went away. Ghulam Ali and I told them to wait, but they said they must seek food and work elsewhere."

"Are we all alone, then?"

"No." The boy shook his head. "The servants are in four tents behind us, but they are afraid. They say they have been threatened by people who think they are spying for the British."

"And what of Ghulam Ali?"

"He is outside your doorway with a musket. He has been there since dawn."

Her chest tightened. "And *he* is our protection?"

Nur Rahman raised his chin. "Ghulam Ali and *I*," he said, pointing to his own, wicked-looking knife, "are *your* protection."

Mariana stood up, tightened her sheepskin across her chest, and pushed the door curtain aside. There was no sign of the courier. The other tents that had dotted the sloping ground in front of her were gone, except for the three menacing-looking ones she had seen the night before.

"Ghulam Ali is not there." She pushed her hands into her sleeves against the invading wind. "Ask the servants to bring more hot coals."

Nur Rahman went out, and returned almost immediately. "There is no one in the servants' tents," he whispered. "They are gone."

"*Gone?*" She stared. "But where would they go, in this weather?"

"I heard one of them say yesterday that he has a Hindu friend in the city. Perhaps they have gone to find him. I found a tribesman standing near their tents just now," he added. "He said that he and his friends had been teasing the servants, threatening to come at night and kill them all. He said they were cowards to run away."

"Perhaps they were not teasing." A shiver ran down Mariana's back. She had seen only two of Hassan's servants since her arrival, but she knew enough of Indian households to imagine them all—at least three personal servants, a pair of cooks, a sweeper, someone to wash Hassan's clothes, grooms, porters, someone to attend to the fire, a courier. . . .

"And what of Ghulam Ali?" she asked sharply.

The boy shook his head. "He has not returned."

"Then we are alone." Panic rose in Mariana's throat.

She put a hand on the tent pole to steady herself. Even the freezing roads would be safer than this vulnerable, unguarded tent. Who knew what horrors they would risk if they stayed.

"We must leave at once," she said urgently.

"No." Nur Rahman shook his head. "We must wait. Ghulam Ali cannot have gone far. Hassan Ali Khan is coming back soon. He will—"

"How do you know Hassan will come?" she demanded, her voice rising. "How do you know he has not been killed? How do you know Ghulam Ali is not lying somewhere outside with his throat cut?"

Her shoulders sagged at the sound of her own terrible words. "We have no food left, Nur Rahman, and only that knife of yours for protection. The men in front of us have seen me here. They know we're alone."

"But where will we go?"

"To Haji Khan's house. He will know what to do. If Hassan returns, he will find me there."

If. The Afghans would have seen that Hassan was Indian. She must not picture him shot by a sniper, lying crumpled by the side of the road.

No one knew where she was.

Nur Rahman threw up his hands. "Khanum," he cried, "we cannot go to the city! It is at war. No women will be allowed on the streets."

She found her chaderi and threw it on. "Then we must join the British on their march to Jalalabad. If we hurry, we can join the vanguard, where the senior ladies are—"

"No!"

"Please, Nur Rahman," she begged, her chin wobbling with fright beneath her veil. "We must get away from here before we are killed. Tomorrow morning the British will have marched away, and the city will be safer. We will go to Haji Khan's house then."

Nur Rahman squeezed his eyes shut.

When she did not reply, he opened his eyes and sighed. "If I am to walk on the road with you," he said resignedly, "then I must fetch my own chaderi."

Like a pair of countrywomen, with dirty, worn chaderis over their sheepskins, they walked together under the high gate of the caravanserai, then turned east, along the narrow, trampled path to the city, and the road to Jalalabad.

A faint thudding came from the distance.

"Heavy guns," Mariana said as they walked. "The British must be fighting a rearguard action, to cover the retreat."

As they neared the city, the sound of artillery grew louder. Mariana walked heavily, weighed down by her sheepskin, her movements hampered by her sodden chaderi.

Her face burned from the cold.

Nur Rahman pointed. "Look!" he cried, over the thundering of the guns.

To their left, past leafless orchards, heavy gray smoke rose into the air.

"The British fort has fallen," he said.

She stared despairingly at the column of smoke. She had never thought the enemy would set the cantonment on fire. Where were Lady Macnaghten and Lady Sale? Where were Charles Mott and Harry Fitzgerald?

"Akbar Khan's men have captured the British artillery," the boy went on. "They are firing after the British as they run away."

Run away. It was a terrible admission, but it was correct. The rising smoke certainly did not speak of tactical retreat, a prelude to future victory. It told only of dismal, hopeless flight.

It had taken the Afghans no time at all to use the captured artillery. . . .

Two boys approached, leading a donkey.

Nur Rahman stopped them to ask for news. The elder of the two pointed east, toward the Hindu Kush mountains. His companion gestured excitedly, a wide grin on his dirty face.

When they had gone, Nur Rahman turned to Mariana. "Those boys watched everything, even the shooting," he said. "They say that Afghan fighters have disrupted the retreating column. They say the British and Indian soldiers are not returning the Afghan artillery fire, and that most of their baggage was plundered before they had even crossed the river."

Mariana shivered. The smoke now seemed to come from more than one fire. Had Fitzgerald lost all his guns? What would become of the poor, desperate column as it tried to force its way through the first, claustrophobic Khurd-Kabul pass? How would it survive that pass, and the next one, and the next? What of the half-starved sepoys who marched in this bitter cold, or the camp followers, the twelve thousand unarmed men, women, and children? What of the shoeless, runny-nosed babies she had seen in the bazaar?

At its narrowest, the Jagdalak Pass was only six feet wide.

Her legs felt weak. Her feet had lost their feeling. She wanted to sit down, but there was nowhere to rest, only snow, gray skies, leafless trees, and more snow.

"We must avoid the fighting," Nur Rahman said thoughtfully. "We will turn north to avoid the path of the British army, then travel parallel to them until we reach the head of the column. At dark, after the Ghilzais have stopped shooting, and dispersed to their homes, we will join the British camp."

She nodded numbly.

"Since it has taken them all morning to cross the river," he said, "they will not have gone far. Early tomorrow morning, before the fighting begins again, we will get away and return to the city. But we must move quickly."

Had they made a mistake? she wondered, as she forced herself to follow the boy. Had they abandoned Hassan's camp too soon? Why, in her panic, had she failed to leave a note for Hassan? Was he searching for her even now?

If he was, then *please* make him wait for her at Haji Khan's house.

Nur Rahman pointed toward a narrow path leading north across the snowy landscape. "This is the road," he said.

It was two more miles before the path they followed was intersected by a second, equally narrow one. Beside that unprepossessing crossroad, a wooden lean-to sat on a patch of packed snow. In its questionable shelter, a red-cheeked man tended a fire beneath a battered samovar.

As she toiled toward it, Mariana looked longingly at the fire and the worn carpets that had been spread on the snow to accommodate the chaikhana's half-dozen customers.

She and Nur Rahman had not a single coin between them.

A second pot stood balanced at the edge of the fire. It was the scent from that pot that drove Mariana to twist off the small gold ring she had worn since she was eighteen, and hold it out to the proprietor.

He pocketed the ring and pointed to a separate place behind the lean-to, out of sight of his male guests. "Wait there," he said, as Mariana and Nur Rahman sat gratefully down on a shabby Bokhara carpet. "I will bring soup."

IT WAS noon before Hassan and Zulmai arrived at the caravanserai, Hassan riding a glossy chestnut stallion and leading a black mare. Behind them followed the eight mules, loaded with food supplies and live chickens in cages covered with felt wrappings. Beside the mules, a boy with a stick drove five nanny goats.

Terrified of what Hassan would say, but desperate to share his burden, Ghulam Ali ran heavily toward them and fell to his knees.

"Bibi is gone," he sobbed, "she is gone!"

"What? When?"

The courier looked up, hot tears standing in his eyes. "I went to relieve myself this morning, out of sight of her tent. I could not wait any longer, Sahib."

"And when you came back?" Hassan sat absolutely still on his stallion.

"They were gone. Nothing had been stolen. The bolsters, the rugs, all are still there. I do not know what happened. I never thought anyone would kidnap them."

"I did not know," Ghulam Ali added miserably, gesturing at the four empty servants' tents, "that the servants had all run away."

"Did anyone see them leave?" Zulmai demanded.

Ghulam Ali's face crumpled. "I did not think to ask. I have been so—"

"Get off your knees," Zulmai ordered, "and ask the tea seller by the gate."

"Two women in chaderis went past this morning," the old man offered when the three men approached him. "I think they turned that way," he added, pointing toward the city. "They appeared to be alone," he added carefully, "and they did not seem to be ladies of wealth."

Before he had finished speaking, Hassan clucked to his new

stallion. "I do not know when I will be back," he threw over his shoulder, as his horse cantered under the gate and onto the road.

"Ghulam Ali," Zulmai ordered, "stay with our baggage. Do not let anyone disappear with our food stores. I will bring more pack animals to carry our tents, and then you and I will wait and see whether Hassan Ali Khan finds his wife."

Chapter 31

January 6, 1842

As she gulped her second bowl of soup, Mariana looked through a gap in the tea shop wall. She elbowed Nur Rahman, and pointed.

A thickly dressed man was approaching the chaikhana. Behind him strode a pair of blond, two-humped Bactrian camels.

Her eyes on the new guest, Mariana reached into the pocket of her poshteen, took out Hassan's medallion, and slid it from its chain and into her palm.

An olive, read its delicate Arabic letters, *neither of the East, nor of the West*.

"Here is what we will do," she whispered.

Half an hour later, when the camel-driving customer put down his teacup and stood to leave, Mariana and Nur Rahman got up and followed him to where his tethered animals waited, their jaws moving rhythmically.

Nur Rahman cleared his throat. "Please," he said sweetly, "will you take us toward Butkhak?"

The man's face was seamed from exposure to the sun. He frowned, his eyes politely averted from them. "But Butkhak is on the road to Jalalabad," he replied dubiously. "Why do you want to go there? Do you not know what is happening?"

"We live just past Begrami," Nur Rahman explained. "We have become late, and now we fear we will not reach there before sunset."

The man shook his head. "I am not going that way."

Nur Rahman held out his hand. Mariana's gold chain dangled from his fingers. "We can offer you this."

The man shrugged, took the chain, and put it into his pocket. "If there is danger," he warned, "I will turn back."

"Once we are past Begrami, we will be sure to find the head of the British train," Nur Rahman whispered.

The man picked up a stick. Making a curious guttural sound, he tapped the forelegs of one camel, then the other.

One after the other, they knelt obediently down, front knees first, hindquarters second.

Mariana's had mild, long-lashed eyes. It smelled warm and musty. Even kneeling, it was tall. She reached up and grasped two handfuls of its luxuriant hair, then, with a discreet boost from Nur Rahman, struggled onto its back, and settled between its humps.

Her plight could be worse, she thought, as they started off. The snow had stopped, although the sky was still heavy and gray. Her stomach was full, and the shaggy humps protected her from the fiercest blasts of wind. She pushed her hands into the sleeves of her poshteen, hunched her shoulders against the cold, hoping she was doing the right thing.

The afternoon light had begun to change. The city and the Bala Hisar were already behind them. Their escort strode rapidly along, saying nothing, the lead ropes in one hand.

As the light began to fade, sounds came from the distance, of a great body of men, carts, and animals on the move.

Their road was taking them nearer to the retreating army. Sounds began to distinguish themselves from the general din: shouts, cries, and shots.

The Ghilzais were still firing on the column. People must have been killed, but who?

She swayed with her camel's stride, listening intently to the sounds of battle. How long, she wondered, was the column? How much farther must they go to find the vanguard?

Their guide stopped and looked back at her. "We will reach Begrami after dark," he announced. "Do you know the way to your house?"

"Oh, yes, of course," Nur Rahman fluted.

Mariana closed her eyes. She felt as if she had been traveling for weeks. The rhythmic chiming of the camels' ankle bells reminded her of something. . . .

She awoke when her camel stopped.

Night had already fallen. Animals blew nearby. A chorus of competing voices combined with the creaks and groans of transport vehicles.

"We have reached Begrami," their guide announced. He was barely visible in the blackness. "I cannot take you any farther. The foreigners and their army have blocked the way. They are all around us. I do not know what to do with you now," he added mournfully. "I wish I had not agreed to help you."

"Oh, no," Nur Rahman assured him. "It is all right. We will get down now. We can walk the rest of the way."

"Impossible," the man declared. "I have taken responsibility for your safety. There is a fort a little way behind us. I must take you there."

Another fort. Mariana held her breath.

"Leave us here!" Nur Rahman's voice held a note of hysteria.

"I will not allow two women to walk through a foreign army camp in the middle of—"

"Leave us!" Nur Rahman screeched. "Make the camels kneel down! Keep the gold chain! We want to get off!"

The man said nothing, but a moment later Mariana heard his guttural noise again, and felt the tapping of his stick.

Her camel dropped, joltingly, to the ground. She slid from its back. Almost at once she felt Nur Rahman tug at her chaderi.

"Run," he urged quietly, "before he changes his mind!"

Clutching each other, they hurried clumsily away.

"Make no sound," Nur Rahman whispered.

At last they heard the man speak to his camels. A moment later the jingling of their ankle bells told them he was leaving.

Groans and cries came from ahead of them. Mariana's heart contracted as they picked their way toward the sound.

When they arrived, she peered around her with growing dismay.

The British camp, if it could be called one, was a disgrace. No cooking fires beckoned them. No lamplight glowed from inside sheltering tents. Barely visible, silhouetted against the pale snow, men lay singly and in groups as if they had fallen where they stood. Sobs and whimpers filled the air.

A shadowy form lay across Mariana's path. She bent over it.

"Where are the senior officers? Where is General Elphinstone?" she asked, first in English, then in Urdu.

The body in the snow proved to be an Indian sepoy. "I do not know where they are, Memsahib," he replied through chattering teeth. "I only know that I am dying from the cold."

Impulsively, she reached down and touched his arm. He wore only his regular uniform, the thin red coat he had worn throughout the summer and autumn.

"I am sorry," was all she could manage.

Afraid to lose Nur Rahman in the darkness, she clutched a handful of his chaderi.

"I think we have found the rear of the column," he whispered. "It is too late to make our way to the front."

"What should we do now?" Despairing, she looked about her. "There is snow everywhere. We cannot stand up all night."

"There is only one thing to do."

His chaderi rustled as he pulled it off his shoulders. "We must take off our poshteens and spread one of them on the snow. Then we must lie down on it, and put the other one over us. That is how we will survive until the morning."

An hour later, shivering against the snoring Nur Rahman, she listened to the screams of the wounded and the groans of the freezing, until her eyes closed.

AT THE front of the column, an exhausted-looking captain put his head around the door flap of the only standing tent. "Is there room for anyone else?" he inquired politely.

"No." Lady Sale pointed to the bodies cramming the floor around her upright chair. "You can see for yourself that there is not a square inch remaining. Is it really true," she added, turning to her son-in-law, "that only this tent has survived the march, of all the ones we brought from the cantonment?"

"I would not be surprised," Captain Sturt replied painfully. "The insurgents fell on our pack animals the moment they left the gate."

"We need only to manage for six more days," Lady Macnaghten offered from her place between Sturt's wife and Charles Mott.

"If your raisins have not been stolen," Mott suggested, "we might have them now."

"You will find them in a leather bag inside the door," she replied, "but do not give me any. I have no appetite at all."

Outside the tent, soldiers lay in heaps, trying to keep warm. Officers called out, trying to find their regiments in the darkness.

"I doubt," groaned someone from a corner of the tent, "that many of us will reach Jalalabad alive."

"Croaker!" retorted Lady Sale.

MARIANA STIRRED, as light penetrated her eyelids. Why was her room so cold? Why was her head covered in cloth? What was that sound that vibrated all around her?

With a sharp intake of breath, she realized where she was. The sound she heard was an army on the march.

She shook Nur Rahman. "Wake up," she ordered. "The column is moving."

It was barely dawn. Shuddering from the cold, they tied on their sheepskins, pulled their chaderis over them, and took in their surroundings.

The corpse of the previous night's sepoy lay a dozen yards from where they had slept, its lower extremities as black as charred wood. In the distance, a ragged crowd followed the bloody path of the retreat, past the carcasses of fallen animals, past their own dying, their own dead.

Mariana shaded her eyes. Far ahead of them in the distance, a concentrated mass of marchers moved over a hill, toward a glorious pink-and-orange sunrise.

Some of the stragglers around them were native soldiers, their faces contorted from the pain of their wounds. Some were unarmed camp followers staggering on frozen feet. Still others were native women, their eyes dazed, their long hair falling down their backs, many carrying babies and small children, most wearing only flimsy shoes and thin shawls. How any of them still lived, even after one day, was a mystery to Mariana.

None of them would be able to keep up with the column. All were doomed.

Not a single British officer was to be seen.

Twenty yards from Mariana, a team of exhausted-looking

bullocks dragged a nine-pound gun up an incline, their hooves slipping, while a dozen native artillerymen struggled to push the gun carriage from behind.

The bullocks meant that this was not Harry Fitzgerald's horse artillery. But where was the wheeled limber with supplies for the gun? Where were the officers who rode beside their men, barking orders, seeing that everything was done properly?

Had they run away, and left these poor gunners to their fate?

Perhaps they had. Nothing, no amount of incompetence or neglect would surprise Mariana now.

Two loud thuds echoed behind her. One artilleryman, then another, spun about and toppled to the snow.

The Ghilzais had returned.

"We must get away," Nur Rahman cried urgently, tugging at her. "Come quickly! We must hide! The Ghilzai horsemen will be here soon. They will do more than shoot. They—"

She did not hear a word he said, for swaying with exhaustion on a gaunt horse, Harry Fitzgerald was trotting toward the lumbering gun and its frightened men.

The bones stood out on his face. His left arm was still strapped to his chest. He drew rein and shouted an order.

Deaf to Nur Rahman's entreaties, Mariana watched two gunners unhook a spike from the gun carriage, and hammer it into the top of the gun barrel, while the others worked to free the bullocks.

They were disabling the gun before they left it behind—the last, most painful action an artillery officer could take.

Without thinking, she threw back her chaderi and ran toward honest, heroic Harry Fitzgerald.

"No!" Nur Rahman wailed behind her.

She had not gone twenty feet before more shots came. A third gunner fell, then a fourth. Fitzgerald jerked in his saddle. His free arm flailing, he toppled to the ground.

He had not seen her.

Heart pounding, unable to scream, Mariana ran on, until some instinct made her turn and look behind her.

Nur Rahman had flung off his disguise. Fully revealed as a young man, he danced, grinning desperately, his feet stamping, his arms above his head, his fingers moving in graceful imitation of a dancing girl.

He did not stop until another shot thudded from behind a pile of rock. Then, in one motion, he dropped to his knees and fell face-forward into the filthy, trampled snow.

Mariana stopped running. Her mind a paralyzed blank, she looked from boy to man, and back again.

Two artillerymen bent briefly over the motionless Fitzgerald, then hurried away to continue their work.

Nur Rahman's arm lifted briefly, then dropped.

She turned, scrambled back to him, and fell to her knees at his side.

He had deliberately attracted the musket ball that had dropped him to the ground. She knew he had done it for her.

She grasped him by his sheepskin cloak and rolled him onto his back.

There was blood on his shirt where his poshteen had fallen open. He had been shot through the chest.

He stared, wide-eyed, into her face. "I am cold," he whispered, fighting to breathe.

"Why did you dance like that?" she cried as she closed his poshteen over his chest.

He shook his head, as if she were asking the wrong question. "Pray for me," he gasped.

"You did it to protect me, didn't you?" she demanded as she stuffed his discarded chaderi beneath his head.

"Take it off," he croaked, plucking at the folds of cloth on her shoulder. "They believe you are a spy, or a dishonored woman retreating with the British army. They will aim at you again, and I will not be here to—"

He coughed, his face clenched.

"*Please* don't die, Nur Rahman," she begged. "Don't leave me alone here."

There was nothing unsavory about him now. He was her lifeline.

"Pray for me," he repeated.

Still kneeling, she steepled her hands together and closed her eyes. "Heavenly Father," she began, thinking of her childhood, "I pray for the soul of—"

Fingers clutched at her. "Not foreign prayers," he gasped. "Pray to Allah."

"But I *am*. I may be a Christian, but—"

His fringed eyes implored her. She could hear air whistling

through the hole in his chest. "You are a good woman, Khanum. The prayer will go from your mouth to Allah's ear. I want—"

She knew what he wanted. *Most of all,* he had told her once, *I long to be made pure again, and to see the face of the Beloved.*

"First," he whispered, "say *La illaha illa Allah, Muhammad Rasul Allah*—there is no god save God, and Muhammad is the Messenger of God."

Have I asked you to recite the Shahada, *the attestation of faith?* Haji Khan had asked her on the day Burnes was murdered, his voice rising.

No, she had replied.

Then I have not asked you to embrace Islam, he had said.

In Munshi Sahib's story of the king's messenger, wise words had set Muballigh free to return to his homeland. Perhaps these Arabic ones would do the same for Nur Rahman. . . .

She glanced skyward. "Dear Lord," she whispered, "Haji Khan told me that You and Allah are the same. If You are not, please forgive me.

"*La illaha illa Allah,*" she intoned, "*Muhammad Rasul Allah.*"

"Now say it twice more," Nur Rahman croaked. She did as she was asked.

There, she had done it.

Imagining the horror on her father's face, she looked down, expecting the boy to smile, but he was already fading.

She bent over him. "O Allah Most Gracious," she shouted over his rasping breath, "forgive Thy servant Nur Rahman, and reward him with the sight of Thy face. Give him loving companions of his own age, and let him drink from the fountain of—"

He stopped breathing.

"—Salsabil," she finished, and dropped her face into her ice-cold hands.

Chapter 38

O thou soul," Safiya Sultana recited, her Qur'an open to the marked page where she had left off the previous day.

"In complete rest
And satisfaction!
Enter thou, then
Among my devotees!
Yea, enter thou
My Heaven!"

After murmuring the proper blessings, she folded the book into its silk wrappings, and stood up.

As she lifted it to its accustomed place on a high shelf in her room, a terrified wail came from the end of the corridor, where the children were waiting for their breakfast.

A moment later, a twelve-year-old girl pushed Safiya's door curtain aside, and carried Saboor into the room.

His screams were deep and throaty. His face was slick with tears. His eyes were focused inward. Beads of perspiration dotted his hairline.

He did not seem to notice Safiya bending over him. He stared through her, as if she were not there.

She made no effort to soothe him. Instead, while his trembling cousin held him, she gripped him by the arm. "Who is it, Saboor?" she demanded, shaking him. "Is it your Abba? Is it Hassan?"

His mouth stretched wide, he shook his head.

"Is it your An-nah?" she insisted. "Is it Mariam? *Speak, Saboor.*"

He nodded.

"Put him down, Ayesha," she ordered.

When he was on his feet, she took his hand. "Come, child," she said decisively, "we have work to do."

Only then did Saboor stop screaming.

"Call all the ladies and older girls," Safiya ordered, as she led him, still gulping, into the sitting room. "I need all of you."

The women crowded around her, staring at the child. "Why do you need us, Bhaji?" they asked. "What is wrong with Saboor?"

Without replying, Safiya took her accustomed place on the floor and drew the child down beside her.

When the ladies had seated themselves, murmuring with curiosity, she cleared her throat.

"Today," she announced, wrapping a stout arm about Saboor's shoulders, "we will perform the Uml of Lost Persons for Saboor's stepmother Mariam.

"Because Saboor is, by Allah's grace, able to see what we cannot," she added, "we have come to know she is in danger."

The ladies cried out. Safiya gestured for silence.

"His gift also allows us to act swiftly on her behalf, so we may hope that our help arrives in time.

"While the preparations are being made," she went on, "you will all learn a phrase in Sindhi which is part of the uml. It does not matter whether or not we speak the Sindhi language, but we must pronounce the words properly.

"If we perform the uml correctly, we will, Inshallah, save Mariam from whatever peril she is facing. In any case, we will, in due course, learn the truth of her circumstances."

Safiya's gap-toothed sister-in-law spoke for the ladies. "Never before," she said formally, "have we been asked to participate in an uml. We are proud to do so, and will try our very best."

"In the meanwhile," Safiya announced fiercely, "no matter how curious we may be to know his story, we may *not* upset Saboor by asking him what he has seen."

Two servants were sent to bring a tall spinning wheel from one of the downstairs storerooms. Under Safiya's direction, it was set up in an unused chamber, and prepared with a continuous skein of cotton leading from the big wheel to the small wheel, and back again.

Other servants found a heavy curtain and hung it in the doorway, to shut the room off from the rest of the ladies' quarters.

A straw stool was set in front of the wheel.

As soon as room and wheel were ready, the ladies began their work.

One by one, instructed by Safiya Sultana, they drew the curtain aside, slipped into the room, and took their turns at the wheel, whispering the strange message that called the lost person home. One by one, after their long, difficult turns, concentrating on their recitations, never allowing the wheel to stop, they withdrew to lie down until their turn came again.

"How long will it take?" asked Hassan's gap-toothed aunt, when her turn was finished.

"I do not know, Rehmana," replied Safiya, "but I can tell you this. For Mariam, the result of our work may come quite soon, but since she is far away, the news of her whereabouts and condition may take time to reach us. Until then we must perform the uml without stopping. It is difficult work, but it must be done.

"And now," she added, "let us wash for our afternoon prayers."

FIFTY FEET from Nur Rahman's body, two Indian soldiers had fallen together, their arms and legs entwined in death. What might be a bundle of rags near them was, Mariana knew, a frozen woman with an infant in her arms.

Nur Rahman's chaderi was still beneath his head. Mariana removed it and spread it over his body.

An elderly red-coated straggler toiled past her, his head drooping. He was a native officer with gray, snow-encrusted mustaches. He looked old enough to be Mariana's grandfather.

Beyond him lay Harry Fitzgerald and the now-abandoned gun.

Before she could go to Fitzgerald, half a dozen Afghan riders appeared from a grove of leafless trees and trotted toward the old sepoy, who trudged on, ignoring them.

"Look out!" she cried, but it was hopeless.

The first horseman bent casually from his saddle, and in one graceful, backhanded motion, sliced the old soldier nearly in half.

He fell, spurting blood, without uttering a sound.

Numb with terror, Mariana watched the horsemen cut down another male marcher, then another. One by one, freezing, starving, and ignored, the wailing women sank to the snow.

Desperate for a place to hide, Mariana turned back to Nur Rahman's shrouded corpse. She threw aside his chaderi, then tugged at his body, her teeth gritted, until she had wrested it out of its sheepskin cloak.

She spread the poshteen open on the snow, then took off her own, covered herself with it and rolled into a lonely, frightened, poorly hidden ball.

If she survived, she would find her way back to the city. To do so, she would have to retrace the army's bloody march, and risk being killed by pursuing tribesmen. But even if no one cut her down, how would she fare, alone in this bitter cold? It must be at least six miles to Kabul. Her hands and feet had already lost their feeling. She had not eaten since the previous afternoon.

Desperately cold and frightened, she waited for someone to come, snatch away her protecting sheepskin, and cut her throat, but in time, the shots ceased, and the cries of the wounded tapered off.

The horsemen seemed to have gone, perhaps to follow the column, looking for more people to kill.

When she sat up, an icy wind burned her ears. She got back into her sheepskin; then, in spite of Nur Rahman's warning, she flung her chaderi over her head, needing its thin cotton to keep out some of the cold.

Praying that the horsemen would not return, she toiled over to Fitzgerald.

He had been shot through the neck. He lay faceup in a scarlet pool of frozen blood, his beard encrusted with snow, his eyes half open.

He must have died instantly.

Of all the British artillery officers, he alone had thought of those abandoned gunners, and come to their rescue.

He had offered her his hand and his heart.

She knelt at his side. "Dear Allah," she prayed through chattering teeth, "take this good man's soul to Thy Paradise. And please," she added, "give him everything Nur Rahman has, but let him be with English people, if possible."

She touched Harry Fitzgerald's stiff cheek, got to her feet, and started back toward Kabul.

No stragglers approached as she trudged along. Save for the dead, she was alone.

At a noise behind her, she turned and drew in a sharp, frightened breath.

She was far from alone. The horsemen had returned. They rode straight for her.

They would kill her now, of course. Nur Rahman had warned her. But what did it matter? Everyone who still lived would be dead soon. Hassan would never find her here. It was too late for hope.

She did not have the fatalistic courage of the old sepoy. Bent double in her dirty chaderi, nauseous with fright, she waited for the horsemen to arrive, to slice her in half with their wicked, curving swords.

They pulled to a halt in front of her, blocking her way.

"You," shouted a familiar, hollow voice.

It was Aminullah Khan, coming to punish her for spurning his asylum. She closed her eyes and waited for the bite of his sword.

"Are you my missing asylum-seeker?" he barked. "Speak! Let me hear your voice."

"I am," she quavered.

"Hah!" He smiled harshly. "I thought you wanted panah."

He gestured with a slick, crimson blade at the carnage around them. "So you have changed your mind. You have decided to die among these infidels after all."

He leaned from his horse. "You did not tell me you were married," he barked. "Where is the husband who has abandoned you to freeze here on this battlefield?"

"Why do you want to know?" Mariana's feet were like blocks of ice. Too hungry and too desperately tired to think, she lifted her chaderi from her face and looked Aminullah Khan in the eye. "Why," she asked resignedly, "do you not kill me now?"

His chin lifted, as if she had struck him. His henchmen looked quickly away from them both.

"Kill you? Who do you think I am?" He smiled unpleasantly. "You are my guest. Why do you suggest that I would kill you? I am no infidel, like your people."

This last was too much to comprehend. Mariana took a step backward, her hands outstretched. "Please do not tease me," she begged, her knees buckling. "Please."

"Come." He sheathed his dreadful sword, edged his horse toward her, and reached down. "Get up," he ordered. "You asked panah, and you shall have it."

Panah. There was no point in asking where he was taking her. After somehow forcing a heavy, numb leg across his horse's back, she noticed only that he and his henchmen had turned away from the city. As before, he galloped headlong, while she bounced behind him, half forgotten, terrified she would fall, her stiff fingers gripping his cummerbund.

They stopped at a place she thought she remembered. There was something familiar in the shape of the sloping ground as they approached the small town ahead of them.

It was Butkhak, the last caravan stop before Kabul on the road from Peshawar, the place where she had seen her vision of the funeral march nearly a year ago.

How true that vision had been.

They clattered under a gate, wound through several streets, and stopped in front of a plain mud-brick house.

Aminullah dismounted, leaving Mariana on his saddle, and hammered on the door. A young boy answered his knock, started back in surprise, a hand over his heart, then disappeared inside, to be replaced by an old, bent man in a huge checkered turban.

Rapid words were exchanged. Aminullah beckoned to her.

As before, she was ushered inside by women, and taken to an empty upstairs room with a string bed in one corner.

A child brought her tea. Never had Mariana tasted anything as good.

Someone else brought her a quilt and a hard pillow. She pulled off her chaderi and sheepskin, rolled herself into the quilt, and fell deeply and instantly asleep.

Chapter 39

The Waliullah ladies had recited without pause since the early morning. Now, with dinner on the way, they huddled on the sitting-room floor, some conversing in low tones, others resting beneath quilts on the bolsters that lay here and there on the sheeted floor. Occasionally, a man of the family put his head around the doorway, nodded, and then took his turn at the wheel.

Steps approached from the room where the uml was being performed. A young woman scuffed off her shoes, pushed aside the door curtain, and entered, heavy-eyed.

"It was difficult, Bhaji." The girl sighed, as the women made room for her to sit beside Safiya. "My mind kept wandering as I recited. I hope," she added in a small voice, "I did not make too many mistakes."

"Have no fear, child," Safiya rumbled, a hand on the girl's knee. "You performed with pure intention, and your pronunciation of the Sindhi was good."

"How much longer will it take?" asked a young mother with an infant on her lap.

"It may be weeks before we learn of Mariam's condition, but Saboor may receive a sign before then."

"But what if she has died?" The girl reached up and touched her ears to ward off evil.

"If, Allah forbid, Mariam has already died," Safiya said carefully, "then we will be told. But we will not consider such a possibility until we must. And now, Asma, go and rest. Lalaji is taking the next turn."

As she spoke the curtain moved aside, and the Shaikh entered. He beckoned to his sister.

"How is Saboor?" he asked, when she had joined him. "Has he seen anything new?"

His sister shook her head. "Nothing that I know of, but at least he has fallen asleep."

She gestured to a corner where Saboor lay wrapped in a quilt, his eyes shut, his lips parted.

The Shaikh nodded. "I will go in, then. Who will come after me?"

"I will be sending Rehmana," she replied.

The Shaikh's gap-toothed sister-in-law looked up, and nodded solemnly.

He nodded in return, then started away.

DARKNESS HAD fallen by the time Mariana awoke. The scent of food wafted up the stairs, but no one came to fetch her. Too exhausted to care, she went back to sleep.

By the time a pair of girls arrived to announce that dinner was ready, male voices were audible elsewhere in the house. The family must have kept the food waiting until its fighters had returned.

As the men laughed and shouted in the room below, Mariana sat warily in a small room with a sandali in the center, watched closely by several women and children.

How many soldiers and camp followers had died of cold and hunger today? she wondered, as she stared without appetite at the mountain of mutton and rice before her on the table, and warmed her feet beneath the family sandali.

How many of the retreating force had Aminullah, and those men downstairs, slaughtered today? How many had Aminullah killed after he left her at this house and galloped away?

She nodded politely to her hostesses and rose to her feet. As she pulled on her boots outside the door, one of them pulled the door curtain aside.

"Make ready," she ordered, in accented Farsi. "You are to leave here soon."

"Leave here?" Mariana hesitated. "Would it be possible for me to go to Kabul? Someone is expecting me there."

Please, please let them take me to Haji Khan's house....

"Kabul?" The woman grimaced and shook her head. "You cannot go there. We are sending you to the British fort at Jalalabad. A kafila will be taking you over the Lataband Pass. You are to join their camp tonight."

Voices shouted up the stairs.

"Get your poshteen," the woman urged Mariana. "They are waiting."

The cold was stunning. A camel knelt in the narrow street, its driver wrapped to his eyes in a shawl. Mariana climbed onto the camel's back and clutched the saddle as it jerked to its feet.

Perhaps Hassan had not died, she told herself as she rode out through the gate of the town, the camel's ankle bells chinking with every step. Perhaps one day she would reach Lahore, and find him waiting.

The landscape sloped away in folds, hill upon snowy hill. It had been here that she had asked Munshi Sahib if she would ever see Hassan and Saboor again.

Swaying on the camel's back, miserable with cold and loss, she closed her eyes and dreamed fitfully of her time in India. She relived her rescue of little Saboor, and her first, moonlit meeting with Shaikh Waliullah. She remembered Safiya Sultana's story about the prince who became a beggar, and her own terrifying afternoon alone on the violent streets of Lahore. She recalled Munshi Sahib's fable of the king's messenger and Haji Khan's beautiful, evocative durood.

She thought of Nur Rahman, begging her to recite the *Shahada*, the attestation of the faith they all shared.

All of them had been her teachers. Surely their lessons meant something. Surely they fitted together to make a whole....

She opened her eyes. A full moon shone through the latticework of her chaderi. It hung before her, its light falling on snowy ground so pale that it could have been desert sand.

Camel bells chinked. The moon beckoned her forward.

They were turning. The moon, no longer in front of her, was now at her shoulder. This was wrong. They were going the wrong way.

Dismount from the camel. The voice in her head was so clear and so commanding that Mariana looked over her shoulder, to see if someone behind her had spoken.

She bent forward to look at the camel driver. Hunched over against the cold, he trudged on.

Dismount, repeated the voice, *and follow the path of the moon.*

They were heading downhill, traversing a snow-covered slope. Soon the moon would be behind her, not in front.

Follow the path to peace, ordered the voice.

Each of her teachers, the Shaikh, Safiya Sultana, Munshi Sahib, and Haji Khan, had spoken of journeys and homecomings. Even Nur Rahman, who had danced for her in the snow, had offered the same lesson—that although the way might be difficult, the goal was beautiful beyond imagining.

Follow the path. She ceased thinking. Moving as if under someone else's volition, she slid one leg over the camel's saddle. Timing her fall so she would not be kicked, she took a deep breath, and let herself slide to the ground.

She landed jarringly on her side. Her thumping fall must have been startlingly loud in that silent place, but by the time she gathered herself and looked up, the camel was already beyond her, striding away as if its driver had heard nothing.

This was madness. If she did not run after it, shouting, she would be—

It was too late. The camel had vanished around a pile of rocks.

She was entirely alone.

Follow the moon.

She pushed herself to her feet. Weighed down by her heavy poshteen, she turned to face the moon, then began working her way toward it, making a new, uphill path through the knee-deep snow.

Had this been a mistake? She stopped to catch her breath, aware that she was tiring rapidly. Had her mind played a trick on her, counterfeiting that voice with its compelling instructions? Unable to go any farther, would she die here on this slope, with only the moon for company?

"*I call to witness,*" her munshi had recited here, at Butkhak, on the day before she entered Kabul,

"*The ruddy glow of sunset;*
The night and its homing, and
The moon in her fullness;
Thou shalt surely travel
From stage to stage."

All the lessons she had learned had brought her to this moonlit landscape where there was no sound but the wind in her ears.

Nur Rahman had longed for the companions of Paradise, but she had found Hassan. He would be her companion here on earth, if they lived to meet again. And there were others—her teachers and Ghulam Ali and Yar Mohammad, and bumbling, talkative Dittoo.

If she did not survive the night, perhaps they would all meet one day in Paradise....

Look up, ordered the voice.

A fire glowed in the distance.

Her exhausted breathing echoed in her ears, but hope offered her new strength. Whoever these people were, she thought, as she started toward their beckoning fire, they would not refuse her warmth and shelter.

The moon shone down on a small encampment. Jezails leaned, steepled together, in the snow. Pack ponies and mules blew and stamped. Tents clustered near the fire. In one, there was light. The silhouettes of two men moved against its wall.

A third male figure huddled at the fire, its light playing on his face. Delirious from cold and exhaustion, Mariana imagined that his pale beard belonged to someone she knew, but that could not be.

He did not see her approaching.

One of the silhouettes stood. A man emerged through the opening of the glowing tent, his head covered in a shawl. He stepped toward the fire.

"Ghulam Ali," he ordered, "go to your tent. Do not punish yourself by staying outside in this cold."

The first man shook his head. "Your wife is lost," he crooned, rocking back and forth. "Bibi is lost, and I am to blame."

"No," Hassan Ali Khan said. "It was my fault from the beginning." He stared into the fire, as if he had forgotten the other man's presence. "I learned too late what she offered me," he went on, his voice breaking. "I did not see clearly—"

Both men looked up, startled, when Mariana began to run.

A moment later, three hundred and sixty miles away, Saboor, the son of Hassan Ali Khan, opened his eyes and smiled.

Epilogue

To the Governor-General of India
Government House, Calcutta

February 15, 1842

Your Lordship,

I am pleased to report that our intelligence officer Adrian
Lamb has arrived in Delhi after surviving the disaster at Kabul.

He and his wife escaped the cantonment shortly before the
retreat, and have come down to India via Kandahar with a group
of Afghan nomads. They arrived in Delhi three days ago. Apart
from what Mrs. Lamb has described as "the unspeakable
squalor" of their journey, they are unharmed.

Although we have no definite news as yet, it seems very likely
that the dreadful rumors we have heard are true: that of the
fourteen thousand souls who left the cantonment on the morning
of January 6th, only one man, Dr. Brydon, ever reached
Jalalabad, where General Sale and the 1st Brigade were waiting.
If this proves to be the case, then except for Akbar Khan's thirty
hostages, all the others must be presumed dead.

It is believed, although not confirmed, that General Sir

William Elphinstone, Lady Macnaghten, Lady Sale,
LadyMacnaghten's nephew Charles Mott, and Lady Sale's
daughter Mrs. Sturt are among Akbar's prisoners, whose number
includes ladies, children, and wounded officers.

We are, of course, making every effort to procure their release.

I should mention a curious part of Adrian Lamb's story—his
niece, a girl by the name of Mariana Givens, vanished from a
caravanserai outside of Kabul while waiting with her uncle for
the nomad caravan to depart.

Lamb insists the girl is in Lahore, under the protection of
someone called Hassan Ali Khan. Having met the man in
Peshawar I can say that I would not put it past him to have
taken Miss Givens there. And since our present difficulties would
preclude any attempt at her recovery, I suppose that is where she
will remain.

I am Your Lordship's most humble and obedient servant,

Major Horatio Wade

GLOSSARY

Note: Four languages appear in this Glossary: Arabic, Urdu, Farsi (Persian), and Pushto. As many of them overlap, I have designated the root language wherever possible. Occasional words from other languages are mentioned specifically.

A

Afridi, *p.*   Pashtun tribe living on the border between Afghanistan and India (now Pakistan)

Akhal Tekke   breed of Turkmen horses known from ancient times as the Heavenly Horses, and prized for their beauty and endurance (Turki word)

Al-Hamdulillah, *a.* Praise be to God

aloo keema, *u.*   spicy stew of goat meat and potatoes

amir, *a. f.*   king, ruler

Ammi-Jan, *u.*   affectionate term for mother

Aryans   people from Central Asia who are said to have invaded the Indian subcontinent from 1500 BC to 100 BC asr, *a.* evening; the pre-sunset Muslim prayer is the asr prayer

As-salaam-o-alaikum, *a.* "May peace be upon you," the standard greeting among Muslims

atta, *u.* whole-wheat flour

attar, *u. f. p.* perfumed oil

Az barae Khuda, *f.* For God's sake!

B

bacha male child; a Hindi word

badragha, *p.* armed escort

Bala Hisar, *f.* palace and fort of the kings of Afghanistan

barat, *u.* bridegroom's procession that comes to fetch the bride after a marriage

bazaar, *u. f.* marketplace

Begeer, *f.* Seize them!

Bhai Jan, *u.* polite form of address for an elder brother

Bhaji, *u.* polite form of address for an elder female relative

Bibi, *u. f.* polite form of address for a young lady

C

caravanserai, *u. f.* stopping place for travelers; a large area, enclosed on four sides, with a large open space in the center, and storage sheds and accommodation for travelers along the walls

chaderi, *f.* woman's long, gathered cotton cloak that starts from a quilted cap on the head, then falls over

the shoulders and to the ground, covering a
woman completely; a separate long flap falls
from the front of the cap to cover the face—
this flap has a latticework hole in front to
allow the wearer to see out

chaikhana, *u. f.*   tea shop

chapan   full-length, long-sleeved coat worn by Uzbek
                        people of northern Afghanistan

chappati, *u. f. p.*   flat whole-wheat bread; in Afghanistan,
                        chappati is a round whole-wheat bread ranging
                        from nine to twenty-four inches in diameter

chappli, *u.*   sandal; also refers to the texture and shape of
                        the spicy kababs of Peshawar, made with
                        ground meat and dried pomegranate seeds,
                        that are said to resemble sandals

charpai, *u. f.*   traditional bed with a simple frame and four
                        carved legs, strung with rope

chillum, *p.*   water pipe in which tobacco is burned by hot
                        coals, and the smoke filtered through water
                        [see also narghile, hookah]

choga, *u. f. p.*   full-length coat, open in front, worn in
                        Afghanistan and northern India; mid-
                        nineteenth-century ones were made of plain
                        wool, the best being of soft camel hair with
                        subtle embroidery

chup, *u. p.*   Keep quiet!

cummerbund, *u. f.* sash worn around the waist; literally: to enclose
                        the back

D

dal	generic name for split peas, beans, and lentils; a Hindi word
Dera Jat	area in India (now Pakistan) along the border of Afghanistan, bounded on the west by the Suleiman Koh mountain range and on the east by the Indus River
dhobi, *u.*	man who washes clothes
dhooli, *u.*	covered chair or palanquin, often used for carrying the sick
dupatta, *u.*	long, wide scarf of thin fabric, used by women to cover the head and chest
durahi silk	lightweight Afghan silk
durood, *a.*	invocation of blessings upon the Prophet Muhammad

E

Eskandar	Alexander: the name used for Alexander the Great

F

Farsi, *f.*	Persian, spoken in both Afghanistan and in Iran
feranghis, *u. f.*	European

G

Ghazi, *f.*	warrior, victor
Ghaznavids	invaders of Turkish origin, who occupied Afghanistan in the tenth through twelfth centuries
gunah, *f. p.*	sin

H

Hafiz	the great poet born in Shiraz in 1326, whose verses are still quoted throughout the Farsi-speaking world
hafiz, *a.*	someone who has memorized the Holy Qur'an
haji, *a.*	someone who has performed the Muslim pilgrimage to Mecca
haveli, *u. a.*	walled city house with a courtyard
Hazuri Bagh, *u.*	the Lord's Garden, a garden outside the Lahore Citadel
hookah, *u. a.*	water pipe [see chillum, narghile], but with a long, flexible pipe that carries the smoke to the smoker's mouth
Huns	warrior tribes from Central Asia who invaded and ravaged Europe beginning in the fourth century
huzoor, *u. a.*	Your Lordship

I

Inshallah, *a.*	God willing—is always used when speaking of the future
ishq, *a.*	divine love

J

jambiya, *a.*	knife with a long, convex blade, originally of Arab design; often elaborately inlaid; used from Arabia to Indonesia
jan, *u. f.*	soul, beloved

jezail, *p.*	long-barreled musket, often with a carved stock, used by Afghans; jezails are well known for their range and accuracy
jezailchi, *p.*	marksman

K

kabab, *a. f.*	fire-roasted meat
kababchi, *u. p.*	cook who makes kababs
kafila, *u. a. f.*	traveling caravan
kameez, *u. a. f.*	long, loose shirt worn by men and women in northern India and Afghanistan; worn with a shalwar
katar, *u.*	Indian thrusting knife with a thick, wedge-shaped blade and an iron handle shaped like the letter H; used since ancient times
khanjar, *a.*	dagger with a curved blade; originated in Arabia, but used throughout the East
Khanum, *f. p.*	polite mode of address for a lady
khelat, *u. f.*	robe of honor, elaborate clothing presented a superior as a mark of favor
Khyber knife	long, heavy knife whose pointed blade can be over two feet long; used by Pashtun tribesmen
Kohdaman, *f.*	fertile valley ringed by brown hills north of Kabul; literally: slope or bottom of the hills
kohl, *u. a.*	eyeliner made of soot and clarified butter or almond oil
kotal, *p.*	mountain pass

kukri knife, *u.* — a heavy knife used by Gurkha tribesmen from Nepal; its blade, which broadens toward the point, has a pronounced downward curve

kundan, *u.* — style of jewelry setting common to India

L

La illaha illa Allah, Muhammad Rasul Allah, *a.* — "There is no God but God, and Muhammad is the Prophet of God"—the attestation of faith of all Muslims

Lalaji, *u.* — affectionate, respectful term of address for an elder male; the Waliullah family children use that term for the Shaikh

lu — Punjabi word for the hot, dry summer wind of the Punjab

M

maharajah, *u.* — one of many words for an Indian prince or ruler

Mairmuna, *p.* — polite mode of address for a lady

Malik Sahib, *u.* — polite mode of address for a chief

masnavi, *p.* — rhyming couplets; the title of Rumi's masterpiece is "Rhyming Couplets of Deep Spiritual Meaning"

matlabi, *u.* — manipulative, interested only in self-gain

maund, *u. f.* — unit of weight used in West Asia from ancient times; the Kabuli maund is approximately eighty-two pounds

Memsahib, *u.* — respectful term of address used for foreigners, i.e., British women

mohalla, *u. f.*	neighborhood of a city
muezzin, *a.*	man who calls the Muslim faithful to prayer five times a day
Mughal Empire	empire founded by Mohammad Babar Shah, the great-grandson of Tamerlane, who invaded India from Afghanistan in the sixteenth century; the empire he founded was known for its art and architecture—the Taj Mahal was built by Babar's descendant, the emperor Shah Jahan
munshi, *u. a.*	teacher
murid, *u. a.*	spiritual student, the follower of a murshid
murshid, *u. a.*	spiritual teacher

N

nahi, *u.*	no
naiza bazi, *p.*	tent-pegging
nan, *u. f.*	thick, flat oven-baked bread
narghile, *f.*	water pipe [see chillum, hookah]

P

Painda Gul	male Afghan name: Everlasting Flower
palanquin, *u.*	long box with sliding side panels used for traveling; a palanquin accommodates one adult, who can sit or lie inside; poles projecting fore and aft are hoisted to the shoulders of four bearers who carry the palanquin
panah, *p.*	part of the code of the Pashtuns: anyone, regardless of caste, creed, or relationship, can claim asylum in the house of a Pashtun

Pashtun, *p.*	group of tribes occupying the northern border between Afghanistan and India (now Pakistan)
Pashtunwali, *p.*	Pashtun code of honor
poshteen	a sheepskin cloak with very long sleeves covering the hands and tied on with a sash
pulao, *u. f.*	dish made with rice, meat, or chicken and spices
Pul-e-Khishti, *f. p.*	Bridge of Bricks, the main bridge leading into Kabul from the north
purdah, *u. f.*	the practice of secluding women; literally: curtain

Q

Qamar Haveli	Moon House, the Waliullah mansion in Lahore's walled city
qaraquli, *f. p.*	fine lambskin, often used to make men's hats
qasid, *f. a.*	Indian courier; relay runners were used throughout India to carry urgent messages
quatlame	fried dough, given to horses in Turkmenistan; Uzbek word
Qur'an, *a.*	the Muslim Holy Scripture, believed to have been dictated to the Prophet Muhammad by the Archangel Gabriel

R

rezai, *u.*	a cotton-stuffed quilt
rokho, *u.*	stop

S

Sadozai   tribe of Ahmad Shah Durrani, the Father of
                                 Afghanistan; Shah Shuja, the British puppet
                                 king, was Ahmad Shah's grandson

Safed Koh, *u. f.*   White Mountains: a group of mountains on the
                                 border of Afghanistan, near Waziristan; the
                                 same mountains are called Spin Gar in Pushto

Sahib, *u. a. f.*   respectful form of address for elders; British
                                 men were also addressed as Sahib

sandali, *p.*   square table with a quilt spread over the top to
                                 warm the legs of people sitting around it; a
                                 brazier of burnt charcoal sits under the table

Sarak-e-Azam, *u.*   Grand Trunk Road built by Sher Sah Suri in the
                                 sixteenth century; runs from Peshawar to
                                 eastern Bengal, a distance of some two
                                 thousand miles

sarod, *u.*   Indian stringed instrument with twenty-five
                                 strings, somewhat like a lute

Sassanians   dynasty of rulers originating in south Persia,
                                 who ruled an empire that included Afghanistan
                                 from the third to the seventh centuries AD

sepoy, *u. f.*   Indian foot soldier

serai, *u. f. a.*   resting place for travelers

shabnama, *u. f. p.*   night letter, used to spread secret news

shalwar, *u. f.*   long, baggy, gathered trousers worn by both
                                 men and women in northern India and
                                 Afghanistan; worn with Kameez

sharab, *u. a.*   wine, forbidden to Muslims

sharif, *a.*   noble, glorious

Sher Darwaza, *u. f.* Lion's Gate, a mountain southwest of Kabul; the Kabul River flows through the Sher Darwaza pass

sirdar, *u. f.*   chief

sura, *a.*   chapter of the Holy Qur'an

Sura Ha Mim, *a.*   Qur'anic chapter whose title is the Arabic letters H and M

Sura Inshirah, *a.*   Qur'anic chapter entitled "Expansion"

Sura Nur, *a.*   Qur'anic chapter entitled "Light"

T

takht, *u. f.*   padded platform, also used as a throne

tandoori, *u. f. a.*   baked in a brick oven

tashreef, *a.*   to confer honor upon an inferior, usually by giving him a gift [see khelat]

taweez, *u. a.*   the Merciful Prescriptions: a series of cures and healings practiced by the Sufis; in this case a silver box containing a Qur'anic verse and worn about the neck

tik hai, *u.*   It is good, it is all right

tujhun, *p.*   white Siberian goshawk, considered the rarest and finest hunting bird in Central Asia

U

uml, *u. f. a.*   Sufi practices that have been described as halfway between magic and miracle

V

vizier, *u. f. a.*   government minister

Y

ya, *u. f. a.*   oh

yabu, *u. f.*   small, hardy pack pony used for mountain
 travel

yakhni, *u. f.*   broth made with mutton or chicken

yar, *u. a.*   friend [also Punjabi]

ABOUT THE AUTHOR

THALASSA ALI was born in Boston. She married a Pakistani, and lived in Karachi for a number of years. Although she has since returned to the United States, her deep connection to Pakistan remains unbroken.